Y0-DNL-651

# unliving
## the
# dream

*Live your dreams!*

*Sandra Woodruff*

Copyright © 2016 Sandra Vischer

This is, in total, a work of fiction. Names, characters, places, and
incidents either are the product of the author's imagination or are
used fictitiously. Any resemblance to actual persons, living or dead,
events, or locales is entirely coincidental.

All rights reserved.
Published in the United States
by Trill Publishing
Portland, Oregon

TRILL

Book Design by *the*BookDesigners
San Francisco, California

Paperback ISBN: 978-0-9969310-0-7
eBook ISBN: 978-0-9969310-1-4

# unliving the dream

A NOVEL

## Sandra Vischer

# Dedication

For my children, who inspired me to keep my sanity

during the most difficult time in my life, and

whom I love from the deepest part of my soul.

And

To my parents, who nurtured a foundation

of strength and confidence and

whose love and support has never wavered.

Thank you for believing in me.

# 1

## Shattered Dreams

# Prologue

I asked my husband question after question, hoping to hear something we could fix. His silence blared within me. Was it work? The last television commercial we did? That music video? One of our employees? Was it his health? The kids? Did I do something wrong and not know it? *Oh, please let it be work!* And why wouldn't he look at me?

As he leaned against the headboard without answering, his hesitation taunted me. What if he said something I didn't want to hear? Would this innocuous hotel room in Victoria become a place I would remember for the rest of my life?

I frantically searched my mind for more questions until there was only one left unanswered. *This is absurd. Don't say it!* I stumbled, not wanting to utter the words.

"James, is it *us*?"

He lowered his head.

In that moment, I ceased to be the Alex it had taken four decades to become. The funny kid, the awesome athlete, the doting mother, the respectful daughter, the trusted friend, and the devoted wife—the person I knew myself to be vanished. Every measured step I had taken to build this wonderful life was in question.

My gut twisted as each passing second became painful confirmation.

"Tell me!" I implored him while struggling to find the strength within me to deal with whatever was coming. "Is there someone else?" I couldn't believe I was asking my husband these questions. This wasn't us. This was other people. We were happy. We had a wonderful marriage, beautiful children, a successful business, a life!

And then, finally, he spoke. "There is someone I'd like to start seeing." His voice was so timid that at first I couldn't comprehend what he was saying. "I just need a little break," he continued. "I want to see what it feels like to live on my own."

The world around me seemed to vanish as I was blanketed in a fog of uncertainty. There was no chair, no dresser, no mints on the pillows. I was suddenly anesthetized by the bewilderment of his words—shocked by the knife that had just been plunged into the heart of our marriage.

"I don't understand, James," I said patiently, praying that I'd misheard him.

"I just want to try something different."

"But dating and moving out?" *What in the hell is happening?* "Who is she?" I asked, expecting to hear a stranger's name.

Without lifting his head, he mumbled, "Mara."

Reeling from his admission, I blurted, "You can't ask her out, James! Are you crazy!"

Mara was the first person I hired into our firm. She was a nice-looking boyish brunette with a bohemian flair, and I welcomed her into our promising organization and taught her about the business of creating miniature environments.

"We're her bosses, James. You can't date one of our employees!" I insisted, hoping to snap him back to reality. "And she's a devout Catholic!" I reasoned. "Even if she

and I weren't friends, Mara would never interfere in anyone's marriage, let alone ours!"

*What in the hell are you doing, Alex? Is this what be-
ing rocked to your core looks like—trying to find a way
out with logic? There's no logic in what your husband just
said. He wants to date your twenty-three-year-old friend
and assistant. Where's the logic in that?*

"I just want to see what happens," he said, his face
now in his hands, as if he'd been suffering a real crisis of
conscience. And I actually felt sorry for him.

"Honey, maybe the stress of the business has taken
its toll on you. You've been working so hard lately. Why
don't you cut back on your hours?" I said calmly. *He loves
me. He adores me. Please look at me.* "I'll stay at the office, and you can spend more time with the kids."

The only reaction he offered was a lame shrug.

*Counseling. Maybe we need counseling. Oh god,
twenty years, twenty happy, laugh-filled, sweet years!*

"Honey, talk to me. Tell me why you feel this way,"
I continued. *Please, James, help me to understand!* Why
wouldn't he look at me?

"I don't know," he muttered. "I just dunno."

"It's all right. We'll figure it out," I encouraged him.
But in the hazy distance of this impalpable moment, I
could feel my body in hardcore distress, my soul knocked
off its axis, and my heart weeping from the thought of an
upended future. I knew then that I couldn't wait to figure
things out. And so, with the hand of fear clenching my
throat, I uttered, "Don't you love me anymore?"

My stomach twisted as I waited for his answer. *Please,
James, tell me you love me!*

"It's not that. I just feel like I need to try something different," he said with a remoteness that left me clinging to the edge of life as I knew it.

"If you still love me, why do you want to start seeing Mara?" My frustration with his thoughtless confession began to swell. "You promised that if our marriage was ever in jeopardy, we'd do everything, even give up the business, to save us. What happened to that promise?"

James offered no explanation. No reassurances. No comfort.

I sat alone on the balcony of our hotel room that night, staring at the impassive moon's reflection on Puget Sound, telling myself my husband's revelation was just an aberration. We were under a lot of pressure at work. This was something we'd figure out together. Our love was too special.

But after that weekend, I learned the true meaning of rage and betrayal. Their toxic venom boiled beneath my skin, their fervor threatened my very soul when I discovered that Mara and James had been having an affair for months—and that I, mild-mannered, rock-solid Alex, could explode into the dark side.

*CAN YOU LOOK AT ME NOW?!*

A week before James planned on moving out, we still hadn't told Lily and Jack about their Dad "needing a little break."

He asked if I would be the one to tell them. "I think *you* should do it," I said. After all, he was the one firing bullets into our precious family. "But I'll be there to help the kids after you tell them."

"Lily and Jack will be fine," he said. "It's not like I'm dying."

When did the man I love turn so clueless?

Perched comfortably on the fireplace hearth, James called the kids into the den. I sat across the room, distancing myself from the misery he was about to unleash. Lily and Jack ran through the kitchen and bounded onto the couch.

"What's up?" Lily asked.

"Your mom and I need to talk to you about a little change that's going to take place next week," he said, wielding a smile.

The kids waited with excitement, eagerly anticipating good news, perhaps a family vacation or a day at the beach. Why would they expect anything less in their idyllic lives?

Without warning, James pulled the trigger. "I'm moving into my own apartment," he said like he was running out to pick up a paintbrush at the local hardware store.

They looked at me. My anguished face confirmed their fears.

Lily howled, "Nooooo!" and began sobbing.

Jack started to cry silently.

They'd witnessed enough of their friends' broken homes to know what their dad's words really meant. Lily sprang into my arms, seeking comfort. Jack soon followed. I hugged my kids tightly, slowly rocking them, hoping somehow it would ease their pain.

Their reaction was so searing I wanted to scream at

James, "Look! Look what you've done! Your stupidity and selfishness have crushed their world, and they will never be the same again!"

My children wailed, begging him not to leave. "Please don't go, Daddy. Pleeease!" they cried. "Why are you leaving us?"

And through their pleas, James calmly blew the smoke from the barrel of his gun, explaining that his move was no big deal—that he'd still see them.

As I held my kids, I knew I had to stay strong. I promised them everything would be all right. But how? How could anything be all right again?

James moved into a modern two-bedroom apartment, leaving his wounded family behind. He meekly asked what furniture he could have. I graciously offered our hefty hide-a-bed sofa and oversize armoire. He gladly accepted my generosity, unaware it was laced with ball-busting revenge as I visualized him in groin-pulling agony heaving the colossal pieces up three flights of stairs to his new bachelor pad.

My husband fulfilled his fatherly duties on an every-other-weekend basis while dating the woman my friends supportively called Mara the Maggot. Every Monday through Friday I'd send the kids off to school and drive into work listening to Wilson Phillips, blinking back tears as the song *Hold On* encouraged me to make it for one more day. Once I hit the freeway, I fought to regain my composure, knowing that within ten minutes I'd be facing both my husband and the other woman, who sat at her desk just outside of my office.

Yes, Mara was still James and my assistant three months after I found out she was sleeping with him. She didn't have the decency to quit, and I couldn't fire her. What if their affair turned sour? A woman who would betray a friend might also sue for sexual harassment, saying James used his position in power to force her into unwanted sex. So day after day I pretended that everything was okay, knowing the other employees were aware of our dirty little scandal.

I lived out my childhood fantasy of becoming an actress, performing the role of a dignified woman, rising above the situation I found myself in, all the while believing James would come to his senses. But my portrayal took its toll. I moved through the world in an altered state of numbness, comforting my demolished ego by telling myself, "I'm funny and smart, tall and blond, and, well, really, really nice. And her? She's a mousy little waif."

Finally, Mara's sister-in-law, a friend of mine, convinced her to resign. At last I had room to breathe, and more important, I had hope. For the first time in months, I didn't have to fight off nausea and migraines. The shroud cloaking my spirit had partially lifted. There would be no more feigning civility for eight hours a day. Mara would be out of our lives, and my husband and I would have a chance to find our way back to each other.

Not long after she quit, James and I were invited to attend a movie premiere in Los Angeles. After just two years in business, our firm, Xtreme Perspectives, had skyrocketed to success, supporting twenty employees and receiving impressive industry accolades. With my management skills, James's design talents, and my family's financial investment, we'd quickly catapulted to the top of our profession. Our intricate models were being proclaimed throughout the entertainment industry.

The atmosphere at the film's debut would be electrifying, the perfect opportunity for rekindling our love. For one night, Alex, businesswoman and suburban mom, would be red-carpet ready in an outrageously expensive black, figure-hugging dress.

Our flight to Los Angeles consisted of cordial job-related discussions punctuated by uncomfortably long pauses. I pretended to be composed—sipping my drink as my mind readily dismissed the multitude of things I really wanted to say. *Keep it light and humorous,* I told myself. Unfortunately, the weight of my desire to reclaim our life together thwarted any hope of finding the funny.

James and I checked into our hotel and said we'd meet in the lobby at six. It was so strange to see the love of my life, the man I'd cherished for the past two decades, putting his keycard into the lock across the hall from me. *Wake up, James! Please, wake up! It's me, your wife!!* And then his door clicked shut.

I spent the next few hours preparing for the moment when I hoped to see the look my husband had given me every day until Mara came into our lives. My hair, makeup, jewelry were all perfection. I slipped into my dress and stared into the full-length mirror. *What if this doesn't work?*

Taking a deep breath, I put on my heels and grabbed my clutch as I left the room to face what would either bring me tremendous joy or insufferable heartache.

I spotted James across the lobby looking incredibly handsome in his rented tux—his dark, wavy hair and tall, swimmer's physique reminding me how much I missed the harmony of us.

The only sound I heard was the pounding of my heart as he turned toward me. I smiled, and in that slow-motion instant while I kept moving forward, the smile still on my face, I died inside as he gave me a dispassionate nod and moved to open the door.

A nod! What the hell was that? Didn't he want to tell me how great I looked, put his arm around me and breathe in my perfume? Wasn't he weak in the knees from the jolt of memories that just came flooding back? *For god's sake, James, look at me! I'm the woman you've always said you adore!* And yet, my face did not betray me.

Once again, I became a thespian, acting out an Oscar-winning performance of denial. As we sipped our bubbly and beamed over the praises of the high-society partygoers, I blocked that awful moment in the hotel lobby from my reality. Yes, I pretended that everything was as it should be, and hung on to some semblance of hope. Maybe after the highs we were experiencing, and the expensive champagne, I'd feel him gently take my hand and lead me into his room.

But in the hotel hallway, James said a polite good night. I heard the sound of his door sealing our fate as I entered my darkened room. I slipped off my shoes and sank slowly onto the foot of the bed, finally allowing the mortality of our future together to hit me.

Just two months after our trip to California, James asked for a divorce. Shattered by the end of our marriage, I became lost in a frightening abyss. All I could see was the blackness of an unimaginable future. Nothing was certain anymore. I ached for all of the things that would no longer be a part of our togetherness: dancing at our kids' weddings, holding hands as we explored the streets of Paris, the supportive touches, the silliness under the covers, babysitting our grandchildren, gracefully navigating the inevitability of aging—everything was gone. The promises of our future together wiped clean of the years they took to build.

My public façade became expressionless. I never slept. I experienced bouts of feeble intelligence. And my face was decaying from the ravages of stress. *Robotic, sleepless, simpleminded, scary mug. My god! I've just described a frickin' zombie!*

Even though I appeared devoid of emotion, I noticed my contemplative vocabulary had become quite salty. Curses, long absent from my word stock, became one of my internal stress relievers, along with constant sighing and throwing phones at my unsuspecting fireplace.

But I told myself I would survive this implosion. And so I focused on my children and my recovery and tried to move forward into the next phase of grief, from denial into—I'd forgotten what came next. Was it loneliness, depression, low self-esteem? Ahh, there were so many inviting personal-growth opportunities that lay ahead of me.

Down the street from Xtreme's Seattle office, James and I had our weekly lunch meeting at Bacall's Brewery. Only this time we weren't discussing the particulars of a new business deal—we were politely negotiating the conditions of our breakup. A yellow legal pad listing the details of our separation leered back at me from beside my bowl of chili.

First bullet item: Alex gets the equity in our house, along with the mortgage; James, our modest investments. Second bullet: Alex has the kids on Christmas Eve; James, on Christmas Day. Third bullet: Alex keeps the Volvo; James, the company car. Bullet, bullet, bang, bang, blah, blah, blech. How sickeningly civilized of us.

I lifted a spoonful of cheesy beans halfway to my mouth, but nausea prevented me from eating it. Hurried strangers passed by on the sidewalk outside the window. Patrons conversed and laughed all around us. Our regular waiter stopped by for some friendly banter with James.

*People, people, look at me! I'm dying here!*

"I'll get these notes over to John's office. He'll have his secretary add the necessary legalese and submit them to a King County judge for approval. Thirty days from when he signs, it will be official," I said mechanically. It was true. I had become a zombie, detached, dispassionate. *Hmmm, come to think of it, a pound of Mara's flesh might go down a bit easier than this Tex-Mex fare. Can I get a nice pinot to go with her, please?*

"Thanks for taking care of everything, Alex. I know we'll be able to move forward together as business partners," James said in his own tactless, pseudo-compassionate way.

I offered a faint-hearted smile. *You bet your sweet ass we're going to continue as business partners! Our marriage may have failed, but I'm not giving up the kids' and my financial futures, or my family's investment in this goddamn dream of yours!*

*Holy acrimony! I must have blown right past loneliness and depression! Always the overachiever, Alex.* But this passive-anger phase felt a bit unsettling. I wondered how long it would last.

Nine months after that hideous night in the Victoria hotel room, I was . . . Jeez, I couldn't say it. It was way too painful.

*Come on, Alex, you can do this. Remember, acceptance is a part of healing. Just say it, for god's sake!*

Hi, my name is Alex and I'm a . . . *Crap, this sucks! I'm . . . Shit! . . . I'm a . . . Say it already! . . .* I'm an—EX-WIFE! *Oh man, I think I'm gonna hurl.*

Growing up in a home where the epitome of wedded bliss resided, I found it terribly difficult to fathom that I wouldn't be dancing at my own fiftieth anniversary celebration. That ingrained virtue would be a hard one to overcome.

However, I was not someone who sat on the pity pot for long, at least not beyond what it took for me to get up off the couch, throw on some makeup, and drag myself to the mall to score a sedative retail fix. Of course, I was well aware this alternative therapy was no substitute for the real thing, and not very practical either. Nevertheless, I discovered that when my life was sinking, I shopped, worked out, and organized closets. Unfortunately, the enormity of divorce was going to require something much bigger than a pair of Italian boots and downward-facing dog. And I knew just what to do—at least to start.

# Chapter One

I call my friend, Nat, a sailboat captain in the British Virgin Islands, to take her up on her offer for the kids and me to come for a visit. The constant strain of adjusting to the abruptly altered course of my life, facing my ex every day at work, single parenting, and being strong for all of those around me begins falling away as we descend toward Tortola's Terrance B. Lettsome International Airport. Ground personnel are going to need a forklift to remove the extra pounds of angst-ridden baggage that just fell off of my shoulders.

I exit onto the airplane's stairs, inhale a deep breath of sweet deliverance, and am blissfully enlivened by the warm, tropical smells.

Always an entertaining character in Lily's and Jack's lives, mom's eccentric friend, Nat, blows into Seattle once a year during the charter off-season, bringing plenty of spellbinding stories of her harrowing voyages.

I first met her at a party while attending the University of Illinois. James and I were on our first date when he suggested we drive over to the mobile home park where some of his friends lived.

I followed him up the metal steps of the rundown trailer and into a dimly lit living room. The air was thick with the smell of cigarettes and pot. *Marrakesh Express* blasted from the huge JBL speakers, and quart bottles of Old Style beer littered the coffee table.

One of the guys sitting on the couch was in the midst of offering up a supercharge to the girl next to him. She was someone you were quick to notice even while sucking up some weed. What's Julie from the Mod Squad doing here, I wondered. Dressed in an artistically patched pair of bell-bottom jeans and scoop-neck peasant blouse, Nat had an intimidating vibe. But even so, it didn't take long for our friendship to blossom.

"Welcome to the BVI!" Nat exclaims while squeezing each of us with a bear hug that says everything is going to be all right. She doesn't even raise an eyebrow at Lily's dark eye shadow. Why would she? To Nat, Lily's just a kid being a kid. I find comfort in that interpretation.

"Nat, you have no idea how great it is to be here. It's as if I've come to the surface and gasped for my first breath of air after nearly a year of holding it."

"We're gonna have such a great time! Right, kids?" she says with her usual zeal.

"Right!" The excitement in their voices is heartening for me, especially from Lily.

We grab our duffels and make our way to the parking lot, where a few small, rusty cars brave the hot asphalt. Nat heads toward a bright-yellow, bumperless military-like vehicle—basically a metal box with an inhospitable, six-inch shelf that doubles as a backseat. A moment of panic strikes when I realize there are no seat belts. And jeez, part of the floor is missing!

We pile into the car and take off down the bumpy coastal highway. Jack and I cling to the roll bar while balancing on our bags as Nat hits another pothole. Meanwhile, up front, Lily's downright giddy when she spots pigmy goats along the roadside.

"Does this thing have a roof?" I yell over the sound of the disgruntled engine.

"Naaah, lost that a long time ago," Nat responds with the guttural expressiveness of Blackbeard. I half expect an *Argh, Matey* to follow.

"What do you do when it rains?" I ask as the resuscitating sultry wind blows past me.

"You get wet! And then you air-dry when the sun comes out. We usually have a quick shower every day this time of year."

*Oh great. There goes the old crowning glory.* I've already noticed the humidity has given my coif a fuller, wavier look. *Go with it, Alex. It's kind of sexy—something you haven't felt in a very long time.*

We wind around the south end of the island next to the water's edge and head toward Soper's Hole, where Nat has a one-bedroom apartment.

Crossing over a wooden bridge, we venture onto a small dirt road where lush island foliage envelops us. Nat slowly maneuvers the car into an open area that reveals a charming marina to our right and a three-story concrete apartment building adjacent to the hillside on our left. She parks the car next to the building, and we follow her up the stairs to the second floor.

Nat opens the door to a simple but tidy place decorated with batik fabrics, seashells, and native plants. The balcony's serene view of the harbor filled with sailboats and yachts, framed by palm trees, reminds me of a picture-postcard come to life. Just across the narrow road is Pusser's Landing, a local eatery and vacationers' nightspot. The sound of reggae gently emanates from the outdoor speakers as bathing-suited boaters enjoy their late-afternoon Heinekens and burgers under green and white table umbrellas.

"This is so spectacular, Nat! And you get to wake up to it every morning. Lucky you!"

Lily and Jack soak in the stunning vista, their faces revealing the same carefree buoyancy as the boats in the harbor. They've been through so much this past year. I've tried to do all of the right things by taking them to counseling, maintaining their routines and activities, and being unfailingly present in their lives. If I'm not at work, I'm at home, nowhere else. Yet because their pristine lives were mucked up by divorce, I've been struggling to hold on to my once happy, lighthearted children—especially Lily, who has been dangerously testing her boundaries.

Jack's response has been heartbreaking at times but at least sweetly manageable. One chilly Saturday afternoon, I spotted Jack by the fireplace with a lit match in his hand.

"Tiger! What are you doing?" I gasped.

"I'm making a fire."

"You know you're not supposed to be using matches."

"But it's my job to take care of things now that Dad's gone."

I took his hand and gently pulled him onto the sofa next to me. "Listen, sweetie, just because he's not around, doesn't mean you take on his responsibilities. Your job is to just keep doing the same important stuff that you've always done—like going to school, playing with friends, and leaving your smelly, balled-up socks on the bedroom floor," I teased. "I'll take care of the rest."

Not sure he was totally convinced, I leaned in close and cupped his chin with my hand. "I mean it, Jack. You're my son, not the dad. And while I appreciate your help, what I really want is for you to be happy." Feeling his body relax, I added, "Now, why don't you go over to David's and see if he's got that new remote control car you've been telling me about." With those few simple words, Jack was out the door and back to being my Tiger-Bear.

A simple heartfelt conversation won't heal the wound that Lily has. During one of my many sleepless nights, I read that experts say the child most affected by a father's leaving is the adolescent daughter, most noticeably when there's another woman involved. In our case, this clinical observation couldn't be truer.

Lily has always been a sweet, friendly kid. One of her teachers remarked that in her thirty years in education, she'd never seen a student more well-liked by all of the other children. "And I mean *all of them*," she emphasized. But our divorce is slowly changing all that.

Time after time James chooses romantic getaways with Mara over his designated kid weekends. And then when he is available, she tags along, intruding on Lily and Jack's limited time with their dad.

Oh, sure, Mara tries to be Lily's friend. Why not, they're almost the same age. And Lily makes a real effort too. But little by little, my daughter's anger is revealing itself. She slowly morphs from Pollyanna into, well, needing a polygraph—ratting and lacquering her beautiful blond tresses while wearing black clothes and dark eye makeup. Her grades are slipping, and her choice of friends concerns me. And on Parents' Night, her teachers describe someone I don't recognize.

At least now, for a little while, the kids will be transported from their sorrow.

"Senwe's coming over with some monkfish he caught for tonight's dinner. In the meantime, let's walk over to the marina, and I'll show you my boat and some of the funky little shops. Then tomorrow we'll spend the day sailing."

"Wait a second." I stop her. "Who's Senwe?"

"My guy," she says matter-of-factly. "He's a local from Jost Van Dyke."

"Ahhh, we have a guy!"

It's been a few years since Nat divorced her second husband. She has a knack for finding great men, but the wrong ones for her. I haven't figured out what her particular type is yet, and I don't think she has either. Her first husband was a college friend of ours, a rock 'n' roller, tall and lanky, with a sweet disposition. Her second, a hunky Irish Catholic from Boston, had a great sense of humor and an endearing boyish charm.

Nat always seems to need a man in her life, if for nothing other than stud service. She has a theory that all men should be confined to one state, say, for instance, Idaho. In her scenario, women would be able to cross the border into Idaho anytime they'd like to have sex, but men wouldn't be allowed to leave. As she points out, her system permits us to screw them without giving them the chance to fuck us. I'm curious to find out what Senwe is like.

Dressed in our new vacation attire, we scope out our balmy environment. The quaint marina is an exceptionally charming place with its two-story shops painted in

Caribbean pinks and blues and with colorfully tiled roofs, shuttered windows, and wraparound, second-story verandas. Palm trees shade the pristine wooden decking.

Nat stops to introduce us to a muscled man wearing a tight, sleeveless T-shirt.

"Berwick, this is my good friend Alex and her kids, Lily and Jack. They're visiting from Seattle." She turns to me and with obvious sarcasm says, "Berwick's a fairly decent captain around these parts. He tries his best to beat me in some of the island regattas." Turning back to him, she adds, "Maybe one of these days, huh, Berwick."

His white teeth gleam against his gorgeous black complexion. "Mm, you wish you could win one, Not-a-lee." He chuckles, his Tortolian accent making his words as slow as honey.

"Hey, we're taking *Seabiscuit* out tomorrow. You want to join us?"

"Mm, yes, that would be nice," he says, beginning each statement as if he's taking a moment to think out loud.

"We're planning on getting underway around nine o'clock."

"Mm, all right den. Mm, nice to meet you," he says with a wink to Jack, who appears to be mesmerized by Berwick's shiny, ripped body. And, by the way, if any flies are looking for a place to land, my gaping mouth's available.

Nat leads us to *Seabiscuit*, a beautiful forty-five-foot Beneteau. She has a polished fiberglass hull; teak decking and trim; three double cabins, each with its own head; a large main salon; and a roomy galley. Nat says she was built for speed and comfort. Jack and Lily check out every inch of her while my friend explains the basics of sailing.

"Tomorrow we'll go to Sandy Cay, hike around the island, and do a little snorkeling. Then we'll cruise over to Great Harbour on Jost Van Dyke," Nat says. "But right now, we need to go back and meet Senwe for dinner."

Jack and Lily run ahead while Nat and I stroll along the pier. "Nat, thanks for having us. I haven't seen the kids this happy in a long time. And you are literally saving my sanity."

"I can't imagine what it must be like for you, working with him every day. Even though James has been my friend since high school, and I love him, that doesn't mean he's not an asshole. And that bitch, Mara!" Nat fumes, suddenly red-faced. "After all you did for her!" Like many of my friends, Nat has helped to release me from my anger by spewing obscenities and loathing toward my ex and Mara. I haven't been able to do it for myself, fearful of unleashing something frighteningly ugly in me. But my dear friends have circled the wagons in a protective way. I don't think they realize how much their supportive rancor allows me to take the high road and relieves me of the undignified bitterness that is so often the unwanted offspring of divorce.

Softening, she sighs. "How the hell are the rest of us supposed to have any hope if you and James couldn't make it?"

"I know," I say, feeling like a disappointment to her. "You just illustrated the roller-coaster ride I've been on. You went from melancholy about your friendship with James, to rage against Mara, to sadness over the loss of the dream."

She chuckles. "I did, didn't I."

"I wish I could express my feelings so openly, but I can't because James and I are in business together. Seeing him every day and maintaining a pretense of professionalism is smothering the real me. But I can always count on you to say exactly what you're thinking."

Nat takes hold of my arm and asks, "What went wrong, Alex?"

"I wish I knew. I'm still trying to understand it. There's a part of me that feels our divorce is just some huge mistake, that James will wake up one day and say, 'What have I done?' Yet, working together, I've seen a different side of him—one I never experienced before. I knew he was capable of cutting people out of his life. He did it to his parents and his best friend years ago. But as my husband, he was always loving, compassionate, and fun to be around.

Nat," I say, stopping to look her in the eye, "when he's at work, he's so intense. He's impatient and driven and really feeds on the power of his position. It's like he's two different men. I mean, in the past I always wondered why he wasn't close to the people he worked with. Now I know."

"They must have experienced the *other* James," Nat says. "I'm sure that you being an equal partner must irritate the hell out of him, especially now that you're divorced!"

"He tries to intimidate me like he does our employees, but I'm not afraid to challenge him when I disagree. I have no illusions, certainly not anymore, of his greatness. After all, I've seen his less-than-impressive junk . . ."

Nat grins.

"Honestly, I've been living in such a funk. I'm forgetful and have constant headaches. Half the time I don't know what I'm doing. I just keep forcing myself to put one foot in front of the other. I feel like my brain is floating in a jar of Dr. Frankenstein's formaldehyde, waiting for a lightning bolt to shock it back to life. Yet here I am raising two children virtually on my own, running a business, and having the audacity to supervise twenty people when I can't even get my own shit together.

"Which," I continue, "helps keep everybody fooled into believing I'm doing just fine. But if I hear one more person say how amazing I am, I'm gonna yak. I don't want to be amazing—I just want to completely fall apart. I actually fantasize about going to the airport and buying a ticket to France, changing my name, and living a fictitious life. Even getting falling-down drunk sounds like a wonderfully self-indulgent escape. But you know me, responsibilities always come first."

"We'll have to see what we can do about that while you're here. The Bomba Shack is celebrating its Full Moon Party next week, so we can take care of your drunken fantasy. I think a little mushroom punch may be in order. And don't worry, I'll look after the kids so you can be overserved. As far as the fictitious life in France goes, why don't I just start calling you Monique?"

Nat's man is a total surprise to me. A good-looking, jet-black beanpole with four-inch dreads sprouting from his head like a koosh ball's spikes, he wears a constant smile.

Senwe grew up on Jost Van Dyke, one of only a few hundred inhabitants, most of them related in some way, and is a man of few words. Chalk up another altogether different type for my feminist friend.

During our dinner of West Indies fish, for the kids' entertainment, Senwe savors the eyes, rolling them from cheek to cheek and licking his fingertips one at a time as Lily and Jack stare at him, equally grossed out and in awe.

Afterward, Nat and I each hold an end of a broom for an impromptu limbo contest. Lily, Jack, and Senwe take turns arching under it while Bob Marley and the Wailers encourage the sway in their hips. Even though Senwe stands six foot six, he manages to defeat my inflexible offspring.

As our first day on Tortola comes to an end, we say good night to Senwe, who leaves to take his dinghy back to Jost by moonlight. Jack inflates a couple of air mattresses for us to sleep on while Lily claims the couch. I'm exhausted after a long day of travel and ready for a night of untroubled slumber.

# Chapter Two

I wake to the sound of a gentle breeze caressing the palm fronds outside the open balcony door and breathe in the beauty and tranquility of the boat-filled harbor. Lily stirs on the couch, stretching her arms overhead, while Jack peeks out from beneath his sheet.

Nat shuffles into the kitchen to put the kettle on for her morning cup of tea. "Hey, kids, how'd ya sleep?" she says, her puffy eyes still half-shut.

"Great. Better than I have in ages. How 'bout you?"

"Delightful, just delightful. Are we ready for some fun today?" she asks, followed by her morning throat-clearing ritual.

"Can't wait!" I respond with a long abandoned excitement in my voice. "It seems like we're on a whole different planet down here," I add, amazed at my sensory revival. "I know this sounds silly, but it's incredible how different I feel. Like I'm so alive!"

Within an hour, we're provisioning the boat for our two-day trip. In addition to Berwick, Nat invited a couple of other locals, Jelly Belly and Ontie Deedee, to go along with us. Jelly Belly is, as one might expect from his name, a jolly guy who apparently enjoys too much rum cake. Ontie Deedee, a Caribbean Queen Latifah look-alike, is boisterous, funny, and wears hot pink from head to toe. She even drives a pink jeep!

I love observing my kids as they experience new

cultures and characters, and never worry about them in social situations. Both born expressive, they have outgoing personalities. Even at their young ages, and despite the divorce, Lily and Jack can schmooze with more charm than their dear old analytical mother. Jack's already flexing his muscles for Berwick (though the difference between flexed and unflexed on his pubescent body is not apparent to me), and Lily and Ontie Deedee are gabbing like long-lost girlfriends. I notice that Lily's so relaxed she hasn't even unpacked her hairspray!

Nat motors away from the dock as I situate myself atop the rim of the cockpit, relishing this opportunity to be a spectator.

Thinking is all I've been doing for so long. Thinking about my forever-changed future. Thinking about my children's well-being. Thinking about my business and facing James every day. Thinking about my failed marriage. Thinking about my family and their investment in my business. Thinking about being alone the rest of my life. Thinking about my employees. Thinking about which friends will stick by me now that I'm no longer part of a couple. I used to pride myself on the fact that I'm a thinker. I even use the word *think* five times in the personal mission statement I carry in my wallet. Ha! I am one sick puppy! Now I envy the leap-before-you-look mindset.

As soon as we're out of the harbor, we hoist the sails and point *Seabiscuit* toward Sandy Cay. Berwick's at the helm, though it isn't long before he has Jack in charge of maintaining our course. Lily, Ontie Deedee, and Jelly Belly are laid out on the foredeck, soaking up the sun.

*Ahh, this is the life. It's truly heaven on earth. . . . He could be here with us right now if he wanted. What does she have that I don't? Jeez, Alex, shut up!* Warm sun, cool breeze, and the ever-important deep, cleansing breath.

Sandy Cay is an uninhabited island you can hike around in half an hour. We drop anchor fifty yards from shore and prepare to jump off of the stern.

When the others enter the water, I lean in close to Lily and Jack, whose faces are adorably smooshed by their masks and snorkels, and instruct them, "It's very deep here, and there are strong currents. You have to stay close to me at all times. Do not, and I repeat, do not leave my side!" They both nod in agreement. I brace for Lily's rebuttal, but she's still acting like her old self. "Okay, let's do this!"

As soon as we hit the water, the kids take off, following Nat and the gang while I swim a couple of feet behind, herding my little lambs like an Australian shepherd whenever they stray. Every now and then I glance at the beauty below me, but mostly I'm in mother mode.

Neither Nat nor her friends have children; consequently, they don't realize how out of my comfort zone I am. My first priority is the safety and happiness of my kids. It's my job to protect them from the dangers of the world. Yet here we are, on a small boat in the vast Caribbean Sea, diving blindly into unknown waters as if we did this every day. And I'm operating without backup, for god's sake!

On the beach, the kids shed their gear and are off and running.

"Hey, you guys, wait for me!" I yell, struggling to remove my fins as Lily and Jack leave to explore the island without even a whiff of their devoted mother.

We check out the flora and fauna and then chill on the beach for a while. On our way back to *Seabiscuit*, Nat dives toward the ocean floor, pointing out sea cucumbers, anemones, and triggerfish, and then motions for us to re-surface, where she explains what they are.

Our next destination is Great Harbour on Jost Van Dyke. We cruise around the south end of the island and jibe our sails to head into the bay. The surrounding green hillside is sparsely dotted with tile-roofed homes. Straight ahead, a small village borders the white sandy beach.

After mooring *Seabiscuit*, we prepare to board *Hard-tack*, the dinghy. Yes, even the dinghy has a registered name—causing me to wonder why we don't practice this seaworthy tradition with other forms of transportation. Say, for example, one day I wiped out on my mountain bike, rendering myself unconscious. When emergency personnel arrived on the scene, they wouldn't know who I was, only that I'd been riding a Schwinn. But if bikes were licensed, the paramedics would be able to determine that the *Elmira Gulch* was registered to an Alex Fisher, thus giving them much needed information about the cold-cocked woman lying on the ground before them.

"There's Foxy's over to the right," Nat says as we step off the pier onto the beach. "It's a famous night spot—food, music, reggae concerts. There's Foxy himself, sit-ting under one of the big grass umbrellas."

"Nat, are we supposed to know who Foxy is?" I ask.

"Let's just say there are people from all over the world who've had some memorable times at Foxy's. On New Year's Eve, the harbor is so jammed with anchored vessels ready to party, you can walk from boat to boat without ever touching the water!"

Right now, there's little activity other than a few locals wandering about.

A row of mangrove trees with rope hammocks tied between them lines the beach. Just beyond are a few souvenir huts, a couple of canopied eateries, and a white-clad immigration center/post office/mini-market.

Nat, her friends, and I take shady refuge at the closest beach bar and order cold beverages. Meanwhile, Lily and Jack wrestle with the inviting hammocks. I'm still pinching myself as I curl my toes into the sand beneath my white plastic chair. Within twenty-four hours, we've met Senwe, Berwick, Ontie Deedee, and Jelly Belly—people from an entirely different world. Who are these folks with such unusual names? Who else will we be meeting? I'm astounded at how remarkably light I feel. And yet, I'm quietly pained by the presence of a phantom limb.

We sail west to White Bay, where Senwe is caretaker for a New York architect's vacation property.

"There it is," Nat shouts in her land-ho voice.

"That's quite a house!"

"I know. The guy owns the whole hillside, but he's never around, so Senwe has the estate pretty much to himself."

We lower our sails, and Nat patiently gives orders to her inexperienced deckhands. Lily and Jack are quick studies while they work the winch together. Unfortunately, my limited nautical abilities consist of knowing the words to *On the Good Ship Lollipop*. But if we ever need to make a *happy landing on a chocolate bar*, I'm your girl.

"We'll have to be very careful when we set the anchor here. The bottom is quite sandy," Nat cautions. "I've had one pull loose before."

Our first attempt is unsuccessful. Nat grumbles under her breath, bringing the boat about for another try while Berwick and Jelly Belly man the anchor. She eases *Seabiscuit* into reverse, testing the hold. "I think we've got it."

We climb aboard *Hardtack* and make our way to shore, pulling the dinghy well up onto the beach when we land. White Bay is more open to the sea than Great Harbour. The long, pristine beach, with large breaking waves, has a few open-air seaside bars at the far end but not much else. Our crew begins the twenty-minute hike down the shore and up the hillside to the main house.

When we arrive, Senwe's waiting for us. He leans down to give Nat a hug and smiles at the rest of us, but no words pass his lips. Standing next to him is a tall, black Adonis with shoulder-length dreads and a chiseled body. *Holy hunk! Not another beautiful man! I want one! Yeah, right. Like that'd ever happen. Middle-aged woman, single mother of two. Do the math. He's hot, you're not.*

Hmm, I think I may need to analyze my postdivorce self-esteem issues. But here's a news flash: my dormant libido sounds like it's rallying after a rather lengthy sabbatical.

"This is Culture," Nat says. "And these are my friends Alex, Lily, and Jack." She points across the large, airy room and adds, "That's Newman over there, messing with the music."

In no time at all, Lily, Jelly, and Ontie Deedee, whose booming voice punctuates their fun, are huddled together in front of a colorful mural depicting life in the islands. Meanwhile, Jack, Berwick, and Culture are stretched out on the oversize floral-print couches, deep in conversation. Nat and Senwe work behind the bar, popping open Heinekens and blending Painkillers. And me, I'm swiveling on a bar stool, drinking in the action around me like I'm in a West Indies production of *Stranger in Paradise*.

*James would love this. He'd enjoy seeing the—Dammit, Alex! See how you did that! Now you're not smiling anymore. Be in the moment. James made his choice—now you make yours.* Lily, Jack, and I will be our own happy family, and no one is ever going to screw with that again!

"Mom, Culture wants to take me fishing," Jack says, snapping me out of my private pep talk. "He's going to teach me how to catch dinner without a pole! Can I go, pleeeease?" he pleads with his hands clasped together in beggar repose.

"Where?" I ask calmly while simultaneously experiencing *mom*-stinctive distress.

"There's a ledge out on the point not far from here," Culture says.

I envision huge waves crashing against a massive jagged rock wall with my ten-year-old perched precariously on its precipice. Nat, wise to my way of thinking, shoots me the "don't be so damned overly protective" look. All eyes wait for my consent.

I know there will be nothing else on my mind until his

safe return, and yet I find myself saying, "You can go, but stay close to Culture." As Jack races out the door, I shout after him, "And be careful," like those three words will give him any extra protection he might need. In the real world I'd never let my son go off with someone I'd only just met, especially to play on rocks hanging out over the sea. But hey, we're not in the real world—we're in paradise, mon!

Both Jack and I manage to survive the next couple of hours. He returns triumphant, proudly showing off his butt-ugly fish. In the meantime, I also bagged my limit, reeling in a few gray hairs while he was gone. All keepers, I imagine.

As dusk rolls around, Nat informs me that Jack and I will be spending the night on the boat while everyone else sleeps at the house.

"What do you mean? Aren't we all staying on *Seabiscuit*?" I conceal my sudden apprehension.

"I like to get off of the boat whenever I can, so we might as well make use of the bedrooms. Lily and Ontie Deedee can share a room, Jelly and Berwick will bunk in another, and Senwe and I have his room. You and Jack are gonna have to crash on the boat—otherwise it will be too crowded up here," she orders.

Feeling intimidated by her captain-like command, I resist the urge to snap my heels together and give her the royal salute. Captain Bligh, along with several Heinekens, has taken control of my friend. This is no time to argue, but I totally get what's going on. The party people, including my thirteen-year-old daughter, are going to let loose at the villa while the reserved mother and her young son are being set adrift at sea!

"All right," I say, acting like it's no big deal. "Are you going to take us out to the boat or should we use the dinghy ourselves?"

"Senwe and I will go with you and pick up our overnight bags. Then we'll leave the dinghy on the beach for us to use in the morning."

And just like that, I'm back to thinking. Thinking, thinking, thinking! What if something happens? Jack and I won't have a way to get to shore. Will we be safe alone on the boat? Might someone try to board her during the night? What if we need help? Who will be looking out for my teenage daughter while I'm confined to quarters? And will the anchor that Nat *thinks* is set actually hold?

Ever the pleaser, I reply, "Okay—but you *are* going to watch out for my kid. Right?"

"She'll be fine," Nat assures me.

The last remnant of daylight illuminates the horizon as I watch Senwe and Nat motor away. Below in the captain's cabin, Jack gets ready for bed.

"Hey, Tiger, how's it going down there?"

"Great, Mom!" he says and then climbs up into the cockpit with me.

We nestle together in the cool night air, quietly talking about our fabulous day, my arms wrapped around him as he leans back against me. The wind gently rocks *Seabiscuit*, and before long, we're blanketed by the light of the brilliant Caribbean moon.

"We're fortunate, Jack. Very few people in the world get to live like we do. We should never take it for granted." I squeeze him tightly in the cool night air. "But nobody gets through life without facing challenges. What's important is how we handle them. Tough times can be an excellent opportunity to grow and become a better person. While this past year has been difficult, we have to focus on the good we have in our lives. You understand what I'm saying?"

"Yeah, Mom, I get it."

Even at his young age, I can tell Jack is going to be a tenderhearted man. He has a maturity I haven't noticed in other boys his age. But I'm not a parent who thinks that James and I can't screw him up with our own stupid choices. At this critical time in our lives, it's my job to make sure his father and I do our best not to derail his sweet, gentle soul.

As he fights to stay awake, I whisper, "Tiger, go to bed. I'll be down in a while."

I gaze up at the star-filled night sky and wonder what constellations I'm looking at, maybe Cassiopeia or Orion. *Who am I kidding? I haven't a clue.* Nat would know. I remember her telling me about how she got caught in the middle of the Atlantic by a wicked tropical storm that knocked out her navigational system. After the storm passed, she used the stars to steer herself back to the islands. Maybe, if I bask in the beauty of their brightness, these same stars will guide me back to my own safe harbor.

I never pictured myself sitting alone on the deck of a sailboat in the Caribbean, questioning where my life is headed. I thought I knew exactly where I was going. It's a helluva lesson learned. How presumptuous of me to think I was immune to adversity. I guess in some weird way, James is one of my spiritual teachers. Though his schooling is decidedly painful, he has presented me with a chance to grow. And the good news is—I'm the one who determines what direction that growth will take.

Above us in the distance, the architect's house lights up the hillside. I bet they're having quite a shindig, blasting reggae tunes, dancing, and indulging in beverages. But the only sounds I hear are the unsociable wind and indifferent waves lapping against the side of the boat.

Soon the waves begin cresting higher than before. And the wind, it's picking up! Uh-oh, this can't be good.

I look into the cabin, past the galley to where Jack is sleeping. Whoa, the boat's really rolling below, but my boy is completely unfazed. Part of me selfishly wants to wake him so I'll have someone to share in my worry. Fortunately, my motherly sanity grabs hold.

The waves start to thunder as they hit the distant shore. The rigging clangs against the mast's metal shaft. I can't sit sideways in the cockpit anymore without losing my balance. Bracing my feet, I gauge our distance from the beach. I'm a strong swimmer, but what about Jack? These have become seriously troubled waters. Storm clouds move overhead like they're on fast-forward. Should I leave Jack below or bring him topside with me? Once again, I shine the flashlight toward his bunk. He couldn't be more oblivious to the peril we're in. And what about the dubious anchor?

I stare up at the house on the hill, silently cursing my

friend. *Are you noticing the imminent storm?* This would be just another daring chick adventure if I was alone on the boat, but I'm with my kid, and that makes everything different.

The air is thick with the smell of oncoming rain. I gauge *Seabiscuit*'s back-and-forth pitch to be about ninety degrees. Oh god, are those trees along the shoreline getting smaller?! *Calm down, you moron! Panic won't help.*

I take a deep breath and decide this might be a good time to close my eyes and meditate. I repeat my mantra, *ah-im-ah,* exactly twice before being forcefully thrown off of the bench.

The moon and stars have disappeared behind the threatening clouds. A gigantic raindrop hits me, and then another. *Yikes! Those suckers are huge!*

In seconds, the full impact of the squall hits *Seabiscuit.* I duck below, falling into the galley under the violent sway. I quickly find my footing as the storm beats down on me and pull the overhead hatch closed. Flashing the light over to the bunk in the fore cabin—yep, still asleep. Oh, how I wish I could sleep.

I stare out a porthole toward the beach. Fear and fatigue mess with my mind as the violent motion of the boat makes us appear to be moving farther away from shore: See the beach. Don't see the beach! See the beach. Don't see the beach! We're okay. We're *sooo* not okay! *AND WHAT ABOUT THE GODDAMN ANCHOR?!*

For the next several anxious hours, my eyes continue to play tricks on me. Finally, the rain stops. I open the hatch and climb topside. The wind has returned to a soothing tropical breeze, and yes, the anchor has held. A sigh of relief blows past my lips as a glimmer of daylight heartens from the east. I reach into the storage bench and pull out a couple of dry cushions to stretch out on, at last closing my weary eyes.

Jack and I watch as the others load their bags and themselves onto *Hardtack*. When they motor toward us, we notice the boat is barely above the waterline. There must be a leak in the partially deflated dinghy. Still, their nervous laughter, coupled with the buzz of the struggling Evinrude, make for a sweet sound.

"Ahoy, the *Seabiscuit*," Nat yells, waving her arm.

"Ahoy, the *Hardtack*," I shout back.

As our crew begins to board, there's a skirmish when Ontie Deedee tries to abandon the sinking skiff before Lily does. Deedee bops Lily on the head with her flip-flop, bellowing, "I'm gonna bust your head like a melon!"

"What?!" cries Lily with exaggerated anguish.

"Ju know what I'm talkin' bout. Don't be splashin' Ontie Deedee."

A whole new storm has blown in, but this is one I'm going to enjoy.

"How was your night?" Nat asks.

"We did some rockin' and rollin', but everything was fine."

There's no way I'm divulging how scared I was. I have my strong-woman image to maintain, plus I know Nat will just flip me some serious shit about it. Both my chicks are safe with me again, and that's all that matters.

"Where are we off to this morning?" I ask.

"A friend of Senwe's stopped by the house last night and told us about a place on the other side of the island that only a few people know about. They call it the bubbly pool. We thought we'd check it out."

With the anchor raised, we set sail around the east end of the island, heading into the Atlantic. There's a definite shift in the water as we move from the protection of the Caribbean toward the open ocean. The power of the deep blue sea is thrillingly evident by the sheer wind speed and the extreme heel of the boat. Wow, what a ride! It feels as if we might tip over as we cling to the deck's hardware.

Nat assures us that the keel, which provides the boat's stability, weighs about a bazillion pounds. "There's no way we're going over."

Berwick spots the broken-down pier last night's local described to them. It extends about twenty yards into the water and looks as if it were abandoned decades ago. Some of the planking is missing, and the remaining wood appears to be old and rotting. With no signs of life on this part of Jost, we question what this structure is doing smack in the middle of nowhere, and, more pressing, how the heck are we going to tie up to it? The wind and current are pushing the boat into the dock with tremendous force. I see the tension in Nat's face, but she's a pro and manages, with a little help from her crew, to maneuver in safely. After securing the lines, we make our way to shore, carefully jumping over the missing sections of dock and hoping we won't break through the boards we land on.

"There's supposed to be a path off to the right. Let's see if we can find it," Nat says.

We follow our captain into the brush. The air turns thick as we move inland. Nat discovers a path overgrown with vegetation. We swat away annoying little bugs and question what we've signed up for.

"Are ju sure ju be going dee right way, Miss Notalee?" Ontie Deedee says with her diva-like attitude.

"No, but this is the only path we found, so let's keep going."

Just as mutiny is at hand, our band of buccaneers steps out of the vegetation and into a small clearing of crystal-clear, ankle-deep water. Our eyes lift to see, smack in front of us, a wall of gigantic boulders with an opening the size of a Mini Cooper through to the Atlantic. The huge rocks frame the ocean so pristinely it's as if Rembrandt himself painted the seascape.

Suddenly, our sense of marvel turns to panic. Through the hole, we see an enormous wave heading straight toward us. With no time to run, the wave forcefully smashes against the ocean side of the rock formation, sending water exploding through the opening. The surge knocks us backward onto our butts, and we're left toppled in what is now two feet of white, fizzing water.

Our fear turns to exhilaration. "Man!" I exclaim to Jack and Lily as they adjust their wave-battered swimsuits. "That was so cool!"

Everyone feels a rush of excitement, except for Ontie Deedee, who doesn't like that she's gotten wet. Thousands of nature's salty champagne bubbles burst under our chins, tickling our faces and leaving us awestruck. We're

astounded by the wonder of it all and frolic in the intoxicating, effervescent water, letting wave after wave send
us tumbling.

# Chapter Three

With Nat as our expert tour guide, Jack, Lily, and I spend the next few days exploring Tortola. We sunbathe and snorkel at Brewer's and Cane Garden Bays. We boogie board at Josiah's. We dine at dives along the water's edge where Nat knows the cooks, feasting on fried conch and roti. The four of us sail to Norman Island, where we spot barracuda and sea turtles from atop the *William B. Thornton*, an old vessel anchored in the bay that now serves food and libations to vacationing boaters. On Friday night, we attend a fish fry where the Tortolan high school principal plays lead guitar in a local fungi band. And we are the only white folks placing bets at the island's horse track.

One evening while Nat and I relax at her place and Lily and Jack are, supposedly, eating ice cream across the road at Pusser's, the apartment door bursts open.

Out of breath with excitement, Jack rushes in. "Mom, this is Eric and Megan. They're from California. They live on a boat with their parents. Can we go for a ride in their dinghy? Just around the harbor. Please?"

"Whoa, pardner, slow down," I say, making a motherly assessment of the Scandinavian-looking kids by judging them on their appearance—something I always preach against but, hey, Lily and Jack don't know that I'm doing it.

"Hello, Eric and Megan. It's nice to meet you." I continue my evaluation by asking a few pertinent questions.

They're halfway through a two-year around-the-world vacation with their parents and, yes, they're experienced boaters.

Satisfied with their answers, I complete my safety analysis by looking to Nat for her opinion. Her let-them-go look isn't totally unexpected.

"Wear your life jackets and don't be gone too long. It's getting late." I check my watch to mentally set my worry alarm. Lily and Jack disappear with their new friends as quickly as they arrived and head out to explore the world without me.

After a very short period of time, I can't stand not having a visual of my kids. "Hey, why don't you let me buy you a drink down at Pusser's?"

Wise to my way of thinking, Nat doesn't hesitate to call me on it. "You just want to keep an eye on the kids," she groans.

"Hey, cut me some slack here. It's not like they're used to hanging around the docks in a foreign country! I mean, yes, I may have dated a few burly longshoremen," I tease, "but—"

"Okay, let's go. It's not like you've heard a word I've said anyway."

The sailboat masts cast silhouettes against the orange sunset as we sit at our bistro table—Nat with a Heineken and me with my new favorite drink, a Bushwacker. Gotta love an icy blend of coconut rum, Baileys, Kahlua, amaretto, vodka, and Hershey's syrup. Mmm, mmm! I pull my camera from my canvas bag to capture the moment.

Nat and I both turn at the sound of a small engine approaching.

"You can relax now. Your children are safe."

Jack jumps onto the pier from the dinghy, barely catching himself before falling into my lap. "Mom, Eric and Megan's parents invited us to spend the day with them tomorrow. They want to take us sailing! You too! Can we go?"

"That's really nice, honey," I say, acknowledging their hospitality with a smile in Eric and Megan's direction, "but I don't know what Nat has planned for us."

"Actually, that works for me. I have a few things I need to do before my next charter."

Four sets of anxious eyes await my decision.

"Well then, I guess we're going sailing!"

Jack slaps Eric on the back and throws his arm around his new buddy's shoulder, while the girls squeal with delight. I find myself with a surprising catch of emotion as I witness the joy that's been missing from my children's lives.

Eric, looking like a modern-day Leif Eriksson, pulls the dinghy up to the dock. I'm amazed at the water skills this boy has and am grateful my land-bound children are sampling his world. We climb aboard and motor into the bay where dozens of boats are anchored.

*Which one is theirs? Maybe that charming catamaran.* Eric changes course. *The sloop with the weathered cabin? The sleek cutter? Wait a second: is it that awesome wooden schooner? Holy herring! That sucker's got to be at least a hundred feet long!*

And there, standing on the deck is . . . gulp! . . . Why, it's . . . *Doooh! Ken and Barbie? Whoa, whoa, whoa! These people are not your typical minivan jockeys! I didn't sign up for this. Crap. Check her out in that biki-ni, looking all Farrah-like. And jeez, he's sooo gorgeous! What a perfectly bronzed body.* Closer, closer. *That's not a . . . Why, yes, yes, it is! He's wearing a frickin' Speedo! Oh lordy, give me strength!*

Ken reaches his hand out to help me onto the boat. Barbie stands smiling beside him. "Hi, I'm Steve, and this is my wife, Kathy. Welcome aboard!" he says, as his teeth give off a matinee-idol twinkle.

*SteveandKathySteveandKathySteveandKathy. NOT-KenandBarbie NOTKenandBarbie!* "Thanks. I'm Alex," I say as he pulls me aboard. "And you know these two."

"Yes, we do. We had a lovely visit with them last night," Kathy says warmly, and we're so glad the three of you were available to join us today. Eric and Megan are excited about hanging out with Lily and Jack. They haven't had many chances in the past year to be with anyone their own age, especially from the States."

Oh man! She's so nice! Now I have no legitimate reason to dislike her. This is surely going to punish my already battered ego. She's beautiful and kind and has a family like I used to have. And me, I'm just a pathetic ex-wife.

"It's definitely our pleasure, and so generous of you to invite us," I say, continuing our pleasantries.

"Before we get underway, would you like to see the rest of the *Pipe Dream*?"

"What a great name!" I say while concealing an ironic chuckle. *Oh, crap! Did my eyes just cross?* "I'd love to."

The main salon's walls are lined with teak shelving, displaying books and marvelous treasures from around the world. Over in one corner is an impressive electronics center including what looks like communication, navigational, educational, and entertainment systems. The galley is a scaled-down version of an ultramodern kitchen with all of the latest stainless-steel appliances. The kids' bedrooms are in a highly efficient five-by-seven space. And the master stateroom is nothing short of luxurious, including a large mirrored wall.

Okay, so I can't help myself. It's the mirror's fault. My mind immediately visualizes Ken and Barbie playing *Adventures in Paradise*, their sculpted bodies reflecting back at them as Kathy rhapsodizes Steve's Speedo-clad *Kon Tiki. Jeez, Alex, you have got to get laid! Ahh, how I loved Gardner McKay.*

"Your boat is magnificent, Kathy. And I'm so in awe of your bravery, traveling across the oceans of the world with your kids."

"Call me brave after we make it back safely to California." Kathy laughs. "It's been a fantastic experience and so educational for the kids. They've learned a lot about life. We all have," she says thoughtfully. I hope she'll elaborate, but instead she says, "Shall we go up and see if the boys are ready?"

Steve and Eric work in tandem, coiling lines, pulling bumpers, and closing hatches—having done it all a thousand times before. Jack, my eager little sailor, follows Eric around like a puppy, tripping over his paws as he attempts to maneuver around the deck's hardware. Lily and Megan, sporting bikinis and Jackie O sunglasses, are stretched across beach towels on the bow. Too bad their skinny, still-blossoming bodies betray their best efforts to appear womanly. I feel pride in my fun-loving, adorable son and my sweet, outgoing daughter. Yes, they are on their way to having a wonderful life. *Oh, if only.*

Once Eric finishes, he joins the girls on the bow while the rest of us relax in the cockpit and get to know one another. Under Steve's watchful eye, Jack takes the helm.

Steve and Kathy, I learn, owned a successful financial investment business in San Diego. Avid sailors, they decided to sell their company and embark on a worldwide family odyssey. I'm mesmerized by the harrowing stories of diving on shark feeds without a cage and escaping pirates off the coast of Venezuela and of Mother Nature hurling her relentless power at them as they crossed the high seas.

I envy this handsome, adventurous foursome who rely on each other to fulfill their every need. Day by day during their journey, they've strengthened the fabric of their family. We're talking Kevlar, baby! I'm inspired to take the burlap state of mine and, thread by thread, build it into the same bullet-proof bond.

We sail to Little Thatch Island, where the current inhabitants are amiable donkeys. The kids dive off the boat and swim to shore. Steve, Kathy, and I load the dinghy with towels and food for our beachside picnic. By the time we land and lay out our grass mats, Jack has begun excavating sand for Eric's burial. Steve and Kathy join Jack in his efforts to entomb Eric. Meanwhile, the girls continue ripening their tans.

*This is your chance, Alex. Their backs are turned. Go ahead. Take off your shirt and shorts. Do it! Everyone else is in a swimsuit. You look like an idiot sunbathing in your clothes. Just because he dumped you doesn't mean your body sucks. Dammit, where's your confidence? Come on!* Somewhere between my husband's rejection and Malibu Barbie here, I'm digging way deeper for my self-worth than Eric's sandy grave.

I find the courage to strip to my bathing suit and quickly sit back down in my best body-flattering position.

Steve and Kathy finish helping Jack and then park their *Baywatch* bodies on the grass mats next to me.

They ask about our life back home.

I fill them in on Xtreme Perspectives. "We design and build miniature environments for movies, TV, and music videos," I say, which inevitably leads to a discussion about my business partner. This, in turn, flows into our personal relationship: "my ex, the kids' dad, yada, yada, yada, cheated with my assistant, blahdy, blahdy, blah." Dang, it's hard to have a lengthy conversation without coming around to my divorce. I feel like such a failure recapping my pitiful downfall to these unblemished strangers. How about we talk politics? Religion, anyone?

My unexpected dissolution seems to touch every aspect of my life. And why am I so comfortable sharing with these people anyway? Surprised by the depth of their empathy, it reminds me that by reaching out, I continue to receive so much in return. For someone who isn't used to sharing her problems, it's been an ongoing lesson.

"It must be terrible to live through a divorce, particularly when you have to work with him. I'm not sure I could do what you're doing," Kathy confesses. "You must have incredible strength and courage."

Here's a woman who has hand-fed man-eating predators, telling me that I have strength and courage! I guess when you think about it, we're not so different. There are all kinds of shark-infested waters.

In the midst of our bonding, a shadow moves over our sun-worshipping faces. Two inquisitive gray donkeys, with white markings around their eyes and muzzles, have caught the scent of our picnic basket. Kathy tries shooing them away, but Steve encourages the party crashers with friendly pats on their noses. As soon as the kids spot the beasts, our serene beachfront property fills with cheerful chaos.

The four-legged creatures indulge us, posing for pictures with us. Jack pets one of the boy burros. The donkey becomes, shall we say, impassioned, showing off his gigantic manhood and making for one great photo-op. My innocent son has no idea from his angle why the rest of us are laughing as he continues to stroke the happy animal and smile, along with the donkey, for the camera.

On our return sail, Kathy asks me to join her below deck. "I want to give you something," she says, reaching for one of her exotic treasures. She places a delicate miniature conch shell in my hand. "This is from one of my dives. I want you to have it, so you remember how beautiful life is. If you look at it every day maybe it will help you to face your challenges when you go back home."

Her kindness and sincerity begin to unmask my, until now, controlled composure. I feel the muscles around my mouth trying to take charge of the emotion I know is about to spill out. "Thank you" is all I can manage to say.

Life, isn't it strange. The person you love most in the world treats you worse than anyone else ever has. Then along comes a total stranger, and she gives you a sublimely compassionate moment that will help sustain you through the days ahead.

Nat's apartment bustles with preparty grooming. Tomorrow will be our last full day on the islands, but tonight we have the infamous Full Moon Party at the Bomba Shack!

Jack sits on the edge of the bed while Lily and Nat playfully style his hair. They step back to admire their work. Nat, armed with a spray bottle in one hand and a comb in the other, winks at me, Monique, as she comments expressively in French for my benefit.

I borrow a short white skirt from my dear friend and pair it with a hot-pink halter top. Then, throwing caution to the wind, I put on one dangly earring and one diamond post. There's something about bright-colored clothing, sexy tropical hair, and a nice rich tan that makes you feel damn good. We are four beauteous blonds ready for whatever the night has in store for us. After more than a week of liberation on Tortola, I can honestly see myself again in the mirror. I remember now. I *am* a fun person!

Nat turns left, heading up over the mountain that divides the south end of the island—climbing and switch-backing on blind, tight curves, she honks to warn oncoming traffic. I think about how astonishingly comfortable I've become in this vehicle the kids and I have affectionately nicknamed the Big-Horned Jeep.

We reach the pinnacle of the mountain and begin our descent. The sun sets over Jost Van Dyke in the distance, and rolling shades of Caribbean blue sweep the beach below. The image is so amazing, it imprints on my mind for eternity.

Halfway down the hillside, we hear reggae coming from Bomba's. There's a reason they call it a shack. Squeezed between the coastal road and the water's edge at high tide, the open-air building is pieced together from scrap wood painted in an array of bright colors and is decorated with graffiti and hanging paraphernalia—everything from hubcaps to women's underwear. The floor is the beach itself. Old pylons support bench seating in addition to holding up the back end of the shack. And dancing takes place wherever you want it to.

But the thing that Bomba's is most notorious for is its mushroom punch. Yes, we're talking psychedelic, baby. Throw a little fungus in a blender with some alcohol and fruit juice and, voilà, you'll be on your knees praying to Bob Marley for morning to come.

This, however, I decide, is not the night to fulfill my inebriated fantasy. If it's true that children learn what they live, seeing their mother buzzed on toadstools is not a class I want to conduct.

As we enter our playground for the evening, Nat leans in and says, "That's Bomba over there."

I glance toward the darkened corner and see a large, shadowy figure in dreads perched on a rattan throne.

It's time to have a little fun with the kids.

"Hey, you guys, Nat told me earlier that since you two are underage, in order to be here, you have to kneel at Bomba's feet and ask him for permission to stay."

"That's right," Nat says, playing along, "otherwise he won't let us in. It's part of their culture."

Jack's and Lily's happy faces turn anxious.

"Go on—we can't insult Bomba," I say, giving them a nudge. "It's our last chance to party in paradise. You don't want to spend our precious time sitting in Nat's apartment, do you?"

The kids begin inching their way over to the Bomba, who looks strikingly like a black Jabba the Hut. I'm pretty sure that I wouldn't even approach the guy! Lily's probably envisioning Princess Leia in a choker collar as she stands before him. Nevertheless, my obedient children drop to their knees. The music is so loud, I can't hear what they're saying, but Jabba, I mean Bomba, suddenly flashes his pearly whites. He looks our way and gives his old friend Nat a wink as his booming laugh rattles the haphazard walls. My gullible offspring jump to their feet, realizing they've been duped. Jack does his best to tackle me. Lily's eye roll and exasperated exhale qualify her to be inducted into the Tortured-Teen Hall of Fame.

We move through a narrow corridor, past a small wooden counter, and hear the whir of the nefarious blender. Nat leads us into an open area lit by dim yellow bulbs attached to conduit along the exposed ceiling beams. The band is on a small platform at the far end of a room filled with crudely constructed tables where locals and tourists are mingling.

The slow rhythmic beat of *Stir It Up* already has our heads bobbing as we drop our things at a table and join the party. Dancing in the cool, soft sand feels like such a guilty pleasure. It can be freeing and romantic and even sensual. But when you're dancing with your friend and your kids, it's just plain old fun.

Before long, Jack manages to become the center of a mambo circle with four middle-aged women from Connecticut. His uninhibited moves have the ladies laughing and giving him the thumbs-up. Nat and Lily pair together, rolling their hips and digging their feet into nature's dance floor. I find myself slightly isolated and worry that if I look alone, one of the unattached men might approach me. While this vacation has renewed shreds of my self-confidence, I'm not ready to brave the dance floor with a strange man.

Well, don't you know: if you think it! *Oh god, here comes one!* I squint in the diming light at my approaching suitor. Gulp, is this what I attract after all these years? *Please don't ask me to dance. Please, please, pleeease, I beg the gods of diminishing self-worth, not him!*

"Would you care to donce?" His accent confirms he's a local. A man in his sixties, I'm guessing, with a coarse-looking, ungroomed salt-and-pepper beard; old polyester leisure-suit pants; and long dreadlocks that haven't been sanitized in perhaps, oh, say, a decade. A real Rasta mon.

"Sure," I say, ever the polite and pleasing woman. I start to reggae rock and roll like everyone else in the room, but apparently this guy's been to the Arthur Murray School of Dance. He wants to hold me as if we're fox-trotting at the Ritz. My eyes bolt from Nat to the kids but they're too busy having fun to notice my predicament. Rasta Mon pulls me closer, hugging me way too tightly.

*Smile, Alex. It's okay. Just a dance. Breathe in, but not too deeply. That's it. You can do this.*

Uh-oh. Wait a minute! *What's . . . ? Is that his . . . ? Oh god, it is! He's got a frickin'. . . ! Shit! Try to ignore it. Oh, so not possible! HELLLP!*

Within a second of my horrible realization, I feel a tap on my shoulder.

"Berwick!" I exclaim, surprised and relieved by his presence.

"Mm, may I cut in?"

I jump back from Rasta Mon's horny limbo stick and silently curse the creep for plunging my self-esteem further into the toilet.

"Mm, you okay?" Berwick asks as he puts his manly arms around me.

"I am now!" I say, followed by an involuntary cootie shake.

For the rest of the evening, when Berwick isn't dancing with Nat, the kids, or me, he waits in the shadows, arms crossed, his eyes scanning the room like a Cylon for our protection.

My mind usually reverts back to the noises of my stress-filled life as the end of vacation draws near but not today. This trip has nourished my soul in a way I couldn't have imagined. Perhaps it's because I've never needed it so bad. My depleted spirit has been transfused with reminders of life's infinite possibilities.

The narrow, rocky road to Smuggler's Cove, our last stop this vacation, is not for the timid. Nat skillfully dodges the rain-ravaged ruts and delivers us safely to what is now my favorite beach. Smuggler's can only be imagined in your best dream. Palm trees, mangroves, and bougainvillea line the soft white sand near the water's edge while two coral reefs welcome the sea like outstretched arms. The gentle surf with its softly bubbled edge deepens to blue perfection.

I stop in the sand, loaded down with beach toys, and watch as pelicans dive for their morning meals just off shore.

"Oh, what a wonderful bird is the pelican. His bill will hold more than his belly can," Nat recites. "He can hold in his beak enough for a week, but I can't understand how the hell he can!"

The kids and I look at her and burst into laughter. We repeat her funny little ditty, committing it to memory, and laugh some more.

"This place is where the remake of *The Old Man and the Sea,* the one with Anthony Quinn, was shot. They used that building over there for filming."

Nat points to a concrete one-story structure, with big arched openings on half walls, buried in a jungle of bushes. A tattered sign over the entrance reads, *Smuggler's Cove Beach Bar.* Weathered scrap wood lies strewn across the corrugated metal roof. Moving closer, we spot a rusty, old cannon ready to take on any pillaging pirates, and a 1960s Lincoln Continental parked smack in the middle of the joint.

"That car was used for Queen Elizabeth's tour of Tortola in 1977. Ol' Bob, who owned the bar, had the only decent four-door vehicle on the island at the time. Believe it or not, this place is still open for business."

"Really." I raise an eyebrow.

"Yeah, it's a working honor bar, run by a ghost," she says with a wink my direction. "Come on, kids, I'll show you."

We enter the eerie, dusty bistro, inching our way behind Nat. On top of the bar is an open cigar box with some change and a few dollar bills in it. Displayed neatly on a table are T-shirts that say *Smuggler's Cove.* A handwritten sign says they are twelve dollars each. We follow our fearless leader into the kitchen and watch as she opens the commercial-size refrigerator fully stocked with beer and soda.

"Are you sure it's all right to be in here?" I say, waiting for someone to appear out of nowhere and scare the heck out of me.

"Of course it is. That's why they have the cigar box. People just pay for anything they take. You can rent the beach chairs and umbrellas too."

"Mom, can we get a shirt?" Jack asks.

"Sure, I think that's a great idea!" We pick up three of the silk-screened souvenirs and put thirty-six dollars into the cigar box. "How do they know someone else won't come along and take the money?"

"*They* don't. That's why *they* call it an honor bar."

"Okay, smart-ass," I say under my breath.

I look around the room for a painting with eyes that move, but there isn't one. Still, I can't shake the feeling that we're being watched, perhaps by an ethereal Hemingway who's grinning at my uneasiness as he hoists a brew at the corner table.

"Let's hit the beach." I'm ready to move on.

We lay our mats down and head straight for the water—Jack wearing his snorkeling mask, Lily carrying her boogie board. Nat and I slowly frog-kick to deeper water and begin swimming parallel to the beach. As I freestyle, each head-turning breath is aimed in the direction of my kids. My undercover glances, camouflaged by the Australian crawl, go undetected by Nat. I've gotten pretty sly over the course of our vacation. Nat thinks I've totally lightened up, and to some degree that's true, but I've also developed some excellent covert kid-surveillance skills in an effort to avoid *the look.*

"Mom, you want the boogie board? I'm getting out," Lily offers, swimming toward us.

"Thanks, babe. Put some sunscreen on." All right, so apparently I haven't completely mastered covert behavior.

I take one end of the board, and Nat swims over and grabs the other. We rest our arms across the top, soaking in the view of the beach, and let our bodies float with the movement of the waves. Jack sits hunched over with his face down in the shallow water waiting for whatever creature might pass his way, while Lily basks on the soft white sand.

The palm trees sway in the easy breeze under the cloudless sky. Does it get any better than this?

"You ready to go home?" Nat says, interrupting my rapture.

I hear the painful sound of a stereo needle scratching across an LP. "Thanks a bunch. Way to snap me back to reality."

"Sor-ry."

"Nat, I can't thank you enough for what you've done for us. I've been able to relax and put some things into perspective. I realize I had a kind of unintentional arrogance about my life. You know what I mean?" I don't give Nat a chance to answer.

"I was raised in a loving family by two dedicated parents, received a good education, married the man I loved, have an exciting career, and am blessed with two great kids. And it all came without any real price."

"So what's the lesson?"

"Well, I haven't figured *all* of them out yet, but the obvious ones are having greater compassion and empathy for others and not judging anyone, because you have no idea what's gone on in their life. I mean, of course I've always known these things intellectually, and even felt that I practiced them. The old Alex would have proudly thought she owned these qualities. But I had no idea how much greater my understanding could be, that I would grasp their meaning so much more profoundly. I feel like I'm discovering a deeper dimension to myself.

"And then, there's the 'never take anything for granted because it can be gone in a heartbeat' gem. It's funny how all of those old pearls hold true."

"You mean, like, 'all men think with their dicks.'"

Laughing at Nat's astute brand of wisdom, I say, "Not quite what I had in mind, but close enough."

# Chapter Four

I return not to cold hostility from James but uncharacteristic friendliness. He starts hanging around my house when he drops the kids off, tossing around his humor and charm. While it's making life more pleasant, I'm not prepared for what happens next.

"Hey, Lex, you want to meet me for a drink some night soon?"

My heart begins pounding so strongly with expectation, I notice my silk blouse quivering. Yes, after all my recent fun and reflection and as much as I don't want to, I still love the jerk.

Since my protective family and friends have verbally annihilated James in their support of me, I decide to keep my rendezvous with him a secret. And more important, I don't want to give Jack and Lily any false hope.

On the drive over to the restaurant, my head swims with questions. *What does he want? Is it good news or bad? Does my tan make me look hot?*

When I enter the dimly lit bar, it takes me a second to focus. I spot James at a corner table and approach him with a confident façade.

"Hi," I say, hoping the sound of that one little word holds all of the strength and composure I intend it to.

"Hi, Lex! Thanks for coming. What can I get you?" he asks while leaning in close to pull out my chair.

Why is he acting so attentive? "Screwdriver, please."

"Hmmm, I'm not sure I want you brandishing what could be considered a weapon," he says, giving me a sly smile. "You might be harboring a few negative feelings."

*Ya think!*

"How about a Slow Comfortable Screw Against the Wall instead?" he jokes.

I feign a smile. *What gives you the right to talk to me that way anymore?* "I suppose you're drinking a Death-wish with a twist?" I rally back.

"We haven't done this in a while," he says, stating the ridiculous.

I've had enough of this coy banter and ask, "James, why did you want to meet like this?"

"No small talk, huh. Okay." Fortifying himself with a sip of his scotch, he begins, "I feel like things have been going really well between us." He looks for confirmation but gets none. "I realize now what an idiot I was to throw our life away like I did."

*Don't change expressions. Control your breathing.* I instinctively adjust my blouse in case it begins vibrating again.

"I want it back, Lex. I mean," he says, reaching for my hand, "I want us back."

I've been struggling for so long to keep moving forward, and in one split second I'm slammed back to the threshold of this daunting ride. *Look! My hand, he's holding it!*

"I've made such a huge mistake," he continues.

*I don't know. What does this mean? How do I feel? What about the kids? What if we don't make it? What would it do to them? And would I have the strength to start my recovery all over again?*

"But what about Mara?" I ask.

"She's not in my life anymore. You're the one I want. I'm just sorry it took me so long to realize it. Lexie, please," he pleads, searching my eyes for reconciliation.

*What do I think? What do I want? Could I ever really forgive him?* I still love the man he used to be, but . . . *Wait: she's not in his life anymore?* I pause for a moment of jilted-wife satisfaction to relish a big fat consoling karmic rush. *Ahhhh.*

"Why should I believe that you and Mara are really through, or that you won't do this with some other woman?"

"I know I've hurt you, but, Lex, please let me try to make it up to you. I love you with all my heart," he says, squeezing my hand and fixing his deep-blue eyes on mine.

Those eyes, I want to believe them so badly. "We'd have to go slowly, James, and even then I'm not sure I'll ever be able to trust you again. I wish I knew, but I honestly don't."

"Can we at least try?"

"It might take a long time to heal our relationship, if we even can. Are you sure you're willing to do whatever it takes?"

"Let me prove to you that we belong together," he says, pulling me closer.

His familiar scent brings with it a flood of memories. How can I throw away this chance to have my husband back, my family together, and my heart healed?

"Are you absolutely certain this is what you want?" I question him, worried about the impact this will have on Lily and Jack. And then I question myself: am I crazy?

"You have no idea." Wait, which question is he answering? "Yes, I want it!" he proclaims.

Over the course of the next few months, James and I carefully and discreetly try to find our way back to one another. The Alex who showed her wounds to all of her friends has closed ranks, sharing with only her inner circle. James is thoughtful and funny and showers me with attention.

> My darling Lexie,
> I'm beginning to realize all over again what a very special person you are. I know that I messed up, and I let you down. Not wanting to work things out was the lowest thing I've ever done, but I'm out of the fog now. What I'm really trying to say is that I love you! My thoughts have been only of you, seeing your pretty face, your beautiful eyes, your smile, and wanting to touch you and be in your presence. I am devoted to loving you. Please let me continue my quest to earn your trust again. I pray that with time and patience, we can be together forever.
> James

James continues to promise me that I can take as long as necessary to resurrect the trust I once had in him.

Ready to open my heart more fully, I suggest we spend a few days alone together. "We're always with the kids or at work. We need to focus on just us."

"I'm in!" he says eagerly. "Where should we go?"

"Let's fly down to Palm Springs. I'll ask Kendall and Tim if they'll take care of the kids for a few days. But, James, I don't want anyone else to know that we're going away together," I caution him. "We'll become grist for the office rumor mill, and there's been enough of that already. I need more time. And I especially don't want the kids to get their hopes up any higher than they already have."

It appears he'll go along with anything I ask. *Oh, by the way, I've decided to have the prongs tightened on the family jewels. The old ones seem to be a little loose.*

"I'll make the arrangements," I say, leaving his office while wrestling with the uncertainty of our future together. Why have I been so hesitant to let everybody know that we're trying again? What's keeping me from shouting it from the rooftops?

Holding hands over the armrest on our flight to Palm Springs, we reminisce.

"Remember how I loved when you would break into song for me?" I say. More than songs, James had a charisma and outrageous wit that had me laughing right up until he sucker-punched me.

He leans in close to my ear. "'If ever I would leave you, it wouldn't be in springtime.' You were so easy," he teases.

"Easy? I don't think so," I say. "But we did have our own Camelot. And I guess you didn't lie about leaving me in springtime, because you left in summer," I add with a note of sarcasm.

"I meant that it was easy to make you laugh. Getting you into bed for the first time took a helluva lot of effort on my part."

"That's because I wasn't buying the *I love yous* you were peddling so soon after we met."

"Well, I tried!" He laughs. "And then spring break happened. Who would have thought that picking cactus needles out of your alabaster ass would lead to breaking the code? I'll be forever grateful for that hike on Sugarloaf Mountain!"

"It's because I knew you really loved me by then."

"And I still love you all these years later," he says so readily.

My delight in recalling our life together is overshadowed by the remembrance of what's been lost, our once-joyful memories now tarnished by betrayal. If I'm feeling this confused, I can only imagine how Lily and Jack must feel. It's no wonder Lily's been challenging me. The safety and security of our family boundaries have been blurred. She has to be asking herself: Are we a family or aren't we? And if we aren't, what's going to happen to me? James and I remind each other of our love all the way to Palm Springs as I labor to repress my thoughts of heartbreak.

Something keeps holding me back. What is it? Something in my gut. Whoa, no, not my gut! Isn't it enough that my heart and head struggle to find synchronicity? Now I've got to contemplate my inner voice and bring it into harmony with the other two? *Crap. This is going to be a lot of hard work.* Maybe if I'd have paid attention to my gut's subtle whispers the first time around, I might not have been so blindsided.

We check into our suite overlooking the resort's pool. "This is really nice," I say, stepping out onto the second-floor balcony to see sunbathers sipping drinks from the poolside cabana bar. I turn to James with a flirtatious grin. "I wonder if this key will be a keeper."

"Ahh, the key." He remembers. "I'm counting on it."

James has a collection of hotel keys he keeps as souvenirs from places we've stayed over the years. The Century Plaza in LA and the Grand Wailea on Maui are two of his favorites.

"Remember the downtown Marriott?" he says. "That was an incredible night, my Lady in Red."

Several years ago when James was working for another production firm, weeks of endless travel and long hours prevented us from seeing much of each other. Knowing his latest project was about to end, I secretly arranged for a quiet evening alone together.

Kendall, my friend and neighbor, offered to watch Lily and Jack overnight. I reserved a room at the downtown Marriott, rented a tux for James, and hired a limo. After shopping for a new red dress, I had my hair styled differently, applied a date-night dose of makeup, and added red lipstick, nails, and lingerie, making the Lady in Red transformation complete.

Late Friday afternoon, James's boss, who was aware of my plan to whisk him away from work, unbeknownst to me improvised his own bit of fun by announcing a quick company-wide meeting over the public address system. As all sixty employees assembled, his boss opened one of the delivery-bay doors, and the black stretch limo I'd reserved pulled into the shop. The chauffer stepped out of the car, asked for James, and handed him a red, scented envelope and a garment bag. His boss, relishing James's discomfort at being center stage, coaxed him into reading the note out loud to the baffled employees.

> Dearest James,
> I've admired you from afar and can no longer wait to be with you. Please allow my driver to bring you to where I anxiously await your arrival. Don't disappointment me. I promise it will be worth it!
> Yours,
> The Lady in Red

From the second-floor window of the Marriott bar, I saw my love arrive. He looked handsome in his black tux as he stepped out of the limo. In mere moments, he would come to me. I tingled at the thought of romancing my husband this way.

His eyes searched the candlelit bar. A smile of recognition came across his face as he found me. At that moment, James Bond had nothing on my 007!

"May I join you?" he inquired, playing along.

"Why, yes," I said, motioning for him to slide next to me.

"Do you come here often?" he asked.

"Actually, no. It's my first time." *This is fun!*

He leaned in close, taking a sip of my drink. "Hmm, a

vodka woman. I'm a scotch man myself." The warmth of his breath stirred me. "Did you know vodka women and scotch men make a perfect match?"

"Oh, really?"

"It's true! It has something to do with their mutually intoxicating spirits."

"That's quite a line. Am I supposed to be impressed by your charm?" I added, feigning resistance.

"I'm hoping," he whispered, his eyes fixated a bit south of my chin. "You smell delicious, and that dress!"

"Why, thank you. Are you staying here at the hotel?" I asked, knowing I had a key in my purse to add to his collection.

"No, no, I'm not. There's a convention in town, and I haven't been able to find an available room. How about you?"

"I've got a suite upstairs."

His eyes widened. "You do?" he exclaimed, temporarily breaking character. He recovered quickly—inched his hand under my dress and leaned in close to my ear. "Do you by any chance have a bed big enough for two?"

"Maybe," I teased, enjoying the excitement of his touch as my finger lightly stroked the back of his hand.

Well, apparently that was all James needed. He reached for his wallet, threw some cash on the table, and pulled me out of the booth. Thank goodness I have long legs, because his stride would have toppled a shorter woman.

The elevator doors opened. *Good, nobody inside.* I pushed James against the side wall, hit the tenth-floor button, and laid my body against his. We kissed passionately, my lips craving his as my hands impatiently reached beneath his jacket. *Ooo, these reflective walls are niiiice.*

*Are there cameras in here? Is some security guard enjoying this?* Just then, the elevator chimed, and the doors opened.

But now, here in Palm Springs, a sudden awkwardness comes over the room as we both glance at the bed.

"You want to go into town? Check things out. Maybe get something to eat," James says.

"Sure," I answer, anxious to leave behind the silk-covered elephant in the room.

I know why I'm avoiding our hotel room—it's called rebuilding trust. But why is he? Didn't he beg for our reunion? Isn't he getting exactly what he wants?

James and I finally find our way into bed in the early-morning hours. We have sex, but we don't make love. Later I try talking to him about it but feel the same frustration with his answers as I did that horrible night in Victoria. This time, however, I am a different woman. I'm not a happily married wife unearthing a lie she's been living. I'm an independent woman who's protecting herself and her children. Unfortunately, choosing the right course of action for our future will not be easy. I'm still in love with James. My heart and gut are throwing punches at one another. Can I get my head back in here please?

Not long after our trip, I impulsively walk into James's office and ask, "Is there something going on that you're not telling me about?"

"What do you mean?" he says as he leans back in his chair, clasping his hands behind his head.

"Are you and Mara still seeing each other?" My voice falters.

"Why are you asking me this?"

"Please, James, just answer the question."

"Of course not."

No sooner does he issue a denial then his pants begin to bulge. I blink my eyes in disbelief as his groin inflates, blowing up bigger and bigger until . . .

*Oh god! Look out! It's going to burst!*

His zipper explodes, and a gigantic, erect penis the size of Babe Ruth's baseball bat springs from his pants! I'm so stunned, I can't move. He points the monstrosity at me and discharges liquefied truth all over my face!

I bolt upright in bed and survey my darkened room. *Oh my god! He's cheating again!*

Later that morning, with James away on a two-day business trip, my assistant, Carol, pops her head into my office looking flustered. "Mara's on the phone." Though Carol didn't know Mara, she's heard so much office gossip, I'm sure she feels she does.

"For me?!" I say, blown away that she'd call me just hours after my dream.

"You want me to get rid of her?"

"It's all right. I'll take it."

Carol closes my door as I turn to the phone on my credenza. I calm myself and reach for the receiver. Why is *my* heart pounding? She should be the anxious one. *Show confidence, Alex. And don't let her hear anything in your voice but a strong, together woman.*

"Hello."

"Hi, Alex. It's Mara."

"What can I do for you?" Now, there's a really stupid question. Like I'm gonna do something for her. *Hey, need a facial?*

"I was wondering if you would meet me for lunch. There's something I have to tell you."

*Don't be a pleaser, Alex. Don't do it. She could go wacko on you.* My imagination flashes to her lunging at me in our local eatery with a deadly salad fork as patrons slurp their Friday afternoon clam chowder.

"Whatever you have to tell me, you can say over the phone."

"I just thought you ought to know that James and I have been seeing each other again."

And there *it* was—that *something* holding me back.

"We only broke up for two months and then got back together. James didn't want you to know, but I thought you should."

The false compassion in Mara's voice sickens me. She's telling me for her own selfish reasons, and we both know it.

What's my next move? Do I scream at her? Call her a home-wrecking whore? No, not me. Instead, I actually express gratitude. "Thanks for telling me. Is that all?"

"Yeah, I just thought you should know."

I place the receiver back on its cradle and stare at the phone, not believing I'm still living this drama. *Why is it in my life? What more am I supposed to learn? Help!*

I want to throw the phone through the window as my blood boils on its way up to my face, but I don't have the luxury of falling apart here, not in front of my employees. I'm their leader and must be professional. I also know Carol, the office Louella, has already gotten word out about the phone call, discreetly sharing her scathing opinion of Mara.

My eyes fall on the Caribbean seashell Kathy gave me when I was visiting Nat. I need to give James a chance to explain himself when he returns from Arizona. Maybe Mara is lying. James said she couldn't be trusted. *Stuff your feelings one more time, Alex. Do your work; take care of the kids; and when James returns, you can engage your heart again.*

After our morning managers' meeting, I ask James to stay in the conference room with me. As co-owners of Xtreme, there are plenty of business reasons why we'd meet behind closed doors.

I look directly into James's eyes and take a deep breath to steady myself. I've tried not to think about Mara until this very moment.

"James, I got a call from Mara while you were out of town," I say, beginning to let myself feel the agony of her words. "She told me the two of you have been seeing each other again."

His face twists and flushes with rage. "That bitch! She should never have called you! You don't deserve to hear it from her! Goddamn bitch! Who in the hell does she think she is? I swear I could kill her!"

For the first time in our lives, James scares me. I've never seen him this angry. He's mad at her for telling me? Shouldn't I be the one screaming at him?

"Forget about her, James. What about us? I thought you wanted to get back together," I say, feeling myself begin to break apart. "And I believed you."

"I know, I know," he concedes. "But, Alex, it was taking too long."

"You said you would give me all the time I needed." Then it hits me just how short my trust-building timeline had been. "Mara said you broke up with her for only two months and that you've been together ever since." The realization jars me as the words come spilling out of my mouth, the pieces quickly falling into place. "Oh my god, that means you were back with her when we were in Palm Springs!"

"I'm so sorry, Lex. I didn't mean to hurt you," he says, reaching for my hand across the conference room table, but I quickly pull it away.

"Was it all lies?"

"No, I really wanted us to make it," he says, giving me his "don't be mad at me" face. The same pitiful look he used when I chastised him for eating Oreos for breakfast.

"We never stood a chance. You couldn't make up your mind, so you tried to have it all, without even thinking about the devastation it would bring to the kids and me." Each word is like a knife wound in my throat. "Why would you do this again?" I begin to cry, swatting away my tears like annoying flies. "Well, you don't need to worry any longer about deciding for yourself. Fool me twice, goddamn shame on me!" I can't speak anymore and swallow hard to regain my composure. I squeeze my mouth to stop it from doing what it wants, from completely unleashing a stream of obscenities. *Get a grip, Alex. You can't fall apart here at work!*

"I don't know what else to say, Lexie. I never wanted

this to happen," he says pathetically.

Clearing the painful daggers from my throat, I manage to utter, "There's nothing else *to* say! I have a choice to make, and I choose to move on. We will continue to have a business together and parent our children. Nothing more."

James mumbles another inadequate "I'm sorry," as I open the door to leave and come face-to-face with my assistant's pitying gaze.

I head straight to my office, grab my purse, put on my sunglasses, and hurry out the front door.

I've got to go somewhere! Anywhere! *When the truth is told to be lies, and all the joy within you dies.* My fingers practically snap the radio knob off as I drive up the hill toward the park. Blinded by my tear-filled eyes, I pull into an empty parking lot and slump behind the wheel of my car. At last, I indulge my sorrow and grief by letting the salty toxic pain fall away.

# Chapter Five

Once again, I begin to accept life without James and move forward by focusing on my blessings, which include my wonderful girlfriends.

When Lily was a toddler, I joined our neighborhood babysitting co-op. Through the years, seven of us mothers have welded an unbreakable bond and, to this day, find plenty of ways to continue nourishing our friendships. Our annual junkets to Black Ridge Ranch are a unanimous favorite.

This year, our road trip is the same weekend that Lily and Jack will be visiting Mount Rainier's Paradise Inn with James and Mara. Yes, they're together. Apparently instead of, and I quote, "that bitch . . . I could kill her," he's decided to punish her with his wayward love.

Kendall, Kate, and I, always partners in crime, are driving over to the ranch in my car. Whenever we're together, there's plenty of laughter. Kendall, an Iowa black-haired beauty, is district manager for a large pharmaceuticals company. Kate, a tall, salt-of-the-earth Montanan with short, curly, brown hair, is a pediatric nurse who exudes an aura of warmth and positivity. I can laugh just looking at her!

Liz is following behind us in her black SUV, with Annie, Elise, and Tammy. All of my gal pals and their husbands are hovering around the twenty-year-anniversary mark. Without them intending to be, my happily wedded friends are another reminder of my failed marriage. Once a member of the neighborhood fourteen, I've reduced that number to an unlucky thirteen, adding yet another psychological adjustment to the endless stream of paradigm shifts we divorcées have to make.

In the past, my friends and I have driven straight through to the ranch, but this time, after a late start, we decide to stop for dinner. Places to eat on Highway 2 are few and far between, and most of them challenge one's culinary palette. It's our first time at A River Runs Through It.

Situated along the Skykomish River, the setting is brimming with rustic charm. At first glance, the place appears to have potential; however, my childhood training and German genetic code have made me acutely wary of wayside eateries. I begin my assessment by looking for signs of neglect as soon as we approach the restaurant. When we enter, I scan for cleanliness. After being seated, I do a discreet visual smudge check of the table, condiment jars, silverware and, yes, even the menus.

Kate senses my *anal*-ytical thinking. "What's going on in that head of yours? I see your wheels turning. Come on, tell me. I know something's up."

Kate loves to hear how my mind works. It's so diametrically opposed to her way of thinking. In the past, she has gotten cheap thrills out of secretly vandalizing my über-organized closet. Once I went to work wearing one black shoe and one navy because of her fun-loving ways. She, on the other hand, is lucky to find a matching pair of flip-flops on her cluttered closet floor.

"Well, have you really looked at this place? It's pretty dirty. Check out the salt and pepper shakers and the plastic menus. They're all slimy from food and goo—goo that's come from other people's germ-laden, diseased fingers."

Tickled by the extent of my meticulosity, her eyes squint as she chuckles.

"I'm serious," I declare with a grin. "How can you trust the food in a place like this? The stew's probably been simmering since Sacajawea put it on the stove for her fur-trading friends."

"So, what you do when you're in a situation like this?" she says, humoring me.

I jump at the chance to exaggerate my philosophical perspective for Kate's amusement. "Well, you shouldn't order anything with meat. Around here, they probably have a different meaning for the term *aged beef.* And definitely keep away from the New England clams," I say affecting a gag reflex. "Hmmm. At a place like this, I'd order the grilled cheese."

Kate unleashes a comical snort and then feigns serious contemplation by tapping her index finger on her chin.

"I mean, how can you screw up bread and cheese?" I add, pausing for effect. "That's right, when there's no other recourse, you can always eat the grilled cheese. And besides, any restaurant with the word *runs* in its name can't be good."

Black Ridge Ranch, in the heart of the Cascade Mountains, is a beautiful resort embraced by several snow-capped peaks. A thousand acres of Ponderosa pines, fresh-water ponds teeming with trout, and spring-fed streams rippling through a meadow where cattle graze all serve as the backdrop for secluded high-end vacation homes, a golf course, tennis courts, pools, endless bike paths, and horse trails.

An old business associate of mine has been renting me his cabin for years. Every time I pass through the gated entrance and round the bend to the first awesome view, I say out loud with impassioned emphasis, "God, I hate this place!" Of course, nothing could be further from the truth. It's one of those rare locations where you get a feeling of immediate peace—and with my girlfriends in tow, the prospect of uninhibited good times!

For the first couple of years I brought the girls here, I ran the group ragged, organizing outdoor activities from morning till night. My efficient methods, while useful in my career, simply took us from one of life's treadmills onto another. I'm surprised the girls didn't strip me of my counselor's whistle and lock me in the outhouse. As the years have passed, I learned that all we need for our weekend adventures are the right alcoholic beverages and each other.

We pull into the two-story retreat's red cinder driveway. After unlocking the house to the first level where the bedrooms are situated, we head upstairs to the main living area. The entire second story is one big, vaulted room with floor-to-ceiling windows. Comfy couches face a stone fireplace. A redwood coffee table acts as the perfect platform for our nightly beverages and spread of hors d'oeuvres. This cozy furniture has been privy to all sorts of important conversations.

A bar and a game table, where serious bouts of Texas

Hold 'Em, Spoons, and Spite and Malice have transpired, occupy another corner of the room. The modern kitchen and massive dining table inhabit the other half of the upstairs. Outdoors, a wraparound deck among the treetops looks out past the twelfth hole to a pond loaded with Canada geese and to the wilderness beyond.

The cars have been unloaded, and we're immediately in party mode. Most of our group took time off from work during our kids' formative years, but all of us have since gone back. After all, as I've learned, the bottom line is that we have only ourselves to rely on. Liz, Elise, Annie, and Tammy set up the beverage counter and take our drink orders. Crammed in and around the kitchen, we move to the cranked-up beat of Donna Summer's *Bad Girls.*

Kate and I, the jocks of the group, start a game of indoor football with a roll of Bounty paper towels. I boogie my way across the great room to Donna's disco beat as Kate rifles a pass, keeping it low so she doesn't take out any hanging light fixtures. Kendall shimmies her way in front of me for an interception. The Friday night freedom train is rolling, cocktails are flowing, conversations and laughter are ringing from the rafters as we dance and sing to *She Works Hard for the Money.*

In this moment, I mentally transport myself outside the cabin and look in from the darkness to this glowing cathedral of joy. There's no sound, but there is such a rich aliveness to the happy activity inside, I can feel its radiating warmth. Life is so big that I'm suddenly overcome by the highs and lows of it. I take a long inhale of gratitude and return just in time for . . . *so you better treat her right.*

"You okay?" Kendall mouths to me.

I give her a nod and a wink.

Kendall has a psychic ability to read people. She's taught me how to accept help from my friends, a very challenging lesson for me. After all, I try to live up to my name. *Alexandra* is Greek for "helper of mankind," an honorable mission I proudly serve. But Kendall knew from the beginning of my trouble that I was the one who needed help. She forced her way past my façade and elevated me to a new level of understanding. Once she did, I was able to see a world of loved ones with their hands stretched out to me.

Jumping up on the bar, I do my own interpretation of *Coyote Ugly.* Annie grabs her camera for future blackmail purposes, and Kate sneaks up from behind to pants me. *Damn sweats.* Long ago, we took an oath of secrecy regarding some of the incidents that occur on our getaways. Unfortunately, Donna Karan warm-ups around my knees don't qualify as classified.

The next morning, one by one we crawl upstairs from our bedrooms. The rising sun blinds us through the wall of windows. I grab a pair of sunglasses off the counter to protect my vodka-infused eyes. Thankfully, Tammy was up early and brewed a pot of rich Colombian blend.

"How'd everyone sleep?" I ask, knowing it's a loaded question.

Over the years, these ladies have been duct-taped to their beds, found creatures under their blankets, had red powdered tempera paint put in their shower heads, been forced to liberate Liz's shrink-wrapped Suburban, and, the pièce d' résistance, had to recover Kendall's stolen company car filled with pharmaceuticals.

"How could we sleep?" Elise complains. "We were waiting all night for you to shave off our eyebrows!"

"I told you guys I'd be kind this year. I really meant what I said. I just don't have it in me to plan a worthy practical joke," I say, playing off of their sympathy.

"Yeah, right," Annie grumbles while giving me a dubious glance.

"Look, did I do anything last night? No. I said I wouldn't, and I won't," I reiterate with all sincerity.

We curl up on the couches around the fireplace in our pajamas, relishing every sip of coffee.

While Friday nights are strictly for partying, Saturday mornings revolve around conversations about school, health, community affairs, and neighborhood gossip. I'm always amazed by the extent of my friends' knowledge on these subjects. Where do they find the time to learn about these things?

"So, what's going on with you and James?" Elise asks with a note of enthusiasm.

"Well, ladies," I say feigning a smile, "it looks like we're over again." My words sound cavalier, but the devastation in my voice can't disguise my true feelings.

"He's still with the bitch," Kendall says, so I don't have to.

"Oh, Alex, I'm so sorry. What are you going to do?" Liz asks as she tucks her ombré-colored hair behind her ear. Up until my divorce, Liz, the owner of a midsize civil engineering firm, and I lived parallel lives. She manages a thriving company, has a good marriage, and is raising great kids. And damn her, she always looks good doing it.

"I'm just going to keep moving forward one day at a time, taking care of Lily and Jack and running Xtreme. Eventually, I'll be able to work through the emotional bull-shit. But in the meantime, I've got to be smart about the kids' and my futures." I respond positively even though gravity is having its own way, drawing my face downward.

"I'd be so angry!" Annie says. "Don't you just want to scream at them?"

"Yeah, but I can't go off on either one of them because I'll end up paying for it." My nausea begins to kick in, so I attempt to lighten the mood. "But I had a lovely daydream where I kicked Mara's scrawny, sorry ass. It was quite healing."

Kate senses my need for a break from the James and Mara discourse. Constantly hearing *her* name paired with his is just one more painful swipe of the sandpaper that erodes my soul. I've been half of James-and-Alex for all of my adult life. I hadn't realized how often my name was linked to his until it wasn't anymore.

"What time is it?" Kate asks, checking out the clock. "Oh my gosh, it's almost eleven. Who's on breakfast committee?"

"That's us," Liz says, acknowledging Elise and Annie. "I guess we'd better get started if we want to eat by noon."

Cooking isn't a chore when you've got your friends working in harmony with you. As we shift through showers, the smells of eggs California and glazed sausages fill the house.

Ready to indulge in our meal, Kate raises her glass. "To the Black Ridge Babes, may we still be doing this even when we have to remember to pack our adult diapers."

"Hear, hear!" we agree, clinking our glasses and savoring the taste of the icy rum-infused cranberry drink.

Just as we're about to take our first bite, the house phone rings for the first time in all of our years of being on the ranch. Startled, Annie jumps up to answer it. As she listens to the voice on the other end, her expression turns serious.

"That was the resort's property manager," she says after she hangs up. We breathe a collective sigh of relief knowing our families are fine. But the news that follows has us gasping anyway. "There's been a couple of bear sightings!"

"What?" Elise says with panic in her voice.

"He said we shouldn't be alarmed and that we should just make a lot of noise when we go outside, so the bears will hear us coming," Annie says earnestly.

We debate whether or not to stay indoors on such a gorgeous day.

"Let's just keep together in a group, and everything will be fine," Kate declares.

"Of course you'd say that—you're from Montana," Elise frets. "You probably shared a locker with Gentle Ben. But I've got my period, and you know what they say about *that!*"

"Don't worry. We'll put you in the middle of the group," Kendall says, trying to reassure her.

"The guy on the phone said homeowners usually keep noisemakers around the house for situations like this," Annie continues. "Apparently it's not the first time this has happened."

After breakfast, Kendall, Kate, and I clean up the dishes while the others search for some sort of auditory bear repellent. It isn't long before Elise yells from downstairs, "I found it." *It* turns out to be a cigar box filled with jingle bells.

"Let's tie them onto our shoes when we go for our walk," Annie declares.

"Good idea," Elise agrees, somehow convinced that these little bells will ward off a big, angry bear. I suppress a tiny smile.

As we begin our walk, generating enough noise to make Santa think it's time to load the sleigh, we notice no one else appears to be around, causing additional distress to the group. While discussing the topic of bears above the intrusive sound of our feet, we keep our eyes peeled on the woods around us, just in case. Annie and Elise make sure to stay inside our protective formation, releasing nervous giggles every now and then.

We move out of the forested area into a clearing about a hundred yards from the pro shop and golf course. To our surprise, Black Ridge is hosting a men's golf tournament smack in the midst of a bear scare!

Our chorus of jingles begins to attract attention the closer we get. Soon, all male eyes are upon us.

"I wonder why they aren't worried about the bears," Elise says.

"And how come they're not making any noise?" Annie chimes in.

My dear, sweet, gullible friends have such perplexed looks on their faces, and I'm trying hard not to laugh.

Then one of the golfers jokingly yells, "What's going on? You afraid of bears or something?"

The once-comforting sound of their deafening feet has now become the reason for their mortification as fifty men stand, clubs in hand, grinning at them. My pals can't seem to get away from the jingling of their feet. In a moment of shared realization, they turn and face me. I try to appear innocent but am too pleased with myself to effectively continue my performance.

"Alex!" Annie shrieks and then charges after me with Elise joining the chase. I'm laughing and running as their annoying bells quickly deter them from pursuing me any longer. They stop to remove the hideous reminders that, yes, once again the Queen of Practical Jokes has been victorious!

The quaint town of Brothers is only a few miles from the ranch. It's complete with Old West storefronts, decent restaurants, and an assortment of art galleries and boutiques. The community isn't big enough to have a stoplight, but it's big enough to welcome all sorts of outdoor enthusiasts who enjoy hiking, horseback riding, whitewater rafting, camping, cross-country skiing, and snowshoeing.

My friends and I begin working our way down Main Street. However, moving seven women in unison through stores is like herding sheep—except that we're wearing lipstick and carrying credit cards. Then again, I vaguely remember a lipstick-wearing sheep—but that was an entirely different weekend. We decide to split up and rendezvous for margaritas later.

After browsing a few shops, Kate and I park ourselves outside on a log bench next to a life-size cedar cowboy. "Now, this is my kind of man," I kid, "the strong, silent type. And he's packin' some mighty fine wood in those jeans."

Kate chuckles and winces simultaneously.

"Are you ready to face the dating scene?" she asks, going all serious on me.

"Not really," I answer, knowing I'll need considerable courage to put myself out there again. "But I want to be at some point."

"So what's on the must-have list?"

"I don't have a clue. I thought I knew the first time around, but obviously, I need some work in this area." Then, deciding to take her on another one of my philosophical journeys, I say, "But when I do, I'll be sure to check out his shoes first."

My pal puts her fingertips over her mouth, covering her "I can't wait to hear this one" grin. "Shoes first. Hmm. Interesting. And that would be because . . . ?"

"When I was seventeen, I spent the summer visiting my grandmother in Germany. Neither one of us was fluent in the other's language, so consequently, we had a few minor gaps in communication. One day we were talking about boys, and I'm pretty sure she told me to look at their shoes as an indicator of their character. You know, like the old saying, 'hooey on the outside means phooey on the inside'—something like that. Anyway, I think it's a smart strategy. Don't you agree?" I ask her, knowing she'd never consider checking out a guy's footwear in order to discern his desirability.

She nods in agreement and barely stifles her laughter. Getting a kick out of the absurdity of my pearl of wisdom, I proceed to expound, or should I say make stuff up, to see how far I can take this one. I quickly look away, trying not to lose control of my performance.

"For example, see that guy coming down the street?" I ask her.

"Yeah, what about him?"

"Well, even though we can't see his feet because of the fence, by the looks of the rest of him, I'd say he's wearing some ratty, old, hmm, probably gray running shoes."

"Oh, really."

"Yeah. I'd venture to guess he needs a new pair but feels there's tons of wear left in the ones he has on. Yep, he's single, lives in a cluttered old cabin that he doesn't own, and has a cat named Anarchy." I pause for dramatic effect and continue with my eyes glued to him. "He has a daily breakfast of high-fiber cereal eaten with organic yogurt and a sprinkle of flax and then pops a garlic pill and puts baking soda under his armpits—which, as we all know, doesn't really work." I take a deep breath and offer one final observation. "Yeah, I sure did learn a lot from my Omi that summer in Deutschland."

As soon as I glance over at Kate, we both begin to laugh. And then the guy we've been talking about passes by on the sidewalk in front of us. Kate's shoulders begin moving up and down so fast they could power a freight train. Her hysteria escalates as she tries to say something but can't. She inconspicuously points to his feet. I take a look, and I'll be damned if he isn't wearing ratty, old, gray running shoes!

That does it—we can't contain ourselves. Her eyes squint, forcing tears to puddle. We're leaning into each other, falling apart. I'm trying to salvage my mascara, but every time we glance at each other, our outburst is refueled.

"You are too much," Kate says.

"Me, what? There's some kind of silliness aura surrounding you. I get sucked in by its powerful magnetic force. Thank you for that. It's a great place to be."

Kate checks her watch. "Come on—let's get going. It's margarita time."

# Chapter Six

"**H**i, you guys. I missed you," I cheerfully say to my kids while my mind flashes on maracas and a sombrero. *No such thing as too many margaritas.* James is dropping them off after their weekend at Rainier. Lily rushes by me without a word, trailed by a draft of tumultuous air. Jack follows, rolling his eyes as he throws his arms around me, and retreats to his bedroom.

"We need to talk," James grumbles with flared nostrils.

"Come in," I say, averting my eyes from his angry scowl, afraid my face might twist to reflect his. *Stay cool, Alex. Don't let the bastard age you anymore than his lies and deceit already have. The kids are safe, so how bad can it be? Jeez, James, I could park a Hummer in those raging nose holes! Which, by the way, could use a little tweezing. She obviously doesn't take care of you the way I did.*

"Lily was such a fuckin' bitch this weekend!" James seethes, sending my neck muscles into spontaneous lockdown. "She had Mara and me tied up in knots with the shit she pulled!"

Knots? They were in knots? Poor things. I remember when Nat taught me all about knots on our first sailing trip together. Let's see if I can recall their names. The halfhitch. But that's not the one that I'm thinking of right now. The bowline. Nope, it's not that one either. Hmm, oh yeah, now I remember! It's the noose! Ahhh, yes. What an ingenious little knot. I wonder what Mara's neck size is.

Why do I do that? Why picture *her* with a rope choker around her neck? Why not a nice scratchy sisal necktie for *him*? Why does she always bear the brunt of my hostility? Every cognitive shot I fire is aimed at her. Why? Why? Why?

Oh sure, she's partly responsible for destroying my idyllic family, but James is the one who vowed to love me forever. I think it's just easier to blame her than to accept the shredding of my heart as his personal choice. James chose her over me. That's a deep, internal wound I haven't been ready to acknowledge, a bleeder I put a temporary clamp on. But from now on, I plan on redirecting 50 percent of all fury away from Mara and toward my ex-husband. After all, I'm a fair-minded person.

"What happened?" I ask, my motherly concern trumping my spurned-wife revelry just as the moral lawbreakers' scaffold doors are about to swing open.

"She and her friend disappeared until three in the morning!" he fumes, his mouth pulled taught with tension.

"I didn't know that she was taking a friend." I feel a flutter in my heart over the 3:00 a.m. tidbit, but Lily clearly made it home. So I'll focus on the lingering issue.

"I let her bring Renée along. When I went up to their room at eleven o'clock to say good night, they were gone."

"How did you find them?" I ask.

"After we searched around the lodge, Mara and I stayed in the girls' room and waited. When Mara left to check on Jack, she ran into them in the hallway. At three in the fucking morning!" His anger rises. "And Lily had the nerve to storm into her room with an attitude! I could smell booze and cigarettes on her!" He grows more red-faced by the second. "So I had Mara take Renée out to one of the sitting areas to give me a chance to talk to Lily alone. Things got worse from there. It turned into a god-damn blood bath!" he says, launching some spittle my way.

Does he finally understand the depth of anguish and helplessness I've been feeling about the change in her? I'm horrified if she really was drinking and smoking, but I'm, sadly, not surprised.

"Then security showed up because someone reported us. What a fucking nightmare! I was so embarrassed."

"Did she say what went on in the boys' room?" I hope drinking and smoking were the worst of it.

"Teenage partying, I assume."

*Exactly my concern.* "James, we have to do something. I've tried reasoning with her, but obviously logic is having no effect. Maybe she needs to spend more time with you. You haven't done much together as father and daughter since our divorce. And *I* certainly haven't been able to figure out how to get to the heart of her anger. I've got the name of yet another therapist, but we can't expect this one to be the answer to our problems. We have to stop this now before it gets worse." *We—ha! There hasn't even remotely been a "we" through any of this!*

"I need your help. I think Lily may be feeling aban-doned," I say and then add, "whether it's warranted or not," in hopes of not infuriating him any further but be-lieving she has every right to feel forsaken by her father.

When I was growing up, I was given a solid founda-tion for life by parents who personified the values they believed in. In the '60s, at a time when most fathers' attitudes were still "marry them off," my dad's mantra was "girls can do anything." I want so desperately for Lily to have the same belief in herself that I did. But her inner light seems to be dimming. Is it my fault? Did I not give her a father who will nurture her with the same love and respect that I was given?

Having learned the moral teachings of my parents, I try to be someone who thinks before I speak, doing battle in my head with any disagreeable thoughts—in some cases to my own detriment. Over the past few years with James, I've become the Obi-Wan of nonthreatening communication. Unfortunately, because of our work situation, it's an exhausting day-in and day-out achievement, leaving my head littered with the unspoken remains of slanderous sentiments. Someday when I'm finished with the mess my unsuspecting life has become, I'll find the energy for a good cranial cleansing.

I offer a suggestion. "How about taking her out, just the two of you? Try to connect with her. Maybe have some sort of regular date night. This book I've been reading says that daughters get a lot of their self-esteem from their fathers. You could be the one to help her through this."

Apparently, I'm willing to say anything to save my daughter, even stroke the already inflated ego of the man who ripped her self-worth from her in the first place. I feel a twinge of nausea at my hypocrisy but don't really care. I will do anything to save Lily.

"I'm not sure spending more time with me will solve her problems. I think she just needs more discipline, but I guess I can give it a try."

*You guess? Her problems? Just needs discipline?* Thank you for your professional advice, Sigmund. Make sure you don't trouble yourself too much helping your own daughter. She's only at a major crossroads in her life. We certainly wouldn't want you to disrupt your unaccountable lifestyle. Go ahead and be on your merry way like you have from the very beginning of all this bullshit, and I'll continue to handle the raising of our children . . . alone!

Whoa! There's another load of verbal refuse to add to my cerebral landfill. I guess I mastered my pledge to spew equal fury at James. I'm slamming him pretty good. Mara, take a vacation. Have a mai tai! Now, if only I could shake the words out of my head so someone could actually hear them. *Coward!* The ever-present burden of knowing I have to work with James continues to prevent me from unleashing my anger at him, fearful of the fallout. We continue to be civil to one another, even occasionally finding warm and funny moments to share. When you're with your ex forty to fifty hours a week, the best choice is to make nice. And, of course, it's the right choice for our children's sakes. But that doesn't mean I wouldn't benefit from one good vocal rage. *Owww, my head. Crap, not another migraine.*

"By the way," he says, changing the subject, "I thought you should know—Mara and I are engaged."

I feel a sudden air-gasping blow to my midsection and exhale a raspy, "Congratulations. When's the wedding?"

"We haven't made any definite plans—probably not for a while."

"Do the kids know?"

"Mara and I told them on Friday."

And there it was—the likely motive for Lily's late-night insurrection! *Did you tell them with the same compassion you just used on me?*

"I'll talk to Lily about her behavior," I say, getting up to escort him to the door. I want him gone! Now! *RIGHT NOW!!*

"Good luck," he mocks.

"Thanks," I say, barely missing his ass with the door.

*They're getting married. Oh god, that feels awful, but I can't think about it now. I have more important things to deal with.*

Not quite ready to face Lily, I pay Jack a visit. My remarkable son continues to hold on to his good-natured disposition. He gets excellent grades, is a terrific athlete, and is a kind kid. Whenever he's confronted with a questionable adolescent situation, we talk about it, and he understands the right choice. When he's done something wrong, I discuss it with him, and he doesn't do it again. Yet part of me is anticipating some sort of fallout from all of this. Will it hit the fan tomorrow? Or worse yet, will there be some unforeseeable long-term damage—maybe in his relationships with women? *Oh god, haven't I got enough to worry about without torturing myself with the what-ifs?* I flash on Eeyore wearing my face, sitting in a thistly corner of the woods. But I shake it off and decide to count my blessings instead: one, two.

"Hey, Tiger, how was your weekend?" I ask, moving next to him on the bed.

"Good," he says, sounding less than enthused. "We went down the alpine slides."

"I bet that was fun. What else?"

"We had dinner at the lodge, but then Lily got into trouble, and Dad was mad after that," he says while nimbly defeating Tetris.

"I'm sorry, Jack. Lily's going through some stuff. We're trying to help her. I know it's hard on you sometimes, and I appreciate how understanding you've been. You're a good man, Jack Branson," I tell him emphatically while patting him on the knee.

Then, in a moment of weakness, I can't help myself. I have to ask, "How did everything go with Mara?"

"Okay, I guess," he mutters.

So far, Jack hasn't had much to say about her. Does he like her but doesn't want to tell me, to protect my feelings? Or does she bother him? My preference is that it's both—that he likes her for his sake and that she bugs him for mine. Not wanting to force the conversation, I leave it for a time when he's ready to share.

"I'm gonna go and talk to Lily. Do me a favor and empty your duffel bag. Got any homework, or did you do it with Dad?"

"Just some math."

"Okay, get started on it."

Crossing the hall to Lily's room, I labor to find the words to make her realize once and for all that she's making frightening choices.

"Hey, Lily-babe," I say, opening her bedroom door, "we need to talk about this weekend."

"There's nothing to say!" she protests, lunging off her bed toward her closet, her body stiff with rage. "Dad's a jerk!" *Well, all righty then, there's something we can agree on.*

I attempt to soothe her. "Honey, come and sit down, so we can discuss what happened. Please."

"No," she barks, bearing a striking resemblance to her father.

"Come on, Lil. Tell me. I want to know your side of the story."

She bursts into tears. "Dad yelled at me, and then he threw my hair dryer and makeup at me!" she cries, struggling to get the words out. "And Mara grabbed me by the arm!"

"Dad threw a hair dryer at you?!" Had he meant a literal blood bath?

"Renée and I went to hang out with some guys we met. We ended up staying there kind of late, and Dad got really mad."

"Lily, Dad said you were in their room until three in the morning. Do you realize how dangerous it was for you to be with them? Nobody knew you were there. All kinds of bad things could have happened."

My heart breaks every time I think about what Lily has lost and the pain she must be feeling. How do I help her? I want so much to make it all go away, but nothing seems to work. "I understand why Dad was so upset. It frightens the hell out of me just thinking about it."

"But he didn't have to throw things at me," she cries, wiping her tears.

I reach for her arm, gently encouraging her to sit next to me.

"No, it wasn't right for him to do that, but, honey, he was sick with worry. And you know he's never done anything like that before."

Lily and James love each other. Unfortunately, they escalate to verbal warfare every time they're in conflict. It's never pretty. I question who the adult is and why *he* isn't modeling fatherly behavior. With the unlikelihood of that happening, I find myself on a solitary journey to heal her feelings of abandonment and low self-esteem, hoping to resurrect mine in the process.

"Why did Mara grab you?"

"Renée and I were in the hallway on the way back to our room when she saw us. She got in my face and yelled at me, saying I really upset her and Dad. Then she grabbed me by my arm. Hard, really hard! It hurt, Mom," she cries again. "I pulled away and told her not to touch me—that she's not my mom!"

"Lily, you've got to understand that your dad and I are worried about the choices you're making. You're a smart girl. You have everything going for you, and yet you're on a road that scares me to death. Every day young women disappear or are hurt under all kinds of horrible circumstances. You think you're immortal, but you're not. Families just like us face the anguish of losing children to vulnerable situations they've put themselves in. Lily, please hear what I'm saying. I don't know how I could go on if anything ever happened to you."

I've said these same words to her before and will keep saying them until she changes her dangerous behavior. With my arm around her, she turns from angry teen to wounded child.

"Mom, I'm in a hole I can't get out of. I've gotten so far behind in school and feel so stupid. I don't know what to do," she agonizes.

"I know it seems that way, but that's why I'm here," I say. "We'll work together. I know we can do it, but you have to start by making the right choices. You can't put yourself in harm's way anymore. I'll help you with your schoolwork and whatever else you need. Just promise you'll never do anything like you did last night again," I say, raising my eyebrows just inches from her face to underscore the importance of her commitment.

"I promise, Mom," she says, wiping her tears.

"Honey, you know that, more than anything else in the whole world, I want you and Jack to be happy. I'll do everything in my power to make sure that happens. There's nothing that means more to me than the two of you. Nothing!"

"I know, Mom, I know."

"Okay, good. Do you need any help with your home-work?"

"No, I got it. Thanks."

I walk out of her room, leaving the door open, feeling reconnected with my beautiful daughter. We're communicating and have another chance to recapture the closeness we once shared.

And then her door closes.

The last few days have been relatively the same. Lily continues to yell at her brother for no apparent reason. Her choice of friends still sucks. And by some miracle, she always manages to finish her homework at school—or so she claims. My level of trust is not rising.

In the meantime, at work, James rants and raves about our best and most talented employee. Brad, a loyal, long-time manager and key player at Xtreme, simply offered James a contrary opinion, but the situation deteriorated into Brad walking off the job and me scrambling to arbitrate the terms of his return. After three days of mediation, using all of my powers of persuasion with Brad and contorting myself to freak-house proportions to keep James's ego intact, all the while absorbing James's misguided anger, Brad agreed to come back to work. The final resolution included James promising to stop intimidating employees and to listen to their ideas, especially when he has asked for them. But I worry that by constantly intervening in these kinds of situations, both at home and at work, I might become the object of his rancor.

Having survived a stressful week, I'm looking forward to a weekend with limited brain activity. Feeling a little hunched over, I wonder, *Atlas, how in the heck did you do it?*

I barely have a chance to set my briefcase down when Lily rushes into the kitchen to ask if she can spend the night at her friend Ava's house. The "rush in and ask" tactic she uses is not a new maneuver. She resorts to it when my defenses are down in an effort to catch me off guard. This manipulative method of persuasion is largely effective when she approaches with a pleasant, positive attitude. I'm so delighted to experience a cheerful teen (an oxymoron) that I've often been unaware of her ploy.

But after falling prey to this scheme on several occasions, I've developed a preemptive warning device. An alarm will sound, much like that of a diving submarine, triggering my "take a moment' counterattack. In this scenario, I quickly back away from Lily and impose a five-minute time-out. However, delivery of this technique is paramount to my success. I use attentive eye contact, a happy demeanor, and the following words: "That sounds like fun. Give me a few minutes, and we'll go over the details." Putting my hand on her shoulder adds a nice touch.

This time I decide to engage the "I'll Be Right Back, Honey, I've Got to Go to the Bathroom" defense. Often there are times when it's essential to separate myself from Lily. And so, sitting on the lid of the commode in *Thinker* repose, I analyze the situation.

Ava comes from a prudent family with parents who are strict and protective. She's been to our house on many occasions and always been respectful. I'm likin' it so far. If you have to pick your battles, this one calls for a white flag.

Ready to approach. One faux flush, a few seconds of faucet time, and exit stage left.

"Okay, babe. Thanks for waiting. I really had to go." It's important to reinforce her patient behavior. (Plus, teens never like to hear their parents say anything about their time in the bathroom. It grosses them out and throws off their game.) "Tell me more about tonight."

"Ava and I want to go to the Gates High football game. She asked her parents if I could spend the night, and they said it was all right with them."

"Okay, Lily," I say, meeting her eyes with conviction, "but be sure to make smart decisions."

"I will, Mom. I promise."

A little while later I discreetly phone Ava's parents,

confirming what Lily told me.

Since Jack's been invited to have a sleepover at his buddy Cole's house, tonight will be a rare opportunity for peace and quiet, and perhaps a little escapism. My choice of decadence for the evening: a Slurpee (half Coke, half cherry), a video, and a pack of smokes. Yes, there's something about sneaking an occasional 'grette that makes me feel like I'm languishing in a Calgon bath. I'll lie in front of the tube, watch a little Meryl, suck on my icy drink, and puff out the back screen door. Man, I'm livin' it up tonight!

After the kids are gone, I think more about James and Mara's engagement. I've been reading another self-help book on divorce. The author uses a mathematical equation to comprehend the value of moving on. I like numbers. Twenty: the number of years I devoted to James—by itself, it sounds like a horrifying number. But in terms of my eighty-year life expectancy, one-frickin'-fourth of my life is all James and I spent together. When I think of everything life has brought me so far, I'm humbled by the prospect of all that awaits me. Am I willing to waste any more time trying to recover from my past with him?

Perspective is so interesting. The smallest things become pleasurable when troubles are monumental. A night off from the ever-present affliction of worry has never been so therapeutic. An icy drink and a three-dollar video feel completely restorative. You'd think I was back on Tortola with Nat. I can almost hear Bomba's blender as I head up to bed and lay my tired, worn-out body on a little piece of *queen*-size heaven.

When the phone on the nightstand awakens me, I immediately remember the kids are not tucked safely in their
own beds and bolt upright.

"Hello?"

"Is this Alex Branson?" an imposing voice asks.

"Yes."

"Ma'am, I'm with the Kirkland Police Department."

*Oh god, oh god! Please don't let her be dead!*

"We have detained your daughter at the corner of Fifth
and Slater, and need you to come and get her."

*Thank god she's alright!* "Yes, sir, I'll be right there." I
don't ask any questions. I have to get to her right away to
see for myself that she's okay. I'll deal with whatever this
is when I get there.

I throw on jeans and a T-shirt and hurry to the "scene
of the crime" a few miles from my house. What in the hell
was she doing out at five in the morning?

I step out onto the pavement and spot Lily and Ava in
the back of a patrol car as one of the officers approaches
me.

"Mrs. Branson," he says, using my married name.

I'm not about to correct him, even though, these days,
I wear *Ms.* Fisher as a badge of honor. *Mrs. Branson* im-
plies there's a man to share life's ups and downs with, a
husband to help face its challenges. Well, honey, there ain't
no man. And the only challenges I've had to get through
were because of the *Mr.!* So don't call me *Mrs.!* Hmm,

bitter? I prefer to think of it as unloading some justifiable resentment for having to stand here alone while the *Mr.* is home spooning his frickin' fiancée.

"We received a few phone calls last night reporting a car driving recklessly down the highway. During our pursuit of the vehicle, we clocked it doing ninety miles an hour. The driver eventually lost control. The car left the road, became airborne, and crashed into that field over there." The officer points to an area where a car is imbedded in a grove of blackberry bushes. "Four people jumped out and began running. We found your daughter and her friend hiding in the underbrush. They've got some cuts and scrapes on them but are otherwise all right," he says in a "just the facts ma'am" way.

Devastated by his description of what happened and the thought of a different outcome, I lock my knees so they don't buckle. *Get ahold of yourself, Alex. This is a cop you're talking to. Badge. Gun. What's happening?!*

I've never even had a speeding ticket, and here I am with my daughter hanging her head like a common thug. I imagine a neon *Loser Parent* sign flashing over my head as the policeman continues his tale of my delinquent child.

"The girls told us they were with two older boys they met at a convenience store last night. After the car crashed, the boys escaped. According to your daughter, none of them were wearing seat belts. They're very lucky, Mrs. Branson," he says, looking me squarely in the eye.

I'm absolutely sickened by what the policeman is telling me. "I'm so sorry, Officer. She was supposed to be spending the night at her friend's house," I say apologetically.

Just then Ava's dad rounds the corner. Our eyes meet.

The look on his face tells me he's a law-enforcement virgin too.

"You can take your daughter home now, Mrs. Branson."

"Thank you, Officer," I say, motioning for Lily to come with me.

But really, this isn't my daughter, all dark and dirty with smeared black mascara defrauding her baby-blue eyes. This is the subject of some hideous mug shot on the nightly news. Who is she? Who are *we*?

While I exclaim all the rhetorical clichés about what she's doing not just to herself but to all of us, Lily stares silently out the window. When I do catch sight of her face, I see it's covered with flecks of dried blood from her battle with the thorny bushes, her cheeks streaked with the blackness of her own disregard. I have to find a way to get through to her, to find someone who will explain the danger she's taunting, someone Lily loves and respects. James obviously isn't the answer. Their volatile interactions won't help her now. And while my family gives me emotional support from two thousand miles away, they can't help with the day-to-day upheaval I'm drowning in. But I'm a fortunate woman when it comes to extraordinarily generous and loving friends. It's time to reach out to one of them.

Ever since I met Will seventeen years ago while working at a large data-processing company, he's been like a brother to me. Back then, James, Will, and I were a tight little family, spending our weekends together, camping, hiking, partying, or just sitting at Mama Rio's eating homemade tortillas, drinking beer, and talking about life.

A divorced father of three whose kids live in Ohio with their mother, Will often crashed on our couch, falling asleep with headphones still cradling his ears. Working and playing together, we spent more time with each other than with anyone else.

Over the years, we've continued to nurture one of the most important relationships in both of our lives. Our consideration of each other reaches beyond the obligations of familial ties, beyond the closeness of favored friendships, to a place that is beyond comparison. We're just a couple of Midwest kids whose core values and personalities are so much alike, I've suggested we have our DNA tested. With unshakable trust, I know in my heart that whatever my kids or I need, their uncle Will is always ready to give it.

Will went through a parade of needy girlfriends. Then he finally met Kaye while he was on a self-improvement retreat. Within a year, they fell in love and got married. I'm selfishly thankful he found someone I really like.

When Lily and I arrive home, I tell her to go and shower off the remnants of last night. I glance at the clock—6:00 a.m.—and decide I can't wait for a reasonable hour to phone Will.

"Hi, Kaye," I say to the sleepy voice that answers.

"Alex, is everything all right?"

"I'm sorry for calling this early, but Lily's got herself into some serious trouble," I say with an obvious strain in my voice. "Can I talk to Will please?"

"Of course, and don't ever hesitate to call. We're both here for you," she says sympathetically. "I'll put him on."

"AJ, what's up?" he says in his consistently upbeat way.

"Hi, Will. I didn't want to bother you, but I need your help," I say as the sound of his voice causes me to falter.

"You're never a bother. You should know that by now—a pain in the ass maybe, but never a bother."

Within the safe harbor of my friend, I begin to crumble as I recount Lily's horrifying night.

"It's gonna be okay, Alex. Just take it easy. I'll be right over."

I swallow hard to fend off the wave of defeat that has stricken me. "You don't have to come now, but maybe later you could—"

"AJ, I'm on my way," he insists, giving me exactly what I need.

Lily and her uncle Will have a special relationship. The kind of father-daughter bond I wish James and Lily had. I know she'll be mortified that I called him, but mortification might be just the remedy for her bad behavior.

A short while later, Lily is indeed humiliated as I describe the whole story to Will. He fixes his eyes on her, filing through thoughts in his head in search of just the right thing to say. He leans forward with his elbows on his knees and his hands clasped together. A look of disappointment comes across his face. He exhales a disheartened, "Wow."

Lily begins to cry.

Will and I discuss with her the impact of her alarming choices and the risks she took. Will speaks frankly about the poor decisions he's made in his own life and the prices he's paid for them. We remind her of what a wonderful person she is and how much she means to us. Honestly, I doubt his visit magically changes her; but it does help her see she has love and support beyond me. And Will's visit reminds me I have it too.

Finally, I send her to her room to get some rest.

The following Monday morning, I share Lily's exploits with James. He offers feedback on what a problem child she is but can't seem to muster up any support or ideas for helping her. That is unless you count wanting to ship her off to boarding school, a frequent suggestion of his. Sending her away would only reinforce her sense of abandonment. She needs to feel the arms of unconditional love wrapped tightly around her, not the uncaring, stone-cold walls of an institution. I'll find the elusive answer, and it won't be by deserting her.

The very next week, Lily's school imposes a mandatory two-day suspension against her because she and a boy were caught sneaking off school grounds. But rather than holding Lily accountable, James is annoyed with me for leaving work to pick her up from the vice principal's office. And it's precisely that kind of reaction that makes me feel like my role as his business partner is more important to him than that of being a parent to our children.

"Don't worry," I say, absorbing his guilt-inducing disapproval, "I'll still have enough time to finish the proposal numbers."

James is highly adept at dumping loads of undeserved guilt. I fed his sick habit during our marriage by playing the role of martyr. It was a codependency we were both unaware of at the time. Guilt: the silent spirit killer. For example, why was it that James assumed he was doing me a favor by, and I quote, "babysitting" his own children? Why did he insinuate I was spending *his* money when I would purchase a household necessity? Why, if I asked him to repair a broken chair or take out the garbage, was I a nag for reminding him about it two days later? Guilt: it comes in so many subtle forms. It's carbon monoxide for the soul. I slowly breathed it in day after day in small doses until finally, unaware of its passing, I laid my asphyxiated spirit to rest without mourning.

I drive to Lily's school, impaired by James's reproachful urgency, and spot the flashing red lights in my rearview mirror. Jeez, I made it past the age of forty without engaging a cop and now, twice in one week!

"Ma'am, do you realize you were going sixty in a fifty?"

"Yes, I do, Officer," I respond with an unfamiliar aggressiveness. "To be precise, I was going sixty-three. Everyone speeds along this stretch. But go ahead and write me up a ticket. Like I don't have enough problems already," I add under my breath. I can't believe my nerve. I'm actually confronting a cop—out loud! Isn't there any room left in my head for angry thoughts?

"Take it easy, ma'am. I'm going to let you off with a warning. But from now on I want you to obey the speed limit."

That's it? A warning? Really? *Oh my god, what a nice guy!*

"Officer, I will. I promise. I'm so sorry. Thank you very much, sir. I really appreciate it," I say, ready to reapply my Pink Parfait lipstick because I've overdone the ass-kissing.

The rest of the way to Lily's school, I'm the only law-abiding motorist on the road. Someone or something is telling me to calm down and take a moment to reflect. The policeman offered an act of benevolence when he had every right not to. He was another reminder to my burdened soul of the goodness that's still out there waiting for me to see it again.

I enter the school's office—and my sweet girl is barely recognizable to me. I want to scrub the anger right off of her and exhume the innocence that lies beneath. *Happy, bubbly,* and *kind* are no longer words that describe Lily. Angry, hurtful, and reckless are her new distinctions. It makes me so very sad.

"I thought we were done with this kind of crap, Lily," I say on the ride home. "Didn't our conversation with Uncle Will mean anything to you?" Not waiting for an answer: "You know it's wrong to leave school grounds," I continue, blind to the road in front of me. "Who were you with?" I demand, glancing over at her defiant face. "Lily, I want to know who you were with!"

"Brian," she answers smugly.

"Who's Brian?"

"You know him. Brian Hunt. We've had classes together before."

Her pissy attitude is really ticking me off. "Don't pretend I'm supposed to know this kid when you've never mentioned him. Why did you leave school?"

"Because I wanted to."

"You wanted to!" I repeat, because I can't believe her

lack of remorse. "What's going on, Lily? I don't know what to do with you anymore. Every time I think we're past the bullshit, you pull something new. What's it going to take for you to wake up and see what you're doing to yourself?"

Lily pretends to ignore me, depleting my patience.

"You're grounded for a week. No phone, no nothing."

"You can't ground me." She sneers. "I won't stay home."

"Oh yes, you will!"

"I won't, and you can't make me." She actually crosses her arms and cocks her head.

"I'll hog-tie you if I have to." Oh god, I never thought that little gem would pass my lips. Quick, Mara, can I borrow the rope that's around your neck?

We roll toward a stop sign. Without warning, Lily tries to jump out of the car. I'm momentarily confused by her insanity, but my protective mom reflexes react. I grab her by the arm. Oh my god, she takes a swing at me!

"Are you crazy?!" I say, yanking her back into the car. "Close that door! Now!"

Lily slams it shut.

"Put your seat belt back on!" Her unashamed look provokes me. "I swear I'm not moving until you do!"

Although it doesn't feel like a win, she eventually succumbs. But when we pull into the garage, she bails out of the car, slamming the door. Then she storms into the house and clobbers that door so hard, the picture hanging in the hallway flies off the wall.

Well, now, that is just a bit too much teen turbulence for my liking. In a moment of true inspiration, I head to the tool box, a woman with a purpose, grab a hammer and a screwdriver, and with the speed and determination of a cheetah hunting down her prey, bound toward Lily's room. Opening her door, I tap the hinge pins out of it. The bewildered look on her face is priceless. A satisfied feeling comes over me as I effortlessly lift the door and walk away with it.

"Mom, where are you going with my door? *Mom! MOOOMMM!*"

How does that old adage go? Necessity is the mother of invention. Well, Thomas Edison's got nothin' on this mother. In my own light-bulb moment, I generate a small but satisfying victory.

Who does grounding really punish? Me, of course. In order to enforce the discipline, I've got to be present. Consequently, my home becomes a prison. Worse yet, my cell-mate is a hardened teen. I am ready to start tying sheets together by the second day.

On Wednesday, while Lily and Jack are at dinner with their dad, the Black Ridge ladies celebrate Elise's and Annie's birthdays. It's the perfect opportunity for me to elicit information from my knowledgeable pals about this Brian kid.

The girls open their gifts—body lotions, candles, and bottles of wine take over the table. I give them each a leather-bound notebook because my own journal has been a source of healing for me, now more than ever. Granted, there are nights when I have to rack my brain to come up with legitimate blessings to jot down, but I always manage to—no matter how lame they might seem at the time.

. Woke up to *Luck of the Draw* playing on my radio alarm clock. Bonnie Raitt is always a good way to start the day.

. Brad and I solved a near impossible problem at work and managed to keep our sense of humor through it all. Thank you, Brad.

. Had a flirtatious exchange with a guy in the waiting room at Q-Lube. A boost for my ego.

. Found a baby toad in the laundry room from Jack's pant cuff after his round of golf. We laughed as we tried to catch the little sucker so we could set him free.

. I still have my parents when many of my friends do not.

. My kids are healthy.

. Had enough energy at the end of the day to hit the treadmill.

. I control the remote.

Could life be any better? Well, yes, but whenever I look at my previous entries, they validate my general good fortune. Ahhh, the power of positive thinking. If only more people knew about Dr. Norman Vincent Peale, the world would be a much happier place. When I was a kid, I stayed up late on the weekends watching old movies. One night, I saw a film called *One Man's Way*. Long before today's spiritual leaders and self-help gurus preached positivity, there was Dr. Peale and his message of optimistic thinking. In this movie, his principles paralleled those of my parents, the ones I gleaned from their example. I was so inspired by his passion for living an affirming life that to this day I'm influenced by his powerful message.

After the girls and I catch up with each other, I seize the opportunity to learn more about Brian.

"I know his mom," Elise says. "She recently moved away for her job and left Brian to live with his stepdad. Brian's gotten into quite a bit of trouble."

Annie adds, "The stepdad's no prize either, but his mom didn't know what else to do. She couldn't handle Brian. He's been running around with the wrong crowd, kids who do drugs and ditch school. There's even been mention of burglaries."

*Oh my god, it just keeps getting worse!*

"Why do you ask?" Elise wonders.

"Lily mentioned him." My friends have known Lily since she was a toddler. They think of her as happy, outgoing, and sweet. I'm not ready to tarnish their view of her. This is one time I won't share.

*Drugs, please, not drugs. And I can't even consider the possibility of burglaries.* In between detached laughter with my friends, I formulate a plan. It's time for me to break my rule about not searching through my children's things. Raised by parents who had complete faith in me, I've wrestled with my conscience about this one. But Lily's broken my trust, and I need to open another door in my crusade to save her.

After the kids leave to spend the weekend with James, I stand in Lily's doorway, saddened by what I'm about to do—betraying her trust is something that can never be undone.

I move to her dresser, fortifying myself with thoughts of her dangerous actions. My hands begin to operate with Mata Hari–like vigilance. I deny my compulsion to straighten her drawers—a clear sign of my betrayal.

*Nothing here. Her desk?* I tug at the cluttered center drawer, finding matchbooks, photos, gum wrappers, and two folded pieces of notebook paper. I hesitate as my conscience wages war against my need to help my daughter. And then I unfold the first paper.

> Mara,
>
> I want you to know how upset my family is with you, especially me! I'm so mad at you! I think it was cruel and inconsiderate of you to betray my mom. She doesn't deserve to be treated so horribly. She trusted and respected you, and you crapped all over her! If you were married for twenty wonderful years to a man you really loved, how would you feel if this happened to you? My parents have had so many amazing memories together.
>
> You should take some time and really think about what you're doing, and how it's affecting all of us, and our relatives too! I really doubt your relationship with my dad will be as loving as my parents'. You're probably just using my dad for his money, and because he's the president of a successful company. Don't lie to yourself. You guys aren't right for each other. If you're really the nice person that my mom thought you were, you will think about what I've said.

When I get older, I want my kids to have married grandparents, and I also want them to see what true love is. It's what my mom and dad have always had until you came into our lives. When my parents got married, they said they would be together forever. You've changed all that.

I just want you to think about everything I've said, and try to understand the way my family and I are feeling. I don't mean to be rude, but PLEASE TRY TO UNDERSTAND!

Sincerely,

Lily

Oh honey, it makes me so sad to know what you're going through. I refold the piece of paper, feeling the weight of her words, and then unfold the other paper and begin reading.

I want to FUCK you, baby! It will be so FUCKING awesome!

Oh my god! What in the hell?

Brian! That little prick!

This is obviously nothing like the sweet love notes of my youth. It's the same wide-ruled notebook paper, but there's nothing pure and chaste about it. My high school boyfriend wooed me with romantic song titles carefully placed within the text of the notes he slid though the vents of my locker door. But this—this is vile!

The devastating weight of it binds me to the desk's chair as my breath escapes me. Years of wishing that my beautiful Lily will fall in love one day and know the rapturous ecstasy of sex fueled by true love have ended. My eyes begin to burn with tears.

*Dreams—screw 'em! They're all delusions built on an arrogant house of cards!*

I inhale a giant breath and unglue myself from the chair by closing my mind off to the reality of what just happened.

I persist in my search for contraband by lifting Lily's mattress. My eyes drop to evidence that my child's innocence is gone.

Now holding an empty condom wrapper, I sink to the floor. At first I can't process whole thoughts. It's way too much to accept. *Lily, what have you done?*

God help me, I visualize some pimply punk sticking his puny dick into my sweet girl. I choke back the revulsion. *Goddamn fuckin' Brian!*

I jump to my feet, frantically pace back and forth across the room, arms stiff at my sides, fists clenched so tightly my nails cut into my palms. What do I do? *Think, Alex, think!*

*Okay, okay.* Lily's with James, still grounded. I'll make an appointment with Dr. Lee. If she's old enough to have sex, which, of course, I don't want, she's old enough to experience the harsh reality of metal stirrups and her first pelvic exam. Make sure she's okay and then, oh god, put her on the pill? I don't want to do that. She'll think I'm condoning *it*.

When Lily comes home on Sunday, we'll talk. Another talk. *Man, my head is killing me!* What will I say? What are the words that will magically end this horror? Sadly, there is no magic. I wish I could channel Confucius for something profound to say, but it's just me, me and my love for my daughter.

I need to meditate. Clear my head. Stop this awful pain.

*Ah-im-ah. Rest your mind, Alex. Come on—you can do this! Focus! Ah-im-ah. Stay with your mantra. Deep breath in—Ah-im. Exhale—ah. Goddamn sex in my house! Stop thinking, you moron! Shake it off. Ah-im. Prick in her bed! Ah—jeez, my head! And exhale out. What am I gonna do? Breathe, you idiot, fucking BREATHE!*

I spend the rest of the weekend alone, trying in vain to escape into my Slurpee and video world. The clock ticks ever so slowly, and the dread and anguish I feel reflects back at me every time I look in the mirror. I keep asking myself why. Why is this happening? What am I supposed to be learning? Compassion? I thought we covered that during the divorce. Judgment? Aren't I good on that one too? Is there something I'm not getting?

# Chapter Seven

**A** metamorphosis has occurred. Alex, former milquetoast mom, is now—*ta da-da-daaah*—Alexandra: Warrior Matriarch! As with Artemis, Greek goddess and, appropriately enough, eternal virgin, a great spirit has taken over me, and I'm ready to kick some major juvie ass.

Imagining myself as Ripley from *Aliens*, I descend in a cage-like elevator, belts of ammunition crisscrossing my chest, flame thrower in hand, ready to blast the hell out of the salivating alien and rescue my precious Newt. Fuck the calm intellect!

I confront Lily about the wrapper that was under her mattress. ". . . And what about the risks that you've been taking with your body? Do you know if Brian has been with anyone else? Does he always wear a condom?"

She clearly hates this conversation but can tell the Warrior won't back down any time soon. There's been a decisive change in command, and she knows it.

"I guess I should also ask if there have been any other boys," I say while holding my nauseated breath.

"He's the only one," she confesses, finally revealing shame and embarrassment.

"What if you get pregnant? Your life would change forever. Please, Lily, you've got to end this reckless behavior."

*Oh, shit! Did I just say, "please"? Damned manners!*

*Keep going before she senses weakness!*

"You're too young to fully understand the consequences of your decisions."

I've got to remember exactly what I'm doing because she actually seems to be listening. Could this be the right balance of *tough* and *love* that will save her? It's been so elusive. And will I be able to re-create it when I need to? *Pay attention, Alex! Quit wandering!* Firm voice, steely eyes, strong body posture, and just a pinch of understanding.

"I'm going to make an appointment with Dr. Lee. I want him to make sure that you're okay, and"—*Oh god, how I hate saying this!*—"have him put you on the pill." I quickly follow with "I'm not condoning you having sex. In fact, if you hear nothing else that I'm saying, hear this: I want you to stop! But it's my job to protect you, even if it's from your own stupid choices.

"I'm not a fool, Lily. I won't close my eyes to the possibility of you making another error in judgment, one that could bring devastating consequences. Do you think Brian worries about you getting pregnant? I don't. You and I will be left to deal with the repercussions. Try to remember that the next time he wants to put his dick in you!" *Hey, I actually said that out loud! And with emphasis on the "dick" part! Man, my head is throbbing.*

"Do you have any homework?" I ask. What a conversation, from teen pregnancy to world history. Yes, we moms do it all.

"No, I finished it."

"How come I never see you cracking any books?" Always an A/B student, Lily's grades have fallen to Cs and Ds.

"I get most of it done in study hall."

I'm too drained by our coitus conversation to battle with schoolwork. There used to be a time when a little sex talk was actually a stimulating thing. But those days are gone. I have neither the time nor the energy for a playful romp of *Oh baby, yes, . . . YES!* Now it's all about the worry. Am I saying the right things? Did I forget any important points? Are we making progress? It's goddamned left-brain genocide!

Lily and I sit silently in Dr. Lee's office—a place where I've anticipated the news of my pregnancies, waited to listen to the heartbeats of my babies for the first time, and had postdelivery checkups with my newborn in tow.

As I glance at the parenting and baby magazines strewn across the coffee table, I ache for the life we were supposed to live. Instead of watching Lily win a tennis match or congratulating her on her grades, I'm questioning whether or not to put her on the pill? I've never felt so intellectually and emotionally inept.

"Lily," Dr. Lee's nurse calls out.

Linda's been with Dr. Lee since he first began his practice. Lily's birth was his first delivery. Now the adorable infant he once helped bring into this world is paying him an unseasonable visit. Maybe I should ask him to hang her upside down and give her a good whack on the popo. I'm willing to try anything.

We follow Linda into one of the examining rooms.

Lily doesn't question my participation. After all, this is foreign soil, and she doesn't know the protocol.

My baby sits on the examining table, a cloth sheet covering her naked lower body. This is awkward on so many levels. But my face is masked with conviction. I was twenty years old the first time I had my privates inspected. And I didn't have an audience.

I feel bad for her. Still, she needs a healthy dose of reality. Unfortunately, my motherly compassion is interfering with my determined façade. At the very least, I can explain to her what to expect. This is a big moment in my daughter's life. As much as I hate the timing of it, I want Lily to understand how important an annual exam is to her long-term health. So many women avoid the gynecologist, choosing the "ignorance is bliss" school of medicine instead, and I—

Wait just a frickin' minute!! What in the hell am I doing?! Isn't it bad enough that I have to worry about her teenage sex life without having to consider whether or not she'll get a pap when she's forty! Help! Brain overload! My gray matter is getting grayer!

The sound of the door opening redirects my attention. "Hello, Alex," Dr. Lee says, entering the room. "And who do we have here?"

"Hi, Dr. Lee. This is my daughter, Lily."

"Ahhh, yes, I remember you. But I believe you were bald the last time I saw you," he jokes, causing Lily to smile for the first time in a week.

"Dr. Lee, we're here because Lily recently became sexually active. I felt it would be a good idea for her to see you and have her checked out—possibly put her on the pill."

He pauses for a moment and then says without judgment, "If you're having intercourse and don't want to get pregnant or contract a disease, then it's important you protect yourself. And in order to proceed, I'll need to examine you." Then he adds, "Lily, what do you want?" This is why everyone I know in Seattle has such awe for him. He's calm and attentive but practical. If you must have someone you didn't first have dinner with perusing your hoo-ha, it should be this guy.

I look at my beautiful child. She has such an innocent presence. If she hadn't been born in rainy Washington, you'd swear she was a sunny California girl.

"I don't want to get pregnant," she answers softly.

"Okay. Before we do the exam, let's talk about contraceptives and sexually transmitted diseases. If you're going to be active, you need to be informed."

That's right, Dr. Lee, bombard her with all the gory details. Tell her about the three Cs. Clap, crabs, chlamydia. Then hit her with genital herpes. Ooo, ooo, mention the seeping sores. How about HPV and hepatitis B? Then finish her off with HIV and AIDS. Let's really scare the crap out of her! Do you need any help with this?

On the way home, I decide to take advantage of Lily's weakened condition. "Honey, you know I only want what's best for you. Everything I do is because I care. There's absolutely nothing in this world that comes close to the meaning you and your brother bring into my life.

Lily-babe, I want you to really listen to what I'm saying. You're an amazing person. You're kind and compassionate, smart and funny, and so much more."

She stares blankly at the road ahead of us. What is she thinking? I want to reach into her head and pull out the thoughts that keep her from healing. How can a youthful mind possibly comprehend the complexities of life's shattering events?

"Lily, I'm here for you."

The awful truth is Lily doesn't know what she needs, and neither do I.

After dropping her off at school, I head downtown to work.

Why is it that I feel most vulnerable when I'm in my car listening to the radio or taking my morning shower? Perhaps it's because I'm alone with my thoughts. Every sad song that plays when I'm driving seems to have been written just for me. And lord knows my water bill has skyrocketed from all of the crying I'm doing while trying to get my hair washed. Maybe I should use public transportation and restrict my hygiene? Wait a minute! I think I've just progressed from a mindless zombie to a frickin' bag lady! How many hideous stages of grief are there?

When I tell James about Lily's appointment with Dr. Lee, I feel his compassion. Then the phone on his desk rings, and it's over.

I know James loves our kids. He just can't deal with the difficult stuff. He's Mr. Fun Guy, not Mr. Go-To Guy. He offers lame solutions and critical judgments based on misguided assumptions, thinking he's helping in some way.

While witnessing his lack of emotional intelligence

throughout our divorce and during Lily's troubles, I'm grateful to be the primary one raising our children. Yet along with my gratitude comes concern for my mortality. It's not something I thought about when I was happily married. But now that I no longer have faith in James, I need to live long enough for Lily and Jack to have a strong foundation based on the values and principles I trust in. It sounds incredibly dramatic and arrogant, but I sincerely believe it to be true. I can't go now. I have more work to do. Please don't let some wicked twist of fate take me too soon.

Lily and I enjoy a fragile honeymoon period after the whole condom nightmare. Then her report card arrives in the mail.

I stare in disbelief at the Cs, Ds, and a disheartening F, and notice that Lily was, unbeknownst to me, absent for eight days during the grading period. My heart predictably quickens as I call her into the kitchen.

Apparently pissed off by my tone, or maybe the shade of lipstick I'm wearing, she immediately responds with aggression. "What? I was on the phone!" she snarls.

I thrust the paper at her. "Explain this," I demand, now furious with both her report card and her attitude.

She's not surprised by her grades and has the nerve to give me an impertinent pose.

"Your grades suck, and you missed eight days of school!" I say loudly, now livid. "Where were you?"

"With my friends," she says with her hand on her hip

and her nose in the air.

"With your friends doing what?" I can't believe she isn't apologetic.

"Hanging out," she says coolly.

The blood coursing through my veins becomes dangerously pressurized, and I vent through my mouth as I yell at the top of my lungs, "That's bullshit, Lily! I want to know what you were doing and who you were with! Was it Brian?"

"Some of the time and with other friends too." She flares her nostrils like her father.

"Did someone write notes to excuse your absences?" I want names. I have to know who's aiding my incorrigible daughter.

"One of my friends wrote them and forged your signature," she answers with a look I want to smack off of her face.

"What in the hell were you thinking?!" I scream so loudly that I strain something in my throat, forcing me to rely upon vehement body language to convey my outrage. Strangled by my own temper, my arms flailing with dramatic emphasis, I strongly whisper, "I'm sick of this crap, Lily!"

"You can't stop me from being with my friends!"

Am I hearing her right? The little bitch is challenging me. I grab her by the upper arm, gritting my teeth two inches from her face, and fume, "Oh yes, I can."

She screams back, "No, you can't," and then pulls away while kicking me sideways in the thigh like some ninja, knocking me backward. I reach for her again and miss as she runs toward her bedroom.

"Goddammit, Lily, come back here!"

I catch a glimpse of a horrified Jack as I race by his room. *Oh, Tiger-Bear, I'm so sorry.*

"Leave me alone, Mom!"

"Lily, you can't kick me like that. You hurt me." And not just physically.

She doesn't care and begins dialing her phone.

"What are you doing?" I ask, flabbergasted at her nerve.

"I'm calling Jennifer."

"Oh no, you're not! Put the phone down!" I demand as she holds the receiver to her ear. "I said to put it down!" I yell while squeezing the pain in my throat.

She ignores my command and gives me an insolent shit-eating grin. I charge across the room and pull the phone cord from the wall.

"Give me that, Mom!" she shrieks, grabbing for it.

I snatch the phone from her unsuspecting hands and march out of the room.

She follows me into the kitchen, stomping her feet at my heels while trying to pry the phone from my clutches. I hunch my body like a running back to keep it in my grasp. Her nails scratch my arm as she claws to liberate it.

Though I'm caught in the moment, I'm also dumb-struck by the absurdity of it. This is not my kind of role. I'm comedy, not tragedy. At least, I used to be.

"Stop it, Lily! Let go!"

She backs away seething and then thrusts her head forward with demon-like fury. Have I just opened Carol Anne's closet in *Poltergeist?* "I hate you! I hate you!" she spews and then runs to her room in tears.

She hates me! Holy cow, did I really participate in that? That went so terribly wrong. What happened to my Lily? What happened to me?! I'm not handling this warrior thing very well. Dammit! I know better than to be drawn into such hysteria.

How in the hell do I fix this one? Thinking . . . pacing . . . thinking . . . staring out the kitchen window . . . thinking. *Oh man, not another debilitating migraine. Hurry, Alex, before the throbbing completely engulfs your thinker.*

First, I'll let her simmer down, and then we'll find a strategy for raising her grades. Maybe hire a tutor. That could work. It certainly would better than me trying to help her. We've gone that route before. Schoolwork is such a source of frustration—frustration breeds anger, and I don't need to be the recipient of any more than I already am. She won't yell at a stranger, especially if I choose the right one, a healthy role model she can relate to, maybe a senior from her school.

*Oh maaan, where are my migraine pills?*

An attractive, sturdy brunette, Sonia, who emigrated from Russia as a small child, has a marvelously solid way about her. And more important, she's cool! Yes, she has to be or Lily and her teenage hubris will shut down this new opportunity.

Sonia and Lily get right to work. I find myself eavesdropping and am pleased to discover they're actually studying. From that day forward, Sonia comes to our house every Tuesday and Thursday to help Lily climb out of her proverbial hole.

And then a neighbor calls to report an incident that she heard about. Some kids were sniffing gasoline at the home of a boy who lives down the street from us. She wanted to let me know Lily was one of them. Who thinks of this kind of stuff? Whatever happened to prank calling somebody to ask if their refrigerator was running?

I maintain my composure long enough to thank her for getting involved and then hang up the phone. I fall into the recliner, lean my head back, and close my eyes—numb to the pain of this new revelation. It has all become too much. Immobilized, I can't react yet. I need not to feel anything, just for a moment. Slowly I rock back and forth, my arms limp at my sides, and push away thoughts of Lily intentionally snorting poisonous fumes.

My eyes begin to burn with tears. When will it end? How can I save her? I allow myself a small indulgence of self-pity and then, grabbing the arms of the chair, force myself to my feet and into her room.

"It made me sick, Mom. I'll never do it again. I promise," Lily says in earnest.

I tell her she won't be allowed to go over to Justin's anymore.

"Why can't I?" she questions. "I just said I wouldn't do it again."

"Because, Lily, Justin is home alone a lot. His mom works long hours to support his brother and him, and I don't want you over there unsupervised. It's as simple as that," I say calmly.

"There's no reason I shouldn't be able to go to his house. And you can't stop me." She raises her voice.

"I'm tired of hearing you say that. You're not going over there, and that's final."

Hoping to avoid another painful martial arts lesson, I leave her bedroom. Unfortunately, my volatile daughter follows me.

"I have a right to be with my friends, and there's nothing you can do about it," she yells in my ear.

"Lily, I'm done with this discussion, and I won't change my mind."

"You're so stupid, Mom. You can't control me. *I mean it!*" She shouts so loudly that our dog, Trixie, takes cover behind a chair.

I resist the urge to get sucked into her anger and try to leave the kitchen, but she grabs hold of my arm, pinching the skin.

I move in nose-to-nose with her and say, "I don't want you to ever touch me in anger again, and I mean that!"

"Lily's school is on the phone," Carol says, giving me a sympathetic look as she closes my office door behind her.

"Hello," I say, bracing for another arrhythmic disturbance.

"Hello, Mrs. Branson. This is Mr. Bigelow. Again."

"Yes, Mr. Bigelow, what can I do for you?" I ask, hoping he wants a chaperone for the next school dance.

"Lily and another girl intimidated a student on the bus

today. We have a zero-tolerance policy for this kind of behavior and are suspending Lily for three days."

Once more, I'm disgraced by the voice of authority. Why can't Lily feel the same disappointment in herself that I do for her?

On the short walk over to James's office to give him the news, I feel like Hermes about to be riddled with bullet holes.

"I know you don't want to hear it again, but we need to find a boarding school for her. Aren't you tired of this?" James says, regurgitating the same old solution.

"Yes, but I won't send her away. At least, not yet."

Hoping to find another possible solution to save my combative child, I ask James something I swore I never would—something that my friends suggested as an alternative, but my intuitive voice kept warning against it. This time, however, I'm desperate. "James, what do you think about Lily moving in with you for a while? Maybe I can't give her what she needs right now."

His response is quick and decisive. "Sure, she can live with me, but"—*Oh no, was my gut right?*—"she'll probably be out on the streets within a week," he says coldly.

His words send shivers down my spine. *Be out on the streets! Are you kidding me? What kind of dad are you?* I can't possibly send my kid to live with a father who's prepared for her to fail. He just slammed the door on that alternative forever. And maybe that's exactly what he wants.

"I'm leaving to pick Lily up from school and bring her back here."

"What do you mean?"

"Just what I said. And I'll be bringing her to the office for the next three days. I'm certainly not going to allow her to be at home on her own," I reason, while acting like his disapproving face doesn't bother me—but it does. "Don't worry. I'll put her to work."

"I don't want her here. She'll be too disruptive," he orders, pursing his lips to show he means business.

"Who will she be disruptive to? There are things she can do to help us. Everyone here knows Lily, and it's not like they're unaware of our family drama. I'll be back by lunchtime," I tell him, refusing to argue the point any further.

For some reason, I still allow James to make me feel guilty. Guilty because I can't find a quick fix for Lily. Guilty because I'm pulled away from work because of her. Guilty because one of our employees isn't living up to James's unrealistic demands. Guilty because someone jammed the copier. Guilty, guilty, guilty! Stop pounding the gavel already! I'm the one who wants order. And anyway, I thought Mara got all of the rights to the *G*-word in our divorce settlement.

Sadly, my daily exposure to the perpetrator, and the twisted feelings I have for him, leave me vulnerable to his ways.

For the rest of the day, James's words echo in my head. *She'll probably be out on the streets in a week.* What a messed-up thing to say! That's not tough love—it's fatalistic. When did the funny, sensitive man I married turn into such a cold-hearted, selfish bastard?

That night while washing dishes at my kitchen sink, I hear small children playing nearby. A glass slips out of my hand and shatters against the tile floor. I'm worried that the kids might get cut and ask James to help clean it up. Instead, he intentionally grinds the broken pieces with his shoes, crushing the glass into hundreds of shards, and then purposefully walks over them, spreading the dangerous slivers everywhere.

Fearing for the children's safety, I'm filled with utter frustration and shove James in the chest with both hands, yelling and crying, "You're worthless, damn you, worthless!"

"Mom, Mom, wake up. I'm going to be late for school," Jack whispers, gently shaking my shoulder.

"Oh, Tiger," I say, wiping a tear from my eye, "my alarm must not have gone off. Let's hurry so you don't miss the bus."

On the way to work, while tormenting Lily with more of my wisdom, I imagine all she hears anymore is *Blah, blah, blah, Brian, blah, blah, blah, bullshit*. Hell, I don't blame her. I'm just regurgitating the same old sermons.

> *Oh, child, my sweet child,*
> *Take my hand, and I will show you the road to morality, to the value of right and wrong.*
> *Let me lead you into the kingdom of principles, where the laws of humanity shall guide you onto the path of righteousness.*
> *Yes, I have a dream.*
> *A dream built on love and honesty.*
> *Come with me now.*
> *Let us end our suffering,*
> *And walk together from the bowels of teen damna-*

*tion into the Promised Land.*
*Can I get a big "hell yeah"?*

And then a Baptist choir sings *Oh Happy Day,* but I know my rebellious daughter isn't listening.

I put Lily in a discreet cubicle, away from James's disapproving eyes. Through my office window, I notice our staff stopping by to chat with her. I've always tried to make Xtreme a family-friendly place. Christmas parties, summer picnics, road trips, and help with personal problems are all part of the culture I've initiated. It's my job to keep the workplace happy.

Later that morning, I witness James cheerfully interacting with Lily as if she were his praiseworthy daughter, but as soon as he turns in my direction, his face sucks up tighter than a vacuum-packed gargoyle.

He marches into my office, teeth gritted, and says, "This is the last time I want her here!"

*Holy schizophrenia, Mr. Hyde! Weren't you all jovial just a minute ago?*

I'm determined not to buy into his intimidation tactics and lean forward with my elbows on my desk, insisting, "We'll do whatever we have to for *our* daughter."

His eyes narrow. "*I mean it,*" he snarls, and then turns to leave.

Where have I heard *that* before? *Mean* seems to be the operative word with James and Lily. They're certainly mean to me, and I'm definitely paying a price for it.

A couple of semiuneventful weeks pass before I spot something suspicious. The screen from Lily's window is askew.

I decide not to reveal the damning evidence to her, knowing she'll offer some deceptive excuse. Instead, for the next few nights, I set my alarm clock at two-hour intervals to check whether or not she's in her bed. It's a tiring process, but I'm fueled by the prospect of catching her in the act.

On Friday, at one in the morning, my alarm clock wakes me to the sound of *I've been searching for the daughter of the devil himself. I've been searching for an angel in white.* Yikes! That has got to stop happening!

I creep down the stairs and into the hallway, carefully avoiding the floor's creaky spots. Slowly, I turn the doorknob to her bedroom and inch it open. Complete darkness forces me to tiptoe right up next to her bed. I lean down, holding my breath, to see if she's in it.

*Aha! She's gone!*

I check the window. It's unlocked. Now it's just a matter of waiting. While lying on Lily's bed, I try to come up with a new and, hopefully, effective punishment. Unfortunately, I'm exhausted from the past few nights of sleuthing and lack any creative energy to devise yet another strategy. For the time being, I decide to use my own brand of shock therapy and scare the hell out of her when she climbs back through the window.

The illuminated numbers on the alarm clock seem to mock me, taking more than sixty seconds to pass each minute. I can't believe I'm surrounded by my daughter's stuffed animals, trophies, and dolphin collection, while she's out doing who knows what kind of god-awful things.

The hours tick away. I try to keep my headache at bay by massaging my scalp and inhaling deeply. Finally, the window slides open. I still my breathing. The curtain billows as Lily struggles to replace the screen. The window lock clicks shut. She undresses and moves toward her bed, oblivious to the fact that I'm on it.

Just as she's about to lie down, I use my deepest voice to say, "What are you doing?"

Lily screams and falls backward onto the floor. I wait for a moment and then flip on the light.

"Mooom, you scared me!" she howls.

I look sternly at her but can't hide the fact that I've gotten pleasure out of frightening her.

Shaken and angered by my tactic, she cries, "That wasn't very nice. You're mean!"

*Oh yeah, I know, I'm the mean one.* It's time to get real.

"What are you doing sneaking out of the house in the middle of the night? It's dangerous out there! You could be in terrible trouble before I even realize you're gone," I scold her. "And not only that, but you're endangering Jack and me! We're innocently sleeping in an unsecured house. We could be murdered in our beds for all you know!"

Lily regains her composure and lays on the attitude.

"Trixie would bark," she says of our springer.

"Are you not getting this? What is it going to take for

you to understand? You're risking your life!" *Why won't she hear me?* "Who were you with?"

"Brian," she says smugly.

My head goes right to where it doesn't want to be, to a graphic image of her and that pimply-faced prick. Like the fleeting high of an addict, my momentary rush from victory has vanished. Crashing back to reality, I don't have it in me to concoct another lifesaving plan. "Go to bed, Lily. We'll talk in the morning. And from now on, leave your door open. If I hear it close, I'll be back with my tools."

I lay my pounding head on my pillow. My eyeballs throb as an ice pick stabs the left side of my brain. Why is it always my left side that suffers? Have I finally depleted myself of all logic and reason? Is this what happens when emotional turmoil requires constant resourceful thinking—all that remains is a void of agony?

I try to calm myself with meditation, but the pain is unrelenting. What's the goddamned answer? I gently press on my eyes, attempting to relieve the pressure. I'm nauseous and fight to swallow the revulsion away. It's too late. I run to the bathroom just in time to heave into the toilet, and then slip onto the tile floor, too weak and broken to move.

While we have serious issues to contend with, it's still important to maintain a sense of normalcy. So, with some annoyingly happy birds chirping outside my kitchen window, I make breakfast while the kids take care of their weekend chores. Which leaves me asking, why is it that I can get Lily to clean her brother's pee off of the toilet rim but not make good life choices?

Will's and Kaye's familiar voices are at the back door. I slide open the screen to greet them.

"It's such a beautiful morning, we thought we'd take a drive over to see you," Kaye says as they enter the house.

It isn't long before the five of us are feasting on German pancakes while I saturate myself with the love and laughter surrounding my table. I can't believe how happy Lily seems. Why can't I sustain this elusive moment?

After breakfast, with the kids off cleaning their rooms, I replay last night's alarming behavior for my friends. "I don't know what to do anymore."

Will looks at Kaye and then at me and says, "What if Lily were to move in with us for a while?"

"We've been talking about it." Kaye assures me that though it may sound crazy to offer, they've put a lot of thought into it.

I'm flabbergasted that my dear friends would actually disrupt their kid-free lives to help us! "You guys are amazing. That you would even suggest such a thing is incredible!" Their selfless gesture unexpectedly energizes me. "I really appreciate that you would do this, but I'd feel like I'd be abandoning her. Thank you, though! Your support means more than you know."

"I have another thought," Kaye says. "I met a woman who sent her son to one of those camps for troubled teens. She found a great one in Utah that's run by Mormons. They do a really great job with the kids. It's not cheap, but she was really pleased with it. I can get her phone number for you."

Other than the short time Kaye worked at Xtreme Perspectives, she's run programs for at-risk teens for the State of Washington. While I trust in her knowledge and experience, it's still a daunting possibility to consider.

"I don't know, Kaye. That seems so drastic. Anyway, Lily would never agree to it."

"Sometimes the kids don't go willingly. The camp has people who escort them for you."

"What do you mean?"

"There are various methods they employ," she says. After hesitating for a moment, she adds, "Occasionally the campers have to be kidnapped and taken forcefully."

"Oh my god, that sounds horrible!"

"But then, so is what Lily's been doing," she reminds me. "It's just an idea."

She's right, and I know it. Another door has opened but, for now, I'll wait. There's something in me that still thinks I can reach Lily with my words. Reason used to be the only discipline I needed—before divorce.

You don't solve a problem by banishing it to some remote canyon in Utah. And as much as I hate to admit it, shipping her off for others to help would mean that I've failed. How can I not succeed at the most important job I'll ever have? I hug my friends good-bye and thank them for strengthening my resolve.

Later, with the waters still calm, I decide to find out more about Lily's friends.

When I enter her bedroom, she's on the phone with one of her accomplices. Since I don't want to incur her wrath, I smile and mouth for her to come and see me when she's done. Then I add an extra teaspoon of sodium pentothal sweetener by whispering, "No rush, honey."

When I was five years old, way before there were film ratings or concern about a movie's content, my parents took me to see *The Seven Voyages of Sinbad.* During one of Sinbad's crusades, he traveled to the land of the hideous Cyclops. Well, holy crap, if that didn't scar me for life!

I mention this because, when Lily's enraged, she mimics the primitive, herky-jerky special effects of the horrifying creature. I want to run screaming from the room, but the beast keeps coming—grabbing and smashing everything in its path, until finally, it catches me. As I flail in its bone-crushing grasp, I look into the Cyclops's eye and ask it nicely to put me down. "Please, sir, if you would be so kind as to let me go." When am I going to learn?

Lily knows she screwed up big time last night and is willing to make nice for the moment. Our temporary truce gives me the perfect opportunity to shine the interrogative light in her eyes.

"Hey, babe," I say when she emerges, "I'd like to know more about Renée, since she's become such a good friend of yours. Have you met her parents?"

"Yeah, I have, but I don't really like them."

"Why do you say that?" I ask, keeping it mellow.

"They're her foster parents, and all they do is use Renée and her older sister to take care of their real kids. Plus, they do drugs," she says openly. "She and her sister have to do all of the laundry and cleaning too."

"Do her parents work?" I question, hoping to find a redeeming quality.

"Not very often."

This is not the kind of information I was hoping to

hear, but at least Lily's talking. I keep digging while the Cyclops sleeps.

"How many brothers and sisters does Renée have?"

"She has her biological sister who is a couple years older, and then her foster parents have two little boys and a baby girl. But her older sister hates living there and plans on moving out in a couple of months, when she turns eighteen. Then Renée will be left alone to look after the others."

I love that my daughter is showing compassion for her friend—I just wish it would be for someone from a healthier environment. "What kinds of drugs do her parents use?"

"Mostly marijuana, but other stuff too."

"Do they smoke it in front of the kids?" I continue, trying not to overreact.

"Sometimes," she admits. "It's sad. And Renée doesn't like it either."

"Maybe you shouldn't go over there anymore." *Doh! I did not just say that!*

"Mom, you're not going to stop me from going over to her house!" she snaps.

"I know I can't stop you," I say calmly, gently patting ol' One Eye on the head. "But why don't you invite her to come here instead? She can bring her little brothers and baby sister along."

"She can't. Her mom won't let her," she says, growing more impatient with me.

"How do you know her mom won't let her?" The woman sounds like she'd be thrilled to be rid of her kids.

"I just do!" she argues, demonstrating her familiar posturing.

Uh-oh, now I've gone and done it! Run, Sinbad! Run!
"I would rather you didn't spend time at their house, Lily."
*"Would rather?" Shit!*

"Mom!" she says, spitting my name like it's a curse
word. "Renée's my friend. She can't leave her house, so I
have to go over there!"

How can I prevent her from being with her friend? It's
impossible to monitor every move she makes. Maybe I
*will* have to do something drastic after all.

Alone in this life-altering decision to send my daughter away, I know Lily and I are the ones who will have to
live with whatever the consequences are.

"What do you mean, you're not coming home?!" I repeat into
the phone while I pace the kitchen. "It's two in the morning!
I've been worried sick! Where in the hell are you?"

Recently Lily's gone missing more often than before,
forcing me to make humiliating late-night phone calls to
the parents of her friends. The dark and lonely hours are
insanely distressing. My heart billows to the brink of rup-
ture as I wait for news of my daughter's body being discovered alongside the highway. I persist pacing in vacant
darkness from room to room, the flicker of our tired street
light my only salvation. So far, she's come home safely, but that doesn't keep me from going out of my mind,
thinking this could be the one time she doesn't.

"I'm staying at Brian's," she says, sounding distant.

"You can't do that!"

"I think we need to take a break from each other," she says, emotionless.

"A break? Lily, you're my daughter. There's no break."

"Yes, Mom. I'll call you tomorrow."

"Lily, wait!" I protest, but it's too late.

*Oh god, what are you doing, Lily?* I have to persuade her to come home! She didn't even give me a chance! My words, my precious words, are they no longer the vehicle for our redemption?

Panicked by the abrupt ending of our phone call, I quickly look at caller ID to retrieve Brian's number. Frantically, I dial it. No one answers. I try again and again, leaving all kinds of messages: demanding ones, angry ones, then begging and pleading ones. How can she ignore the pain in my voice?

Fueled by a surge of out-of-control anger, I slam my fist hard on the kitchen counter. I turn to see Jack as he collapses against the wall. He covers his face with his hands and sinks slowly to the kitchen floor, crying. My sweet son, the wholesome young man who lives in the shadows of our home, is paying his own harrowing price.

I move onto the floor next to him and put my arms around him. "Everything's going to be okay, Jack. I'll fix this. I promise."

I feel my hand swelling up like a blowfish as I help Jack back to his room.

I have no idea where Brian lives. I don't even know his stepfather's last name! How will I ever find her? Oh god, I'm a horrible mother!

I head into Lily's room, search her desk, dresser, shelves, notebook, hoping to find something with an ad-

dress on it, but there's nothing. I hurry back to the kitchen
and open a folder filled with years of phone numbers from
the kids' classes, team rosters, and every activity they've
ever been involved in. Again there's nothing.

I spot Renée's name and realize I have no other choice.
I don't want to call her, especially not after what Lily's
told me about her foster parents, but I have to. I've thrown
away so many of the rules of propriety and manners since
my daughter's fall from grace. Balancing a book on my
head, gliding through life, is no longer the way I live.

A groggy, gravelly man's voice answers the phone.
"Hello."

"Hello, this is Alex Fisher, Lily's mom. I'm sorry to
bother you at this hour, but I'd like to speak with Renée,
please."

"She's asleep," he grumbles.

"I know, and I wish I didn't have to ask you to wake
her, but it's urgent. I need to get some information from
her. Please."

Irritated but apparently willing to help, he mutters,
"Hang on."

Once again, I have hope. Hope that Renée knows
where Brian lives. And hope that I'll be able to convince
Lily to come home.

It takes forever until I hear her voice. "Hi, Renée,
this is Lily's mom. I'm sorry to wake you, but would you
please tell me where Brian lives? Lily's with him, and I
need to bring her home."

"I don't know," she's quick to answer.

There's no way she doesn't know. She's obviously
covering for Lily. Desperate to find my daughter, I plead,

"Please, Renée, I'm really worried. She might be in danger, and you're the only one who can help."

The resistant teen gives way to a sympathetic young adult.

"You did a good thing, Renée. Thank you."

I check on Jack, who's fallen back to sleep. The thought of leaving him alone in the middle of the night upsets me. If you'd asked me a few years ago if I'd ever do such a thing, my answer would have been "Absolutely not, never! How could any mother ever?!" But in my world today, I don't have a choice. Please turn to page thirteen in your Moral Lessons Hymnal. Let us rise and sing. *Mine eyes have seen the people who are judging all the world; they are trampling out the village where the grace of man is stored.* Enough already! I get it!

I have to go quickly and return before he knows I'm gone.

I leave Jack a note, lock up the house, and drive toward Brian's place a few miles away. There's no more thinking to be done. Protective-mother adrenaline surges through my body—propelling me toward what I must do. I can only hope my instincts will guide me through this nightmare. My fear deafens me to the sound of my tires. I feel like I've been thrust into life's underbelly. What might I encounter? It doesn't matter. My love for Lily is far more powerful.

No one inhabits the suburban streets in the early-morning hours. The cold night air seems hollow and reticent. As I pass the darkened homes of my neighborhood friends whose children are snugly nestled in their beds, their comforting support seems so very far away. I've never felt the isolation of being a single parent quite as cruelly as I do at this moment.

The illumination of my brights on the black pavement is the only thing guiding me. It's as if there's no one else on earth—just me going to rescue my firstborn.

I turn into Brian's cul-de-sac and spot his house among the five modest ranch homes. With a rusted-out truck sitting on concrete blocks, broken garage door panels, and scattered yard debris, its foreboding appearance is so cliché. My fear escalates as I shake my head, thinking, *What more?*

I step out of my car and quietly close the door, careful not to latch it just in case I need to make a run for it. Moving from under the glow of the street lamp toward the darkened entrance, I remind myself why I'm here. *Get in, get Lily, get out.*

Raising my finger to the doorbell, I push it with conviction and wait—and then wait some more. No one comes, so I push it again, this time holding it a little longer, hearing it ring inside. Still no one comes.

Nervously I survey the bushes and the corners of the house to ensure I'm not going to suddenly be attacked. Then I jam the button three or four more times. *Shit. Come on—open up, for crissakes! Don't make me be a crazy lady!*

I reach out my hand, feeling every petrified beat of my heart, and slowly pull back the screen door. The pulsing in my ears is so incredibly loud, I look around again to see if I've woken any of the neighbors.

My fist hammers on the scuffed wood-paneled door. What is it with me and doors? They always seem to be closed. James and his hotel door at the movie premiere in California; Lily and her bedroom door or any other door within her reach; and all of the metaphorical doors that have been slammed in my face since that unhinging night in Victoria.

Without warning, this scary door opens. A tall, shadowy figure looms in front of me. It steps forward and becomes a man, his hair scraggly and wild, his face unshaven, his whole being reeking of armpits and alcohol. He is shirtless and fills the entryway with his sinister presence. I instinctively take a step backward.

"Do you know what time it is, *lady?*" he barks. "What in the hell do you want?"

"I'm sorry to bother you in the middle of the night. I'm Lily's mother," I say, fortified with *mom*power. "I've come to take her home. Would you please get her for me?" My voice is firm, but I have to squeeze my hands together to stop them from trembling.

"She's not here," he says coldly and then starts to close the door.

"Wait, wait! Please! Brock, right?" Using the name I'd heard Elise say, hoping my familiarity will soften him. "Listen, I know she's here. She called me from your house."

"*Lady.*" He spews the word so salaciously I can smell the bile blasting from his mouth. "I'm telling you, she's not fuckin' here."

*Oh maaan, he just ruined the word* lady *for me forever.* Even if it were superlatively used, say I were to become Lady Alexandra one day, it will forever conjure this vulgar sack of shit. The hairs on my neck stand up at his callous, intimidating attitude. I hold my ground as my face reddens and my blood begins to boil. Jesus, my heart is about to fucking explode! This lunatic isn't going to help me! And he's being a prick about it too!

*Don't mess with a mother protecting her young, you asshole!*

Fear and anger battle within me. I'm so pissed off, I want to shove the bastard aside and scour the house for my Lily. But the potential for disaster keeps me from kicking him in the balls and running inside. What might he do? I flash on Lily's and my bloody corpses, her on the bed, me splattered against the wall.

Finding the one lone rational cell I have left, I use it to control what every other part of my body is crying out to do. "Stay calm, Alex," I hear a faint voice urging me.

"Sir, please, I know she's with Brian. I want my daughter to come home with me. Can I step inside and get her?" I continue with my patient, pathetic rhetoric. *Fucker! If only I were a man, I'd kick the livin' shit out of you!!*

Provoked by my persistence, he roars, "You're not coming in, bitch! If you don't leave right now, I'm calling the cops and having you fuckin' arrested for harassment." And then he seems to take pleasure in sneering. "Your fuckin' daughter's not here."

The police—do I want him to call them? Hell, yes! But Lily's already had her run-ins with the law. Would I be drawing more negative attention to my daughter? Would this leave another black mark on her already tarnished record?

Frustration from my inner turmoil is finding its way out of every one of my pores. I'm so goddamned angry, I'm ready to unleash my own crime of passion! *Go in, dammit! Get her out now, you wimp!*

But what if you're wrong? She might *not* be in there. As I stand alone in the dark, eerie night, the asshole's menacing body language and threatening words force me to shamefully back away. *You can't do this, Alex. No, God help me, I can't.*

With watery eyes and neck veins surely bulging, I unleash a teeth-clenched threat of my own. "If any harm comes to my daughter, you're going to pay for it!"

The vehemence of my delivery is frighteningly primal. I'm stunned by this savage, unfamiliar woman. I can physically feel fire so deep in my gut it's like the earth's core is burning inside of me. In this moment, my own potential for violence scares the hell out of me. I had no idea the barbaric lengths I might go to in order to protect my child. My heart is begging me to vomit obscenities, but instead, I turn my body and walk toward my car, all the while locking a murderous look over my shoulder on the hellish man leering at me.

I don't remember driving home. My first recollection is looking in on Jack, still safe in his bed. My two beloved children pull me back and forth between heaven and hell.

I can't take this anymore. It's time. *Kumbaya, my Lil, kumbaya.*

# Chapter Eight

*A*ll I wanna do is have some fun. I hit my alarm clock. Love you, Sheryl, but right now I don't want to hear about anyone else's good time. Dragging my exhausted body into the bathroom, I squint into the mirror. *God, you're looking old!* These life lessons sure speed up the aging process. I close my eyes and inhale deeply. *Remember, Alex, you're becoming a better person as you face these challenges. Personal growth, yada, yada. What doesn't kill you, yeah, yeah, right, right.* And then I open them, hoping by some miracle . . . Nope. Still look like crap.

I do what I can to salvage my appearance, get Jack off to school, and arrive at the office in time for an important meeting with a client from San Francisco. Yes, life does go on even when your child is in jeopardy.

A few minutes before the team is supposed to gather in the conference room, Carol discreetly whispers, "Lily's on the phone."

I quickly duck into my office, closing the door behind me. "Lily!"

"Hi, Mom. How are you?" she says, as if my recent trip to hell had been just another night spent in front of the boob tube.

"How am *I*? How are *you*?"

"I'm fine, Mom. I just want to let you know that I've decided to take a couple of days off and hang out at Brian's house," she announces as if she were an adult in charge of her own destiny.

*I knew it! That bastard!* "Lily, why didn't you come to the door when I was there?"

"You were here? When?" she asks, sounding surprised.

"Last night, at two in the morning. Didn't you hear me talking with Brian's stepfather?"

"No, Mom, I promise I didn't know. Brian and I were asleep in the back bedroom." I quickly flick the image of the little prick in bed with my daughter out of my head.

"Brian's dad is such a creep. He lied and said you weren't there," I say, and realize I'm just as agitated about my failed attempt at rescuing my child as I am at being reminded of the son of a bitch who scared me away. "Lily, you need to come home so we can work things out."

"Mom," she says firmly, "I want time to think. Nothing's changed. I'm going to stay here, but I promise I'll call you later."

"But we need to talk now. And what about school?"

"I'll call you this afternoon. I promise. Bye, Mom," she says with some compassion, but not enough to change her mind.

Fortunately for me, I'm not the lead in our meeting with the San Francisco group. That's James's job. One he's very good at. Watching him present with such ease and confidence, I'm unaware my heart has taken control of me.

*How did we get here? Why aren't we still married? We had such a wonderful life.* For a moment, I let myself want it all back. I want to return to our joyful family—to the excitement of our new business, and to our soulful love.

*Jeez, you idot, snap out of it! What in the hell are you thinking?!*

"Alex has the modifications for your review," James finishes, and my professional posture snaps to attention.

During lunch, I phone the camp in Utah with an armload of questions and fears. The professional's answers, along with Kaye's recommendation, give me enough confidence to follow through with my decision. Summer break starts soon, and Lily will have way too much idle time on her hands, time to put herself into more danger. One way or another, by next week my self-destructive daughter will be on a plane to the Alpine Academy.

After signing a contract to absolve the camp of all liability, causing me to experience a tremor in my already shaky resolve, I receive a list of clothing and personal items Lily needs for her lengthy expedition. With James's uncustomary support, I leave work to shop for top-of-the-line hiking boots and the latest in fashionable outdoor apparel. Somehow, purchasing high-end protective gear unburdens my troubled conscience.

It's become quite apparent to me over the past few years that subconscious mind games soothe my unbearable pain: Enjoy fantasy revenge on those who've done

me wrong, and I'll stay out of jail. Take the high road even
when it sucks, and my friends will ride on the low one for
me. Buy designer field wear for my daughter, and maybe
she won't notice that she's shitting in the woods.

When Lily phones later, I'm ready to begin my reluctant treachery. "Hi, babe." *Be nice, Alex, no lectures.
There's a greater plan at hand.* "Thanks for calling. How
was the rest of your day?"

"Good."

"What'd you do?" *Nothing you were supposed to, I'm
guessing.*

"Just hung out here," she says.

My stomach churns over the "hanging out" possibilities. Drugs? Sex? But I move on with theatrical composure, offering her a poisoned apple.

"Listen, babe, I don't want to fight anymore. We need to
make things right between us. So I've been thinking, since
we haven't had a chick adventure in a while, how would
you feel about going to Scottsdale for a long weekend? Just
you and me. No heavy discussions, no pressure, just fun."

The kids and I have gone to Scottsdale on a couple
of occasions so that Jack could play in some tennis tour-
naments. While he was with the other players, Lily and
I spent our time shopping and sightseeing. I'm hoping
those happy memories will outweigh her anger. Besides,
if I mention a trip to Utah, somewhere she's never been
before, she'll be suspicious.

"I don't want to fight anymore either, Mom. Let's do
it," she says, sounding excited by the idea.

God, how I hate myself! What kind of mother tricks
her child into thinking she's going on a pleasure trip and,

instead, is having her kidnapped and carted off to bear country?

"How about if we go next week? I'll make the reservations. We can leave on Thursday and return on Sunday."
*Traitor, traaaitor, TRAAAITOR!*

As far as Lily knows, the plan is for us to fly to Salt Lake City and then drive to Arizona from there. She thinks it's the only flight I could get on such short notice and believes everything I tell her to perpetrate this horrible betrayal. After all, she trusts me. Sadly, I'm painfully aware that once we step off of the plane, that trust will be broken.

My girl doesn't come home again that night, further fortifying my intention to send her away. Finally, on Friday, she walks through the front door. I reach out to hug her as if it's the last embrace we'll ever share.

And then it hits me. The simple duplicity of my phone deceit is now elevated to eye-to-eye hypocrisy. For the next six days, I'm going to have to live in a world of false principles. Honesty and integrity, at the very core of my values, will be buried under a pile of pretense. No wonder I've been sick. My stomach is twisted by the perversion of my morals.

The following Wednesday, before Jack and Lily leave for their weekly dinner with James, I ask Lily to pack her bag for our trip the next day.

But as soon as she's gone, I remove her things and replace them with the items from the list.

After that, there are no more mind-numbing tasks to perform—giving me time I don't want. I stare at the wall clock as my mind tortures me. Thirteen hours until we leave for the airport, fifteen hours until we take off, seventeen hours until . . . *Stop it! Stop thinking about it! You have got to go through with this!*

The atmosphere surrounding me is heavy with the weight of my aloneness. How I wish I had someone to lean on. My parents, Will and Kaye, and my sisters all called earlier in the day, offering words of encouragement. But this time I need more: someone's arm around me, a sympathetic hug. Like Popeye's energizing hit of spinach, the power of human touch would surge through my body. It happens so rarely anymore, my body craves it.

Just then, the phone rings. It's Kendall. "Hey, you, how ya doing?" she asks.

My heart lifts at the sound of her voice. "Man, you're spooky."

"Why?"

"Your timing is impeccable."

"I thought you could use a friend."

"You have no idea," I confess.

"Meet me at the bridge by the school in ten minutes," she says, catching me off guard.

Unprepared to actually see her face-to-face, I'm afraid of losing control of my emotions when confronted with her compassion. But this time I don't listen to the discipline of my head, and I relinquish control to the aching need of my heart. "Okay, thanks, Kendall."

As I walk down to the creek, I offer thanks for having this merciful person in my life. Counting my blessings has become a routine necessity. The pathetic woman who sat on the couch in despair just moments ago is up and moving toward the comfort of a true friend.

Kendall's waiting for me when I approach the bridge.

"Hi, you," she says, reaching her arms around me for a big, healing hug—an embrace that means more than anyone could imagine: atomic fuel for the soul.

We head toward the playground at the grade school as I recount the details of my deception.

"I can't imagine how difficult it will be sitting in the airport after they've taken her away," she says.

Even though I hear Kendall's voice, it's as if I'm completely desensitized to it. My body is in protective mode. If I were stabbed by some psychopath, I would feel nothing. I'd only be capable of bearing witness to the blood draining from my wounds.

"Listen, I was thinking—why don't I go with you to Salt Lake City? I can sneak onto your flight or take a different one."

Once again, I'm sustained by the love of a dear friend. "That's so incredibly generous of you, and I would like nothing better, but I should do this myself," I say. "Thanks, though—it means a lot to me that you would even offer."

We sit on the swings, my eyes transfixed on the wood chips beneath my feet, as Kendall does her best to raise my spirits. I blink recognition like a catatonic vegetable and begin rocking back and forth, trying to comfort myself.

"I feel like I'm leading a lamb to the slaughter."

"Alex, listen to me. You love your daughter more than anything, and that's the only reason you're doing this."

"But what will Lily think of me when they drag her away?"

"You have so much courage, and someday Lily is going to realize what you went through for her."

*Control, Alex, keep control. No falling apart. Not until*

*after you're done.*

Fearful of the emotions that will overcome me if our eyes meet, I distract myself by gently kicking the wood chips. "I'm in such a funk, and yet, somehow I'm still logically able to go through the steps I need to take. My intellect is fully intact, but my soul, my spirit, and my emotions have been tied up, gagged, and thrown into a closet. I can't risk letting them out. Otherwise, I won't make it through this."

"It's okay to let go," Kendall says, putting her hand on my shoulder.

"No," I protest, more for myself than for her. "Not yet."

She recognizes my need to hold fast to my strength and asks, "Jack doesn't know anything, does he?"

"James is going to tell him tomorrow after Lily and I leave."

"Do you trust him to handle it tactfully?"

"I'm hoping. These past couple of days, I've caught glimpses of the old James—the one I married."

Once more, sleep evades me. In the shower the next morning, I remind myself why I'm betraying Lily: she'll be safe; she'll receive intense counseling to regain her self-esteem; she'll remember how fortunate she is and re-discover gratitude; and she'll be away from her trouble-making friends and their pathetic parents.

As for Jack, he'll have my undivided attention. And me, I'll have time to nourish my soul. Best of all, when

Lily returns, we'll be a loving family of three. *Oh, if only.*

I squeeze Jack tightly to fill myself with his energy before he heads off to school. *My sweet boy, what will your teen years bring?*

"How long will it take to drive to Scottsdale from Salt Lake City?" Lily asks on our way to the airport.

I fight off a reflex bout of nausea and deceive her once again. "About three to four hours."

Lying to her is killing me. Will my daughter ever trust me again?

If I turn the car around right now, we could be back at home in a matter of minutes. *Hold the wheel steady! Don't even look at the exit ramp!* I feel my right arm flexing to steer to the right, and yell, *Don't do it!* Fortunately, the shouting is just in my head.

Look at her. She's so happy we're taking this trip together. How will I survive them pulling her away from me?

*Oh man, I'm gonna yak. Stop thinking about it, for crissakes!* My eyes begin to well. *You can't cry now! She'll see you! Look! Look at those beautiful evergreens. God, how I love Washington.*

Lily's excitement over the anticipation of our weekend grows more painful as the miles pass under us. *Jesus, this sucks!* Where's my power coming from? It's as if I've been programmed to complete the mission. Alex, loving mother, is no longer in control. *Lillll—y, Lillll—y, give me your answer, do. I'm half cra—zy, over the love of you.*

After we board the plane, I pull the Sky Mall magazine from the seat pocket. I don't want to talk—talking means more lies. I don't want to look—looking means breaking down. *Keep staring at the page. Lily, I'm so sorry. I love you more than you know.* My eyes begin to flood again. *Stop it! You can't give it away now! You're so close!* I look up from the page of garden Yeti statues to restrain the tears cresting in my eyes and quietly swallow the lump in my throat. *The lavatory's vacant again. Hmmm, wonder if that guy washed his hands.*

After our plane lands, I'm deafened by the all-too-familiar sound of the pounding in my ears. Just a few minutes more.

"Can we go to the Cheesecake Factory tonight?" Lily eagerly asks.

"Sure, babe," I say, following her down the aisle.

*Are they waiting? Breathe, Alex, breathe!*

We walk out of the gangway. A muscle-bound man steps in front of us. "Are you Lily?" he questions.

She looks at me. I rip my eyes away from her bewildered gaze, knowing I must do this quickly or I won't be able to do it at all. I nod yes to her escort and the brawny man next to him.

"I'm Jeff. Please come with us."

He removes her purse from her shoulder and hands it to me. The two men take her by the elbows and begin leading her away. It happens so fast, Lily's stunned—her frightened look begs me for help.

"Mom!" she cries, struggling to get away. "Mom, Mooooom, pleeeease!" she screams as they force her toward the main terminal.

My heart breaks as I watch my daughter fight to be with me. I want to run to her, to hold her in my arms and tell her, "If you stop your dangerous behavior, baby, we'll go home right now." But instead my voice cracks as I choke out the words, "It's going to be all right, Lily. I promise. I love you."

"Mom, please!" she howls. "I swear I'll be good! Pleeeease, Mommy!"

Within moments, my girl is out of sight, but her desperate cries in the distance pierce my heart. I fight off the agony of what I've just done. My pain becomes more than I can bear as I stand alone in a cone of isolation. Passengers are everywhere, but they're all a blur. Their presence doesn't penetrate me. All I can hear is my broken daughter howling for me, her mother, her protector.

A female voice announces a flight over the public address system, jarring me from my trance. Just as quickly as they left me, my senses return, and I am angry at the hundreds of strangers surrounding me. *Why didn't anyone help her? What if we're bad people?* I'm shattered and broken.

I hurry away from the gate, bolting toward something, anything. *I have to get out of here! Don't look at me! Don't talk to me!*

I flee to the nearest hideaway, a low-lit bar, and collapse into a chair.

"What can I get for you?" asks the young server.

"Nothing, thanks," I say, sending her back to chat with the bartender.

I want to pour my guts out to her! *Do you have any idea what a horrible thing I just did? Any clue what my life has become? I just gave my daughter away to complete fucking strangers!*

Droves of commuters pass by. *I can't sit here and think. I've got to keep moving.*

I step out into the flow of passengers, and—*Oh my god! Lily's still here.* She's sitting on the floor along the concourse wall, about forty feet from me, with Jeff crouching beside her. I quickly step back into the bar. But I can't resist the urge to take a peek. She looks so sad and alone as she wipes away her tears. Jeff helps her to stand and puts his arm around her, but not in a restraining way.

It will be two long months before I hear her voice again. *Lily-babe, please hear me, feel my arms around you. Know that I love you more than life itself.* And then I blink away my tears.

Mind escape. I need mind escape. *Check the departure board. Gate B12.*

*Now, just sit and people watch. There sure are a lot of blonds in this airport. And tons of children . . . Oh, how I wish I was consoling you, honey. . . . They seem like a nice young family—kids are well behaved. I remember when James and I took Lily and Jack to Disneyland. The flight attendant commented on how polite they were. We were a nice young family too. Shut up! That was a lifetime ago. You've got to stop thinking about that shit. And for Pete's sake, don't look at families! . . . Hmmm, attractive guy, expensive suit. Ooo, niiiice shoes.*

"Hi, Trix. How was your day? Better than mine, I'm guessing," I say, reaching down to pet my lovable springer. "I had to send Lily away today, girl." Her brown eyes console me as I stroke her silky ears with my thumbs. "We've got to get her back on track. We can't lose her." She cocks her head with recognition. "Did anyone ever tell you you're a damn good listener?"

Just then, I notice an envelope on the kitchen counter. Inside is Jack's undeniable printing.

> Dear Mommy-Bear,
> How are you doing? I'm doing good. I heard what you had to do today. I don't think I could have done it. You are very brave. I think it was the right choice for everybody. She was probably very scared, but so were you. I want you to know how much I love you. OK, so now what's the deal? Do I have to do her jobs too?!
> Love, Tiger-Bear

I stare at Jack's card, the warmth of his empathy joining the other countless conflicted feelings I have within me.

I did it. How horrible of me, and yet there is a ray of new hope—oh, but that agonizing scene at the airport. I abandoned my daughter when she needed me the most. Is she still crying? Is someone comforting her? *Lily, what are you thinking? What are you feeling?*

Somehow it seems befitting that on this dark and forsaken night, with a thousand miles between us, we are the same—alone and afraid.

So deep into my lamenting am I that I barely hear the sound of the doorbell.

"Surprise!" exclaim my Black Ridge cohorts, their arms loaded down with wine bottles, pillows, and overnight bags.

"What are you guys doing here?" I say, swinging open the screen door.

"We thought you might need us, girlfriend," Kendall says, giving me a hug.

"And we couldn't think of a better time to have a few therapeutic margaritas!" Liz adds. "Where are the glasses?" she says, moving past me.

"I'm here for you," Kate whispers in my ear as she gives me a big squeeze.

Elise, Annie, and Tammy follow right behind with compassionate hugs.

I recount the hideous events of the day to my sympathetic friends, whose love, support, and humor lift me. By 3:00 a.m. my family room is filled with overindulged women who will surely need strong cups of coffee and deep-tissue massages by morning.

# Chapter Nine

I lean in toward the speaker on James's desk as if it will bring me closer to Lily and hunger after each morsel of information from the academy's counselor like a starving urchin devouring a bowl of gruel. *Please, sir, I'd like some more.* As foolish as it sounds, it's as if Lily were safe when I'm telephonically connected to this chosen stranger.

"She's doing fine. We're taking good care of her," says the counselor. "I'll have more to report next week."

*No, don't hang up! Does she miss me? Is she sad? Does she like her boots?*

I hold cerebral pep rallies to quell the anxiety that fractures my peace-seeking mind as each day I eagerly flip through my mail to see if Lily has written. It's been an eternity since my home was a sanctuary. Living in a tranquil house is a gift no longer lost on me. Still, the more time that passes without hearing from her, the more apprehension and fear again outweigh my serenity.

Finally, on day eight, a manila envelope with Alpine Academy's return address arrives. I hurry into the house and tear open the seal. Three dirt-stained letters pour out.

My eyes dance at their radiance! There's my name! *Mom!* And in her beautiful handwriting! That's my baby!

READ THIS AND THINK SERIOUSLY, PLEASE!

The first letter begins as my excitement quickly vanishes.

Mom,

I need your help! I'm in so much pain, physically, mentally, and emotionally. Every day we're up at sun break and hike until 8:00 pm with heavy packs made out of plastic tarps. They don't give us any food until we get to our final destination, and then it's only cold, uncooked oatmeal and one banana! We can't talk, and for every word we say, they add an extra mile. We hiked until midnight yesterday! I fell off some rocks and sprained my ankle. It's 90 degrees and we're in the desert, going up mountains, with dirt in our mouths. We can't take showers, and have to drink water from the same muddy ponds that cattle drink from!

Just being here for a little bit, I've learned my lesson. I swear I can't do this. If you would try to really trust and believe in me, then get me out of here. All I do is cry, and so do the other eight kids in my group. When we cry, they make us walk extra miles. I'm so homesick. If you would please have me released, I'll work at Xtreme everyday this summer or do whatever you want. I'm so sorry for everything. Not being able to sleep, eat, or talk really makes me think about how good I have it at home. I just want to see you, Mom. I love you and miss you. No more grief, I promise.

This place actually makes me more upset inside. I feel like my body's deteriorating. PLEASE HELP ME FROM THE EXTREME PAIN I'M GOING THROUGH! I'm begging you, Mommy, please (I'm crying), get me out so we can be mother and daughter again. I was truly ready for us to get back together in Arizona. Come and get me and we can spend lots of time talking things out. I love you.

Please tell Jack and Dad I said hi. MISS YOU ALL! PLEASE HELP!

I rip open the next letter, searching for words that will unbreak my heart.

Mom,

I can't say enough how much I'm hurting. They made me and this girl pass out, throw up, and hyperventilate, and they didn't even care!

There are a couple of things I want to remind you of. First is that you know how much I love softball, and I'm missing it! It's so disappointing. Also, I have Aerosmith concert tickets for next month.

I don't know if you believe how bad things are here because when you talk to my therapist, he probably says everything's fine. But to tell you the truth, I've never been so honest and scared in my life. I think this program can't fix our problems because we're not together dealing with them. So why don't you, Dad, and I go somewhere and work on things as a family? If you get me out, you should do it as soon as possible so the people here don't get mad. See, they won't let us leave without your permission, even if we're hurt.

You can send me to some other program. I mean, this one isn't even healthy. We've all been really sick and exhausted. We have to put drops in water that cows have peed in and then drink it, and it has bugs and crap floating in it. I need you more than ever, Mom! This would be the best summer if I learned my lesson, got to spend time with you, stayed out of trouble, and played my sports. Please don't let me down. Don't make me stay and suffer. The other girl here might be leaving and then I would be the only one with seven boys! HELP! I'm really counting on you.

Love, Lily

I frantically open the last letter.

Mom,

Please take into consideration that we could work out our problems together instead of being apart and, also, growing apart. I'm serious! If this lasts much longer, I don't know if I will ever trust you and Dad again for putting me through this. You wouldn't believe all the hurt and damage it's doing to me inside. If you really care, call the office and have them contact me as soon as possible so I know when I'm leaving. You're my only way out. Why are you separating the family when we could be together? It's not too late!

*Stay calm, Alex. Don't panic. "Never trust you again!" Honey, don't you get it? For three long years I've done everything I could think of to make things better. How can you blame me for not trying hard enough? "If you care." Lily, you know I care, don't you?*

> Yesterday my spleen was so enlarged, the pain was going into my back, and I could barely breathe for hours. Nobody would help me. I seriously felt like I was going to die. They said they called my doctor at home and he told them I've never had an enlarged spleen, but that isn't true because I did. I swear everyone here is so sick and depressed, and as time goes on, things are getting worse.

Aren't they taking care of her? Why didn't they call me? And why did they lie about calling her doctor? She *did* have an enlarged spleen last year. Have I just swapped one life-threatening situation for another? The image of Lily curled up in pain, despondent over her family's rejection, punctures the deluded bubble I've been floating in.

*You've got to stop beating yourself up for sending her away. Remember why you did this, Alex. She stands a better chance in the woods than she does on the streets.* Somehow the possibility of confronting a rattlesnake seems far less dangerous than spending one more night with the stepfather from hell and his stepspawn. Stick with Mother Nature. *She* won't let you down.

> Mom, I'm asking you one more time from the bottom of my heart to please forgive me and take me home. No kid should have to go through this. We're out in the middle of nowhere, and when I was really sick (I still am), they thought I was faking. What is this, Mom? I have no more tears left in my body because I've cried them all out thinking of home. I know if I was there with you, I would be improving

in a positive way. Please give me another chance. I
swear I won't let you down, so please don't let ME
down! It would mean more than anything to spend
time with you, Dad, Jack and, okay, friends, too.

"Friends"? You mean the flunkies who helped trigger this
desperate act. Lily, you are not coming back until you're
purged of their wretched influence.

Mom, if you knew how I was feeling, you'd take me
home in your arms right this minute. I give you my
promise that I'll do whatever you want.
      Sorry to swear, but this is pure HELL! So far I've
learned nothing except how much I miss everything,
like you guys, food, toilets, civilization, clean water,
etc. I haven't showered since I got here, and bugs
are swarming me and eating me alive. So please
consider how I'm feeling. I know you sent me here in
my best interest but, Mom, I'm begging you, please
help me. If you wanted me to get better, why couldn't
you have forced me to do something else nearby?

"Forced me to do something." Have you baked too long in
the Utah sun? Day after day I tried and failed to let you
make your own good choices—failures that led to more
and more alarming behavior. Don't you remember, Lily?

I've changed for the best in this short time because I've
never been put through so much pain. Now I know what
I've done to you and Dad, and I'm truly sorry. I can't
take back the bad actions, but I can start somewhere.

Get me out now and we'll have a new beginning.

She's acknowledging my pain. Is she starting to get it?

I love and miss you, so come and get me before I die! Do me a favor and tell Brian I ♥ him and miss him, and he'll be the first person I call when I get out. Tell him not to leave me and that I'm thinking of him constantly.

Write back. No, just come and get me. I've had diarrhea for three days. Don't put me through this if you love me.

♥ Lily

She almost had me. I was so close to jumping on the next plane and searching the wilds of Utah for her. I was Mel Gibson in *Ransom* ferociously screaming, "Give me back my daughter!" The mountain lions would have ducked for cover! But then: "*Do me a favor and tell Brian . . . love him . . . he'll be the first person . . .*" Big mistake, baby! Huge! I *will* complete the mission!

I read her letters over again, and even though they distress me, in some weird way, they're strangely validating. She's obviously suffering, but more important, she's alive and thinking about her reckless behavior. Focusing my thoughts on the positive aspects of her words, as few as they are, I manage to find the humor in some of them: no talking (must be torture for my social butterfly), cow pee (ewww), diarrhea (keep away from the poison oak, honey), and love Aerosmith (oh yeah, you've been *Livin' on the Edge* all right).

I remind myself how my own personal challenges have made me a better person and hope Lily's time away will do the same for her. And when worrying about her safety, I cling to the Mormon foundation of her boot camp—knowing their commitment to home and family.

> My darling Lily,
> July 2nd
> I hope you've received my other letters and that you realize how much I love you. My sweet daughter, I know this is difficult for you. It breaks our hearts to have to do this, but you left us no choice. Dad and I only want what's best for you, but too often you've refused to listen.
>
> I'll call Alpine to talk to them about your spleen and find out about getting you some medicine. When one of the medical staff is there with you, be sure they thoroughly check you over.
>
> Dad and I will be there in August to bring you home. I'm counting the days and can't wait to hug you so tightly your head might pop off! Please remember at night when you're trying to fall asleep that I'm at home thinking of you.
>
> Though your letters are heartrending to read, I long for them so I can learn about the things you're doing. You'll be a real wilderness woman by the end of the summer!
>
> The weather here has been totally crappy. It's in the low seventies and raining. Anyway, we're not officially starting summer until you come home. Jack and I have no plans for the Fourth of July. If it's still raining, we'll probably go to a movie, or maybe I'll finally paint the downstairs bathroom.

Jack's turning into quite a golf pro! Dad took him to Newcastle, and Jack beat him by seventeen strokes! Oh, and your brother said to tell you that Trixie misses you, but I think it's his way of saying that he's the one who misses you.

Well, babe, I'll write more tomorrow. I know Omi and Opa, Uncle Will and Kaye, Nat and your aunts are sending notes and cards too. Hopefully you're being inundated with love and support. If I wrote a letter every time I thought of you, I'd need a stack of paper from here to the moon! Take care of you, honey. You're so very precious to me.

I love you,

Mom (or am I Mommy Dearest?!)

When James and I have our next conference call with Robert, Lily's therapist, I ask him about her health, her spleen, sprained ankle, and bug bites. He assures me that she's just fine and that most kids initially write home with horrifying stories of mistreatment and sickness because they're away from their friends and their creature comforts and, in some cases, their addictions. He encourages us to continue writing to her about our home life and daily activities—saying they're happy reminders that will foster gratitude and her desire to return to the open arms of her family.

I focus my time on work, Jack, and writing to Lily every day. Life seems amazingly untroubled. What kind of mother is happy that her daughter is gone? While it would be easy to swim in self-loathing, I remind myself what brought me to this point and squelch the persistent fears that creep into my thoughts: Is she safe, or will I receive a devastating phone call about some horrible cliff-falling accident or ferocious bear attack? Is this working, or will she return full of rage? Was this the right choice to save her, or am I closing yet another door—perhaps once and for all locking away my hopes for Lily's future?

A new batch of letters arrives four days later.

Mom,

I have thirteen bug bites on my face alone. One on my eye, and I can't open it! Mom, I know you talk to my therapist every week, but I don't know what he says because he doesn't even talk to me. You might think he's nice and that he cares, but he doesn't. Honest to god, take my word, I wouldn't lie about something this painful. If my letters can't convince you, I don't know what to do. I lie here under the stars thinking of what a great family I have and wish I was there with them. If that wonderful family wants a new and improved daughter, COME AND GET ME NOW!

I can't express enough how dead I am inside. I'm not just homesick, I'm really sick. We hike so much my spleen is bothering me again, and our stupid fifty-pound pack is causing such extreme pain. I know that you know I'm not faking. All the kids here are sick, so get me out before I catch some horrible disease.

The leaders have told us this program is too expensive to waste your money on getting me out, but I promise you'll see a great change already— better than if I stay here the whole time. We haven't been able to clean our clothes or body (private parts) for a week, and I stink so badly! I have a total of for-

ty-eight mosquito bites! Please help me, Mom. Get
me out! Call Brian.
💜 Lily

And there he is again. *Lily, Lily, Lily! I know you're hurting, but the teen fiend is obviously still beckoning. We've
made it this far—we're not turning back now.* Then, as I
begin to read the next letter, I notice a change, a yielding.

Mom,
Here I am writing to you again at six in the morning
cause that's when we get up. I miss you so much. I
wish you could visit me or something. It really stinks
because I totally want to see you. I know you want
the best for me, what's safe and healthy. I do admit
that it's safe here but definitely not healthy. We do so
much work, we can barely move. The food is gross,
and I'm so dirty I don't even know what color my skin
is anymore. My clothes smell and the bug bites keep
multiplying.

Thanks for trying to help me. It's just hard to deal
with. We can't ask any questions so if you know anything about what we're doing in the future, tell me.
Say hi to Jack. Tell him I love and miss him. Mom, my
hair is falling out and I have the biggest knots ever.
We can't brush our teeth or anything. I just can't get
all of my emotions out on paper.

This program has four phases and I always complete what has to be done, but some of the other kids
slack off, and that means for every day they waste,
the whole group has to stay here longer. When you

talk to my therapist, tell him what Brian said when you called him. Robert makes me feel a lot better. I know you care, and I'm on the right track again so please release me. You probably won't, so just be here in August. I count down every day until I get to hug you again. I'll always love you and I'm sorry for asking so much, but it would mean a lot to spend the rest of my summer with my best friend, you Mom!

I feel a lot better when you, Dad, and Jack write to me all the time. I cry when I read your letters, but at least I know you're thinking of me because I get a weird feeling. Anyway, give Brian the address and tell him to write.

All my love (your best friend), Lily

At last, a letter sparking optimism, tiny morsels of promise for a better future. There's no anger in this one. Dare I dream? I have to write to her about Brian. I know she wanted me to call him, but I didn't. Robert feels it's best if she takes this time to focus on herself, and James and I couldn't agree more. We don't want any contact or reminders of Brian. And if I have my way, she'll never hear from him again. Better yet, that by the end of her journey, she won't want to.

The next letter comes addressed to both James and me.

Mom and Dad,
I just had therapy with Robert and it was very relieving. I'd like to thank you both for caring about me. I'm sorry for whining so much in my letters but it's the way I feel. I told Robert a lot of stuff and opened up to him

like never before. I need to tell you both why my life has been going downhill.

I've been lying about the divorce. All these years, I've been hoping that I could somehow bring you back together. Whether it's been bad or good, I've been trying to help.

Dad, please don't be upset with me for opening up because I feel a lot better about my life. It's Mara! I really can't stand how she hurt you, Mom, and I'll never forgive her for what she's done. Dad, why did you do this? I'm mad, but I still love you. I just don't understand how you could do this to Mom.

There's a lot I need to say but will wait until you guys come for our last few days here together. I feel better now. I can make it through this. I'm stronger already. I promise it will be okay. Trust me. I'll fix this problem about Brian, too. I'm glad I'm here because I realize what I have to do to make things right. It's truly helping. I love you.

♥ Lily


My eyes glisten with happy tears. Yes, this is the sound of my girl. *Oh, honey, have you come back for real?* Maybe, just maybe, this *was* the right choice.

She'll never forgive Mara. *Lily-babe, thank you for finally acknowledging her part in this whole nightmare.* . . . Hmm, that feels kinda good. Relishing for just a moment. Mmm, mmm. *Okay, that's enough.* I've kept my mouth shut for so long—not placing blame on Mara in front of Lily and Jack. There were times when I bit my tongue bloody trying not to spew vitriolic criticisms about what she'd done. I knew that one day my children would be mature enough to recognize the emotional devastation she caused.

I read Lily's letter again to confirm that she's not upset with me. Nope, just James and Mara. This is so good for the ego. Ego? Do I still have one? My husband left me, my daughter tormented me, bad wife, bad mother, self-esteem in the crapper. *What ego? I thought you were dead and gone! But here you are, popping up like some narcissistic jack-in-the-box who hasn't been cranked in a while.* I'm feeling a little cocky. *I feel good! Na-na na-na na-na na! So good!!* I've waited a long time to hear Lily confront her anger over our divorce. *Oh, baby, you have no idea what a huge step this is!*

It might seem a bit silly to send a small, white stuffed teddy bear to a hardened fifteen-year-old, but I don't care. This cuddly creature takes Lily and me back to when she radiated sweetness—to when she would let me love her, and she showed me respect. It's symbolic of repairing her shattered childhood innocence. I hear it in her letters. I know I'm not dreaming it.

> Hi, Lily!
> My name is Benny. Yep, that's right—Benny the Bear. I'm here to make you feel better. Your mom says you're a very special person, and that you've begun an impressive process of healing. She, along with your dad and Robert, think the picture of you and Brian you wanted your mom to send should stay at home. It's not a good idea for you to have it right now. It would be too distracting, keeping you from dealing

with your own issues, which I know you want to do. But I'm pretty good company, and I like to get dirty too! I promise I'll behave and won't make a fuss riding in your backpack.

Please feel free to talk to me as much as you want. I'm a beary good listener even though I don't have a lot to say. Your mom told me you've seen some of my relatives out here, but it's okay if we don't run into them again. I've never been that fond of the Grizzly side of the family!

Okay, Lily, let's have some fun. And just in case you forget, I do so love to be hugged!

The next day, I left Lily's letter on James's desk. This is the first time she's confessed her true feelings about his affair with Mara.

*And what a delicious thought it is! Come on, Alex. That's not very nice.* But why should I feel guilty about finding satisfaction in their long-overdue retribution? James and Mara don't live with the repercussions of their doing or the moment-to-moment angst, nor do they deal with the cleaning, feeding, shopping, laundering, chauffeuring, homeworking, nurturing, disciplining, and the overall responsibilities that I, the Lone Parent, have. I have no faithful sidekick.

Their lives consist of snot-fucking fornication (I'm just guessing, but only in a nauseating way) in a cozy, luxury love nest, romantic getaways, the best restaurants

in town, time for a social life, and all of the other pleasures that freedom, money, and no children bring. *Jeez,
Kimosabe, wallow, why don't you!* At long last, they'll
have to face the truth about their culpability. And to that
I say, *"A hearty hi-yo, Silver, to you two!"* No longer
can James blame Lily's behavior on her being a "horrible
little bitch."

I know her time away has softened him, made him
more introspective. In our conference calls with Robert,
he's loving, supportive, and concerned, just like he used
to be. It's the most compassion he's shown Lily since he
walked out the door.

During the next couple of weeks, Lily's letters continue to peel away her emotionally damaged layers. Her attitude becomes distinctly positive. In fact, it's downright
bubbly. And after a while, she stops mentioning Brian.

When she's ready, I write to her about a second visit I
made to Brian's house—the day after I took her to Utah.
I needed to find a way to let go of that corrosive night
with Brock and my pathetic attempt to rescue her. Hard
as I tried, I couldn't shake it. How could I have failed us
both so miserably, letting some creep defeat me like that?
Only this time when I faced him, I wasn't unarmed. I was
packin' righteousness, my hard-fought feminist battle
scars, and most important, daylight.

I knew it wasn't an exercise in logic. There was no
reasoning with him. It was simply my chance to say, "I'm
still standing, and my daughter is safe and healing." I
knew he wasn't worthy of my energy. I knew he didn't
give a shit about what I had to say.

In fact he spewed something obscene about duct-tap-ing my daughter's legs together, but after I'd finished with him, I walked taller to my car.

Dear Mom, Dad, and Jack,
July 10th
I'm sitting here on a very high mountain where I can see miles of canyons, plateaus, desert, the Henry Mountains, and all the way to Colorado. It's so breathtaking! I wish you were here with me. In a few days we move into phase three of our program. Each phase gets easier and more fun. The staff has a lot more trust in us. A couple of people screw up once in awhile and, unfortunately, we all get punished. I'm really hoping we don't have more days added onto our time here. I can't wait to see you!

I've accomplished so much already and we're only half way through. I know you'll be proud of me. My life is so happy right now. I can't wait to share all of my phenomenal experiences with you. Only one month left and we can be together again! Yessss! I'm so excited for our new beginning!

I can't express enough how much I've changed. I know for a fact that I'm going to spend all of my time with my family. I could care less about my friends back home. All I want is you guys. Thank you, Mom and Dad, for putting me back on the right track.

Now I want to tell you about some of the activities that have helped me change so drastically. It's really weird because, first of all, we only have the bare necessities. Our first phase was called Impact, and this one is Survival. Impact was the most difficult thing I've ever done in my life. I thought to myself, if I made it through that, why can't I deal with problems and decisions at home that are so easy? I realize I've made many wrong choices, and made little problems extremely hard. I blew everything out of proportion.

I never knew how much of an effect hiking and not having food could change you! I feel so lucky for all that I have. I know I haven't been appreciative, but I want you to know how grateful I am for everything you do.

Anyway, during the Survival Phase, we're called The Clan of the Coyotes, because coyotes are the best survivors and leave no trace or evidence of where they've been. We're low-impact campers. We crush the coals from our fires, dig latrines, and don't leave any sign that humans have been here. We also make our own bow drills to start fires, otherwise we don't eat. It's these types of things I took for granted at home. Now that I have to work for everything, I know how you guys feel when you do stuff for us kids and we don't thank and respect you.

Right now I'm sitting about 100 yards away from everyone. I've already finished my work so I can write to you. I just want to get my point across of how much I've changed. Every day I set myself a difficult goal and I've achieved all of them. And I've made a future goal for this whole family to stick together, no matter what.

Speaking of sticking together, if you saw me or smelled me right now, you'd probably die! I'm so dirty, stinky, and totally scratched up, but it's okay. I'm getting help and that's all that counts. I don't care if I smell like a pound of limburger cheese, you better be ready for me to hug and kiss you a million times! My friend, Sasha, the other girl here, and I cleaned up in a lake once, but then she got a leech! Gross huh!

I've seen so many animals while I've been here, coyotes, rattlesnakes, mountain lions, yellow-bellied marmots, and many more. I saw two bears in one day! I keep thinking about how depressed I was when I got here. Now I just laugh to myself because I was so totally immature. I admit I used every excuse I could think of to try and leave here. Funny how nothing worked! I'm really proud of myself for doing all of this. I know now I can do anything I want to!

I can't wait to see your faces again. Only thirty more days left. Aren't you excited?!

Love, Lily

Hey Mom and Dad,

July 13th

I love you! It's early in the morning and I've been out on solo, you know, by myself for the past day. I got my own fire started last night, made a shelter, and ate some rice and lentils for dinner. I was kind of scared because I kept hearing noises, but everything's okay.

Yesterday was very helpful for me because I really got to think—a lot! I thought about how wrong I've been, and imagined how wonderful our future is going to be. I'm so excited for this change.

I've learned ways to control myself, and they work. One of the things I've been reading is a twelve step plan for addiction. Even though I don't have those problems, this book has daily wisdom and action that is helping me. So don't worry about any more fights because that's over. When I think about all of the minor issues I turned into big raging arguments, I realize how immature I was. I can't wait to see what I'm like when I come home. This is a major life change for me, and I feel so proud. I didn't think I could feel this much happiness again.

♥ Lily-babe

Dearest Mom, my Mommy Dearest,
July 19th
How's my best friend? I'm doing great because we transitioned into Frontier Phase. Jeez, Mom, I can't believe my growth here at Alpine. I never in my life thought I was capable of doing everything I've done. Goes to show ya what I knew!

I've wanted to tell you how much I look forward to and love reading your letters. They make me feel so good inside. I mean, time is just flying by. Before you know it, I'll be squeezing you with everything I have. Oh how much I love you! I really want you to know that, and I want to keep this bond between us forever. I'm looking forward to spending a lot of time together. We have so many good memories, and I want to make many more. Whenever you want to talk, just tell me and I'll listen. I'm a very caring person, but then, you always knew that. I was the one who forgot. Thank you for putting me back on the road to success.

Unfortunately, I have some bad news. Two of the boys from our group went into the staff's tent last night and stole their salt. Now more days have been added to our program. But it's okay. The boys realize their mistake and I know we won't have any more problems. I'll just be that much more excited to see you. The day will come before we know it!

Thank Nat for the pictures she sent as a reminder of our trip to the Caribbean. I look at them every day. Yesterday I got eleven letters! Tell everyone I appreciate their love and support.

All my love, Lily-babe

Dear Mom & Dad,
July 27th
Benny and I had a good night's sleep last night. He's in my bag with me every night. Thanks, Mom. Today I got all of my fires done, and our group accomplished a lot. I've enclosed a couple of pictures that my friend Sasha took with the disposable camera her parents sent. One of our leaders had the pictures developed for us. I know I look dirty and scrawny, but you can see I'm happy! The scenery here is so awesome.

I got a letter from Dr. Herman, and she said how the three of us will be going to her for counseling when I get back from vacation.

*VACATION?! Did she just call boot camp vacation?!*

Mom, I'm glad you went over to confront Brock. I can't believe what a jerk he was to you. I'm so sorry for all of the times I trusted his word over yours. And forget about Brian. I've learned my lesson about giving myself away. Now I want to focus on family fun!

Dad, Robert told me that he talked to you and Mom about the day you moved out. It was very hard for me to relive. I had no idea it had been bothering me so much. We talked again today and I realized some feelings I've never expressed. I also figured out the reasons for my rebelling. I want to explain some of it to you and Mom now.

It all started the day Dad said he was leaving. My heart was torn apart, and I didn't know what to feel. I took it personally even though I know it wasn't my fault. I was hurt, Dad, because you weren't honest about why you left us. When I found out about Mara, it made me mad and sad. Then as time went on, I truly thought that getting into major trouble would bring you back home. After about a year, Dad, you wanted Mom back and I was so happy. Mom, you gave him another chance and he destroyed it again.

I was confused with why, Dad, you said you didn't like Mara, and then you went back to her. I didn't know who to trust. I'm sorry I didn't tell you both how I felt. I think if I had, none of this would have happened. When you were with Mara for the second time, I started to rebel again. After awhile it just became a horrible habit that I couldn't break. I was so uncontrollable, I couldn't even control myself. Being here has helped me to realize the things I've done to all of us.

I'll explain more when we're together but at least you know I'm getting help here at Alpine.

I hope you feel better about all I've said because I know I do. I'm not hiding anything anymore. I love you and I'm so glad we're communicating in a healthy, positive way. I only have a short time left at this fantastic place, and I swear I'll never forget this experience as long as I live.

Love always, Lily, the Wilderness Woman!

Hey, Lily Rose,
August 3rd
You sound mahvelous, dahling, and you look great too! Thanks for the pics. Is that a tan you're wearing or most of southern Utah?!

I went to see Ellie the other day. Remember her? She was my therapist when Dad and I were going through our divorce. I was telling her about how you held all of your feelings inside after Dad and I split. She offered an intriguing insight. She wondered if maybe you didn't share your anger at Dad because you were waiting for me to show mine. It's possible you didn't feel it was okay. She'd told me at the time that I needed to let it out, but I didn't feel I could because Dad and I own the business together. What if I got mad and then he got madder? What if the business suffered or even failed as a result of my anger? Then where would you, Jack, and I be? Consequently, I held my feelings in. Not very healthy or smart on my part, and exactly what I didn't want you to do. Now you're setting a great example for me!

Just think, in two weeks we'll be sharing our monster hug! I'm excited to spend the last couple of days with you sleeping under the stars.

Nat called from Tortola the other day to ask about you. She wants you, Jack, and me to help her bring a boat down from Alaska to Seattle. Sounds like fun, doesn't it? And Uncle Will and Kaye get all choked up when they talk about the letters you've written to them.

Good luck with your last solo, Lily-babe. I'm so amazed you can spend three days alone in the wilderness and do everything that's necessary to survive. What a woman! But don't tell me which three days you'll be doing it. I won't be able to sleep! Tell me after—when you're back safe with your group. I'm counting on you to take care of me when we're out there together!

Say hi to Sasha, my love. I'll see you soon. I'm so excited!

Love you with all of my heart and soul, Mom

# Chapter Ten

James and I arrive in Salt Lake City just after ten in the morning. Even though the awkwardness of what we once shared punctuates the rhythm of our conversation and restrains our excitement, the old wounds have, seemingly, been left behind.

Today we are simply Lily's mom and dad. Two people who are anxious to reunite with the loving daughter we lost three years ago to our broken home. Her letters have renewed our hope for the future. Having been on the brink of absolute despair, I have compassion for the heartbreak of those parents who are less fortunate. I know how close we came to being on the other side of this. *There but for the grace* . . . Another pearl that's taken on a richer meaning.

A half-day of driving lies ahead of us before we check into our motel at the edge of the Dixie National Forest. Our exchanges stay positive, focused on what we still have in common: Xtreme and our children. The scenery is beautiful, reminding me of the last time James and I drove through Utah.

Several months after our Chicago wedding, while we snuggled in our cozy roach-infested love nest, we took out an atlas and imagined the possibilities for our future. James was eager to move to another part of the country. I, on the other hand, was unsure about leaving my family and burgeoning career at an international computer corporation. But I was blindly in love—the kind of happily-ever-after, altruistic love a young woman envisions for herself. We had it, and I knew it. I felt it so intensely, nothing could have shaken my devotion to James.

We asked ourselves where we wanted to live. Let's see: mountains, waterways, nearby city. That very night we devised a plan to keep our jobs and fulfill our new dream to head west to Seattle. The next morning, James went to his boss and told him my job was moving to Seattle, which, of course, it wasn't. Since his company didn't want to lose him, they transferred him. Once they did, I informed my employer that James was being sent to Washington, and my manager arranged for my relocation. After that, it was just a matter of a U-haul truck, a quick good-bye to his family, a tearful farewell to mine, and we left the Windy City for our new life in the Pacific Northwest—just the two of us and a whole lotta love. It wasn't such a different trip through Utah back then: new hopes, new dreams, and new beginnings.

"Are you nervous?" James asks, turning onto State Route Twenty-Four toward the small town of Grover.

"Completely. I'm so excited to see Lily, but I'm scared of what happens next. She's been so positive about how she's changed. I'm afraid the perfect world she's fantasized about all summer won't live up to her reality."

"I know what you mean. She's been safe out here. Will it all fall apart once we go back home?" he says.

Every time I glance over at James, I think about what could have been. It's hard sitting so close to him, away from the trappings of work, knowing he's not mine anymore. I want to reach over and put my hand on his thigh, a familiar place for it.

*What does she do to that body of yours? How is she different? Oh for god's sake, Alex! Bwaaah! Lalalalala. Oh, look! There's a lovely plateau.*

James and I gather with the other uneasy moms and dads outside an isolated brick building just off of the two-lane highway. There's a self-conscious air about us all. Perhaps we're emitting a prevailing sense of shame at our parental inadequacies. As otherwise successful members of society, we find it difficult to acknowledge such a crucial defeat. Because we are reticent to speak to one another, the apprehension among us is intense as we wait to be reunited with our children.

A few tan young men and women in their twenties, wearing heavy hiking boots, baseball caps, and bandanas, smile as they walk by. Alpine leaders, I'm guessing. Moments later, a robust middle-aged man invites us inside. We follow him into a large classroom containing four rows of metal folding chairs.

"Will everyone take a seat, please? We've got a lot of work ahead of us," he says decisively.

*What kind of work? Just give me back my kid. That's all I want. Jeez, why am I so anxious?*

"My name is Ed, and you'll be with me for most of the day," he states. "We're going to be discussing what your sons and daughters have been up to this summer, what you'll be doing for the next couple of days, and what to expect when you go home," he continues in a no-nonsense kind of way.

"Your children have spent more than two months learning about consequences, responsibility, accountability, and making the right choices. Now it's your turn."

*Uh-oh! That sounds scary!* Why does the voice of authority always unnerve me so? I invariably feel like I've done something wrong. *Honest, I didn't mean it. Whatever it was! Man, it's hot in here. Just don't make me talk. I don't want to talk! Oh, shit! He's looking at me!*

Thankfully, the morning passes quickly as Ed offers us information and guidance. "Your kids have hiked over three hundred miles this summer, and each one has completed multiple solos. They've physically, mentally, and emotionally gotten down to the basics of survival. Along the way, a whole lot of feelings have been shared with their therapist, Robert, and the other camp leaders. This afternoon, we'll be talking about *your* feelings," he emphasizes.

*Whoa, whoa, whoa! Wait a second! I'm not going to share feelings with these strangers. My fragility is too close to the surface. I don't want to analyze! I don't want to relive! I've been through so much already! Don't make me talk, I'm begging you!*

*Get ahold of yourself, Alex! Suck it up and find your strength just one last time. Come on—you can do this!*

*Christ, I'm about to hyperventilate! Somebody turn on the goddamn AC!*

"Let's break for lunch. There are sandwiches next door for everyone, and then we'll meet back here in half an hour."

With a morning of uncomfortable familiarity behind us, James and I introduce ourselves over turkey sandwiches to fellow baby boomers from around the country.

But I'm not really like them. My kid doesn't do drugs. *Oh my god! Do you hear yourself? That is so damned arrogant and, dare I say, judgmental! Shame on you, Alex! Who do you think you're kidding? You're just like them!* We all want our kids to be happy and whole again.

Since Lily and Sasha helped each other make it through their male-dominated summer, I've wanted to meet her parents. Doug is a pilot for a major airline, but out of uniform he looks like any other pot-bellied, pasty-white dad in Bermuda shorts, a Grateful Dead T-shirt, and canvas Outback hat. Her mom, Amy, has a kind face. Someone you wouldn't expect to have a wayward child.

Meeting these people isn't like going to your average social event. After introducing yourself, what do you say to each other? *My child has a cocaine habit. Mine test-drives other people's cars when they're not looking. Mine's an alcoholic. Mine decorates private property after dark.* Such proud stories. But there is one thing we all have in common—wanting to be reunited with our newly sanctified children.

During lunch, while navigating our way through awkward conversations, my mind keeps going back to sharing. *It's not gonna happen. Nobody can make me talk.*

The sound of Ed's voice asking us to return to the classroom elevates my blood pressure to stroke levels. Entering the doorway, I stutter-step when I notice the chairs have been rearranged in a circle.

*Oh, shit! You mean we have to look at each other while we're sharing! Okay, okay. Take it easy. Maybe you won't have to say anything. But what if you do? Keep it simple. Don't divulge too much. We've had some attitude problems. She stayed out all night. Joyriding, hood orna-ment theft, yada yada yada. That's it. Nothing that might make you break. Not now. Not here. And most definitely not in front of James! You can't let him see you fall apart! Fucking breathe, Alex!*

"Have a seat, people," Ed says as he takes the twelve o'clock position in our circle.

*Don't sit next to him! If he goes around the room, he'll probably start with the person on either side of him. Clockwise? Counterclockwise?! I don't know, I don't know!!*

"This afternoon we're going to have a shortened session, and then we will be taking you out to where the kids are. Their leaders have just announced to them that they're at their final destination and that they'll be seeing you later today. Needless to say, they're ecstatic!"

We all beam at the thought of holding our babies again.

"But first we have to talk about what brought you here and what happened in your lives to contribute to your kids' problems," Ed says as he eyes each one of us in turn. "I want everyone to be completely honest. We didn't allow your kids to avoid their issues, and we're not letting you either."

*Oh god oh god oh god! This is frightening on so many levels!*

Ed turns to Corbin's parents, on his right, and asks them to begin. *This is good. They're sitting at eleven o'clock, and we're at three. That's one, two, seven, twelve, thirteen parents before he gets to me. Maybe we'll run out of time!*

*Just listen to their stories, and don't think about what you're going to say. You're not making a political statement here. Just relay the facts. Detach, Alex.*

*Oh, she's really sad. . . . He seems kind of distant. Remember the prize. Finish this. Get Lily. . . . They're united in their thinking. . . . Whoa, he's still pissed at his son. Ah, it's his stepson. . . . Look at those two holding hands. Lucky them.* What's the key to all of this, the common thread? They all seem so different.

*Who are you kidding? They're all you, just doing what you are—protecting their hearts and pride, holding it together the best way they can. None of us wants to share. We've all suffered intolerable pain. JUST GIVE US BACK OUR KIDS, DAMMIT!*

*Jeez, calm down! Remember to breathe.* I close my eyes and inhale. *Kuan Yin, Kuan Yin. You have to do this for Lily.*

*Only two more to go before you're up! Just state the frickin' facts. We divorced, she felt abandoned, she rebelled. Oh, look! There's a poster of Smokey surrounded by a blazing forest fire. . . . Why does a bear wear pants?*

*Damn you, Sean's dad! Slow down! I'm not ready!*

Legs comfortably crossed. Hands relaxed in my lap. Back straight. Head held high. *Shit, my heart's beating its way out of my chest! And my eyes—please stop watering! Oh god, it's almost my turn! I don't think I can do this! BREEEATHE! James, you bastard, this is all your fault!*

"Lily's mom, you're next," Ed says, as his and seventeen other pairs of eyes focus on me.

*Oh my god, I'm going to die! I can't breathe, I can't fuckin' breathe!! Say something! Anything! They're waiting!* My eyes search the room for a comforting face, but all I see are a bunch of looky-loos gawking at my car wreck of a life. I don't want to share with these people!

"Our daughter, Lily, began having problems when my husband left." *Oh no, stabbing pain in the throat!* "It's been so difficult, and I've had to—" I swallow hard as I try to hold onto my composure. *My face, shit, it's contorting!* Head down. *Oh, look! Your hands are still neatly folded. Be strong, Alex. Fight it, dammit. FIGHT IT!*

"I've had to deal—" It's too late. My body and wounded soul have seized control! My voice is shrill and in desperate need of air. Tears roll down my cheeks. My hands, still unmoved from their repressed position, are white-knuckled.

I turn to James, the one and only completely safe place I've ever known, and see a tenderness in his eyes that's been missing since that horrible night in Victoria. No longer able to control my anguish, I succumb to it.

"James, I've had to deal with everything on my own," I cry. "Why couldn't you have been there for us? We needed you." The sound of my hideous voice stops me from sharing anymore. I hang my head and impatiently wipe the relentless tears from my face.

Moments, seeming like hours, go by.

"I'm sorry, Alex. I should have helped you."

And there they were, after all this excruciating time, the words I've waited to hear. My eyes lift to meet James's. What we once had, our dreams, our love, and the life we should be living, radiates through from his face.

James begins sharing with the group while I collect myself. He generalizes his mistakes by admitting he wasn't as engaged as he should have been. I analyze the carpet's worn gray threads in the center of our circle, unable to bear the pitying faces that surround me. If I don't look at them, maybe they won't see me. I cracked. I'm mortified. How could I lose it in front of these people?

But there was that one moment with James. The man who was once my everything had reminiscent compassion in his eyes. *Maybe he does remember us.*

When the meeting ends, a few of the other parents offer empathetic words—and I cringe. *Just another one of life's lessons. Way to be humbled, Alex.* Fortunately, there's no time to indulge my embarrassment. *Learn it and move on. Now, let's go and get my kid!*

On our way to where we'll be reunited with Lily, James and I don't discuss what just happened. His shield is back up and his compassion withdrawn. Why was a single moment of understanding from him such a marvel to me? Shouldn't it be commonplace? But for now, it doesn't matter. All I can think about is seeing Lily again.

I gaze out the passenger window, seeing no signs of civilization along the way. If the so-called campers ever wanted to run, there'd be no place for them to go.

We pull off the road into a clearing where we're greeted by the wilderness team—at last meeting the voices from our weekly conference calls. Robert, a more handsome version of Where's Waldo introduces us to Grace and Colton, two engaged Brigham Young psychology grad students Lily wrote about in her letters. We shake hands with the science teacher and three other young, attractive camp leaders assigned to our nine kids.

After we hike a short distance, surrounded by high-desert trees and shrubs, Robert signals for us to stop. "Your kids are a little more than a mile down this dirt road," he says. "When we radio their leader, he'll let them begin their

run to you. You won't be able to see them until they round
the bend down there."

The anticipation of our happy reunion is crazy exhilarating. I can hardly contain my excitement! *My Lily's
coming home!* James and I will soon be sharing an intimate family moment—though in an awkward, divorced
kind of way.

Grace tells us, "Lily's done a great job this summer.
She and Sasha were talking about the run this morning.
Sasha has asthma and won't be able to sprint like the rest
of them. Lily doesn't want to leave her behind but is torn
because she's so excited to see you."

Static crackles over Colton's two-way radio. A voice
on the other end says, "These kids are chomping at the bit.
Can I let them go?"

We all laugh, giddy with the promise of a better future.

"Okay, let 'em run," Colton replies.

The air is thick with our collective apprehension. In
just minutes, we'll be venturing into unchartered territo-
ry. Is this our last chance? Did it work? What if we unwittingly do something wrong and ruin everything? Our eyes
are glued to the road ahead. *Hurry, Lily, hurry!*

Time passes with the swiftness of a hundred-year-old
tortoise. And then, at last, one of the leaders shouts, "Here
they come!" But which ones? As they run closer, he exclaims, "It's Mark, Sean, and Tyler!"

Parents and Alpine leaders begin cheering them on—
whistling, whooping, and hollering with our newfound
optimism. Even at a distance, we notice the boys' clothes
and skin are a consistent shade of dirt brown, and their

hair is long and unruly.

Although I'm fully aware of them as they race toward us, I can't take my attention off the bend in the road. *Where is she?* The boys fall into the arms of their heartened parents, hugging and clutching each other, howling the wounded sounds of deliverance. In all of my years, I've never heard such primordial wails of relieved anguish.

"Look, there's two more!" someone yells.

Boys again. About thirty yards apart. *Come on, Lily-babe. Where are you?* As each one reaches his loved ones, the same scene plays out over and over. They are clinging and crying.

"She must be waiting for Sasha," I say.

"Look! Is that her, behind that boy?" James asks.

I squint to sharpen my focus. "Yes, it is!" I shout, delirious over the sight of my precious daughter. My eyes begin to well as my emotions spill out of my every pore.

She moves closer. I notice her clutching an object. "James, there's something in her hand. Can you make out what it is?"

"No, I can't tell."

She draws nearer. "Oh my gosh, I think it's Benny! She's holding Benny!" I cup my hand over my mouth, trying to control the surge of feelings that come over me. One of the two people I love most in the world, who brings me more joy than I've ever known, someone I would sacrifice everything for, yet someone I thought might die from her reckless choices, is on her way to my open arms. *Please, let everything be good from now on. Please!*

Our girl speeds toward us—each stride bringing more clarity. She looks so frail in her baggy blue T-shirt and army-green shorts. Even from a distance, I can see her tear-stained cheeks. I'm suddenly aware of how pure my baby looks. Even though she's covered in layers of dirt, without her anger, she's all shiny and new. It's her sweetness. She's wearing it again.

*Oh, honey, hurry!*

"Lily!" I shout, waving my arm overhead.

James and I move closer together, reaching an arm around one another while stretching out the other to welcome our beloved daughter.

Lily collapses into us, releasing a wail of relief. She's gasping and sobbing. Our family embrace is so authentic James and I don't realize how intensely we're clinging to one another.

"Lily, I've missed you so much," I say, reaching my hand inside our protective huddle to caress her cheek.

James and I take turns holding her close. He lifts her off the ground, knocking his hat into a Gomer tilt and says, "I'm so happy to see you, Lil! You look magnificent!"

I can't take my eyes off of her or stop touching her, rubbing her back and stroking her face. Affection between us had all but left our lives. I don't remember exactly when. I wasn't even aware it was gone. That is, not until this very moment, when I feel how much it livens me. It's an obvious realization, but one I've been distracted from.

"I see you have Benny. He's so white!" I'm surprised by his newness.

"I know. I kept him in a plastic bag, except for at night when he slept with me," she says, beginning to breathe normally again. "He reminded me of home."

Just then, Robert joins us. "Doesn't she look great?"

"Wonderful!" James enthuses.

"Perfect!" I say with my arm placed tightly around her waist.

Robert doesn't waste time with small talk and says to Lily, "Each family will be in a different location, out of sight from one another. Grace will be taking the three of you to your designated camping area. After you get settled, I'll stop by for our talk."

Within minutes, Grace guides us over the rugged terrain to a small, dusty hillside. This forest is nothing like the ones back home. Ours are green and lush with vegetation and towering evergreens. Here they consist of low-desert shrubs and spindly-looking pine trees punctuated by rock formations.

Grace addresses her conversation to Lily, as if she's the responsible leader of our threesome.

"Get your fire started and your tarp set up. I'll be back with dinner supplies, and then tomorrow we'll be showing your parents our trust-building exercises," she says, sharing a knowing smile with Lily before walking away.

"What does she mean—trust-building exercises?" I ask.

"Don't worry, Mom. It'll be fun," Lily assures me.

"Okay, put us to work. Can I help with the fire?" James volunteers.

"Sure, Dad. Let me get my bow drill out of my pack."

"Do you want me to hang the tarp?"

"No, Mom. Why don't you just relax on that log over there and have fun watching Dad and me try to get a fire going."

"Are you sure, honey?"

"I'm sure, Mom," she says, seeming eager to please me.

I settle onto the wooden stump like I've just been handed a glass of champagne at the Miraval Spa and enjoy the unfamiliar role of pampered mother.

"How do I do this, Lil?" James says as he fumbles with what she's given him: a cattle bone, barkless stick, and handmade bow.

Lily squats next to him and demonstrates her newly acquired skill. James makes several valiant attempts, but apparently he left his be-nimbled fingers at home. It looks like such an exhausting ritual, I'm glad to be a spectator. Lily takes over. I love basking in this moment, sitting and rejoicing in my daughter's revived self-confidence. Could we just stay like this? Send for Jack?

After Lily gets the fire going, she and James tie a tarp two feet off the ground between four trees, and place our sleeping bags under it. That's it: fire and shelter. This is how Lily's been living for the past couple of months. I'm so in awe of her. Before this, I didn't think she could light a candle with a blow-torch, and now she's starting a life-sustaining campfire with cow remains and serious determination.

James and Lily pull up a couple of logs and join me by the fire as the three of us savor her handiwork.

"We're proud of you, Lil. We missed you so much this summer," James says. "And I want you to know, I'm going to do whatever I can to help from now on."

"Thanks, Dad."

"Honey, I'm so inspired by you. What a woman!" I say, beaming at her with admiration. "You've shown such maturity by taking a difficult situation and learning from it when, really, you could have gone the other way and done so many negative things instead. Just think about your achievements, honey! You've accomplished more than most adults would have under the same circumstances!"

"Can anyone join this party?" Robert surprises us as he slips into our campsite with the stealth of a cougar.

"Sure, pull up a log," I say, welcoming him into our happy home.

"Let's get right to it, shall we," he begins. "Lily has worked hard to resolve her issues, and along the way she's experienced some very raw emotions—emotions that she's been keeping inside for a long time." He looks over at Lily, having prepared her for this moment all summer long. "I believe most of what you have to share is for your dad. Why don't you go ahead and tell him what you want to say," he gently encourages her.

She straightens her posture and takes a deep breath. "Dad, I was really hurt and angry with you. I hated what you did to us. It felt like you abandoned us. You betrayed Mom and didn't even try to save your marriage. And then you lied to Jack and me about your affair with Mara. But I want you to know how much I love you, and from now on I'm going to be honest about how I feel. I'm mad at Mara too, but I'm willing to work on my relationship with her."

With the help of her therapist and Mother Nature, the great nurturer of contemplative thinking, Lily's showing tremendous poise and courage.

"Anything else you want to say?" Robert asks.

"It wasn't right for you to hit me, but I understand it

because I've had anger issues too. I forgive you, Dad, and am ready to let go."

"Lily, you're entirely right," James says. "Everything you just said is true, and I'm sorry about all of it. I promise to be straight with you from now on too."

"Is that okay for you, Lily?" Robert asks.

She smiles and answers, "Yes."

I know Lily is telling her truth, but do I trust that James is? He's always been good at making promises, but his actions usually tell a different story. In this moment, I want to believe him.

"Do you care to share with your dad why you've been so angry at Mara?"

"I was mad because she had an affair with you when she was Mom's friend, and she knew you were married. Then later, when you broke up with Mara, she followed you everywhere and constantly bugged you even though you were trying to get back with Mom. And then she took you away from our family for a second time."

James gives her his familiar remorseful nod.

Robert continues, "What about your mom? Do you have anything to tell her?"

Lily turns to me.

*Okay, babe, I'm ready. Hit me with it.*

"Mom, I was mad at you for tricking me into coming here, but I understand it was only because you love me and care about my future. I promise to listen to you, to not lie or defy you anymore. You are really the best friend I have. I want to share my feelings with you, and I want you to do the same with me. And most important, I want you to know how much I respect you."

My eyes well as the painful and desperate times we've had are miraculously healed by her words. "I'm sorry I deceived you about Alpine, and I promise to share my feelings more. Thank you, baby. I love you more than you can possibly imagine."

"Any more you'd like to add, Lily?" Robert asks.

"I want to thank you both for helping me and for showing me what's important in life. I never could have done this without your love and support. And I'm confident about our fresh start. We're going to continue making great memories, just like today." She pauses to clear the lump from her throat. "I swear I'll never forget the feeling I had when we saw each other again. And I know now how smart and capable I am, and I'm going to use it to my fullest advantage." Then she turns to Robert and says, "That's it."

My Lily's back!

That night as we lie on the ground with a thin plastic tarp under us and another pulled tight overhead, Lily snuggles between James and me in the expensive, guilt-ridden, extra-padded, good-to-twenty-degrees-below-zero mummy sack I bought her. Meanwhile, James and I gladly suffer in our childhood, tattered flannel, slumber party bags. The three of us laugh and reminisce together. It's the happiest I've seen Lily since James moved out.

The night is clear and crisp—that is, until about 2:00 a.m., when the skies unleash a torrential storm. The thunder crackles and booms with defiance, and the lightning flashes are so intense I could thread a needle by their brightness. Is this some sort of sign?

One, one thousand, two—oh my gosh, the strikes are

less than two miles away. Holy prairie dog! Is anyone else awake? James? Lily? Nope, like father, like daughter. Oh man, the rain is running like a river next to me. I try scooting closer to Lily to stay dry, but it isn't long before I'm checking my bag for trout.

After a while, James inches in, away from the moat that now encircles our luxurious accommodations. He raises his head, and our eyes meet. I give him an acknowledging look. Lily has spent the past nine weeks dealing with this kind of crap, and much more. We both drop our heads onto the pillowless plastic, hoping to endure the rest of our cold, wet night.

I must have managed to fall asleep because the next thing I know, the sun is shining. James and I gingerly stretch our aching bodies, having put our roughing-it days to rest long ago. Give me a five-star resort with a poolside bar, European spa, and pristine golf course. But today, oh, what fun—a few psychological games, a little Utah grit with our lentils, a ragtag graduation ceremony, and then we're on our way home.

Why is my stomach so tight?

A shower and a burger are the top priorities for Lily. We stop at the only roadside motel within miles so she can remove the acre of national forest real estate she's wearing. James and I listen to the jubilant sounds she emits for the little things in life: clean water, a toothbrush, soap and shampoo, the flush of a toilet.

Who would have thought that sitting in a musty, old motel room with my ex would be such a heartwarming experience?

# Chapter Eleven

Lily reaches for my hand. Her public attachment catches me off guard, making me feel a bit conspicuous as we walk through the mall in search of new school clothes. How many fifteen-year-olds stroll hand-in-hand with their moms? I shake off my silly discomfort but wonder—why such a death grip? Is she simply happy to be home with me or is she holding on for dear life—afraid the lure of her old ways will be too hard to resist?

The next day when Lily returns from her first day at school, I'm anxious to know if she saw Brian and Renée.

"So, how was your day?"

"All right, I guess," she says unenthusiastically.

"Do you like your classes?" I ask hoping for a more inspired response.

"Yeah, they're okay." She shrugs.

"You don't sound very thrilled. Is something wrong?"

"No, everything's fine, Mom."

"You'd tell me if there was, right?"

"There's nothing wrong," she says with just a hint of annoyance.

"Did you see any of your old friends?" I continue.

"Yeah, a couple."

If I've learned one thing during my extensive studies on the care and feeding of a teenager, it's to start with generic questioning, but don't hesitate to go for specifics if you feel like you're not getting full disclosure. Never, and this is vitally important, ever put your head in the sand!

"Did you see Renée or Brian?"

"I hung out with Renée but not Brian."

"Why didn't you see Brian?"

"He has a new girlfriend."

"Oh, honey, I'm sorry." *Yesss!* "Are you okay with that?"

"Yeah, it doesn't matter."

I don't want to grill her too hard on the subject of friends, so I change course and ask, "Got any homework I can help with?"

"No, thanks. If it's all right, I'd like to go over to Renée's for a little while?"

*Holy crap! Not already! Okay, okay. Don't overreact.* "Lily, are you sure that's something you want to start doing again?" I say calmly as I try to hold onto the buzz from our boot-camp high.

"Yeah, I'm sure. Don't worry, Mom, I'm not going to get into any trouble. She's my friend, and I want to spend time with her."

My limited personal experience with Renée has shown her to be a polite and perky brunette, not sullen or angry like one would expect given her history. Unfortunately, the poor kid doesn't have anyone in her life who genuinely cares. And as much as I like her, there was the infamous lodge incident when she and Lily disappeared until three in the morning. On the other hand, she did divulge Brian's address to me in the middle of my night from hell. But then again, her family life sucks. Holy crap, I feel like I'm playing Russian roulette with my kid's future. Is the bullet in the chamber, or can I safely pull the trigger on this one?

The therapists at Alpine explained to the parents how there might be a few hiccups when we returned home, maybe even some serious setbacks, but I've been praying for an unqualified miracle.

"All right, Lily, but please be back by five thirty."

I'm not sure if I finally relent out of fear that the old arguments will return, or if I want to give her the opportunity to earn my trust back—probably both.

Thankfully, Lily shows up on time for dinner, and afterward goes straight to her room to finish her homework. I'm relieved we faced a threat to our family and survived it, but by seven thirty, Lily's ready to return to Renée's.

"Again?" I question, hearing the faint sound of a siren signaling a crash up ahead. "Lily, I'd prefer for you to stay home since it's a school night."

Lily senses weakness. "It's still early. I promise I'll be home by ten o'clock."

Hoping for a win-win, I offer, "Make it nine, and you can go."

"*Mom*," she says firmly, "I'm almost sixteen years old, and I've got all of my homework done. You've let me stay out until ten before when you know where I'm going to be. I promise I'll call you when I'm on my way home."

Isn't it funny how many different definitions the word *mom* can conjure up, falling anywhere between "my guiding light" to "you fucking bitch." In this particular application, I'm getting a visual of an "annoying nag." Progress?

*Crap. Come on, Lily! Take the nine, for crying out loud! Let me flex a little parental muscle, will ya?*

Pre-divorce, I never needed to exert any real punitive brawn on my kids; consequently, I visualized parental muscle as pumped-up biceps. But since then, I've learned it's not your biceps you're flexing at all—it's your brain. And right now, it feels like I'm bench pressing enough weight to give myself a cerebral hernia!

"I want you home at nine, and that's the deal. Take it or leave it—and I'll pick you up because it'll be dark by then," I insist.

She reluctantly agrees.

Having come within inches of a confrontation, I wonder if the honeymoon is over. But why? Am I doing something wrong? Did I slip and not know it? I feel my balance faltering from side to side as I cling to a tiny parasol on this tightrope I've been walking.

As the next few days pass, Lily persistently nudges her boundaries. Not enough so I have to take action, but enough to make me wary.

On Saturday, just two weeks after returning from Utah, Lily asks to spend the night at Renée's. A sick feeling grabs my gut, but I do my best to be reasonable and cautiously pursue the conversation. "Lily, I was hoping you wouldn't want to put yourself in a situation like this."

"Like what, Mom?" she says, knowing full well what I'm talking about.

"Her home is not a healthy environment. And we've had some serious issues in the past when you've stayed overnight at other people's houses."

Growing impatient, she argues, "Mom, Renée's not the problem. Yes, her parents aren't great role models, but you taught me right from wrong. Other than you, she's my best friend, and I want to spend time with her. Since she can't leave her house, I have to go over there."

"How come her mom can get her to stay home, but you won't do the same for me?" *Go ahead, let's see you logic your way out of this one.*

"Because if Renée doesn't do what her *foster* mom says, she might send her back into the *foster* care system. And Renée's been with this *foster* family for a very long time. She loves her *foster* brothers and sister. Who knows where Renée could end up?"

Damn, she's good, bombarding me with a whole new F-word!

"What do you do when you're at her house?" I continue my high-wire walk.

"I help her take care of the kids and do the chores, since her older sister doesn't live there anymore. I've told you all of this before."

"I know you have, but I need more details, so I can feel better about it. I don't want you to put yourself in a position where you might be tempted to do something that you've done in the past. You understand, don't you, Lily?"

"I do," she says, softening her voice.

"What happens when Renée goes to school? Who takes care of the kids then?"

"Her mom makes her stay home a lot."

"Really? She misses school?" I act shocked by such behavior but, really, nothing shocks me anymore. "Do you think that it's right for her mom to keep her away from her studies?"

"No, but Renée doesn't have any choice."

"Does she have other friends who hang out at her house?" I ask, thinking her home might be a teenage den of ill repute.

"No, just me. Her mom and dad don't allow anyone else to come over." Lily is frustrated by my questions but is doing a good job of keeping her cool.

I want to tell her that she can't go but feel like I have to trust her, to give her a chance to show how much she's matured, and to prove that everything we went through this summer has meaning. I've witnessed her personal growth and want to give her the opportunity to use it. I'm proud of her for demonstrating such fierce loyalty and compassion to a friend who's moved from one neglectful mother to another.

"Okay, babe, but I want you home by ten o'clock tomorrow morning. And, honey, please be smart. Call me at any time, for any reason, if you find yourself in circumstances that don't feel right," I say, thinking I may have just thrust my head into some beachfront property.

"Thanks, Mom. And don't worry."

*Oh, I will. It's what I do.*

Thankfully, it's an uneventful night—no conversations with the police. But later that Sunday, after being home for just a few hours, Lily wants to return to Renée's.

"Haven't you been there enough this weekend? I

thought we were going to move onto a better life together. How's that going to happen if we're not spending time under the same roof? Don't the promises we made mean anything to you?"

"They do, Mom. I just don't see what the big deal is. I finished all of my jobs, and we don't have any other plans, so what's wrong with me hanging out with my friend?"

Am I holding on too tightly? Normal teens want to be with their friends. I remember my best friend and I were like conjoined twins. If only Lily was going to a home where I knew the odds weren't stacked against us. Why can't I come up with a logic that will convince her not to go? I'm so tired of searching for new rationales. Give me a corporate financial crisis or a bitter employee dilemma, and I'll fix it. But spar with a teenage mind, and I feel worthless. Maybe I just don't have it in me anymore. Maybe the fight's finally gone.

I was full of hope when we came back from Alpine. Now I feel like Stallone in the opening sequence of *Cliffhanger*, struggling with every ounce of my strength to hold on to Lily's slipping hand as she dangles perilously over a mountainous gorge.

"I think we need to limit the amount of time you spend at Renée's house. I'm not really comfortable with you being there."

Lily and I aren't arguing. We're discussing. It's not like before. She's calm but apparently isn't going to acquiesce. "Mom, I want to go over to Renée's. I don't understand why I can't be with my friend. I know you're worried, but you need to trust me."

I can't think of what to do. Single parenting is such

bullshit! The old "two heads are better than one" gem must have sprung from a taxing teen scenario. *Vanna, I'd like to buy another point of view, please!* If I say no, Lily will do it anyway, and things will slowly spiral out of control. If I say yes, there's a possibility everything could be fine.

"All right, Lily. But when you come home, we're going to have to find a solution we can both agree on, because as it stands, it's not working for me."

"Okay," she says a little too enthusiastically, leaving me wondering if her "okay" was an actual promise to resolve our disagreement or just a brush-off.

"I want you back here by seven."

"How come you're not on your way home?" I anxiously ask Lily over the phone as a frigid wind howls past my gut. I sense my girl is about to sadden me.

"Mom, I've decided to stay here. I'm going to live at Renée's for a while and help her take care of her brothers and sister."

"I don't understand." I say, discouraged by the futility of it all.

"I've made up my mind, Mom. I don't want to fight. It's just what I need to do."

"What you need to do is to come home. Lily, listen to me. We have to talk. I'll be right over," I say, laboring to stay calm but firm.

"I'm really sorry, Mom, but I'm not leaving. I promise I'll keep in touch, and I'll stop by to see you." Damn her!

She's doing a better calm-but-firm than I am!

"I'm coming over, Lily."

I tell Jack I'll be right back and race out the door. I've got just two short minutes to figure out how I'm going to convince Lily that this is oh so wrong. Why is she wrecking everything? We haven't had any fights since she returned from Alpine. I just don't get it. Why now?

Even though I have no idea what I'm going to say, I skip every other concrete step to reach the top of the landing and push the doorbell. Aaand, of course it doesn't work. I knock hard on the screen door, rattling it against the metal frame. I look around and notice the split-entry house is in serious need of a coat of paint, and there's newspaper covering a broken window.

The door opens. Renée is holding a curly-haired toddler on her hip while another doe-eyed one hugs her leg.

"Hi, Renée. I need to speak with Lily, please," I say, peeking inside to catch a glimpse of the shady parents but instead see another child looking down from the top of the stairs.

"Sure. C'mon, you guys, let's tell Lily that her mom is here."

The youngster upstairs runs down the hallway yelling Lily's name as Renée makes her way with the other two in tow.

My heart goes out to this amiable kid who's forced to tolerate such neglectful parents. Yet how do I know they're neglectful? I've never met them.

Do Renée's parents know Lily's about to move in with them? I should talk with Renée's mom. I know I hoped that by not acknowledging her she might go away. I don't want to associate with a woman who uses drugs and neglects her children, if that's even true, but I should, especially since my daughter is choosing to make this her new home.

Lily bounds down the stairs, closing the front door behind her as she joins me outside on the porch. "Hi, Mom," she says sweetly.

"Honey, what are you doing? You can't stay here. You have to come home." I'm not angry. I'm not arguing. I'm just sad we're still trying to find our way through this long, suffering journey.

"This is where I want to be for a while so I can help my friend."

"But what about school?" I question, since I know Renée stays home a lot.

"I'm not going for a while." She's irritatingly composed.

"You can't *not* go. That's crazy. Is there some reason you don't want to go back? I'll talk to the principal, or arrange for you to go to another school, a tutor, whatever. Just come home, honey."

"Mom, I really need to do this. I'm not mad at you. I just want to live here," she says in earnest.

I'm staggered with disbelief. It doesn't make any sense. "Why, Lily?"

"I don't know. It's what I feel I have to do right now."

"You made a commitment to share your feelings with

me. Communication, remember? You promised."

"I honestly don't know why, Mom. I just want to be with my friend because she needs my help."

Isn't it funny how words that used to represent happy things in my life have taken on a negative connotation? The English language assumes a whole new perspective when you view it from the dark side. *Friend, camp, school, sex.* These used to be pleasant terms, even some of my favorites. *Friend:* Will, Kaye, Kendall, Nat, love, laughter, support. From the dark side: Brian and Renée. *Camp:* short sheeting beds, canoeing on the lake, and roasting marshmallows over an open fire. From the dark side: having my daughter kidnapped. *School:* stuffing my best friend into her locker, wearing my boyfriend's ID bracelet, being the last one standing in dodge ball—oh, and an education. From the dark side: stress, frustration, disappointment. And, finally, *Sex:* Huh??

"Honey, if you come home, we can figure things out together. And then we'll find a way for you to feel better about whatever is bothering you. But, Lily, we can't do it if we're living apart."

"I'm sorry if this hurts you, but there's nothing you can say right now to change my mind." Her compassion is both comforting and disheartening. At least when she was screaming at me I felt my logic would prevail. This new sincerity is defeating.

"All right then, I'd like to speak with Renée's mother before I leave."

"Her parents aren't here right now. They're going to be out kinda late, but you can call her tomorrow."

I really don't want to talk to this woman, and breathe

a conflicted sigh of relief. I'm afraid she'll prove to be a monster. It's easier to be ignorant, to pretend she's only a misrepresented, selfish woman.

I put my hands on Lily's shoulders and look seriously into her eyes. "Are you absolutely sure this is what you want?"

"Yeah, Mom, I'm sure."

"Well, then, I guess I'll see you later. Good luck, babe," I say, doing my best to sound like I'm not devastated.

I hug her, filled with despair, and walk to my car parked at the curb. Lily waves as I pretend to be cool and drive away crushed by the senselessness of it all. I remind myself that there's always a grilled cheese sandwich on the menu—but this time I don't see one.

Jack's right where I left him, curled up in a papasan chair, thumbing his video game remote as he attempts to rescue the fair Princess Zelda. *Thank goodness for you, Tiger-Bear. I'd have gone nuts without you by now.*

I need to call my own mom, but it's late in Chicago. I hesitate for a moment and then go ahead and dial anyway.

"Hi, Mom."

"Hi, honey, is everything okay?" she asks, concerned by the nighttime call.

I tell her the story, hoping she'll give me some idea of what to do next.

"Alex, maybe you should consider letting go for a while. You've tried so hard to help Lily, but maybe she needs to stay with these people in order to appreciate what she has at home," she says reassuringly.

"I thought that's what her time at Alpine was for."

"But at the camp, she was removed from everyday

life, protected in a way. Maybe she needs to find out what it's like in the real world, without you around to help her."

"But what about school?"

"So what if she misses some school."

Did I hear her right? Did she just say "so what"!

"Maybe Lily isn't going to take the path you've always hoped she would. Some kids have to find their own way. I think you might need to change your expectations for the time being."

I can't believe I'm hearing this from my mom. She's telling me to modify my thinking—to shift the paradigm for success and family that's been ingrained in me. And *she* did the ingraining!

"You know where Lily's staying, so it's not like she's run away," she says.

"But, Mom, I hate that she's there."

"Give her a little time, Alex. Don't take any action just yet. I know Lily will come home."

"Really? It doesn't seem right not to do anything."

"By doing nothing, you're actually doing something. Once she's had time to experience life away from home, she'll be back. I know it."

I can't believe what a monumental sense of relief I feel. My mother just gave me permission not to fix things. She sounds so sure that everything will turn out all right. And I believe her! After all, she *is* my mom!

I'm able to sleep because of my mother's advice, and wake up with a revitalized thinker. While in the shower, in a soaped-up moment of inspiration, I decide to make one small statement on Lily's poor choice.

"Mom, my key to the house doesn't work," she says, like it's news to me.

"Oh yeah, honey, I had the locks changed this morning."

"But I can't get any of my things!"

"Well, babe, they're not really *your* things, are they," I reply. "I mean, I bought most everything you have, so they're actually mine. And since you don't live at home anymore, I figure you don't need to have a key."

"But, Mom, I need my stuff."

"I'm sorry, Lily, but you made the choice to live at Renée's house, and I'm okay with it. Really! So don't worry about me."

"Moooom, please!" she pleads, trying to rouse the old pansy-ass Alex.

"I'd love it if you'd stop by when you have a chance. Maybe we can go to Zeek's for a bite to eat together."

"But what if I need something from my room?"

"Technically, it's not your room anymore either. Listen, honey, I've got to leave work and pick up Jack from basketball practice. I'll talk to you later. Have a nice evening. Love you."

When I hang up the phone, the tiny parasol I've been balancing with suddenly bursts into a colorful beach umbrella.

During the first two weeks that Lily lives at Renée's house, she visits me every few days. By the third week, she's stopping by on a daily basis. We have nice, nonthreatening talks, and I continue to be cheerful and calm. When we hit the middle of week four, she reveals more of what it's like to be under the same roof with selfish, irresponsible adults.

"It's such a stressful place to live, Mom. Her parents are mean. I feel bad for Renée because they just use her and don't really care about her." She pauses for a moment and then says, "I really don't want to stay there anymore."

I refrain from break-dancing the worm across the kitchen floor.

"Can I come home? Please?" she asks.

I pause for effect and inhale a deep breath of faux consideration. "If you do, you'll have to commit to going to school."

"I will. I promise," she says as she gives me a grateful hug.

"But you won't be going to Gates High School anymore. Dad and I talked about your education while you were gone. You'll be going downtown to Jackson. We'll use Dad's home address to register you. We want you to have a new beginning."

"Does that mean I have to live with Dad?"

"No, you can stay here. Since the school is only a few blocks from work, I'll drive you. At the end of the day, you can walk over to the office and ride home with me."

"Can I move home tonight?"

Oh, how right my mom was!

Toward the end of November, with things otherwise going well, Lily begins having frequent stomachaches and is bothered by constant fatigue. As a result, she's missing a lot of school. A visit to the doctor showed no reason for concern, but I was anyway. While trying to figure out what this could possibly be, a seemingly insignificant memory suddenly pops back into my consciousness. In a painful moment of clarity, I realize this horrible nugget could change our lives forever.

*Alpine Academy. No unnecessary medications. Oh my god! Please, no! The pill! She went off of the pill!*

I hurry into Lily's room, knowing we can't ignore this. "Lily, when you stayed at Renée's house, did any boys come over? Tell me the truth, honey. It's important."

She lowers her eyes.

"I thought her parents didn't allow anyone else over," I say moving onto the edge of the bed next to her.

"They were there when her mom and dad weren't around and the kids were asleep. I'm so sorry, Mom," she says apologetically.

"Who were they?" I ask, realizing that it doesn't really matter.

"You don't know them. Renée was seeing this guy, Josh, and I was kinda with his friend, Jesse. They're sophomores at Gates."

"Kinda with his friend"? Kinda what? "Did you have sex with him?"

Taking her silence as the answer I didn't want to hear, I reach for her hand and say softly, "Honey, I think you might be pregnant." As the words fall out of my mouth, the devastating implications of what this means flash through my head.

Lily doesn't argue. She doesn't defend. She knows this is serious—too serious for her to fully comprehend.

"I'm going to make an appointment with Dr. Lee."

I try not to mourn the loss of my daughter's future or beat myself up for not making the connection sooner. *You can't do it all,* I tell myself. But I should have.

Dr. Lee confirms my worst fear. This is not a time for anger. The enormity of it is far too sad. My sixteen-year-old is pregnant.

"Honey, we'll figure this out together. You know what your options are, and I'll support you in whatever decision you make." As much as I want to decide for Lily, I know guidance and compassion are the only things I should give her. As a feminist and firm believer in *Roe vs. Wade*, if it was me, the answer would be clear, but I'll do my best to leave all doors open for Lily.

Depending on what she decides, who do we have to tell? Will Lily finish high school? Will she go to college? Have a career? And what about my child raising a child? Will she be living hand-to-mouth, trying to support herself and her baby? Of course I wouldn't let that happen. So then—what about me?

Back at work, I close the door to James's office.

"It's positive. She's pregnant."

Not one to mull anything over, he responds immediately. "Let's get it taken care of," he says, as if we're dealing with an employee who pilfered paper clips.

James handles his personal life in much the same way he tackles the business world—just solve the problem, even if it's not the best solution, and then move on. I, on the other hand, think about all of the possibilities, consequences, and feelings—sometimes to my own migrainal detriment—and then make my choice based on all that thinking. He's a mover and shaker. I'm a planner and organizer. For the most part, these different approaches to life have served us well in business. And, at one time, they made for a lovely marriage. We were the perfect team of thought and action. But over the past few years, we've both digressed to the extremes.

"We have to give Lily time to make her decision. She's the one who has to live with it."

"There's no choice! She can't ruin the rest of her life!" he insists.

"I'm going to talk to her tonight. For me, the only option I hope she doesn't choose is adoption. I couldn't stand having a grandchild out there living in the world without us. And I know it would eat away at Lily too. Hopefully, she'll make the decision you and I both want."

Releasing an audible sigh, I remember my first awareness of abortion. Just twelve years old, I watched as Steve McQueen and Natalie Wood, in *Love with the Proper Stranger,* frantically scraped together $250 for a creepy, backroom butcher to end her unwanted pregnancy. My adolescent mind was horrified right up until the moment when McQueen burst through the door to rescue her from the life threatening situation. Back then, a woman's choices were dangerous and unthinkable.

When I arrive home, Jack's in the cul-de-sac playing tennis-ball hockey with his buddies. I cheer for a goal he scores and head inside to confront the decision Lily must make.

Her pallid face peeks out from beneath the covers as I sit next to her and rest my hand on her leg to comfort us both. "Honey, you need to figure out what you want to do."

I can't imagine what she must be thinking. She hasn't even developed a whole brain yet to help grasp the magnitude of this. Why doesn't fertility begin at twenty-five? Who decided teenagers could reproduce? How come I didn't get a say in it?

"One alternative is adoption," I begin, searching her eyes for her feelings on this one. "But I have to say, for me, this would be the hardest decision to handle. I think both of us would have a difficult time dealing with knowing you have a child out there. But even so, if you choose—"

Lily stops me. "Mom, that's not what I want to do. I want it to be over," she says as tears roll down her cheeks.

"Are you sure, honey, because if you have any doubt, we should keep talking. If you decide you want to have the baby, you know I'll help you."

"I'm sure, Mom."

Those three words were all I needed to hear to reinforce her choice. "Lil, I think you're making the right decision, and Dad feels the same way. Having a baby at your age, with a boy you barely know, would change the course of your whole life. You have so much to learn and experience before having a child. Raising kids is difficult enough for adults who are prepared for it."

"Do you know anyone who's had an abortion, Mom?" she asks, looking for validation.

My belief in a woman's right to choose completely takes over. I reach for her hand and say, "Honey, you'd be surprised at the women I know who've had them—women you know and love."

I want to protect Lily from beating herself up with guilt and regret. I hope my encouraging tone and perspective will absolve her of any self-recrimination down the road. Let my soul be the one to take any moral branding. It makes me absolutely sick to be a cheerleader for abortion, and yet, if it helps her, then slap a big red A on my chest and toss me a couple of black pom-poms. But first, can I get a time-out to hurl?

"Have you ever had one?"

"No, but if I was in your situation, it would be the choice I'd make. Someday you're going to fall in love and have a beautiful family, but until then you have a lot of living and learning to do.

"Now, listen to me, Lily. This is not something you want to talk about with anyone. It's your business and no one else's. If anybody at school finds out, then everyone will know. And by everyone, that includes this boy and his parents. The last thing we want is for them to interfere. A woman's right to choose is an explosive subject.

If you need to talk, you have Dad and me. And, honestly, I'll need to talk with someone too. I'm probably going to share this with Omi and Opa, and Uncle Will and Kaye."

"No, Mom. I don't want them to know."

"Honey, we need their support to help see us through this. They won't judge, and they'll be there for us, just as they always have."

Three days later, we enter an unmarked clinic in Seattle. For everyone's protection and safety, Dr. Lee doesn't perform this procedure at his office. With no receptionist or staff in sight, Dr. Lee's nurse leads Lily and me down a barren hallway. The white linoleum floor and monochromatic walls blindingly reflect the overhead fluorescent lights. A macabre thought goes through my mind: it's like a morgue in here.

A cold, sterile chair stationed next to an indistinguishable metal door is where Linda directs me to have a seat. The door opens, and Dr. Lee emerges. His gentle presence is only slightly comforting as he puts his hand on my shoulder and says, "Don't worry. We'll take good care of her."

Wrapping my arms around Lily, I whisper in her ear, "I'll be right here waiting for you, honey."

When the door closes behind them, I take a deep breath and lean my head back against the wall. I close my eyes and try to shut out the reality of this day. Sadly, it doesn't work.

Hoping for some distraction, I look around. But there's nothing to see except the glare of antiseptic white. No magazines. No people. No one to lean on.

*I should stop at the store and pick up milk. Bet I need to tank up too. Write it down or you'll forget. Your mem-*

*ory sucks these days. I wonder if Carol will have the pro-*
*posal typed by tomorrow. FUUUCK!!*

I riffle through my purse for something to do, something to read, anything! *Nothing, there's nothing.* I grab
my wallet and begin digging through the organized com-
partments.

*Hmm, my personal mission statement. Ha! Look at*
*how many times I used the word* think *in it! What a joke.*
Think about how you treat others. Think about what you
say before you say it. Think about the consequences of
your actions. *Think, think, think! Thinking is the last thing*
*I want to do. Hey, one more punch and I get a free loaf*
*of bread. Why in the hell did I just sit like a fucking dog*
*when Linda told me to? I should be in there with Lily!*

Time becomes abstract as I sit in my chair, crossing
and uncrossing my legs—the unnatural quiet begging for
a primal scream.

Without warning, the silence is broken by a hideous
noise. *Jeez, that's loud! It's like a hygienist using a shop*
*vac to suck up saliva!*

I force myself to think about anything and everything
else, all the while knowing I've reached the lowest point
of my life.

When the noise stops, I relax my body, swallow the
revulsion, and ask for forgiveness.

A few days after Lily's procedure, while she's still at home
recovering, the Jackson High School vice principal requests

a meeting with me. Thinking we can finally get back on track, I prepare myself for some minor hiccup with Lily's studies. When the words "expelling your daughter" march out his mouth without empathy, they hit me like a shotgun blast to my academic values.

"What?! But I never received any notification regarding her absenteeism and most assuredly not about the possibility of expulsion! I mean, I know she missed a lot of school, but I called in, and there was good reason." I soften my voice to appeal to him. "Please understand, we had a serious personal issue we were dealing with."

It's obvious he's getting some sort of cheap thrill out of his power trip. "As you are aware, we accepted your daughter even though she lives outside of our district," he continues without missing a beat. "We here at Jackson make it our students' responsibility to attend classes and manage their time, and the vast majority do precisely that. However, your daughter failed to meet our standards. Consequently, we're expelling her," he says as his nose scrapes the perforated ceiling tiles.

That's it! That's all you have to say! No discussion, no nothing! Angered by his condescending attitude, I unholster my own weapon and fire some fully loaded sarcasm his way. "Well, then, I'd like to thank you for your valuable time," I say, getting up to extend my hand to him. "I'll leave so you can get back to your less complicated, trouble-free students. I certainly understand why you wouldn't want to invest any of your precious time or energy into someone like my unworthy daughter." I pause for effect.

"Besides, it would probably take more knowledge and wisdom than you possess anyway," I smile while tightly double-pumping his appendage. "And thank you, too, for protecting my tax dollars. It would be such a waste of money to spend even one public school nickel on a lost cause the likes of Lily."

Then I debate whether or not to close his mouth before exiting his little fiefdom.

After making the holidays as normal as possible, I arrange to meet with Mr. Rogers, a guidance counselor back at Gates High School, hoping to enroll Lily for the winter term. I want him to view her as more than just a laundry list of infractions in a folder.

While filling him in on our history, and emphasizing Lily's commitment to do whatever it takes to focus on her education, I have another out-of-body experience, similar to the one I had at Black Ridge Ranch with the girls. This time, I'm observing myself from above as I make yet one more attempt to help my wayward daughter. It's like I've been separated into my intellectual self, who is fully engaged in conversation, and my emotional self, who looks down on me with compassion. But it's only the emotional me that senses the distinction.

"Is there some alternative education I should be checking into for her?" I ask. "But whatever it is, I want her to be able to attend college."

"Actually, we have a program that allows students to receive a high school diploma through Seattle Community College. Unfortunately, each high school is only permitted to enroll five kids per year."

"Is it a real high school diploma?"

"Yes. Your daughter would officially graduate from Gates even though her classes would be at SCC. Some kids do better in a college environment."

"It sounds like it would be perfect for Lily. Is there any possibility of getting her into the program?"

"These placements are usually reserved for our accelerated students." My heart sinks, knowing Lily doesn't qualify as one of those anymore. "Usually we don't have openings this time of year, but it just so happens one of our students transferred to another district, and we haven't filled his slot yet."

I sit a little taller in my chair, eager to hear his next words. *Please don't let there be some highly qualified brainiac waiting for this opportunity.*

"From what you've told me about Lily, she might benefit from the junior college program, and with my recommendation, we'll be able to go ahead and get her approved."

*On my god, yes! Yes, yes, yes!* Instantly my intellectual and emotional souls are reunited, and I'm fully engaged in this moment of unexpected grilled-cheese triumph.

More than a year later, the wisdom Lily gained from her mistakes, the SCC campus setting, the maturity of the other students, and earning college credits are all working for her. She's thriving in every way.

With everything behind us, I ask her, "Lily-babe, some of my friends have wondered if there was one thing that turned everything around for us. I tell them that I honestly don't think there was one specific thing. I mean, was it the counseling, your time in Utah, living at Renée's, the college environment? Do you have any idea what helped you to find your way again?"

She looks at me with love in her eyes and says, "I've thought about this before, and what I realized was, yes, each one of those things helped, but the truth is they helped because they all had one thing in common—that one thing was you, Mom. It was that you never gave up on me."

# Chapter Twelve

I've decided the kids and I need to shake up our lives in a good way. It's time to shed the crumbled brick-and-mortar trappings of our previous life. Yes, we've made some lovely memories in our home, but I want to breathe in the smell of a new start, and I am ready to fulfill my mission to deepen the bonds of our threesome.

During the past stress-filled years, in order to escape, I perused architectural and interior design magazines, tearing out pages and wishfully keeping them in a folder marked *Someday.* Grateful for the current success of our business, I conceptualize a floor plan for a new home bathed in natural, restorative light. I want to design something that fits us perfectly.

I imagine a great room with a Mexican marble fireplace and floor-to-ceiling windows showcasing the lush Washington landscape; a study with built-ins for my favorite books and an overstuffed chair to read them in; a workout room, since I can't seem to drag my ass to the gym; a game room for the kids to hang out in with their friends; and a master suite with a king-size bed—oh, and no *master.*

After years of dreaming and planning and doing, Jack, Lily, and I settle into our new Mediterranean-style home. Nestled in a quiet neighborhood, it's backed up to a park and protected wetlands. A sense of peace washes over me every time I drive up the road to a home that doesn't haunt me with reminders of the past—and along with that peace comes a new reflection in the mirror. The ravaged face of stress and uncertainty has been replaced by a whole new Alex—not the settled wife I used to be, but a stronger, more confident, and dare I say, adventurous Alex, a me who knows no bounds for what my future holds.

One night, while unpacking a box on the floor of my office, I come across two of my favorite books. Books I read during a different chapter in my life—a chapter when I was living, ahem, the dream. Their discovery brought a flood of memories, along with a grin, as I remember how these books once helped to guide my spiritual compass.

I think back to when I was a young wife and mother, reading Shirley Maclaine's *Out on a Limb*, about her life of adventure and self-discovery. It was what I'd dreamed of for myself—before life's expectations became my priorities. A few years after Shirley's book, I read James Redfield's *The Celestine Prophecy*. It further refined my understanding of the mystical possibilities to life.

Suddenly, it is clear that I'm no longer just trying to survive. We have a new home with new memories. Jack's made new buddies and is a member of the high school basketball and golf teams. Lily, having graduated high school, continues her education at the community college and invites her friends over to the house. And at work, James begrudgingly shares in the growth and prosperity of our business. It is time to get back on the spiritual trail and point my inner compass toward true north.

But apparently I can still be naïve, because, early one morning, James enters my office and declares with his usual lack of tact, "Mara and I have finally set a date. I thought you should know."

*Well, now, my darling ex-husband, perhaps next time we could tap gloves before you throw such a wicked punch. Haven't you ever heard of sandwiching? Ya know, bad news between two slices of good?*

Why is this even bothering me? Did I think that because they had such a lengthy engagement the marriage would never happen? Did some part of me still hope we had a chance? Here I am with my heart pounding, thinking, *That was OUR eternal commitment, you jerk. You can't make it with anyone else!*

God, how I hate when I get jerked back to those old, noxious feelings. Just when I think I've got it all under control, a swift, hard slap stings me right back into the past.

"When's the big day?" I query, as if his words have no effect on me.

"October 2. We're going to ask the kids to be in the wedding," he says, continuing his jabs as I fall back against the ropes.

*I don't want my kids at your lousy nuptials. And by the way, we were married on October 5, remember? October's OUR month, you clueless bastard!*

"That's great. I'm sure they'll enjoy that. Give my good wishes to Mara."

Hoping to shove him out the door so I can have a private moment to roll around in a pile of self-pity, I politely say, "Would you mind getting me the additional scope of work for the music video so I can finish the new amendment?"

Just then, Brad breezes by my office with his brown bag in hand. "Mornin'."

"Morning," James and I respond while flashing disingenuous smiles.

"You ready for a break before the troops arrive?" Brad pointedly asks me.

A tall, skinny redhead, Brad came to Xtreme in his late twenties as a graphic designer. Since then, he's been an outstanding leader, managing people and projects with skill and integrity.

I follow him out to the fabrication department, where he opens the exterior door for some fresh air and pulls a pack of filtered Camels from his shirt pocket.

"Can I bum one of those?" I ask.

He pops a cigarette from the pack.

"Thanks," I say as he flicks the lighter for me.

Brad never questions my need for the occasional smoke. He knows the *ex*-cuse behind it.

"It's only seven o'clock, and I'm having a less-than-tolerable day already," I say, smiling as my minty-fresh breath turns to crap and a nicotine rush dizzies my head.

"Why? What'd he do now?"

Brad is not only an employee but my earnest, loyal friend. We've saved each other on many occasions from James's intimidating ways, always managing to turn his histrionics into an opportunity for humor.

"You might want to send your tux to the cleaners," I say, preparing to drop the bomb. "James and Mara finally set a date."

Brad nearly chokes as he inhales.

Mara and Brad were significant players in Xtreme's exhilarating beginnings. We were a tight little family back then. Brad was disappointed by James and Mara's affair    losing respect for the mentor he once idolized and the woman he once thought of as a friend.

"Well, I certainly won't be going," he says indignantly while staring out the door.

"I wonder if I'll get an invitation?!"

Brad grins before taking a puff. "I'm not goin'," he reiterates, shaking his head in defiance like a two-year-old. "Nope, not gonna do it," now launching into his George Bush impression.

"Listen, if your boss invites you to his wedding, you'd be crazy not to go. We both know you'll end up paying for it if you don't. So snap out of it, buddy—you're going whether you like it or not!"

He continues his gaze outward as he exhales in contemplation.

"Besides, I'll want the scoop."

"Well, all right. But I'm gonna consume as much of his expensive booze as I can."

"That's the spirit. Hey, did you catch *Survivor* last night?"

It is those few moments with Brad that get me back on track. I feel enough compassion, support, and levity from a friend to regain my footing. And here's more good news: my emotional recovery time has been reduced to a matter of mere minutes!

As October approaches, I'm privy to more of the wedding preparations than I care to be. The kids overshare: "Dad found this great band for the reception"; "Mara and I shopped for my bridesmaid dress today"; "I need to buy a shower gift." Holy bleepin' matrimony. But through it all, I smile and say, "That's nice." I even pitch in money so the kids can buy the wedding gift they want to give their dad.

Honestly, I do it all for Lily and Jack. And by doing it for them, I know I'm helping myself. Because of my children, I'm compelled to do the right thing. If they weren't in my life, I might have flung some serious shit at James and Mara. But just in case I ever stray from the path of righteousness, I know a guy who owns a Clydesdale.

My family and friends have asked what I'm doing on October 2. Nat even called from Tortola to make sure I have big plans. But the truth is all I want to do is stay home alone, and I adamantly tell them all so! I've had to be civil and gracious so many times, in every conceivable situation, day in and day out at work, brave face here, brave face there, strong, strong, puke, puke. I'm just plain sick of it. This one's for me. I'm going to lock my doors and just be by myself to feel or not feel, as I wish.

The kids get ready to leave for the rehearsal dinner.

Well, I guess this is it. Tomorrow Mara's going to become . . . *oh god, I can't say it!* . . . my children's . . . *don't make me say it!* . . . *dadada-DUM* . . . step-MUTHA! I try not to visibly cringe while straightening Jack's tie.

Here's what I don't understand. When people remarry, in their blended families, the kids become stepbrothers and stepsisters, and the parents become stepmothers and stepfathers. Why then wouldn't the second spouse be a stepwife or stephusband, thereby defining them as "not the original"? "I'd like to introduce you to my stepwife, Mara." Sounds right to me.

I won't see Jack and Lily again until Sunday, after the deed is done. "Are you going to be okay, Mom?" Lily worries.

"I'm great." Both kids stand by the door wearing concerned looks. "Really! I'm looking forward to enjoying a nice quiet weekend, maybe working in the yard, renting a movie. I won't have to talk to anyone except Trixie. And we plan on having some deep philosophical conversations. Right, girl?"

"Mom, are you sure?" Lily asks.

"Positive. Now, get out of here! And say hi to Grandma and Grandpa and the rest of the family for me."

The thought of my kids, my friends, my employees, my ex-family-in-law all socializing without me leaves me feeling abandoned, as if I've just fallen off the USS *Branson*, completely unnoticed. The people I've come to love are partying on board while I struggle in the cold, black water, watching the ship's lights dim in the distance.

That woman is dancing in *my* shoes! I so wish she could understand the pain of it. Surely if she knew, she wouldn't have done this. Doesn't she have any loyalty to the team? Give me a *W*, give me an *O*, an *M, E, N*. What does it spell? And James, he's going to need a whole other lifetime, maybe a few, to grasp the concept of empathy.

On Saturday, I'm so glad to be alone. I don't have to put on a pretense for anyone. I pull weeds and trim hedges—too busy to visualize their nuptials. There's nothing like manual labor to quiet the mind. By late afternoon, I'm ready for a hot shower and a trip to the video store. Every once in a while my mind flashes onto my ex-husband, my ex-friend, and my kids standing at the altar as a new family of four, but I manage to push that sucker right out of my head by spitting a pox on their house. *Sorry, Trix. Didn't see you there.*

Pulling into my garage, my copy of *Sense and Sensibility* on the seat beside me, I glance in the rearview mirror to see Will and Kaye entering the cul-de-sac.

*Oh, maaan, what are they doing here? I told them I wanted to be alone. Why didn't they listen?*

I step out onto the driveway to greet them.

"What's going on?" I ask in disbelief they hadn't heard my emphatic desire for solitude.

"We came to take you out to dinner." Kaye beams.

Just then the rear car door opens, and a head peeks out from behind the seat.

"Stephanie?"

My sister jumps out with a big, fat grin on her face.

"Steph and I decided to surprise you, so you wouldn't be alone," Kaye gushes. "Will and I just picked her up from the airport!"

Kaye, bursting with her own benevolence, is tickled she's pulled off such a magnanimous deed. My sister does a little ta-da dance step, officially announcing her happy arrival.

I force a smile and walk toward Steph to give her a hug, all the while trying to control the anger building inside of me. Why didn't they listen? I don't want to be cordial. I don't want to make small talk. *Why? Why would you do this to me? Why couldn't you allow me this one moment to retreat?*

But here they are: my wonderful sister and caring friends, doing their best because they love me. They have no idea that by making me the focus of their concern, they're achieving the exact opposite of their well-meaning intention—their sympathetic faces reminding me of what I've lost.

Now I feel awful because I'm mad at my loved ones. Between my resentment and my guilt, I don't remember how I came to be sitting at a table in a Vietnamese restaurant in Bellevue. I'm one big bundle of raw emotion bound up in appearance, my feelings frantically searching for a way out.

I try to take my mind off of *his* wedding but realize that every word coming out of their mouths is meant to make me forget. So I don't.

Even though I can't begin to force food down, I order something just to make my beloved entourage feel good. *Did Will just ask me something? Crap, I wasn't listening. Quick, make some sort of acknowledging expression. I bet the kids are dancing up a storm. They loooove to dance! God, I hate this.*

"Did you get a lot done in the yard today, Alex?"

*Huh?* "Yard, yes. Got a lot done." *Oh man, they left the frickin' head on my fish. Quit lookin' at me! Couldn't we have gone to a burger joint?! I hope Brad's slamming back a lot of Asshole's Private Reserve.*

After I mindlessly mangled the ca basa staring back at me from the painted bamboo plate, my heart finally slows to a hummingbird's pace. There have been way too many stresses for far too long. I can't let myself get upset like this anymore. *Calming inhale. Kuan Yin, Kuan Yin.*

# 2

## Moving On

# Chapter Thirteen

In the past few years, Lily, Jack, and I have shared some memorable adventures, further healing our wounds and strengthening our Musketeerian way. My mission of nurturing indestructible bonds is working. The simple acts of moving forward and holding onto the wisps of promise for something better have brought us to a peaceful place.

In the fall, Jack will be a freshman at Arizona State in Tempe, where he'll study finance. Meanwhile, Lily has completed junior college and is enrolled at the Carsten Institute, also in Tempe, to become a medical aesthetician. Looks like I'll be vacationing in the Sunbelt! Things could not have worked out better. Someday my son will manage my investments, and my daughter will keep me wrinkle-free. It's a boomer's dream come true!

Now that Jack and Lily have successfully transitioned into adulthood, maybe it's time to tune-up my social life. Over the years, I've endured the occasional blind date—the pint-size, tiptoeing shrink; the British face licker; and the freakishly muscle-bound egomaniac, to name a few. Oh, and then there was the executive who was so enamored with himself, I could have been a blowup doll sitting across the candlelit table from him and he would have been stimulated by both the conversation *and* his potential for scoring.

In particular, I will never forget the owner of a lighting

company who took me on a romantic tour of local lamp poles while exulting his illuminative expertise. "This one handles 175 watts and has a cast-aluminum head that we've given a bronze custom coating!" he beamed. Perhaps my greatest performance—feigning excitement over a lightbulb.

Finally there was the hiking zealot whose idea of a hot date was to take me on a relentless climb over steep, treacherous terrain, leaving me paralyzed from the waist down and, horrifyingly, incontinent for a week!

Then one day Kate mentioned her husband Pete's boss. "Gee, I'm not sure, Kate. I'd like to meet someone, and this guy sounds great, but his wife just died nine months ago. Maybe if he'd already gone out with a few other women, kind of been broken in, but to be his first after twenty-five years of marriage seems like a huge responsibility."

I quickly realize how stupid that sounds and immediately change gears. "How do you date a widower anyway?" I tease. "I mean, what's the protocol, the proper attire? Do I have to stay away from black? 'Cause you know I've got the whole black-and-blond thing goin' on."

She laughs. "Nice recovery. Black is good. Just be sure you remember how to showcase the girls properly."

"Yeah, poor things. They haven't seen the light of day in so long, my nips will probably squint."

"This could be their big chance." Then she ups the ante with one of my top five man preferences. "He's very taaaw-all," she says in a sing-song. "And besides, you keep saying all the good ones are married. Well, here's one who's not, and through no fault of his own. You should test him out."

"You mean, like, kick his tires and check under his hood. And then if all looks good, I might want to polish his fender, or maybe buff his bumper—even better, I could lube his joint."

Kate simultaneously winces and grins.

"I've got a million of these. You want me to keep going?"

"No, that's plenty. Thanks."

"Hmm, tall, you say. Okay, tell Pete he can give his boss my number. What's his name?"

"Tom Jefferies."

"Any kids?"

"Three. Two teens and one a little older.

"Yikes, five hormonally charged offspring between the two of us." *Come on, Alex, it's only a date. Probably just another few hours you'll never get back.*

It's been awhile since I dressed to impress a man, splashed on some Chanel No. 5, and revealed a hint of cleavage. I'm feelin' kinda spicy. And, yikes, I've got butterflies!

Punctual as always, I'm outside the restaurant waiting for him. I learned early on that it's essential to have my own getaway car. As the sun sets on this June evening, I gaze up and down the narrow sidewalk through the crowds of weekend pleasure-seekers.

Kate described Tom as six foot three, fit, with broad shoulders and salt-and-pepper hair. It all sounds good, but then Quasimodo could have been characterized as a God-fearing Frenchman who played music and liked to sweep a girl off of her feet.

I look across the street and there, waiting for the light to change, stands a tall, handsome man in dark jeans, linen sport coat, crisp white shirt, and yes, polished black loafers, smiling at me.

He continues to smile as he crosses the street. "Alex?" he says.

"Yes. Tom?" I reply, offering my hand as he takes it in both of his. Our eyes lock. *You've come a long way since that cootie-shaking dance on Tortola, baby!*

Still holding my hand, he whispers close to my ear like we're sharing an intimate secret, "How are you doing with this whole blind-date thing?"

"I have to admit, I've had a little experience in this area, but I understand that you're a rookie," I say, looking into his kind, rugged face. "Don't worry. I'll help you through it. And I promise to be gentle."

He laughs.

I try to quell the blush that flushes my cheeks. *What in the hell are you doing, Alex, falling prey to such charm? Get a grip, woman!*

"Shall we go in?" he says, putting his hand on my back as he opens the door.

"Sure," I say demurely as I float into the restaurant. What in the hell's wrong with me? Demure? Since when? I've obviously been away from this party for way too long. After so many years, I thought I'd never have this kind of feeling again. Dates in the past always felt forced, awkward, tedious. With Tom, I'm instantly at ease, yet strangely . . . giddy? But I don't do giddy. Bubbly? I'm not bubbly! Is there a frickin' cherub hovering around my head?

I must have stock-piled an incredible arsenal of un-used pheromones. The battalion of horny little suckers has unleashed a full assault on my mind and body. *Target the libido, men. Sabotage the intellect. Disarm her restraint and then attack when ready!*

From the moment we're seated at a small corner table, it's as if no one else existed in this bustling restaurant. We each order a glass of pinot grigio.

*Why can't I wipe this ridiculous smile off my face? And look, he's got one too. What a nice face.*

I begin by serving up the first question, expecting his *All About Me* dissertation to commence. *After I graduated cum laude from Stanford, I was recruited by several Fortune 500 companies. Instead, I became a test pilot and race car driver, winning numerous NASCAR events. But after I donated a kidney to a homeless man I met while rescuing a small child from a burning building, I gave up the circuit. . . . Right now? Oh, I'm between jobs.* Why is it always his history that takes center stage? Because oth-erwise it would be called *herstory*! Ba-dum-ba.

But wait! He vollies back. "First tell me about you."

*D'oh! I dunno. I'm the questioner, not the answerer. Why, I'm not prepared!*

"Well, I own a business that designs and builds min-iature dioramas for movies, videos, and commercials. I have two kids, Lily and Jack. Lily's twenty-one, and Jack is eighteen. Kate mentioned that you have kids . . . "

"I do. Michael's twenty-one and is a senior year at Gon-zaga, Summer's eighteen and starting at the University of

Washington in the fall, and Melody's fifteen."

"I bet they keep you busy."

"They do. They're good kids, and we're managing pretty well," he says, acknowledging his loss.

"Kate told me about your wife. I'm so sorry. It must be very hard on all of you."

"The kids pretty much take care of themselves. I'm just the point man who tries to keep track of them and their activities. The girls always have something going on. Besides, I'm not much help when it comes to curling irons and lip gloss." He chuckles. "Fortunately, they have that all under control."

The wine begins warming my face and relaxing my inhibitions. We start talking about free-time activities, and I admit I can effectively live without fishing and bowling. I wait to hear that he's one of the Northwest's avid fishermen or keeps a monogrammed bowling ball in the trunk of his car.

He just smiles. *Nope, we're good.*

"There's something wrong with torturously sliding a wiggling worm onto a dangerously sharp barb, being at the mercy of some smarter-than-me trout, executing a flopping fish-hook extraction, and then topping it all off with gutting the poor thing." I shudder.

His smile grows bigger.

"And as far as bowling goes, don't even get me started on sharing shoes and heavy balls with strangers. That's just not right!" I love that he's getting a kick out of this. *Look at him grinning. And what's up with me!*

"I really like quiet, relaxing times too. You can put me on an exotic beach with a frozen Bushwacker and a grass mat or in a cozy mountain cabin with a Peppermint Pattie and a roaring fire, and I won't complain." *Jeez, Alex, what are you doing, writing a damned romance novel? She heaved breathlessly, her tousled mane draping her breasts, his sculpted body glistening from the glow of the fire's embers as she shamelessly seduced him—*

"Let's go! I'm ready!" he says with real enthusiasm.

"Well, okay. I've got my suitcase in the car. Let's do it!" I tease. But part of me is thinking that if I didn't have responsibilities, I'd be headed to the airport with him right now! I'm astonished at how bewitched I am.

The next three hours go by in minutes. Yes, we share our life stories, but unlike my previous conversational subservience, it feels as if we're celebrating both our histories, riveted to each other's words.

God, I feel good. Feminine, hot, sexy, even, dare I admit, lustful! I've spent so much time in either jeans or a business suit, I'd almost forgotten about the dormant woman in me. She merely needed the right man to awaken her.

I don't think I've ever quite felt this way. Of course, who can remember that far back? My mind jumps to my first meeting with James. It was a sweeter, inexperienced kind of yearning. This is more of a take-no-prisoners kind of hunger. Better yet, take one! Get me my angora handcuffs!

We stroll in the moonlight under the blossoming cherry trees, their scent encouraging our desire as we kick our feet through the fallen pink petals. Tom chivalrously positions himself curbside. How often does that happen anymore? I demand equality in all things, except romance and chocolate.

"I had a great time," I say as he opens the car door for

me.

"So did I. I might have to give Pete a raise!" he quips.

I step between my car and the open door and turn back toward him. "Thanks for a delightful evening."

Our faces say it all. My cheeks begin to ache from perpetually smiling. Tom leans in and gives me a tender good-night kiss—his eyes lingering just long enough afterward to send me into a whole new kind of deep breath!

"Can I call you?" he says.

Holy palpitations! Could this be a more resplendent moment? I'm looking into the eyes of a handsome, charming man, and he wants to do this again. Screw the terrorists! There is hope!

"Yes, I'd like that," I say softly, still inches from his face.

Uh-oh! Body under attack! Pheromones implementing shock and awe tactics! Retreat, RETREAT!!

I decide to introduce Lily and Jack to Tom a few weeks after we started dating. It's a big step, but I'm eager to have them know each other. Although it's been years since James and I divorced, my children's feelings are important to me.

"What do you guys think?" I ask after the meeting.

"Mom, are you kidding? We're excited for you. It's about time!" Lily gushes. "I like him. He's funny and handsome, and he's really hot for you!"

"Jeez, Lily," I blush.

"Well, he is! I can tell! You should see how he looks at you!"

Focusing my attention toward Jack, I ask, "What about you, honey? Be honest."

Lily jumps in again. "Mom, I'm twenty-one, Jack's eighteen. I think you've waited long enough!"

"Jack?" I repeat.

A little more reserved in his enthusiasm, he says, "Tom seems like a nice guy, Mom. If you like him, that's all that matters."

"That's not all that matters. I care about your opinion. I want you to tell me how you feel."

"I think it's great," he says and then adds, "as long as he treats you right."

I wonder what's behind Jack's hesitation. Is it that he's never seen his mom with another man? Is it because he witnessed my pain after James left, and his subsequent anger toward me? Or could he be sensing something I'm not?

James found out about Tom when, after a particularly satisfying "lunch" at the Embassy Suites Hotel, three enormous floral arrangements arrived at my office—generating surprised whispers among the staff. On the one hand, it was flattering to have the attention. On the other, I wasn't sure why everyone was so stunned that I might be seeing someone. Just because my man-drought lasted longer than the one that created the Dust Bowl doesn't mean I haven't been in search of a good divining rod!

Until four of our five children are safely away at school the following fall, Tom and I play a resourceful game of Ditch the Kids: "Jack has a tournament this weekend." "Summer's volleyball team is playing in Sacramento." "Michael's gone, but the girls are here." "Lily and Jack are out of town with James." "I'm sending mine to my cousin's." We develop an ability to manipulate the activities of our kids in order to find time alone together and still fulfill our single-parent duties.

Our secret trysts also occur impulsively: afternoon business meetings at the Westin, extended lunch hours at the Embassy Suites near his work, early-morning doctor's appointments at the Airport Sheraton. We even engage in titillating phone conversation as Xtreme employees pass by my office window. "What are you wearing? What else? Ooo, the black one?!" It's like having an affair without any of the guilt and betrayal.

From our first meeting, our chemistry and lust for one another erupt anywhere and everywhere. It's as if some mad scientist served us the perfect love potion in those first glasses of wine we shared.

One night after a romantic dinner, while strolling through the Sodo district, buried deep in each other's arms, Tom pulls me into a darkened doorway and pins me against the building. *Hmmm, I guess my shoeless massage under the table worked!* His hands reach beneath my trench coat and begin to unbutton my blouse.

"Tom, not here! Someone might walk by," I whisper, not really resisting.

"It's dark. Nobody can see us," he says, navigating my body with the gentle fingertip touch of a blind man.

"I thought you had to be home after Melody's soccer practice?" I softly remind him as he nibbles perfume from my neck.

"Not yet." He breathes deeply, lost in his longing.

Just as I'm about to succumb in this public portal, sanity and modesty grab hold of my racing libido. "Tom . . . Tom, listen. Wait a minute!" I say, gently pushing him away as his hands continue to devilishly torture my breasts. "You realize my office is only four blocks from here, and I've got my keys with me!"

Before I have a chance to fully button up, he's tugging me down the street. "Now, don't go starting anything until I get the alarm turned off," I admonish him. "That's all I need—to have James and the police find us *in flagrante.*"

"Oh, I'm going to be *in* something all right."

I act properly shocked and appalled, when really I love our sex talk. James and I never played like this. We played nice and sufficiently satisfying, with the occasional round of athletic brilliance. But Tom and I, we're undefeated!

The glow from the antique lamppost is enough for us to see our way into the reception area. "Don't turn on any lights," I whisper, both nervous and titillated by our naughty tête-à-tête. "James and Brad both have keys. I wouldn't want either of them driving by and seeing our enraptured shadows dancing on the window shades."

I turn off the alarm at the entry and tell Tom, "It's right over here," as I lead him to my doorway. We stand for a moment, waiting for our eyes to adjust. Illuminated lines from the tilted blinds stripe across my desk.

"Where's James's office?" Tom asks. I point down the hallway. "Let's do it in there!"

I gently slap his arm. "No! That's just too weird. But I'd be happy to straddle you on my credenza," I offer. "Or maybe you'd like to take a spin on my black leather chair. I'll even cling to the frickin' ficus tree if you want," I tease as he begins undressing me. "But not in *his* office."

It's liberating to have someone to be silly with, to feel safe enough to say and do anything I want—to be all of me. And the best part: Tom loves every goofy idiosyncrasy. My anal need for organization and details has become the butt of his adoring humor. It's fun to see myself through his smitten eyes. I don't have to hide behind a cloak of strong mother, steadfast boss. And he flexes his muscles, offering protection when I recount James's attacks on me.

"You want I should take care of him?" he says with Capone-like vengeance. "I'm serious! Just say the word!"

Lately James's disdain for me has escalated. What began as occasional tirades have become daily verbal assaults. His antagonism and constant berating of my abilities are blatant attempts to force me out of the business.

During one of his offensives, I have an epiphany. For the first time, I hear myself as he might hear me: calm, moralizing, righteous. Although I don't intend that, I can see from his perspective how it might appear that way.

Once we began working together, he had nowhere to hide. For a man who was used to being top dog, it must have been annoying to have his wife weighing in on every decision. He didn't want the woman who laundered his boxers to have an opinion about his profit margins. And so, we began a destructive cycle. The more he did things to push the boundaries of what I deemed ethical, the more I became the person who sermonized. I went from annoying him to provoking him. It got to the point where he didn't ask for my opinions anymore. Hell, he didn't want them! But so what—it was my business too!

While in the midst of my epiphany of how James sees me, I realize one of my contributions to the downfall of our marriage: I had the audacity to try and be his moral compass. And yet, I didn't recognize it in myself until this very moment while he's standing over me ranting. Still, we are stuck being business partners. We've lost enough already. Neither of us wants to walk away from the successful company we birthed together.

How do I overcome this way of being with James? I can't stop speaking my mind. I owe it to myself, our employees, and the future of our company to offer my professional opinion. We tried seeing a therapist in order to better manage our business together, but after just two visits, James was done. And our honest revelations brought me to tears. James no longer wants to know me as a woman who needs compassion. When I'm strong and composed, it's easier to see me as cold-hearted bitch, allowing him to excuse his behavior.

There's no other way to say it. Working with James is a daily mindfuck. But fortunately, I have the perfect relationship scenario with Tom—seeing each other a few times each week is perfect, and all I can handle right now.

But soon Tom begins waltzing around us making a more permanent commitment to one another. It isn't long before his subtle moves escalate into a fleet-footed jive. And I, possessing the stealth of a, well, a Stealth, continue to artfully dodge his wish to plunge into the marital abyss, happy with the way things are.

Tom continues to exert more pressure—pressure that, considering my distorted state of mind with James, seems overwhelming. I'm deluded by my corrupted feelings toward James and the thought of what it will take to overcome them. Given the stress I'm under with my ex, Tom's persistence feels oppressive. The added responsibility of a marriage would drain me of what little I have left to give. My emotional plate is already piled high enough with demanding testosterone. Both at work and in my personal life I can't seem to find peace, and it's forcing me to analyze the men in my life.

I realize I definitely have a type. Personality wise, I'm drawn to expressive, dominant men. I like them powerful because I'm a strong woman. But if James and Tom are so much alike, are Tom and I doomed for failure? I begin focusing on their differences in hopes of convincing myself that we're eternally right for each other.

I love Tom. Something I thought I'd never find again. And what's even more amazing, I trust him, but not with the same innocent abandon that I trusted James. When James broke my heart, it was hard to believe it would ever heal. The truth is, it's mended, but the wound is still there.

# Chapter Fourteen

The sounds of Natalie Cole singing *The Very Thought of You* set the mood for a night of romance on this cool October evening. As Tom and I picnic on the floor in front of my fireplace, its dancing shadows give us a radiant, youthful glow. A bottle of a Columbia Valley wine and a few pillows are a welcome relief from another repetitive day of James's rantings.

"How was work today, Slick?" Tom asks as I rest in the comfort of his arms.

"Ah, well, just more of the same," I muse. "When I think about how I never gave up on Lily, I was hoping if I did the same with James, we would eventually find our way back to a respectful relationship. But I just don't know anymore."

"It's still hard for me to believe Lily ever gave you any trouble," he says. "She's so sweet and protective of you."

"Thankfully, we survived those years. But this thing with James, I just don't get it. His attacks have become extremely personal. It feels like he hates me with as much passion as he used to love me." I take a thoughtful sip of wine as if it will bring clarity. "It's a hard thing to comprehend. Especially since our separation was his choice. Doesn't he have the life he wanted? And, to be honest, his hatred hurts. He never treated me like this when we were married. He was considerate and loving. We shared everything."

"I wonder if he shares with Mara," Tom says.

"I don't think he can because I'm so enmeshed in his day. His insecure wife doesn't want to hear about our daily interactions. And maybe that's part of the problem. It can't be easy for him to have to constantly edit himself at home."

"You sound like you feel sorry for the guy. He doesn't deserve your sympathy." Tom pauses to consider what he's about to say next, and then decides to replay one of our recurring conversations. "I don't understand why you don't just leave the business. I've got plenty of money for the both of us."

Oh my god! Here we go again! Is it possible there's a princess-cut dependency ring involved in his not so subtle offer?

"I appreciate you wanting to help, but I need to take care of my own financial future. Plus, I have my parents' and sister's investments to protect, and Jack still has three years of college left. Even more important, I really love my job, and care about the people. Besides, I've put just as much into the business as he has."

"What about your constant migraines? Don't you think they're caused by the stress he creates?"

Tom wants to find the quick fix. Just sell and get out. Problem solved. But it's not that simple. For the moment, the logic of me staying outweighs my reason for leaving.

"Probably," I answer him, "and I know I need to find a better way to cope. Right now I come home mentally exhausted from meeting the challenge of placating his ego and protecting our workforce from his misguided anger. I feel as if I'm in a perpetual state of disarming the enemy. Consequently, when I'm not with you, I've taken to lying on the couch and mindlessly escaping in front of the tube."

I look into Tom's eyes knowing James's constant belittling has changed me on the inside, but I do my best not to show it when I'm with anyone. I don't ever want to be the downer in the room. But I wonder if the weight of it oozes out of me anyway. "Have you noticed anything different about me?"

He smiles in order to charm his way out of whatever he's about to say. "Well, since you ask"—he pauses—"you are a bit overly sensitive."

"Really? Overly sensitive?" I repeat slightly offended because I thought I was doing a great job of coping with it. "In what way? I mean, I like to think of myself as a compassionate person, but isn't that a good thing?" Not waiting for his reply, I defensively add, "You've said you admired my sensitivity toward others."

Tom grins at my response while patting my shoulder. "It's all right. I'm not saying it's a bad thing. But you've got to admit, you're a little hypersensitive."

"Seriously? I don't see it that way. I think you're just saying this because I've been getting on your case about making disparaging comments about others for sport."

Still forcing a grin, he knows he just stepped on a supersensitive landmine. "Take it easy. You're right. I should quit poking fun at others, but remember—you did ask for my opinion."

"I did," I concede, as I sink back into his arms. I've been proud of the growth I've had as a result of my divorce and the challenges with Lily. It's the one silver lining—feeling like I've become a better person.

But in this moment, I just want to forget—to transport

myself away from the pounding of my day. "Let's not talk anymore. I invited you over here to have your way with me, so shut up and start ravaging!"

He smiles and whispers in my ear, "Let the ravaging begin!"

Our playful beginning gives way to a sensual thirsting that rises from deep within my soul. My body does what my mind is not able to—it escapes the emotional weight of my life. Every movement becomes a fluid carnal dance choreographed by my secret self—each erotic caress igniting a yearning I've never felt before as my worlds collide within me. Tom's lips gently graze my breasts while a tear drifts down my temple. I'm not thinking anymore. I'm simply lost in the feelings of body and spirit, my flesh rapturously tasting every intoxicating measure.

Our love is tender and soulful, leaving me breathless from the depth of our connection. Have I found Mr. Right . . . again? Do I trust myself to know? And what's holding me back? The truth is I may never want to get married, but that doesn't mean we can't be together forever.

"What are you thinking about?" Tom asks.

"How can I think after that? My brain is still in an altered state!" I say, not wanting him to know I'm questioning our future together.

"You realize I could be holding you like this every night if we made things permanent."

What the fuck! Enough already! I just spent the whole day doing battle with one overbearing man. I don't want to wrestle with another. "We're already *permanent*," I tell him. "I'm completely committed to you—you know that. I'm just not ready to make it legal."

"When do you think you will be?" he asks as he withdraws from our oneness.

I've spent years taking care of others. And now that Lily is beginning a career she's passionate about and Jack's busy with college, I have the opportunity to focus on what I want. I feel bullied by James to relinquish my half of the business and pushed by Tom to surrender my newly found freedom. Why do I have to give up either one?

And why do I see marriage as giving something up? Maybe it's fear. Fear of the role I fall into when I'm tied to someone else. Caregiver plus pleaser equals one big fat martyr.

My martyrdom had its subtle beginnings in my youth. My parents, while loving and kind to one another, lived the lives expected of their generation. My father was the provider, and my mother took care of home and family, putting herself at the bottom of the list. James was, likewise, a child of a traditional home. Yet even though we were raised in a conventional way, we are also products of the women's liberation movement.

Before we had Lily and Jack, when I was in the corporate world, I had the power and confidence that came along with being a successful career woman. My feminist attributes were strong. When I quit to raise our children, I lost my mojo and easily fell into the role of caregiver—itself not problematic, except that I moved myself to the bottom of the list just as I'd witnessed my mother do. And I was damn good at it. The weird thing is, at the time, I was unaware of how much of myself I'd lost. It wasn't until a decade later, when I went back into the business world, that I realized what was missing—the other part of me. And while the blending of my traditional and feminist sides was challenging, going back to work also had an effect on James—especially since my workplace and his were one in the same.

Now, with Tom, I feel myself being pulled into my old submissive ways. And I don't want to go back there! I need more time to distance myself from what was so ingrained in me—to strengthen and balance this woman I've grown into.

I've spent the last decade as a business leader and guardian of my own home and family. I'm afraid that once I commit to Tom, I won't be able to hold on to the real me—a woman who continues to blossom into her authentic self. I don't want to lose the sweet taste of freedom that has brought me to this place in life. It's hard enough to navigate the stress of my working day with one dominant man. What will happen if I invite another one in?

"I'm sorry. I don't know when," I say, witnessing Tom's mounting frustration. "Can't we just keep things the way they are? They're so good."

"Listen," he says, sitting up. "I know James hurt you, but I also know that I won't. I'm tired of paying for his mistakes. I want more!"

How can he possibly know he won't hurt me? I've heard that promise before. I just want time to be free for a while, to rest my overwrought head on a pillow of unrestraint.

The Black Ridge ladies get together, offering me refuge from the clutter in my head. But toward the end of the evening, I receive some sobering news after expressing my feelings about James and Tom.

"You realize you're in an abusive relationship, don't you?" Kendall says bluntly.

"What?!" Stunned by her revelation.

"James has been verbally abusing you for a long time," Kendall continues.

Oh! I know I've been worried about how Tom sees me, but this! I pause to absorb my friend's disclosure as I look around the table to find concurrence. "I mean, I know he despises me, but do you really think he's an abuser?" I don't want to believe the truth of it, or that I would allow such a thing to happen to me.

"Alex, if you knew someone who was so viciously berated and disrespected on a daily basis, you'd be the first one to say that they were in a verbally abusive relationship," Kendall reasons.

My friends actually see me as one of *those* women. Yes, it's true he's not hitting me with his fists, but he bludgeons me every day with his anger, belittles me with his scorn—and it's making me physically and spiritually ill. But doesn't a battered woman believe that it's her fault? I don't. I prefer to think of myself as a woman who's staying in a sick relationship because she has a lot to lose if she leaves.

Later that night, still digesting my friends' eye-opening admission, I realize I've got to find a new way to deal with James. I can't let him do this to me anymore. Somehow over the course of the past several years, little by little, I've allowed him to chip away at me.

But how? How did I let this happen? The tension between us, eased by occasional business triumphs, built over such a prolonged period of time. I was unaware it was changing me. I recognized it as an unhealthy environment but thought I was capable of handling it. Now his random anger has turned into daily verbal abuse, and those business triumphs no longer protect me from his resentment. In his mind, I'm sharing in wealth that should all be his. It doesn't matter what my contributions are. My friends are right. I'm living in a world of emotional assaults under the guise of running a prosperous business.

The next morning, James marches into my office, reinforcing last night's revelation. "I've set up a meeting with a lawyer for us. I want to change the shareholder's agreement, and I want your family to sign over their stock to me. It should have been mine in the first place," he says, puffing his chest out and spraying his unwarranted disdain for my loved ones all over the room.

"You mean you want to *buy* their shares. Right?" I say, dumbfounded by his presumption. "And why would I ever want to change our agreement?"

It kills James that together with my family, I have controlling interest in our company. If he were to have their shares, he'd be able to take over and, ultimately, get rid of me. "What are you worried about, James? My family has never interfered in our business." But then, James views things through his own underhanded, unethical perspective, presuming everyone will behave without principle, like he does.

"No, they haven't—yet. But they've sure gotten rich off of me!" he scoffs.

"What are you talking about? Rich off of you! That's ludicrous. You've gotten rich off of them! We wouldn't even have Xtreme if it weren't for my family. As I recall, your parents didn't trust you enough to invest in you. And now you expect my family, who believed in me, to just hand over their shares! You're unreal."

He turns furious, his face distorted with rage. My heart begins its all too familiar pounding. "Listen, I'm the one who put my goddamn blood and sweat into this company! Not your fuckin' family! You better tell your parents and sister that I expect them to turn over their interest to me!" He swallows a resentful breath to gain control of himself. "We're meeting with the lawyer tomorrow at ten. Let your family know what they need to do. And I'll have a new agreement for you to sign in a couple of days."

James storms out of my office. Who is this man? Man? What man?! All I see is a green-faced, hook-nosed, flying-monkey wrangler shrieking, "I'll get you, my pretty!" It scared me as a kid, and it scares me now. So why the hell am I continuing to poison my life with him?

I take a moment to quiet my agitated heart and then calmly walk over to his office and close the door behind me. "James, I don't understand. Why do you have so much animosity toward me? What is it that I've done?"

Crazed by my calm, he lashes out again. "I'm sick of you and your family holding an ax over my head! This is my company, and the goddamned Fishers have no right being paid dividends off of my talents!"

I quietly continue as if we're engaging in a civilized conversation, pretending to ignore the hate in his words, yet painfully suffering every soul-battering blow. "Remember how grateful you once were for their help? Besides, you know that you and I get the lion's share of everything. They're just being rewarded for the huge risk they took on us. They've never questioned anything we've done. And I'm sure that if they weren't my family, you wouldn't be making this kind of demand. I just don't understand your problem."

The more rational I am, the more enraged he gets. "My fucking problem is you!" He fumes, and then begins to mock me in a contemptuous voice. "Oh, isn't Alex wonderful! Everybody fuckin' loves Alex! You're just so damn perfect. It makes me want to puke!"

It's all I can do not to shake him by the shoulders and cry, "James, James, remember me, the love of your life!"

And whoa! It bothers him that people like me? "Don't expect my family and me to comply with either of your demands," I vow, ending today's tirade by confidently walking out of his office.

My heart, my poor heart. How he hates me. I don't know how much more of this I can take. Why can't he see the real me anymore? He's obsessed with such loathing. But why? *Why don't you know me anymore, James?*

I'm consumed by thoughts of today's conflict as I walk through the low-lit hotel hallway toward the bar when, suddenly, a hand pulls me into the shadows. I struggle to get away as it covers my mouth. The person attached to it pins me against the wall.

"Oooo, you're lookin' gooood!" he whispers.

I fight to loosen his grip and fume, "Jeez, Tom, you scared the hell out of me! What were you thinking? Let go of me!"

"No. I want you right where I've got you!" he says, tightening his hold.

"Tom, I'm really not in the mood for this." I'm irritated by the bondage and the macho smell of testosterone. "Let's get a table. I need a drink."

"Too bad," he persists, turning me around and forcing his lips against mine as a hotel guest passes by.

"Tom, really!" I protest while glaring into his eyes.

"What's the matter with you?" he says, loosening his grip.

"Nothing's the matter with me." God, he's infuriating. "I just don't want to be manhandled right now."

"Well, I'm sorry. I didn't realize my desire for you was such a problem!"

Oh great, now I'm going to have to slap an ice pack on his bruised ego. It seems like all I do is cater to masculine appetites.

"That's not what I meant. I just want some space," I say, softening my tone. "Come on. Let's sit down and have a drink."

The Tea Room is an enchanting place, especially now with the holidays upon us. The lighting and ambiance are old-world: a tuxedoed pianist plays love songs on a baby grand; large mahogany panels and renaissance murals fill the two-story walls; high-backed velvet-and-brocade furniture provides elegant seating; and a classic Victorian staircase makes for an impressive entrance.

The waiter brings our drinks. I guzzle my screwdriver through the tiny black straw. I'm gonna need another one of these. We listen while the pianist plays *Love is a Many Spendored Thing,* both of us silently pissed at the other. *The golden crown that makes a man a king.* Oh sure! Put him on a throne! *Lost on a high and windy hill.* Sounds like this is me.

It all seems so simple to my way of thinking. James and I should be ecstatic about our mutual business success, while Tom and I could be relishing the perfect relationship scenario. What's the matter with these guys? I don't get it. Why isn't it enough? I'm not about to continue putting their needs above my own, dammit! I'm on the threshold of soaring like the proverbial eagle. Freedom! Give me freedom!

The music stops just as every ounce of my patience is drained.

"Listen, Tom. I'm sorry I reacted that way, but every time we're together, I worry that there's going to be another discussion about making our relationship more permanent. I don't want to continue to feel apprehensive when I see you. I need space right now. You know I'm committed to you. Isn't that enough?"

Perhaps I haven't picked the most opportune time to have this discussion, but I don't care. I have to resolve some of the conflict with the men in my life, one way or another. James is a brick wall, but with Tom there's hope; although, right now his tense body language indicates otherwise.

"I want more," he growls with his heels dug into the Persian carpet. "I know you've dated a lot of losers, and that you were married to one, but that hasn't been my experience. I would never have gone through all that you have. I don't attract *those* kinds of women."

Whoa, whoa, whoa! Did I just hear him right? *You conceited son of a bitch!*

"First of all"—*deep breath*—"James wasn't a loser when we were married. That came later. And what exactly do you mean—you 'don't attract those kinds of women'?"

"Well, good women tend to find me."

"What are you talking about?" I take a moment to gaze at my empty glass, hoping to just let it go, but I can't. "Ya know, you should count your blessings that you haven't had to participate in any of Cupid's little freak shows. It's all been so damned easy for you. Maybe a little one-on-one in the dating world with, oh, say, the Bearded Clinging Vine, or perhaps the Tattooed Two-Faced Diva, would cure you of your narcissism. You have no idea what it's like out there! And, by the way, are you implying that, for some reason, I need help in attracting good men, and that simply because of who you are, the cream of the crop flock to you? If I attract such losers, what does that say about *you*?!" I glance around to make sure my controlled outburst hasn't disturbed the neighboring tables.

"That you finally got lucky!" he says vainly. "You know—other women have been pursuing me."

Okay, I see where this is headed. I hurt his ego, so now

he's returning the favor. "Maybe you should go ahead and take a few of them out!" I say, looking him squarely in the eye. "Arrogant asshole."

Did I just say that out loud? Uh-oh. His wild-eyed look is one I've never seen on him before, yet it's all too familiar. It's the livid, twisted face I see on James every day. "Don't ever call me that again!" he rages in a low voice.

And yes, there's the customary tightening in the pit of my stomach. He's obviously angry. Well, dammit, so am I!

"Look," I say, and then exhale some turbulent air. "I'm sorry I called you an asshole, but I felt like you were putting me down." What I really want to do is tell him to fuck off. "I realize I shouldn't have said that." *Go ahead, squelch what's really on the tip of your tongue, Alex. Play nice.*

In an uncharacteristically reactive moment, I make up my mind to alter the course of my life. There's absolutely no good reason why I should have to face *two* men who think they're God's gift! And since responsibility is my middle name, I'll allow my heart to suffer.

"Maybe we should take a break." I say. "I think we need some time apart." When the words come out of my mouth, I feel sadness—and relief.

"Maybe we should."

After I refuse to meet James's ownership demands, the abuse escalates. His hatred toward me seems to consume him. Thank god I have people like Brad around to give me moments of refuge. But my spirit is deteriorating to the point of losing myself completely. Headaches and restrained anger punctuate my days. I fear a physical or mental breakdown is only one more vile word away. My gut's yelling at me to get out, my head rationalizing me to stay, and my heart weakening from the incessant battering. The pain is real. I feel joyless. Friends and family, self-motivating talks, and daily workouts no longer sustain me.

When I enter the restaurant two months after Tom and I split, he is waiting for me. We hug, and once again I feel the rush that comes with being in his arms.

"How are you?" I ask.

"Good, really good," he replies as we both beam like we did the night we met. "Keeping busy," he says, his smile giving way to a sly grin.

"Been dating, huh," I tease, hoping he'll confess to what a ghoulish ritual it is.

"I have," he answers proudly. "My friends seem to have a lot of women they want me to meet."

"Well, ya know, a good, unattached man our age is hard to find," I say, playing it cool. "Just how many ladies have you squired in eight weeks time?"

Releasing a breathy laugh he says, "Six."

"Wow, you must be exhausted!" I respond as a whiff of his arrogance wafts across the table.

"How about you? Are you seeing anyone?"

"No. I've been busy. Any keepers?" I ask, hoping he'll

confess to new revelations about the superficial world of amour du jour.

"They're all lovely ladies," he says.

*Come on! Admit it! Dating sucks, and trying to find the One sucks even more!*

"I enjoyed getting acquainted with them *but* was hoping," he says, exhaling a nervous laugh, "you might want to try again."

Immediately, the love and lust I felt for Tom stir within me. Nobody makes me feel the way he does. But if we try once more, I'm wary of the commitment coercion that might soon follow. I'm still in the throes of James's daily abuses and am incapable of handling any additional stress.

"If we do this, we *really* have to go slow. No pressure, no promises, just fun, and very, very slow. It's important to me."

"I can do that," he says, sliding closer.

"I really want you to hear what I'm saying, Tom." I reinforce my need for his understanding. "I don't want to feel like we're going back to me having to prove my level of commitment. I need breathing space. You know I'm a one-man woman. I hope that's good enough for now."

"I understand. No pressure. Slooooow! Got it."

I take a sip of my vodka and soda. "Next weekend I'm taking a much needed getaway with Lily and my parents to visit Jack at school. Why don't I call you when I come home?"

"That sounds great," he says, puffing up his chest like he's just made it back to the cave with me.

I breathe easier by putting him out of my mind for the

time being. I just want to be in a happy place, to experience total escape, and to replenish myself like I did with Nat in the Caribbean. Arizona, the kids, my parents—it's all good.

It's only been a couple of months since I've seen Jack, but as he approaches, it's like I'm seeing him as a man for the first time. Not only is he tall and handsome, but more important, he's smart, funny, and sensitive. Yes I said *sensitive*, in a way that's thoughtful and considerate. Still, I worry that he doesn't have a strong enough voice when he needs one. After listening to so much conflict at a young age, he avoids the tough conversations. But I'm confident he'll get there because he is a seeker of self-improvement.

I'm so looking forward to some sunshine with the people I love. Boy, how I need this! A little lying by the pool with the kids, some quality time with my parents, maybe a spa treatment or two, and a couple of margaritas with a side of table-made guacamole. Abso-frickin-lutely nothing else. No thoughts of James, no thoughts of Tom, no pressure.

When I open the door to our suite, I notice a huge floral arrangement and a hefty basket of wine and gourmet samplers on the counter. *How nice! They sure know how to make a guest feel welcome.*

As I move my suitcase into one of the bedrooms, Jack says, "Mom, there's a card with it. It's from Tom. He misses you and wants you to hurry home. He can't wait to see you again."

I have no idea what in the hell comes over me, but I snap. "Are you kidding me? I told him I wanted to go slow! This isn't going slow!" I fume, waving my arm at the pressure-packed goodies. "He didn't hear me at all! Was I talking to a blasted wall?"

My family is perplexed by my overreaction, shocked by the woman they've always known as composed. I turn crimson and am instantly mortified by exposing my feelings. To diminish my embarrassment, I pull a bottle of Cabernet from the basket and say in a nasally voice, "Whine anyone?"

I don't call Tom when I return home. Something I'm not proud of. It's not like me to treat anyone that way. Then again . . . who am I?

James continues his attempts to get me out of Xtreme. The business grows at a phenomenal pace, and of course we disagree on how to manage its success. Now, not only does he hate me because I'm his successful ex-wife, but he vehemently opposes any ideas I have for our company's future.

In a management meeting while discussing our growth, with the tension between us palpable, James asks everyone but me to leave the room. As they file out, Brad sends me a look of support before closing the door.

The moment it shuts, James fury explodes. "I am so fucking sick of you preventing me from taking this business to the next level!"

"James, lower your voice."

"*I DON'T GIVE A SHIT IF THESE PEOPLE HEAR ME!*" he roars.

"James, please."

"Every time I try to make a move, you fucking get in my way," he seethes, his face red with anger, "acting all high and mighty, like you know better than me when you don't know shit! You're too stupid to realize what I can do with Xtreme!"

Alarms begin blaring inside my head. *This is bad! Really bad! Get out, Alex!* Yet here I sit, hands folded on the conference room table, quietly observing his lunatic ravings. Part of me feels strangely removed from it, but my heart races, absorbing every psychotic punch. *I was married to you?*

"James, I'm not trying to get in your way," I say calmly. "I just think we need to manage our growth carefully. Yes, we have enough contracts to get us through the next eighteen months, but you know this business as well as I do—it's riddled with peaks and valleys. We have to be smart about how we maneuver our way through it."

His eyes are crazed as his fury seizes complete control of him. "I'm fed up with you blocking me from fulfilling my vision!" he shouts. "And you better stop brainwashing our generals! No one, and especially not you, has any right to mess with my business!"

"I'm not brainwashing anyone. It's just that, after reviewing the numbers, they agree with me. If we lease the new expensive property and move the whole company, we could lose everything. Our managers recognize that. I still think we should rent a nearby warehouse on a temporary basis to finish the contracts we currently have, and then we can downsize when we need to," I say, pretending this isn't personal.

"I'm through discussing this bullshit with you! You and everyone else are going to do whatever the hell I want, and anyone who doesn't can get the fuck out! So you better get 'em all on board! I won't stand for this shit any longer! You and your family have been a goddamned thorn in my side!

"You'd be nothing if it wasn't for me. I could replace you with a fucking monkey, and for a lot less money! Money that should be in MY pocket!!"

*Breathe, Alex, breathe.* I think of our employees within spitting distance and try to keep my composure as James rants over me, his body tensed like a pit bull ready to attack, his nightmarish face and pointing finger intimidating me, unleashing blow after lethal blow.

"I really wish I didn't disagree with you, but I'm only looking out for our business and the people that depend on us for their livelihoods."

"When are you going to get it through your fucking head," he shrieks, repeatedly jabbing his index finger against his own temple. *"IT'S NOT YOUR BUSINESS!* The only reason you're even here is because we used to be married! My biggest fucking regret!"

I'm absolutely shocked by his cruel admission. *You can't mean it, James! That's the one thing I held on to— that you knew in your heart what we once had.*

"You think you're so fuckin' valuable because everyone likes you—so goddamned what! Go be a greeter at Walmart if you're so fuckin' likable. Just get the hell out of my company!"

Intensely sharp pains force my abdomen to convulse as if something inside of me is fighting to get out. Slowly, whatever *it* is begins to move upward within my body, causing such unbearable spasms I cover my mouth to muffle my cries. *What in the hell is happening to me?* My hands clutch my stomach, trying to stop the convulsions.

I look at my body in horror as whatever *it* is crawls up through my chest and into my neck, forcing it to bulge with excruciating pain. My skin is stretched taut in agony as I choke and cough to dislodge it. I gasp, desperate for air. Gagging and heaving, my mouth is savagely forced open—my body fiercely rejecting the mysterious demon that possesses me. Finally, my tongue thrusts it into my palm, instantly relieving my pain.

Bewildered by what just happened, I stare at it. Why, it's an egg? But not just any egg. It's all slimy and soft, like jellied cancerous pus with hideous black swirls.

The light of day breaks through my bedroom window as I stare up at the ceiling, thinking about my dream. I recall the litany of hateful words, the disrespect, and the endless attacks I've swallowed from James. A smile comes across my face as I realize that all of that ugliness has just been purged from my body—I just yakked up a frickin' abuser's hairball!

I remember the books I used to read and believe in, the ones that asked me to trust my unconscious mind, and the promise I made to get back on a spiritual path.

In deference to my enlightened regurgitation last night,
I know what I must do.

I tell my parents and sister it's time to sell our share of the
business. I can't stay any longer and protect our investment. Yes, we could oust James with our controlling interest, relegating him to a mere shareholder, but I need to
leave and determine who I want to be. This business has
given me many good things, but it was also the catalyst
for the death of my marriage, plunging my life out of control. I need to start fresh, to begin a whole new chapter. I
don't know what it is yet, but the thought of unburdened
freedom brings excitement to the anticipation of my journey—whatever it is.

While sitting in the conference room with James, Brad,
and the rest of Xtreme's management team, smoke rises from the chimney of the white study model on the table. Awed by such a preposterous sight, I look around the
room to see if the others have spotted this strange development. Seemingly oblivious to what I'm witnessing, they
continue with the meeting.

    As the smoke billows, an image of a hand holding a
gold-banded cigar, its ember cleanly smoldering, comes
into focus. For some inexplicable reason, I'm utterly tran-

quil—unafraid of this absurd apparition.

Slowly the form takes shape, and details of the hand emerge. Its nails are perfectly manicured with ruby-red polish, and a diamond solitaire adorns its right ring finger. The pristine cloud ascends to reveal the upper body of a heavyset brunette with short, silky hair, flawless in a tailored navy-blue business suit, a string of dignified pearls complementing her neck. *You guys, don't you see this?*

While marveling at her beautiful, radiant face, gilded with garnet-colored lipstick and a glorious smile, I realize, her smile, it's for me! I can't believe how divine I feel as I bask in her loving glow. Her presence lifts me, making me light again.

When I mention the woman in my dream to Nat, she says that she represents my guardian angel. "Don't you know that she's a reflection of you and what you need in your life right now? She's telling you to rely on your own strength, and her brilliant smile is to let you know that everything is going to be alright. As for her look, she presented herself as a well put-together business woman, something you are. The short-haired brunette part characterizes your mom, Kendall, and Kate—all women you lean on for support, besides me, of course. And the cigar—that's your power, girlfriend!"

# Chapter Fifteen

It has taken time to adjust to the new road that I'm on. To this day, I mourn the loss of the work and people I so loved. And although I said good-bye to Tom in the process of rehabilitating my life, the beauty of it is in focus again. I was unaware of just how distorted my view had become. It's amazing how the mind can be so deceived. And yet, what I've learned to appreciate is that each challenge brings me closer to the woman I strive to be. James's abusive treatment actually fueled my revival, forcing me to look at myself and make a difficult choice—a choice I am now thankful for. The colors of the world have sharpened to such an intensity I can't remember when they seemed so vibrant. My mind is clear, my body strong, and, the icing on the cake, I feel years younger!

Grateful as I am for all these blessings, something is still missing. I haven't found the elusive synchronicity of heart, mind, and spirit I've been seeking. I went from a woman everybody needed to someone nobody needs: not my children, not my employees, and not a man. I want balance, dang it!

Might I find it in Peru? It's an oddly specific question I've been asking myself lately. Both of my favorite books, *Out on a Limb* and *The Celestine Prophecy*, took place there.

My internet searches about international volunteer organizations have been successful. I've contacted a New

York City group called Cultural Response Partnership that supports humanitarian work and promotes cultural exchange. I'll finalize the arrangements by mid-January and be on my way to Peru in early March.

Yes, Shirley, it's my turn to go *Out on a Limb*! After reading her inspiring story over two decades ago, the longing for my own journey has not diminished. In fact, the wisdom of my years has made it that much sweeter.

Along with the information packet from CRP comes pages of warnings about the dangers volunteers are exposed to in the area where I'll be working. I've traveled quite a bit in my life but not to many Third World countries, in particular not to one such as Peru, where political unrest has thrived for the past hundred years. And not to one where the Shining Path, a Maoist group that's listed as a US-designated foreign terrorist organization, was responsible for the deaths of over thirty-five thousand people in the 1980s and '90s.

Just before completing my travel arrangements, I let the kids know about my trip. I call Jack in Arizona, and he congratulates me on fulfilling a lifelong dream. Lily's initial reaction is also just as I expected, and the reason I waited so long to tell her.

"Mom, you can't do this! It doesn't sound safe! What if something happens to you?"

"Don't worry, honey, I'll be fine. I've done my homework, and I promise to be smart about what I do."

I see that Lily's spirited wheels are turning.

"Well, then, if you're going, I'm going!"

"Yeah, right. Like you could protect me." I tease my wisp of a daughter.

"No, I didn't mean that. This is an opportunity for us to have an adventure together! Come on, Mom! What do you say?"

I automatically jump into mom mode by thinking of excuses why she shouldn't go, and then just as suddenly realize: who better to join me on this journey!

The night before our flight to Peru, my doorbell rings. When I look through the peephole . . .

*Oh my god! It's Tom!*

I immediately fly into a tizzy. Excited? Yes, I'm excited! I'm thrilled! It's like the Three Stooges have possessed me! *Woowoowoowoowoo! Oh man, was there garlic on those halibut cheeks I had for dinner?* I breathe into my cupped hand. *Well, soitenly!* I sprint to my purse for a mint while my tongue urgently searches for any rogue parsley remains.

Quickly, I check my attire. *Crap, comfy.* At least I've still got on my "just been out to a fancy dinner" underwear.

Back at the door, I fluff the girls to perk them after a long day's gravitational pull. I close my eyes and take a deep, principled breath. *He's probably still with that woman I heard about so be strong, Alex.*

With an air of composure, I swing open the door. But I'm so frazzled by his presence, all I can manage is a breathy "Hi."

"Hi, yourself!" he says, looking oh-so-fabulous. *God, he's such an attractive man!*

"What are you doing here?" I ask as my blood pumps like a Texas oil rig. "I heard you transferred to San Francisco, got a new girlfriend . . ." *Shut up, Alex!*

"I'm sorry to be stopping by so late. I actually just moved back to Seattle and thought I'd come by to see you. I hope that's okay."

"Of course it's okay. Come on in," I say cheerfully. Holy bleepin' body heat! Is my fantasy coming true? Will he take me right here in the entryway?

"God, Slick, you look great!" he says, hugging me tightly.

"So do you!" I resist my awakened desire and withdraw from our embrace. *He said he's moved back, not that he'd gotten single.* "Come and sit down," I say, showing him into the living room. "Can I offer you a drink?" *Look at those jeans. They fit like they were custom-made.* My mind flashes on what lies within. *He's not available! Focus.*

"Sure."

"What's your pleasure?" I ask, suddenly hankering for a good stiff beverage myself.

"What are you having?" He follows me into the kitchen.

"Hmm, I think I'm gonna have a vodka soda." *With a ten-count pour!*

"That sounds good. I'll do the same," he says, parking himself on one of the island's bar stools.

*Look at the wicked grin he's wearing. Maybe I shouldn't have a drink. Stay in control, Alex. You can do this.*

"So, how are the kids?" I make small talk while having scintillating thoughts of our sexcapades.

"Great! They still live in the Northwest, so it's nice to be back."

"Did work bring you home?"

"Work, kids, Seattle," he answers as I try to clear my head of erotic images. How is it I can carry on a conversation while my mind shamelessly indulges in carnal images? "What about Lily and Jack?" he asks.

"Lily works for a plastic surgeon, and Jack's finishing up at ASU. Everything's good," I tell him as images of our naked bodies flicker in front of me like those on an old newsreel.

"I bet you love having Lily close by," he says with his eyes transfixed on me. "Goddamn, you look good! Did I say that already?"

I hand Tom his drink and move onto the stool next to him. The energy between us flares like passion-fueled propane. *Holy shit! Hang on, Alex! Stare at his chin. Count the pores. Just stay away from his eyes!*

"Where are you and your girlfriend living?"

"Oh," he says with a chuckle, "Barbara and I broke up some time ago. She still lives in San Francisco."

"I'm sorry. I didn't know." I try my best to sound sincere. "Are you seeing anyone else?"

"You're funny," he says, confidently jerking my bar stool close to him. "No, I'm not seeing anyone else. I'm here for you!"

His sudden move excites me, sending my thoughts

one step closer to shameless lust. I allow myself to listen to the howling from deep within me.

*Look at how that shirt hugs his broad shoulders, his muscular arms, and that chest that I love to press against my uncovered breasts.* My breathing deepens. The girls inflate with anticipation.

His hand slides up my thigh, his thumb landing dangerously close. His mouth is on mine, the kiss deep and forceful. He lifts me onto him. His generous hands encompass my ass.

He unbuttons my blouse and growls, "Mmm, I've missed these!"

I grab his hair, pull his head back, and whisper, "I've missed *you!*"

We lock onto each other's eyes.

The feverishness of our rapture erupts as we give in to our temptation. We tear at each other's clothes, flinging our final restraints to the floor. The strap of my bra circles the nearby blender like a horseshoe finding its mark. Tom dives into my breasts, his aggressive hands squeezing them as he feasts on me. The wildness of our attraction erases all thoughts other than to have him within me. He pins me against the kitchen wall, and my head hits the framed lemon photograph.

He turns me toward the wall, driving me insane, and plunges himself inside, slow and deliberate.

"You're mine now," he whispers in my ear.

"Fuck me."

My words incite his vigor, hastening him.

Tom kisses my tingling flesh while I ache for more. Breathless from the potency of our connection, I feel all of me smoldering with a long-forgotten delirium.

We collapse against the wall and stay there, simmering in our contentment.

I turn, and we look into each other's eyes. "Come with me," he says, taking my hand and leading me to the bedroom.

He stops in the doorway, spotting my luggage. "What's this?"

"Oh, I almost forgot," I laugh. "I was obviously distracted! I'm leaving tomorrow morning for a place just outside of Lima." I pull back the covers on my bed and slide on top of the sheets.

"Oh! How long will you be gone?"

"A month. I'm going with Lily."

"You used to talk about wanting to go there," he says, and then pauses to process this new information. "Listen, it's pretty late. Maybe I should leave so you can finish packing and get some rest."

"Oh no you don't," I say, pulling him onto the bed with me. "There will be plenty of time to sleep on the plane. I've been waiting much too long for this," I confess, "and I'm not finished with you yet!"

This time our lovemaking is tender, sweetening our desire for one another. I savor the taste of his hardness as I bring him to the brink of ecstasy. He pulls me on top of him, and we look into each other's eyes as we ascend to the moment of breathlessness, lost in the pleasures of our bodies.

I collapse onto Tom, moistening his ear with my breath, and then rise up and exhale a blissful sigh of exhaustion. "Talk about nirvana!"

"Hell, yes! It always has been!" he says as he clutches my alabaster ass and rises for a nibble on my breast. "So, is it possible that this time when you return from your trip, I'll hear from you?" he teases.

I close my eyes and wince with embarrassment for how I behaved the last time I said I'd call. "I think it's not only possible but probable. That is, if you want me to."

He hesitates, "Hmmm, let me think." I start to uncouple our bodies, but he tightens his grip. "Yes, I want you to call!"

"That's more like it, Jeffries. Just remember who's on top!"

"Oh yeah!" he says, muscling us over so he's in the power position.

I try unsuccessfully to roll once more.

"Okay, all right, I guess I'll *let* you drive. But just for a while."

# 3

## Living a New Dream

# Chapter Sixteen

Staring out the grimy windows of the old cream-colored van, I take in the harsh reality of this distressed nation. My breathing is shallow to diminish the stifling smells of pollution and foul humidity. The sky is gray, but not from the weather, and the streets are gritty with dirt and sand. There's no greenery here. Airports are never in a good part of town, I tell myself. Even pristine Seattle has its flaws.

We drive toward Surco, the middle-class section of Lima where we'll be housed. Lily chats with Diego, a stocky Mexican American volunteer from California whose brassy-blond hair is a curious style choice, and Armando, the Peruvian CRP director. An attractive man with an inviting smile, distinguished salt-and-pepper hair, and a neatly groomed stubble beard, Armando has an ease and sense of humor that comfort my mild apprehension. Behind the wheel, Mario, with his two-tone baseball cap, denim shirt, and over-the-shoulder canvas bag tucked up tightly under his armpit, expertly navigates the busy city streets.

Silently, I'm electrified by the rush of stepping into an unfamiliar world—here to embark on a pilgrimage to expand my heart, enrich my mind, and nourish my soul. I can't believe I'm finally living my dream. And I'm sharing it all with Lily!

The city reveals signs of a country that's suffered from constant turmoil. Storefronts have expandable iron

gates and bars on their windows. Guard stations sit on
street corners. Piles of rubble lie in ruin like post–WWII
Germany. And indiscriminate urban sprawl clutters the
view. There seems to be little order, or maybe there is, but
it's not like any system that I've ever seen.

I'm not surprised by the bleakness of it all. In my re-
search, I discovered that Lima holds more than a third of
this vast country's population. Eight million people live
here, almost six million of those having arrived in the past
thirty-five years—displaced by terrorism, natural disas-
ters, and rampant poverty. If you're not a farmer or a min-
er, Lima offers one of the few prospects for work, though
the odds of finding it are highly unlikely.

Peru was once a country replete with gold and silver, the
most powerful and developed civilization in South Amer-
ica. That is, until Pizarro and his Spanish conquistador
thugs arrived in the early 1500s, bringing with them small-
pox and initiating the slaughter, starvation, and slavery of
the people here, most notably the Incas. Within a hundred
years of the Spanish invasion, Peru's entire population fell
from over ten million to under one million. A civilization
and its rich history were virtually destroyed, and the political road to recovery has been bumpy ever since.

The caste system thrives here—where once the Incas
were the elite upper class, Spanish pure-bloods have replaced them. As for indigenous people, more than half of
them fall below the poverty line, and the majority of those
live in abject poverty. The disparity between the two
classes hasn't changed as the country struggles to become
a democratic nation, fighting pervasive election fraud and
corruption. Many of the impoverished masses live on the

outskirts of Lima in shantytowns, each housing hundreds of thousands of people. Villa El Salvador, where Lily and I will be working, is one of these towns.

Mario turns onto a quiet residential street with flat-roofed homes butted up closely next to one another. Although they're situated within ten feet of the narrow road, most are concealed behind fortified fences. Mario stops the van in front of a mustard-colored walled fortress punctuated by a mahogany, speakeasy-style door. I half expect Al Capone to peek out of the porthole and ask for the secret password so I can enter and order my first pisco sour. A wooden gate rolls open as our van pulls into a modest courtyard. One of the guards immediately seals the entrance behind us and returns to his station along the perimeter.

Armando shows Lily, Diego, and me around the large two-story house. He introduces us to Lucilla, our cook, and Consuela, the housekeeper. Diego quickly endears himself to the women by conversing in fluent Spanish. Meanwhile, Lily and I smile and courteously bow like Japanese geishas.

The main floor has a small front office and half bath with a window open to the courtyard from where the smell of smoke wafts, as Mario and the guard sit on a bench puffing their unfiltered cigarettes. In the back of the house is a meeting room with vinyl couches, adjoined by a dining room with two long, wooden tables. We pass through the dining room and enter a humble kitchen that includes a two-burner stove, a mini-fridge, and a two-foot-by-two-foot painted table—the only apparent workspace. As Lucilla hand-washes dishes in an old 1940s-style basin, I wonder how she prepares food for all of the volunteers with such limited resources. I mean, I've seen Northwest campsites outfitted more lavishly!

The floors throughout the house are highly polished brown linoleum, and the furniture is clean and unfussy for easy maintenance. The back of the house has large windows and glass sliders that open onto a small terrace and quaint backyard. The yard is surrounded by towering, thick stucco walls, adorned with razor wire to protect our little piece of heaven.

We head upstairs to where there are eight bedrooms and four baths, with separate quarters for the men and women. Armando shows Lily and me our room. A wooden bunk bed, metal-framed twin, and small nightstand leave little floor space. Lily immediately claims the bottom bunk. I look at the top, flashing on the short-sheeted summers of my youth, and drop my backpack onto the twin. Six small wire shelves serve as our dresser. Two entrances, across from one another, make our domain a communal passageway to the back stairs that lead to the rooftop—a place for doing laundry.

A yellow-tiled shared women's bathroom has blackish grout, the result of years of mold and dust-covered feet, I'm guessing. The fixtures include a 1960s mint-green toilet and sink; a stained, out-of-order bidet; a wall-mounted distilled water dispenser for brushing our teeth; and a modest shower. Armando instructs us that the garbage pail, no bigger than a generous bowl of ceviche, is for our used toilet paper and feminine hygiene products—noting the plumbing has difficulty with anything solid. *Hmmm. Which brings me to my next question . . .*

Lastly, we're assigned a hallway locker to secure our

money, passports, return airline tickets, and cameras.

After Lily and I get settled, we head downstairs to learn more about the people we already know and to meet with the other volunteers.

Diego, who will be offering his services at the senior center, is on his second tour of duty with CRP, having volunteered in Tanzania a couple of months ago. A district sales manager for See's Candies, he spends his vacations helping others. This warm and outgoing man in his midthirties, the youngest of eight children, is eager to confess to us that his crazy hair is not his doing. His teenage nieces insisted on dying it the day before he came here. He laughs good-naturedly at their color choice.

Lily connects with twenty-year-old Henry, a lanky Brit who's spending three months at one of the elementary schools before finishing up at Cambridge in the fall. His spectacles, quiet presence, and obvious intelligence are reminiscent of Harry Potter.

Since Diego is the only one who speaks Spanish, Chanda, a physical therapist who immigrated to the United States from India, and Crystal, a thirtysomething business woman from Chicago, are glad to be working with him at the senior center. Michelle, a fresh-faced twenty-one-year-old blond from Nova Scotia, beginning a career in health care, will be helping at the hospice center. Three other volunteers, expected to arrive shortly, have chosen to participate at the elementary school along with Henry. Meanwhile, Lily and I are assigned to the government-sponsored children's institute. Although the majority of our group is only volunteering for two weeks, Diego, Henry, Lily, and I will be staying longer.

Lucilla rings the dinner bell. We move into the dining room for chicken-and-rice casserole and sweet white corn that appears to have been fertilized with growth hormones. Yowsa! Has Iowa heard about these mega-kernels?

After the main course, Lucilla brings out a tray of seriously over-the-hill guava and passion fruit. *Is this supposed to be dessert? Don't they know fruit's not really a dessert unless it's wrapped in a flaky pie crust or smothered with buttery streusel? This could very well be my most challenging adjustment!*

But wait! There's no need to panic. Much to my delight, my dear, special, light of my life, new best friend, Diego, surprises us with a box of See's chocolates. *Love your hair, buddy! Really! Mmm, brings out, er, the yellow in your eyes!? Just one more piece. Thanks!*

After a long day of travel, I'm ready to say good night to the others. Fortunately, none of the youthful recruits have been assigned to the top bunk in our room. I am especially thankful since Lily reminded me I make a puffing noise in my sleep that sounds similar to a ball machine popping out tennis balls. Oh to be young and inaudible again.

The two CRP vans follow one another out of the city and onto the freeway where old ravaged cars and trucks race alongside of us without lane recognition, sometimes three across, sometimes four or five, depending on the daring of the drivers. Buses stop without warning in the middle of speeding traffic to pick up crowds of people. Horns unmercifully honk, and tailpipes visibly spew carcinogens that coat our throats.

Hundreds, perhaps thousands, of helter-skelter shacks cling precariously to the steep, gray, unstable hillsides. Stacked so perilously, they look as though they've already been toppled by an earthquake. Abandoned dump trucks and mammoth concrete drainpipes sit idle on the side of the road like decomposing dinosaurs waiting to fossilize. Meanwhile, the occasional palm tree goes unnoticed because of the overshadowing desolation.

Twenty minutes into our drive, Mario turns left off the main thoroughfare at the entrance to Villa El Salvador. I'm overcome by an increasingly malodorous stench in the air. I try to hide my revulsion, having never breathed such indescribably vile air. Lily looks at me, acknowledging the foul odor with her eyes.

*What in the hell is that?*

I take a shallow whiff, trying to pinpoint its composition—separating the scents like I'm dissecting the flavors of a fine merlot. But it's such a horrid blend of pollution, raw sewage, rotten garbage, and god knows what else that I decide it's better to pretend that I don't smell it. It's most certainly not buttery or oaky, but there is definitely a hint of anus.

We drive in a cloud of dust behind buses, cars, and ancient three-wheeled motorcycle taxis that bump along the crumbling roads. Stray dogs roam everywhere. Most of the homes and businesses are partially constructed, with their second stories left unfinished for years or, in some cases, forever, Armando tells us. Many of the buildings are made from whatever scavenged materials the locals can appropriate, while several extended family members stay together under one roof, or second-story floor, as it were. Poverty and suffering are everywhere. I stare out my window, not wanting Lily and the others to see my emotion as tears well in my eyes.

It's all so tragic. *Why do people have to live like this?* I'll never be able to convey the grim truth of this place to my friends back home. The assault on my senses is truly unutterable.

Our first stop is San Sebastian, where we're greeted at the gate by Manny, the energetic, middle-aged director of the senior center. As soon as we enter the single-story brick building consisting of a large, sparse room with scattered plastic tables and chairs, the local seniors surround us, conversing as if we understood their every word.

Dark, friendly eyes search for a sign of warmth and compassion in our faces. We offer it, reaching back with our hands, hearts, and reassuring hugs. Three grandmas approach Lily and touch her long, blond hair as they swoon over her pale beauty. I bend down to be embraced by a petite (though I'm starting to assume everyone in Peru is shorter than I am) woman in a white straw fedora as I observe my compassionate fellow volunteers out of the corner of my eye.

After a two-hour class on customs and cautions given by Manny, we board the vans for our next stop, the primary school, the work site of Henry, the astonishingly composed British lad; Bob, a handsome, pushing-forty, perpetually smiling volunteer from Michigan; Spencer, a bewildering young man from Maine who chooses to avoid eye contact with me; and Mary Lee, in her late twenties, a seemingly proper Southern girl from North Carolina with an endearing impish streak.

When we arrive, Armando leads us through deep, filthy sand and debris, reminding us to be careful not to step on any feces. The concrete building is protected from the elements by a corrugated metal roof that hangs four feet above the top of the uninspiring walls. Rope climbing nets dangle halfway around the room. A couple of wooden tables, a few chairs, and the reverberating squeals of fifty rowdy children complete the loud picture. I wonder where the interactive play stations and the ABCs on the wall are—any of the educational tools necessary for learning. And such chaos!

After a quick visit, we make our way back to the vans, where Armando tells us we're returning to home base for more orientation. *But aren't we visiting my site? I want to see where I'm going, so I can prepare. I need to know what to expect. Take a deep breath, Alex. No—wait!*

That afternoon we receive another *Don't* lecture. *Don't* leave the confines of your volunteer facility. *Don't* drink the water at your work site. *Don't* bring your passport, camera, money, or other valuables with you. *Don't* wear sandals because of human and animal excrement. *Don't* consume salads, uncooked vegetables, undercooked meats, reheated food, fruits without a peel, ice, and juices made with unboiled water. *Don't* wear shorts. Women must dress respectfully. No scoop-neck tops. It's a macho world here in Peru, so *don't* attract unwanted attention.

Armando's warnings make me a bit uneasy, especially for my gorgeous daughter—but then it occurs to me: yes, we need to be careful—something bad *could* happen—

but CRP might very possibly be doing a little CYA. As a former business owner, I know all about covering your ass, which, by the way, isn't on the *Don't List.* I resolve for us to be cautious but fearless.

After the midday meeting, our group decides to have a drink before dinner. Since alcohol isn't allowed in the house, Diego, who shared a smoke earlier with Mario in the courtyard, scored the inside track on one of Lima's hot spots, an oasis for gringos.

We head en masse to the corner of a busy street and hail two cabs. Taxis in Lima are about the size of Spanish peanuts. Diego asks the drivers to take us to an area known as Miraflores, but first he barters for a good fare. He negotiates a twenty-minute cab ride down to thirty cents per person, and the nine of us cram into the vehicles. Talk about getting friendly with your fellow volunteers! *Hey, Bob, is that a chorizo in your pocket?*

Well, now, Peru might just be the place where the old adage "you get what you pay for" originated because— holy crap!—what a hair-raising ride through the free-for-all streets of Lima we're having! Forget about seatbelts— there aren't any. Air-conditioning? Not an option.

One minute we're racing through the city on a wild adventure, laughing at the craziness while inhaling incessant exhaust fumes. The next, we're at a dead standstill, sweating it out in a massive traffic jam while being harassed through the car windows by an endless stream of road vendors selling bananas, Inca Kola, and Chiclets!

We enter Miraflores. The smell isn't quite so bad, the architecture's improved, and people, here and there, look somewhat prosperous. Sure, the pollution's still heavy, and it's no Park Avenue, but I can tell we're in uptown Lima.

As we turn the corner, my eyes gaze upward. A heavenly chorus sings a note of *Ahhhh!* as a beautiful, black-glass monolith rises majestically above the gray city skyline. It's the Marriott! *Hallelujah . . . hallelujah, hallelujah!*

We round the circular drive and tumble out of our cramped *coches*, falling at the feet of the hotel doorman. I look up to see his stiff, unimpressed face. He's all military-like in his bellhop uniform; I immediately feel underdressed in my capris and Keds. *Hey, man, we're not here to cause any trouble. We're just a bunch of hot, tired do-gooders looking for a little relief.* I straighten my dignified, middle-aged American woman posture and my pink Columbia Sportswear T-shirt, and stroll past him as if I'm on my way to a formal event.

Inside the resplendent, lofty entry, coral-colored marble floors shine under our feet and continue in the distance to our right toward an open-bar area. A grand piano and clusters of comfortable couches and coffee tables face soaring windows that frame a view of the Pacific shoreline. Our voices echo through the lobby, turning heads as we walk toward our respite.

We add a few more chairs to one of the cozy sitting areas and seat ourselves next to the windows. A pretty waitress asks for our order in Spanish. Diego translates and eagerly suggests we try the famous pisco sour, a popular Peruvian cocktail. After he rattles off its ingredients, including raw egg white, I decide to go with a margarita. Yes, I know it represents an entirely different country, but, hey, I like 'em. And after sweating all day, I can use the salt! Lily, Chanda, Bob, Mary Lee, and Henry brave the pisco sour. Meanwhile, Diego orders, hmm, a beer.

As I take in the panoramic view, I get my first real look at the Peruvian coastline. Carbon-blue in color, the ocean reflects the persistently gloomy sky. A black water-line runs the length of an uninviting beach that stretches for miles. What is that stuff—the remains of some oil tanker leak or just more general waste and pollution?

Global environmentalism hasn't found its way to Peru. I think about how the people of the Pacific Northwest are such tree-huggers, recycling anything and everything—so conscious of the air we breathe and the land we love. And then I hastily excuse this underdeveloped country because it's poor and the government is deficient. Still, it pisses me off that they can get away with destroying our planet while I'm constantly being chided by hypocritical politicians and righteous celebrities who ought to be preaching to the bureaucratic South American choir, with shouts out to China and India too!

"How's your margarita?" Lily asks.

"Great! Your pisco sour?"

"Awful," she whispers, wrinkling up her nose.

"No kidding," I note sarcastically under my breath so only Lily can hear me. "Didn't the first syllable of the name clue you in?!" She scrunches up her face. "And right there," I say, discretely pointing my index finger toward her twisted mug, "is where the *sour* comes from!" "Hence the name. Not very smart on your part, my love. Sip?" I offer up my glass.

"Funny, Mom," she whispers as I mouth her an air kiss.

Soon our group learns that Henry is not only a scholar but also a musician.

"No one's using the piano," Diego says. "Why don't you play for us?"

Henry's face flushes as the others coax him. I certainly understand his hesitation. Not only will he be performing for us, but for the hotel guests and employees who fill this immense lobby and bar. It reminds me of the time I was strong-armed into playing Christmas carols on my accordion at the Palatine Elks Lodge. I can still feel my ten-year-old nerves! Henry's music will reverberate throughout this glass and marble palace. And besides, we don't really know him. What if he sucks? Our gang might be booted out of here—and I haven't finished my drink yet!

Henry rises, forced into submission by the urging of our group. In his recital-quality cargo pants, short-sleeve shirt, and a kilo of Villa dust, he humbly walks over to the bartender, leans in for a quick chat, proceeds to the grand piano, and adjusts the leather-tufted bench to his liking. *Oh god, Henry, please be good!*

He sits erect, hands poised perfectly on the keys, and begins to play. A delighted grin crosses my face as I listen to the most dulcet arrangement of *Moon River* I've ever heard. His long, narrow fingers gently roll up and down the keyboard as if he's channeling Mancini. I swoon as Andy Williams sings within me. Henry's good! Shit, he's great! What an impressive young man! *Are there any more like you back home—perhaps, say, with a touch of gray?*

*Koo-koo-ka-choo, you little Renaissance hunk!*

# Chapter Seventeen

ily and I know little about our volunteer place-
ment aside from the fact that we'll be hanging out
with kids. On any given day, the National Family
Welfare Institute takes care of close to one hundred at-risk
children, ranging in age from one to twelve—children
who are the poorest of the poor, whose parents may have
mistreated, neglected, or abandoned them.

Repugnant smells still hang in the Villa air. Pedro,
riding up front with Mario, is a young man we met this
morning. Proficient in English, he'll be showing Lily and
me around the institute.

After dropping Diego, Crystal, and Chanda off at
San Sebastian, Mario turns onto a narrow dirt road.
Ramshackle structures made from earthen bricks, scrap
wood, corrugated metal, and old tires ironically have steel
gates safeguarding their dilapidated doorways. Our driver dodges haphazard piles of gravel and large boulders.
Old wooden streetlights stand in isolation like weary sen-
tries keeping watch over the dispossessed—their loosely
strung wire uniting them in common purpose. Our open
car windows draw in a brownish haze of dust that sticks
to my perspiring skin.

Mario stops in front of a secured entrance along an expansive concrete wall. Pedro, Lily, and I roll out of the van.
Sun-parched dirt flies up around our ankles as we approach
the guard, who is amusingly a featherweight of a man.

The diminutive guard nods to Pedro and opens the gate. As we enter, we're immediately overrun by a swarm of chattering kids. Like three fat frogs thrown into a piranha tank, we're picked clean as they push and shove to be near us.

I say, *"Hola,"* showing off my limited Spanish skills, and smile. They assume from my simple gesture that I know their language and engage me in conversation. *"Señorita, señorita—"* The rest is an incomprehensible blur. Lily laughs at the high-spirited confusion. I continue smiling, a perpetual state I've been in since our arrival in Peru, wanting to show that I'm open and friendly. For now, a big, warm grin is all I've got. Pedro shushes the children and nudges them in the direction of the cafeteria.

We are inside the custodial walls of a two-acre complex. The U-shaped one-story building located at the front of the complex has a shaded outdoor walkway that runs along the inside of the horseshoe. A kitchen, a cafeteria, an administrative office, and classrooms bustle with early-morning activity. The rest of the property includes a large arid garden cultivated by local seniors that produces root vegetables for the kids' lunches; a cracked-concrete soccer field with sun-faded lines and rusted metal nets; a small building housing time-worn bathroom facilities; and a narrow open area with a few desert shrubs and a single destitute tree.

Pedro escorts Lily and me to the first childcare room, where two young women are tending to several one-year-old infants. A few metal cribs, without protective bumper guards or stimulating mobiles, hug the back wall. Otherwise, there's nothing to speak of in the room. No toys, no pictures, no motivating incentives for development. Every surface is hard and unforgiving.

The babies sit precariously on small chairs at a child's table, some of them barely able to hold themselves upright. Their faces are vacant of emotion as the caregivers coax them into eating a breakfast of unpasteurized milk and dried biscuits. Suffering and sadness hang in the air. A feeling of melancholy strikes my heart, making it painfully heavy. *Oh god, I hope I can do this.*

We look through the windows of the next room. A woman in her thirties cares for nine two- and three-year-olds, who sit quietly at a table. How adorable these delicious toddlers are. I want to hug them and steal them away to a better life.

I stifle my emotions as Pedro leads us to the next room, where we observe four- and five-year-olds.

"I'd like to be with these children," Lily says without hesitation.

Pedro takes her inside and introduces her to the caregiver. Filled with pride, I wave to her through the glass as we leave her to fend for herself.

Pedro and I continue under the overhang to a small alcove that holds the entrances to three classrooms. The kids inside spot us and come charging out of their rooms, mobbing us with their enthusiasm. They begin pleading with Pedro for something.

"What's going on?" I ask above the sounds of pandemonium.

"All children want you," he says loudly.

Their hands begin pulling at me. A tug-of-war with my arms ensues. Pedro pretends to admonish them, but our smiles suggest otherwise. Over the ruckus, he tells me, "This room is for six- through eight-year-olds, that one is for nine and ten, and the next is eleven- and twelve-year-olds."

Suddenly a woman with wildly permed hair bursting from beneath a bright-yellow visor comes out of one of the rooms and tries to establish order. Even in her four-inch wedges, she's more than a head shorter than I am. Her tight skirt and spandex tank top, partially covered by a smock, challenge more than one of the *Don'ts*.

She speaks intently to the children, seemingly unaware that Pedro and I are even there. I watch her sprinting lips, hoping for some word recognition from my old high school Spanish days. My focus is so intense, I feel my eyes might start spinning like the reels of a slot machine. My heart begins to race. She talks with her hands, her whole body showing such consuming passion toward the children. The kids argue with her, but she'll have none of it. Her tone and demeanor are decisive as she shakes her reprimanding finger. My anxiety level, already in a heightened state because of my First World naiveté, elevates.

In the midst of the mania, this tigress suddenly turns, looks at me like she knew I was there all along, and gives me an intentional wink. I'm caught off guard, having a moment ago been frightened by her fiery energy. My anxiety vanishes with just one knowing look—a look that, for some reason, was familiar and funny. I immediately feel a destined opportunity for friendship. It doesn't matter that we don't speak the same language—we already have a connection.

"That's the one, Pedro," I say, tilting my head in the direction of her room with my arms still occupied by the spirited *niños.* "The six-through-eight-year-olds."

Pedro and I make our way through the sea of yakking dolphins into her classroom while the older children head back to theirs, groaning with disappointment.

He introduces me to Marina, who reaches out her hand adorned with lumpy silver nail polish. Her grip is firm. She pulls me close for an embrace and says something.

Wrapped in her arms, I glance over at Pedro for the translation. "She say she happy you choose her."

"Please tell her it's my honor."

He does, and then she adds something else while looking up at me, causing them to laugh.

Pedro explains, "She say she need taller shoes!"

I had been prepared to be respectfully somber the whole time I was here, thinking those who live in such deplorable conditions must be perpetually sad. Did I really think people who are poor don't have a sense of humor? That we couldn't relate?

Soon Pedro will make an abrupt exit, leaving me to massacre the local vernacular, so I quickly ask him what Marina would like me to do. Their lips fly with incredible speed, increasing my concern about my limited language skills.

She tells Pedro not to worry, that we'll figure things out together. *Gulp! You don't understand.* I'm a person who likes to anticipate, have a direction, and conduct myself with decorum. What if I accidentally do something inappropriate for their culture like, say, bend over to pick up a paper clip, completely unaware I should be facing south, and inadvertently curse the classroom with Plantar warts? Or maybe I misinterpret something she asks, and instead of cleaning the chalkboard, I, ah, do the Chicken Dance! I don't want to disappoint her or unwittingly respond incorrectly. *Are you sure we can wing this? Deeeeep breeeaaathhhh, Alex. Oh man, I have got to stop doing that!*

Pedro leaves, and Marina pulls out a chair, inviting me to sit at one of the kid-size tables. There are three such crudely made wooden tables, all painted brown, each with six matching chairs—chairs that have no molded butt impressions or rounded backs for long-term comfort—simple, uncraftsman-like plywood, so-called chairs.

Up front, a green chalkboard is riddled with jagged holes as if some slate-hungry rodent has been gnawing on it, and is coated with a white film, making it difficult to see what's written on it. Marina has a small metal desk facing the classroom. Rudimentary shelves run under the windows and across the adjacent wall, holding the kids' backpacks, a game of Monopoly, a tub of Legos, and an empty plastic Pepsi bottle. On a small table in the corner, a black cloth covers a mysterious object.

As I lower myself onto the chair, the kids scramble to sit on either side of me. The unsuccessful ones climb onto the table in front of me and shove each other out of the way to get closer. Marina scolds them and eventually manages to harness their zeal. I'm embarrassed to be a disruption to her class, but she appears unfazed by the commotion.

Through gestures, and with a bit of understanding on my part, I realize she wants me to write my name on the chalkboard. After I do, Marina says it out loud for the kids to repeat in unison. "Eye-licks." *Perfect!*

Now it's up to me to figure out who they are. My

powers of observation have been hard at work since entering the room. I've successfully matched a few names and faces. There are ten boys and two girls in the class. I've already deduced that chubby, demonstrative Mirella likes to be in charge, while petite Emelia is quiet and shy. I'm having more difficulty matching up the names of the boys. With ten of them, all having black hair and dark-brown eyes and clothes with less individual personality than the girls', it's going to take me a little longer to figure them out. To make things even more difficult, it seems like most of them go by both their first *or* their middle names. So a kid who's called Carlos one minute might be José the next, and one who's José is then Luis, and Luis can be Carlos. But maybe it only appears that way because they've been in a constant state of motion. Three of the boys have names I've never heard—Edson, Lezandro, and Grimaldo. These I can remember. And then there's a Kevin. Go figure.

When I return to my seat, Marina has the kids take out pencil and paper. While the institute isn't really a school and Marina's not really a teacher, she apparently tries to give the boys and girls some sort of education while they're here. I notice most of the kids have only nubs of pencils with no residual erasers and tattered spiral notebooks they've pulled from otherwise empty backpacks.

Marina writes a few math problems on the chalkboard. Five of them appear to be for the older kids, and five, I assume, are for the six-year-olds. By looking at their papers, I see that Lezandro and Grimaldo, the smallest in the class, must also be the youngest, because the rest of the kids begin working on the more difficult assignment.

One of the boys runs up to Marina's desk and asks her something. She removes a jar of Pond's face cream from her drawer, opens it, and gives Luis, José, or Carlos—I'm not sure yet—a well-worn eraser. He hurries to correct his paper and returns it to her. This scenario repeats itself each time one of the kids makes an error.

I notice that Lezandro is having difficulty, so I move onto the seat next to him. I smile and put my index finger on the first problem, which he has wrong. Gently shaking my head no, I hold up seven fingers and then take three away. While pointing to the four that remain, we count together. *Uno, dos, tres, cuatro.* A big, toothy grin lights up his face. I acknowledge his success by exclaiming, "*Perfecto.*" And then he bolts to Marina's desk to fetch the priceless eraser.

Enrique, an eight-year-old with a real charm about him, walks over to the small table and uncovers the mystery underneath the black cloth: a pitcher of water and a glass. He pours himself a drink, puts the glass back, and then covers it again. *Must be to keep dust and dirt out. Lord knows it's everywhere! But do they all share the same glass?*

Meanwhile, a couple of kids who've finished their work snuggle up next to me. One puts his arm around my shoulder, another leans against me, touching my blond hair. I reach around their waists and smile eye-to-eye with them. Soon five more *chicos* are huddled close by, giving off the collective fragrance of Eau de Sweaty Little Boys.

Jack and his buddies wore the same prepubescent scent. I used to enter his bedroom and make a beeline for the window to counteract the nearly fatal aroma. Now, here I sit in Tom Thumb's chair with my knees up to my chest, nose-to-nose with that same smell, except this time, the windows are already open! And I'm lovin' it!

Mirella takes the Legos from the shelf and disruptively dumps them onto one of the tables. She and a few of the other kids begin fighting over the pieces. I glance at Marina, wondering if this is acceptable behavior. It must be, because she doesn't look up from her desk. Lezandro, who's just finished his work, runs to seize his share.

I move to their table to get a closer look at the treasure. There are about fifty pieces in all, each one an uninspiring shade of gray. *Hmm, twelve kids, fifty pieces. That's not gonna work.* I think about the thousands of brightly colored Legos I have stored in the attic for my future grandchildren, who are already blessed in countless ways.

A few of the kids snare only four or five pieces, with Mirella being the clear winner. Poor Lezandro wasn't quick enough to grab any, so he sulks his way over to the shelves and reaches for the grimy, plastic, double-amputeed SpongeBob SquarePants.

Emelia, not wanting to engage in combat for the Legos, takes the old Monopoly game from the shelves and brings it to the table where I've returned to sit. The box is battered, and many of the pieces are missing. Like everything else, it's covered with a gritty layer of dirt. Using my miming skills and an occasional Spanish word, I ask her if I can join her. She smiles sweetly and hands me the thimble.

Our pleasant exchange ends suddenly when a few of the boys descend upon us. They snatch the remaining tokens and fight over the money. Once again I glance at Marina, who is unstirred.

I do what I can to make things better and gently pull Emelia out of the line of fire. I ask if she wants to sit on my lap and share the thimble with me.

She says, "*Sí*," and bashfully looks downward.

When the boys finish arguing, we begin the game. After a couple of turns, I realize the kids are making up their own rules. The more aggressive the child, the more the rules work to their advantage, and the quicker my Monopoly bucks end up in their pile! For today, I'll play along and try, as much as possible, to help the nonaggressive ones survive the blatant pickpocket hands of the local Lollipop Guild.

When we finish, Marina comes over and says something to me. I shrug and tell her, "*No entiende.*" She tries speaking slowly, but when that doesn't work she uses synonyms in an effort to find one I might understand. I feel bad for not knowing, but she doesn't give up. Smiling in her passionate way, she increases her volume level just in case I've been to one too many Loggins and Messina concerts. And still nothing.

She holds up her index finger, indicating she just remembered something, and walks quickly over to her desk. Rummaging through her drawer, she pulls out a small pamphlet. After flipping through the pages, she shows me a Spanish word followed by its English phonetic pronunciation and the correct English spelling.

"*Semana,*" I say. "Week?"

"*Sí,*" she says, happy that I finally understand. Then again, I could have said "pig's feet" and she would have agreed with me, after which I'd be trying to figure out how pork fit into our conversation.

Week what? This week? Did I arrive this week? Do you want to know if I'm here all week? *Yes, thank you, ladies and* gelatina frijoles. *How many weeks? Crap, I'm so sorry. I'm not sure what you're asking me.*

I make the assumption she wants to know how long I'll be staying in Peru. "*Yo, cuatro semanas . . . aquí.*"

She smiles big and says, "*Bueno!*"

Tomorrow, *Don't List* be damned! I'm bringing my electronic translator with me.

Since the kids solved their math problems earlier this morning, they've been crowded around me, constantly touching me and talking to me. I feel a bit overwhelmed. Time passes slowly with such limited resources for entertainment, not to mention the language barrier.

Occasionally, Marina exits the classroom, leaving me alone with the kids. After her second departure, I push through my fear of doing something wrong and reach into my bag of tricks for a way to entertain them. Not actually having brought a bag, I have only my wits to rely upon.

When I was young, my dad would pretend to detach his thumb at the knuckle joint. Naturally, my sisters and I were awestruck by his inspiring talent. Having learned from the master, I proceed to whack my hand on the table, feigning terrible pain. The kids' eyes bulge in horror. I prolong my suffering for dramatic effect, and then, just when they're about to run for help, I expertly put my hands together so my thumb appears to be in two separate pieces. Their concern changes to bewildered awe.

Next, I cup my hands over my nose and mouth and discreetly pop my thumbnail against my front tooth while jerking my nose to the side, pretending to break it. This one's always a crowd pleaser. The munchkins cringe with pain while waiting to see if I'm okay. I prolong their worry and then unmask a teasing grin.

Having spent my high school and college summers as a camp counselor, I reach deep into the recesses of my memory to dazzle the troops with all sorts of comic buffoonery.

After my triumphant performance, Marina returns and says something to the kids. Lezandro runs to the back of the room and grabs the liter Pepsi bottle. I notice it's not empty like I previously thought. It appears to have been cut in half and made into a toothbrush storable containing twelve moisture-laden, bacteria-growing toothbrushes that have been baking in the sweltering Lima sun. Is this what Pepsi meant by the Same Great Taste? Didn't we experiment with this in Miss Nahigian's fifth-grade class? Gut a frog, birth a fruit fly, germinate an Oral B.

Lezandro runs to the front of the class as he pulls off the roughly cut top half of the bottle. He trips and sends the brushes flying across the dirty floor. No one flinches except for me as several unwashed hands pick them up by their worn-down bristles and put them back into the bottle. As a woman who can't live without the vigorous caress of her Sonicare, it takes me a moment to recover.

The kids march outside to a communal trough filled with stagnant water and brush their teeth without toothpaste. Some of the boys dip their heads into the same water and smooth their hair with their hands.

At just before noon, Marina shouts another directive over the classroom commotion while Enrique pulls at the skin on my elbow.

"*Pollo,*" he says, grinning coyly.

I tickle him and grab for his elbow, but his supple, young flesh won't stand at attention like mine. A couple of the other kids join in, giggling while they pinch my chicken skin. Pretty soon the entire class is having its way with my funny bones.

I encourage the silliness with a few "Buck, buck, buckees" and then realize we'd better follow Marina's instructions, whatever they were. So I put my finger over my lips to quiet the kids. They take my hands and lead me outside under the overhang to where the two older classes have already lined up. On our way to lunch, my arms gently wind like maypole ribbons as several children dance and twirl from them.

Our merry band enters the cafeteria where the seniors, who've been working all morning under the forbidding sun in the garden, ardently wave to me from their lunchroom table. I wave back with equal enthusiasm. What an oddity Lily and I must be around here. I've never felt so tall and blond before. Between the pint-size kids and the petite old-timers, I feel like Gulliver in a world of toasted Lilliputians!

And there's my fellow giant now! Lily smiles as she helps seat her adorable class.

The kitchen staff brings trays of food to the five long tables filled with hungry kids. Mirella immediately turns up her nose at what is put in front her. I can't say that I blame her. With its overcooked turnips, questionable meat product, and compost-ready pear, it doesn't look very appetizing. While some of the boys begin to dig in, Enrique and Grimaldo struggle to choke it down. I gather from Marina's tone that they can't leave until they're finished.

Marina pours what appears to be room-temperature milk, but I'm not sure because it has a nasty gray tinge to it. Mirella picks up her metal cup, smells it, and drops it back onto her tray. In an effort to prove that it tastes good, Marina takes a sip, barely touching the ambiguous milk to her lips, and exaggerates her delight. When Mirella looks away, Marina makes a face like she's just eaten a worm. I try not to laugh—relieved I wasn't the one who had to sample it.

The children finish their meals right before it's time for Lily and me to catch our ride back to the CRP house.

"*Hasta mañana!*" I say. "*Muchas gracias por todo, professora y chicos.*"

Marina reaches up to give me a hug. She says something *más rápido* with a big smile on her face. I pretend to understand, assuming it's something akin to "Thanks for a great day." But who the heck knows—it could be "Beware the Ides of March." What is a soothsayer anyway?

The kids sing out, "*Hasta mañana, Señorita Ojos Verde.*" Yes, they've nicknamed me Miss Green Eyes. Lezandro chases after me, putting his hand in mine as he looks up with that big toothy grin of his. I rub his close-cropped head and say, "*Mañana*, Lezandro."

Lily and I wait on the bench inside the gate for our van. "I'm drained."

"Me too," she says.

"I thought maybe it was just me. I mean, we've only been here four and a half hours, and I'm already spent."

"Were kids hanging on you all morning?" she asks, looking overheated.

"Yeah! With the noise level, the fighting, the struggle to figure out what they're telling me, the challenging smells, and the heartbreaking visuals, I feel like I'm on sensory overload."

"I must be dehydrated. I'm afraid to drink anything." She sighs. "But, Mom, it felt good today."

"I know what you mean, babe," I say as our eyes connect.

When Lily was away at boot camp, she called me her best friend. Back then I didn't see it that way from my side of things. But now it's true for me too. I love the woman she's become. I know I can count on her for absolutely anything. She doesn't judge me and takes pride in our relationship, and we have a helluva lot of fun together! The profound potency of our time here will only serve to enrich what we've worked so hard to achieve.

# Chapter Eighteen

*E*arly the next day, Mario drops Lily and me off at the institute well before the kids will be arriving. Without our interpreter to direct us, we're a little unsure as to how we should pass the time until then. Should we go and sit in our respective rooms? Stand here in the entry? Or try to figure out how to milk a guinea pig?

"Mom, we've got an hour before we need to be in class. I'm going to see if I can help the seniors in the garden."

Lily's daring inspires me. I wasn't as gutsy when I was her age. It's taken me years to gather my mettle.

"And I think I'm going to check out the kitchen," I say. We high-five each other. "Way to be fearless, my love."

My eyes linger on Lily as she heads toward the desert garden.

I turn toward the kitchen and tap into the courage the last decade of events have fostered in me. I stride across the vacant cafeteria toward the mysterious room that Pedro so carefully avoided showing us yesterday. It's a bold move on my part, particularly since I may be breaking the rules. I don't know the kitchen staff, and I can't really communicate with anyone. *Okay, Alex, be brave. You didn't travel five thousand miles to languish within the walls of your comfortable self.*

Slowly, I push the swinging door open. A wall of heat assaults me like a raging brushfire. It's as if I've stepped into Dante's inferno. Giant bubbling cauldrons, licked by reckless, open flames, sit atop two charred, archaic stoves fueled by chunks of firewood. A monstrous oven, straight out of the Dark Ages, expels heat like a fire-breathing dragon. Steam rises from large, tarnished sinks lined along one wall, where an old woman washes dishes. The pungent odor of unfamiliar spices shocks my unsuspecting nose, sending it into a reflexive twitch. In the corner of the windowless room, an antique fan, about as effective as a ninety-year-old asthmatic blowing on a four-alarm blaze, hangs as the only source of ventilation in the sweltering, stagnant air. And overhead, a tinny, distorted speaker screeches high-pitched folk music above the deafening kitchen din.

Holding a long, wooden fork half his size, a scrawny, sour-faced man—perhaps Dante himself—shouts orders at four weary women wearing tattered aprons and green surgical caps. They look at me and then turn away. Uh-oh, that didn't feel very warm and fuzzy. My instinct is to flee, but I persevere. *Don't be a frickin' chicken, Alex. You can't possibly be the first volunteer to have come in here. What's the worst that can happen? Hey, man, whatcha got cookin' in those big pots anyway?*

I tread lightly and head toward one of the sinks, where a young woman is peeling carrots the size of Manhattan. Running through my head is the litany of warnings we received in our CRP information packet, the recent terrorist history of Peru, the *Don'ts* spelled out for us at orientation, and just plain old fear! Man, this is so out of my zone. I press on, surveilling Dante's movements out of the corner of my eye.

I engage my fluent pointing skills, asking the young

woman if I can help. She hands me what looks danger-ously like a shiv some prison cook has fashioned to gut a rival convict. Carefully, I begin paring, hoping not to slice myself open or, perhaps, need to wield it at some Peruvian dirty rat!

After the carrots are done, the young woman gives me an old rag and demonstrates how to vigorously scrub some sort of mud-caked root vegetable. All the while, I keep my wilting head down, hoping Boss Man is too busy stirring his pot to notice that I'm still here. *By the way, nice necklace. Are those bones?*

With the gargantuan veggies clean, I follow the young woman out of the kitchen and into the cafeteria, instantly relieving my senses as I relish the cool ninety degree air. She stations me behind a counter, demonstrates my next task, and then retreats through the swinging door. Suddenly I'm alone and in charge of making breakfast for the masses.

For the next fifteen minutes, I slit open more than a hundred small, white rolls and deposit two tiny green ol-ives in each center. As it turns out, one of these delectable canapés is the only sustenance the children will have until lunchtime. And for some of them, it's their only nourish-ment since noon here yesterday.

Over the coming weeks, I'll discover every breakfast is the same roll with different, painstakingly rationed fill-ings. One day it's a thin layer of mashed avocado; the next it's dry, canned tuna and onions, followed eagerly by the kid-pleasing strawberry preserves. And then the cycle re-peats itself.

When my little ones enter the cafeteria, they run across the expansive room to greet me. I say in a confident voice, "*Buenos días, mi chicos.*"

With blurring velocity, Spanish words whiz past me like Speedy Gonzalez on his way to a cheese festival. *Arriba! Arriba!* Aaaaaand I'm back to smiling.

When Marina arrives, she reaches up for a big hug while reeling off something in Spanish, something extraordinary, I'm sure. What must my tilted, perplexed face look like to her? Maybe like my dog Trixie's does when I ask her about the meaning of life—only she comes up with better responses.

Today Lily and I brought our goody-filled backpacks with us. Inside mine, I have an electronic translator, Spanish/English flash cards, and, after a quick walk over to Wong's Department Store last night, erasers, toothbrushes, and a bucket of six hundred colorful Legos.

I discreetly show Marina the contents of my pack, which, it turns out, she's thrilled about. Apparently, she doesn't mind breaking the rules either. I ask her if it would be all right to teach the kids some English, and with her usual display of enthusiasm, she makes it clear that she'd like me to instruct them about something new every day.

*Todos los días? Really! Okay, yeah, yeah. In Spanish? Right, I can do that!?*

Let's see, so that's two days remaining this week; five next; Easter week they're closed on Friday, so four more there; and then four the last week. That's two, seven, eleven, fifteen: fifteen days of trying to convey fun and interesting lessons—all with a decisive language barrier. My head begins its typical race to achieve the goal. I've got to talk to Diego. Visual aids will be important. I'll use the book I brought from home that shows Washington's gorgeous landscapes, the pictures of my family and home life, more flash cards, art supplies, what else? *For the love of Pete, Alex, take a shallow breath and quit worrying. You'll figure it out. Now, get your ass back in the moment!*

Marina's face brightens when a teenage boy enters the classroom. She beams as she brings him over to me. *"Este es mi hijo, Javier,"* she says.

"Your son! *Mucho gusto, Javier,"* I exclaim while extending my hand to him.

Marina radiates pride while rattling off a flurry of information. I manage to pick up that he's thirteen, goes to school, and has stopped by to see her.

*Quick, what's the Spanish word for* handsome? Schön? *That's German! Come on, Alex, you know this. Crap, now all I can think about is schön! Let's see,* bonita *is pretty* . . . I do a quick mental debate whether to use *bonita* and instead offer up my broadest smile yet—hoping for Julia Roberts but fearing it's more like Chucky.

After Javier leaves, Marina whispers, *"No padre,"* indicating Javier's dad abandoned him when he was little, and adds that his father's behavior is typical of the men in Peru. Then she launches into one helluva man-bashing moment, which I completely understand!

*"Yo también.* Me too, well sort of," I answer, confirming our sisterhood. *"Yo tengo una hija, Lily,"* I say while pointing toward the room that Lily's in, *"y un hijo, Jack. Yo no hombre."* We want to pour out the details of our lives to one another but, for now, savor the taste of our growing connection.

Marina writes questions on the chalkboard for the kids to answer in their notebooks. Most of them work independently, but Lezandro and Grimaldo look painfully frustrated as they labor to put something down on paper. While witnessing their struggle, I wonder what their home lives must be like and what their futures may hold. Do they have parents? Do they love and take care of their kids? I recently read that children who live in poverty are more likely to act out, to be impatient and impulsive, and to lack gratitude—totally understandable. Even under the best of circumstances, Lily did these things. Without food, shelter, and education, they are often deprived of security, stability, and nurturing. I imagine the earthen floors of their ramshackle shanties, those that have one, and the sparse, filthy furniture they contain. What will become of you all, my new little friends?

I try to encourage the two youngest with their assignments but can't find the right words to help them. I ever so quietly unzip my backpack—not wanting to attract the others' attention—in order to retrieve my electronic translator. Well, ever so quietly, ha! Within seconds, a dozen twining hands, like curious serpents, coil all around me.

"*Momento, momento!*" I say, hugging the pack tightly so the kids will finish their work before discovering the treats inside.

Once they've completed their assignments, I remove the bulky container of Legos. Mirella tries yanking it from my hands. The others quickly join in. But this time, I'm prepared for their eager offensive.

Clutching it like I'm safeguarding a piece of my grandmother's strüdel, I instruct them, "*Sientese, por favor!*"

Marina smiles from her desk. The kids quiet down, their eyes like saucers, as I divvy up the colorful pieces.

Lezandro and I construct a robot, after which everyone, except Mirella, who's pissed off because I intentionally made her last when doling out the portions, wants me to help them build one. I'm having more fun than they are, watching their happy faces while they create cars, spaceships, and bugs. Suddenly I'm reminded of what's been missing from life as my spirit overflows with joyful purpose.

At 11:00 a.m, Marina interrupts our playtime to escort us to a hot, empty classroom. We gratefully sit on the cool linoleum floor. I refrain from pressing my parboiled face to it. A spindly senior with an unfriendly demeanor enters the room carrying an old record player and an album. He talks to Marina without any notion of pleasantry while he sets up the phonograph. Marina waves *adios* to the children and me as she heads for the door. *Wait! What are we doing?*

The scowling music man instructs the children to stand and begins spacing them at arm's length. I jump in line with the back row—the man virtually ignoring me. *Hey, Napoleon, I'm up here! You been talking to Dante?* Then he places the needle on the scratchy record, beginning some sort of piercing, whistley music.

The kids begin dancing, stepping from side to side and turning in circles. They giggle as I try to imitate them. As soon as Napoleon turns his back, I do a few funky disco moves, making them laugh all the more. The Little Colonel halts the music. I panic, remembering my class-clown school days when I was put in the corner to ponder my third-grade crimes.

*Nope, we're good.* He's just instructing us on the next few steps.

The sound of the grating ditty fills the room. We listen to the same shrill bars over and over aaaand over again. This one's gonna stick in my head forever. Like the time I got trapped in Disneyland's *It's a Small World* ride. *D'oh, I shouldn't have done that!* It's a small world after all. It's a small—*shit, not again!*—world after all. *Please make it stop! Quick, think of something else! Hmm, I wonder if Diego has any more chocolate.*

The door opens. Marina enters carrying a pitcher of water. The kids take turns sharing from the same glass. Enrique offers me a sip, but I smile and say, "*No, gracias.*" As much as I'd like to encourage his kindness by drinking it, we've been repeatedly warned, *bottled water only!* Then again, I've ignored a few of the other rules. But somehow this one . . . well, let's just say, I don't want to have to spend anymore time *not* flushing toilet paper than I have to.

Marina and Napoleon leave the room for a few minutes. I seize the opportunity to have some fun with the kidlets by *du-du-duing* a little jitterbugging with them two at a time. I spin and twirl them, throwing in the occasional lift and over-the-shoulder move. Their little hands reach up to me. My throat catches as I swallow the conflicted feelings of joy and sorrow that wash over me.

By the time we return to our classroom, the kids scurry to get ready for lunch—making it time to break out the new toothbrushes! Mirella quickly snatches the pink one. Somehow I don't see her as a pretty-in-pink little girl. She's more of a hothead red.

They run, one after another, to the trough to polish their ivories.

As we march toward the cafeteria under the shaded overhang, I'm amazed by how at ease I feel compared to yesterday. Yes, I'm hot and tired, but I feel like I belong. In a matter of just a few days here in Peru, I've experienced a wide range of emotions—from utter despair over the human condition to the great satisfaction of it. I can't remember the last time I've felt so alive!

# Chapter Nineteen

After boogieing with the kids in the blistering heat this morning, I decide to skip lunch and indulge in a second shower. Pouring cold water over my still-smoldering head is a luxury I can't forego. *Ahhh, it's the little things.* If only I lived in a perpetual state of awareness for the infinite daily blessings I'm given.

Water. Clean, fresh water. A necessity for good health and survival. Yet I rarely stop to realize how precious it is. I simply turn on a faucet and, voilà, have purified water to meet my every need. Oh, sure, I limit my lawn watering and run the dishwasher on energy-save mode. Once I even had to live without running water for twenty-four whole hours because of a burst pipe! And I had two small children at the time! God forbid! But I've never fully comprehended what life-threatening deprivation might be like until I came here to Villa—a place where clean, safe water is scarce and often inaccessible. It's having the opportunity to bear witness that intensifies my enhanced awakening.

I can't remember when I've been so grateful for a cool, rejuvenating shower. My thirsty body responds to each drop as it revives me. I let the water cascade over my steaming head and watch as the crystal beads dance on my heated skin. Tremendous relief and pleasure rush through me as the fire within retreats.

I bounce down the stairs a new woman. It's time for our group to tour one of Lima's museums. The gang's pretty beat and would much rather hang in the coolness of the house for a couple of hours, but like good soldiers, we climb into a small bus driven by Mario. On board, a slightly built man sporting a pencil-thin moustache and wearing an oversize uniform adorned with red epaulets and gold buttons awaits us. Armando introduces him as Ramiro, our translator and tour guide, and then leaves us in his care.

As soon as Mario starts the engine, Ramiro, a serious guy with an animated face enhanced by his heavy black eyebrows, begins his informational spiel. I'm confused for a few seconds as I try to figure out what language he's actually speaking. Finally, I recognize a couple of English words. *Are you kidding me? He's speaking English!* This guy's accent is so comically thick, Lily and I make eye contact and quickly look away in order to fight off the urge to bust out laughing. *Focus, Alex. This is important historical stuff. Try to understand what the commandante is saying.*

"Tree oonthred jeers ive pas sed zinch . . . "

I glance over at Diego for some help, and he whispers, "Don't look at me! I haven't a clue what he's saying!" Inside, I'm doubled over!

For a while I struggle to understand him but finally give up and turn my attention outside the bus. A sprawling, windowless building blanketed in a thick layer of soot catches my eye. The four-story stone structure, though relatively modern, is rapidly aging from the city's heavy pollutants, making it appear slightly sinister. And, of course, the entire thing is surrounded by the ever-present ominous wall. I wonder what scary things go on in there.

Just then, our bus turns into the security checkpoint along its perimeter. *Is this it?* Mario shows the guard some papers, and the wrought-iron gate swings opens. We pull into a huge, empty parking lot. *Why isn't anyone else around?*

My imagination jumps to all kinds of possible scenarios, none of them good. Remember *Missing*? American Charles Horman was murdered in the aftermath of a 1973 Chilean coup. Isn't Chile just a bit south of here? Didn't Jack Lemmon and Sissy Spacek go looking for him in a big, eerie stadium where everyone kept disappearing? That place didn't have windows either! *Proof of Life*: Meg Ryan, Russell Crowe, husband kidnapped by South American drug-dealing guerrillas! Doesn't Peru export massive amounts of cocaine?! *Under Fire*: Nicaraguan insurgency! *Oh god! There have been rebellions and revolutions all over this continent! WHERE IN THE HELL ARE THEY TAKING US?!*

Ramiro instructs us to put away our cameras and stay with the group.

An inhibiting atmosphere of oppression, a sense of recollective paranoia that exists throughout Peru, permeates this place. They say it's a free country, but it never occurred to me there are different kinds of freedom. Here in Peru, it's a crude, fragile thing cloaked in the fear that it may vanish at any moment. The political haunting of a corrupt and sometimes violent past lingers—the road to real freedom is slow and complicated. And the magnitude of necessary change is almost incomprehensible, primarily to those of us who have never known anything other than liberty. For the people here, their perspective is that which comes from a glimmer of new hope. Yet it will be a long time before true democracy trickles down to the masses of poor.

We follow Ramiro into the main entry, where he checks us in. It's odd that no one else is walking around this enormous place—no local families taking their kids on a cultural outing, no tourists, no school groups. No one but us.

The first hall we enter is filled with casework displaying ancient tools and crude carvings of figures, all of them male—distorted phallic gods of fertility with spiked penises extending from their toes to their chins. *In your dreams, baby.* These symbols of male dominance and entitlement fill the room, hundreds of them. This is why women all over the world are still fighting for equality. This shit's been going on forever.

The next hall we enter is filled with casework displaying ancient tools and crude carvings of figures, all of them male. *Wait a second. Didn't we just . . . ?* Yep. We did. It's more primitive men with grossly exaggerated manhood. And somehow, Ramiro continues to have a lot to say about them all. Is anybody tuned in to this guy? I look around to see the disenchanted faces of my new friends as they wander aimlessly from case to case, worn down by the struggle to assimilate our leader's pathetic articulation.

We survive five more exhibit halls of endless artifacts: a dish, a spoon, a pot, an idol, and let's do it all again. This country is literally buried in archaeological history. I realize that I've become tired and cranky. On any other day, with an intelligible guide, I would view twelve thousand years of civilization as awesome.

When we return to the house, Lily and I hurry to catch a cab to Lima Tours to arrange for our trip to Cusco. Crystal and Chanda decide to tag along so we can have dinner together afterward.

For the past five days, Diego has been our Pied Piper, leading us through town as we follow merrily behind him. If we need to go to the store, exchange currency, find a place to have our laundry done, or even cross a busy street without getting clobbered, he's always ready to lend a hand. But this evening, we women are venturing out on our own.

And since I'm the only one with any sort of Spanish-language experience, though admittedly limited, the others seem eager to let me take the lead. It's not long before an itsy-bitsy, toxic taxi pulls over. I barter with the driver, just like I saw Diego do when we went to the Marriott. We agree on a fare. Lily, Crystal, and Chanda squeeze into the backseat, and I lower myself into the cramped cockpit.

I'm still getting used to the fact there aren't any seat belts in the vehicles here. Do the owners intentionally remove them or are they not factory equipped? Where's Ralph Nader when you need him? Sitting in the notorious death seat of this Campbell's soup can, another radical driver at the helm, I'm forced to let go of the years of Volvo-like restraints that have ruled my life.

"Are we having fun yet, girls?" I ask, looking back to see the same aliveness on their faces that I'm feeling.

The travel agent with enviable rich, dark hair, and a more understandable accent than the museum's mustachioed commandante, types away on her computer, organizing arrangements for our trip to Cusco and Machu Picchu.

"Meez Feesha," she addresses me, "the ten o'clock flight on that Friday morning is available. I will confirm it and dispatch a driver to collect you from the CRP house. When you arrive in Cusco, there is a very nice hotel, the Posada Del Inca, which can accommodate you. I will reserve your first night there, if this meets with your approval, Meez Feesha," she says while showing me the brochure. "You will have time to rest and acclimate to the eleven-thousand-foot elevation before you travel on to Machu Picchu. Many people have trouble with this but, do not worry, the hotel will offer coca tea, and this will help you."

Lily and I give each other the ol' wink-wink at the thought of a hot cup of loco brew. "It looks good to me. What do you think, babe?"

"Let's do it!"

"Yes, Meez Feesha," the agent continues, "and then early on Saturday morning, you will take the four-hour train to its last stop, the town of Aguas Calientes. I recommend the Hatucha Towers Hotel, which is a short walk from the bus that will take you up the mountain. By noon, you can be visiting the Inca ruins. Upon your return to the town, you will spend the night at the Towers before going back to Cusco the next evening."

Dinner at Huaca Pucllana, a lovely restaurant in Miraflores, is set amid the ruins of an ancient civilization that dates back to approximately 400 AD. The pink glow of the elusive sunset casts a mystical quality over the ruins.

As I gaze upon it, I wonder if a thousand years from now people will look at our cultural remains and think about how primitive and savage we were.

I imagine myself back in time among the highly evolved women of the Nayca tribe, painting pottery, weaving baskets, and talking about the latest in kitchenware: a granite mortar and pestle set. Our children laugh and play with their handheld sticks. I throw a little more alpaca dung on the fire as the girls and I sip fermented camu camu nectar. Life is good.

Suddenly, with their dark, frightening faces streaked in barbaric white markings, spears in hand, and screaming war cries, our tribesmen charge toward my gal-pals and me in a heathenistic macho frenzy! Fearing for our lives, the woman and children scatter. My BFF, Luchadora, stumbles! They grab her! She fights to get away but can't break free of their madness!

"May I take your order?" the waiter asks, waking me from my musing.

# Chapter Twenty

Over the weekend, Lily and I enjoy a couple of quiet days in Lima while most of our housemates, who return to the States next Saturday, visit Cusco and Machu Picchu. With each passing day, I feel more self-assured and unexpectedly content. My sole purpose for being here is to help others. None of life's daily distractions beckon, diverting me from my mission. I'm fully immersed in a month-long gratitude moment.

And it gets me to thinking: what if all of my girlfriends could have an opportunity like this? My analytical mind immediately calculates the possibilities. Let's see. Women over fifty are the largest demographic in the United States. With our children raised, careers established, or retirement ready, we have both the time and the desire to do something philanthropic. We want to nourish our souls and revel in an enlightened sensibility. The women I know are a generous congregation who want to share their wisdom, and their innate nurturing genius, to help others.

But I digress. Back to the numbers. Let's take half of the 25,000,000 women over fifty in the United States and have each of them embark on just one two-week charitable mission. Go with a girlfriend or a group of girlfriends, to Toledo, Tanzania, or Timbuktu.

Suppose we volunteer for twenty-five hours each week—that would be twenty-five hours times two weeks times 12,500,000 women, equaling 625,000,000 hours, or 71,347 years of giving! What an amazing crusade that would be!

I decide not to wait. I can totally get this started—right here, right now. I'll begin by picking Armando's brain as soon as I get back to the house. I've already got a ton of questions floating around in my head. We'll need a name. Women United. Eh, I'll work on that later. Running a foundation must be similar to running a business, so I should be okay there. When I return to the States, I'll figure out the administrivia, start networking with my business connections, and begin a grassroots campaign with my women friends, and their women friends, and so on. *This is it, Alex! This is just what you've been looking for!*

*Oh maaan! That's just plain disgusting! Damn maggots.* An involuntary shudder hits me as I flick the slimy, legless suckers from the potato with the shiv I've become modestly adept at wielding. Here in Villa, nothing goes to waste. But I'm telling you, if one of these vile creatures ever found its way into my kitchen, I'd hurl the revolting spud with such force, astronomers would have solid confirmation of life on another planet! Yet with Boss Man comfortably tolerating my presence, I don't want to antagonize him by tossing out what he thinks is perfectly good food. But ewww!

Then again, perchance these aren't just any ol' maggots! And maybe Boss Man isn't just another ol' sourpuss! Maybe—*dadadadummm*—I'm smack in the middle of an X-File!

What if these mutant organisms are really—holy shit!—alien larvae unearthed from some recent archaeological dig?! Uh-oh! Did I just see Boss Man's tattoo move her lips?

And what if I accidentally touch one of these paranormal parasites? Will it find its way into my body and slither up to my brain? Maybe I'll be doing the Chicken Dance after all—or running in right-hand circles like an afflicted wildebeest!

I wonder what Mulder and Scully would do—check to make sure they still have their livers! I give one final shake to shed any residual revulsion and then just keep on a-flickin' and a-peelin'.

After kitchen duty, I head confidently toward my classroom. As I pass the window through which Lily cheerfully teaches her kids, I smile and feel tremendous pride for my daughter. Things could have turned out so differently.

And with each stride, I realize I'm not so emotionally overwhelmed anymore. A sense of purpose and fulfillment has replaced my feelings of helplessness.

I anticipate the usual bedlam on my way to the classroom, but when I round the corner, I'm stopped in my tracks. My typically unruly rascals are sitting quietly poised at their tables, hands neatly folded, while beaming at me.

*What's going on?*

On Marina's cue, my darlings cheerfully say in unison, "Good morning, Meez Eyelicks!"

Instinctively I raise my hand to my heart as the celestial harmony of their sweet voices welcomes me in English. I flash on them wearing white choir robes— with tilted halos. They look so proud of themselves. I'm touched by their simple gesture. It's like these wild Peruvian angels have taken my scarred heart and healed it in their clammy little hands—and it's beating more joyfully than I ever thought possible again.

"*Muy bien, mi chicos! Buenos días,*" I say, beaming right back at them. Then, acknowledging Marina, I add, "*Buenos días, mi amiga. Como está?*"

Enrique, Carlos, and Edson rush from their seats and begin tugging at my backpack in search of the electronic translator. I admonish them with a wagging finger and a sly smile, telling them they have to wait until *la professora* says it's okay. In the meantime, Lezandro and Emelia reach for my hands and gently pull me onto the seat they've saved for me.

Marina asks if I've prepared lessons for today.

"*Sí,*" I reply, having studied the Spanish phrases I need to communicate the activities.

With the institute not having any curriculum to speak of, it isn't hard to figure out why these kids are so untamed. There is way too much idle time and not enough structured programming. While Marina makes minor attempts to educate the *chicos,* I've gathered her own schooling wasn't much more than the basics of reading, writing, and arithmetic.

First, we'll practice our English. After that, I'll tell them about life back home in the Pacific Northwest. And finally, after having made another trip to Wong's last night, I'll teach them how to play bingo.

Before Lily and I came to Peru, we were advised to bring pictures and share stories about our personal lives. Now that I know the harsh reality of this world, I'm feeling uncomfortable, even guilty, about flaunting my remarkable life.

But I begin anyway to show pictures of my family. The kids immediately react by oohing and aahing. They can't believe there are more people like me, an entire family of fair-haired giants, especially Jack. Their eager questions and enthusiasm wash away my self-indulgent guilt.

When I open the new photograph-filled book of the Northwest, I realize I hadn't really taken a good look at it before. And even if I had, I wouldn't have seen it with the same depth of clarity that I have now. My view of the world has become appreciably more lucid.

After only a short time in Peru, my new perspective has sharpened the beauty of so many places back home: the wildflowers that bloom beneath the Cascade Mountains; the panoramas of the Columbia River Gorge with its world-class windsurfers, endless stream of hikers, and evergreen forests; the rolling vineyards and farmlands of the Yakima Valley; the fresh air and clear water of Puget Sound teeming with whales and other sea life and punctuated by the lushness of the San Juan Islands; the canyons, buttes, and volcanic rock formations of Eastern Washington; and the rainforests, rugged cliffs, and beaches of the Olympic National Park and Pacific Coast. Yowsa, it's all so magnificent!

The kids continue to ooh and aah, and in my head, I'm right there with them!

Mirella wins both games of bingo. I reward her with two sheets of stickers. She immediately brandishes them in front of the other kids like Zorro about to make his signature mark. Naturally my sense of good sportsmanship is annoyed, so I reach into my backpack and give the other kids their own sheets of the coveted gems. My fiery friend stomps her foot, puts her hand on her hip, and cocks her head defiantly.

This petulant pistol is going places. She's smart, independent, a leader, and a total pain in the ass. I hope someone can guide her into the successful woman I know she can be. Then I remember where I am and wonder if she'll ever have the opportunity.

Opportunity: that's what we have in spades back in the States, and I've taken it for granted. Opportunities are everywhere. They present themselves each day in so many ways. Yet I haven't noticed them. I enjoy a hot shower, slap on some scented body lotion, reupholster a chair with a lovely fabric, take an art class, dine out with friends two nights a week, go to the dentist, and volunteer in Peru—my possibilities are endless. The choices I have, no matter how small, are daily opportunities to be grateful—because most of the world doesn't possess them.

I decide to quit wasting time. *Fulfill your dreams, Alex. Fly in a glider, run the Hells Canyon rapids, visit New Zealand, start the foundation, paint landscapes— even take a frickin' yodeling class if you want! Whatever! What are you waiting for?*

After we play bingo, Marina heads to the administration office, leaving me in charge.

At one table, Grimaldo, Kevin, Edson, Luis, and José

quietly build architectural marvels with the new Legos. At another, Emelia and Lezandro devise their own version of Monopoly—happy the bullies are too busy to commandeer their game. The ever-charming Enrique leans up against me as I sit in one of the butt-busting chairs I've grown accustomed to, wanting to learn more new words from my pocket translator. Across the room, Mirella and Carlos engage in a spirited exchange of ripping stickers out of each others hands. I keep a watchful eye on them, anticipating their fun is about to teach Carlos a painful lesson.

Within seconds, I hear a chair fall over and turn just in time to witness Mirella lunging toward Carlos, who's holding one of her sticker pages. He turns and runs, circling the classroom. Mirella flies after him in hot pursuit. I ask them to stop. Well, not really. I can't remember the word for *stop*. Fortunately, I remember how to say *no* in Spanish.

"*No!*" I declare firmly, but Mirella ignores me. The look on Carlos's face tells me he'd listen if he didn't fear for his life. I can't really blame him. Mirella's an intimidating ball of fire, and since she won't stop, I do the only thing I can think of to diffuse the situation. I grab her from behind as she whizzes by and engulf her in a big bear hug.

At first she struggles to get away, but I hold on, hoping my clinch will calm her down. I whisper, "It's okay," in her ear. Once her body yields, I relax my grip so she can break away. But to my surprise, she doesn't.

Marina returns just in time to witness our awkward embrace. Mirella quickly leaves my arms and doesn't look back.

But what is so interesting is that from that moment on

we seem to have a new understanding. She doesn't behave like a complete snot, and I, well, I cut her some slack.

After Marina and I seat the children for lunch, instead of waiting with the kids like I usually do, I decide to follow her into the kitchen to help carry the food trays.

She bursts through the swinging door like a breath of fresh air, bringing new life and vivacity into an otherwise dreary place. My kitchen coworkers laugh as she touches each one on the back and speaks to them above the kitchen clamor, all the while making sure that I'm by her side. Our connection seems to have elevated my status. I notice a shift in the faces of my fellow culinarians. I'm actually receiving engaging affirmation for the first time since braving the galley. Even Boss Man bestows an acknowledging nod.

Is it possible that tomorrow morning when I show up for duty, they might actually consider me a part of the team? And to that I say, "Put me in, Coach—I'm definitely hot!"

Today's lunch is rice, some sort of green soup, a questionable meat covered in gravy, another root vegetable, a severely battered, overripened banana, and—woohoo!— lemonade. Most of the kids polish off the meal quickly, though Mirella feigns a dry heave before each spoonful of soup.

Kevin, the little professor, as I've dubbed him, with his studious demeanor, wire-rimmed glasses, and neatly tucked-in shirt, struggles to eat. I slide over next to him and gently coax a bite, but he refuses. Even my sad puppy dog look doesn't work. A devilish grin crosses his face as he slaps the back of his hand, mimicking my thumb-splitting trick. *Oh, I get it! You want me to entertain you! Well, all right, here's the deal, one broken finger for every heaping mouthful of food.* "Una grande boca," I say, reinforcing the heaping part of it. *Hmmmm, did I just tell him he has a big mouth? Oh, well, he seems to get the point.*

Without hesitation, Kevin begins to eat. Wow! Who knew it would be so easy. I remember when I was a kid, my mom loved to prepare all kinds of unique dishes for us. Unfortunately, to my mind, I experienced way too many kid-unfriendly vegetables, like kohlrabi (puke), rutabaga (barf), and cauliflower (hurl). Consequently, I'm quite familiar with the gag reflex. And when Brussels sprouts stared back at me from my plate, fugetaboutit. My parents couldn't have bribed me with a Beatles lunch box filled with Clark bars to get me to choke down one of those nasty-smelling booger balls.

It took more than a dozen finger-splitting illusions before Kevin finally finished his meal. He laughed every time. I even drew a crowd of interested onlookers from the older students' tables. With an audience of thirty huddled around me, I simulated my nose-breaking trick and finished my performance with armpit farts. From that day forward, every kid in the place was my friend.

# Chapter Twenty-One

After the other volunteers leave Lima for home, Diego, Henry, Lily, and I continue to forge friendships sure to transcend the fickle memory of time and distance. Lily and Henry are even taking nightly Spanish lessons from a tutor who comes to the house—but I suspect there may be something else going on in addition to learning the local lingo.

We also cultivate our worldview by confronting its harsh realities. We visit seniors like Trini and Dimitri, who live in deplorable conditions—their home is a seven-by-seven windowless structure consisting of old stacked bricks. Trini, bedridden because of a crippling case of arthritis, lies on a filthy, sheetless mattress shrouded by a scrap of tattered felt that Dimitri straightens in a sad but loving attempt to keep her warm. In the tepid morning hours, seventy-six-year-old Dimitri, afraid to leave his wife home alone, places her deformed body in a rickety wooden wheelchair and pushes her through the uncompliant streets of Villa while futilely trying to sell candy bars.

We visit a woman who cries in desperation because she can't afford medicine for her husband's life-threatening illness. Another weeps as she tells our translator about nighttime thieves who repeatedly break into her indefensible home, stealing what little she has while she lies terrified in her bed.

"I think I would feel such a paralyzing sense of hope-lessness knowing there's no way out," I tell Lily. "At least when we face challenges, we have options."

"I've never been more grateful for my life, Mom."

"Me too, Lily-babe. Me too."

We learn from the personal stories of our new Peru-vian friends about the injustice and hardship that decades of rampant political corruption have led to. Yet somehow these seemingly impossible obstacles have not broken their spirits.

We laugh at Henry who, after tending to his mountain of laundry on the scorching CRP rooftop, requires Lu-cilla's homemade sunburn remedy: being blanketed from shoulders to toes in tomato slices. He blushes an even brighter shade of red when Lily catches sight of him and teases him unmercifully. Meanwhile, later that day, we dine on, hmm, caprese salads Lucilla prepared for us.

It is with both sadness and appreciation that today is the end of this volunteer journey. We'll be leaving behind the privilege of sharing in the lives of these wonderful people but will also move forward with newfound wis-dom, deeper compassion, and profound gratitude.

Mario's head bobs up and down in the resilient driv-er's seat as he takes us, one last time, through the streets of Villa. I focus intently on the sights and smells I've be-come accustomed to, hoping to recall the abundance of this pilgrimage whenever I'm preoccupied with the mundane stresses of my life. I never want time to diminish the awak-ening that has so enriched me. Today is a bittersweet day.

After dropping Diego and Henry off at their sites, Ma-rio pulls up to our facility. I listen to the amplified sound of the van door sliding open and stare at my feet as they hit the incessant dirt, sending it drifting onto the tops of my no-longer-white tennis shoes. I examine the friendly face of the pint-size guard. He smiles broadly and unlocks the gate for us. I breathe in the kitchen inferno's pungent air ever so deeply and take pride in Boss Man's reluctant acceptance of me. My heart inflates as the children run to greet Lily and me. We hug them tightly and relish the symphony of their frenzied chatter.

Later, I languish in our classroom rituals of thumb breaking, nose cracking, elbow pulling and the laughter that always ensues, and savor the smell of sweaty little boys. Finally, I honor the harrowing reality of my new friend, Marina, as she shares her passion for life with these precious children. *Remember this, Alex. Remember all of this!*

Today I plan on venturing outside the classroom. It's time to take our party outdoors, to brave the persistent Peruvian sun with the Frisbee and balls that are stuffed in my pack. I'm a bit hesitant because I've never seen any of the children play outside. But since my arrival, I've cultivated my courage and confidence. The annoying voice in my head that always tells me to play by the rules has been silenced. Just as my mom said "so what" when Lily moved into Renée's house, those words continue to be the mantra that keeps me boldly going forward. It worked then, and I'm hoping it will work now. *So what* if the institute's director doesn't like it. *So what* if she asks me to stop. *So damn what!*

The *chicos* tug at my bulging backpack, hoping new treasures await them. Once again, I subdue their enthusiasm with a wagging finger and a smile, saying, "*Estudio primero.* Studies first."

"*Oh no, señorita!*" they respond with conviction.

But I'm wise to their ways, "*Sí, mi niños. Vamos!*"

Their heads hang as they dramatize their disappointment, slowly pull out their chairs, and begin working on the chalkboard assignment. I take this opportunity to tell Marina how sad I am that this is our last day together.

The surprised look on her face tells me that somewhere along the line we had a lost-in-translation moment. She repeats,"*Hoy?!*" in disbelief.

Yes, today. "*Sí. Yo va Machu Picchu mañana,*" I say, thinking she was aware of my flight to Cusco tomorrow.

Without another word, she turns and runs from the room. Several minutes pass before she returns and tells the children to put away their work. Marina whispers to each one as she hands them something. Soon the entire class is huddled together, not so secretly working on farewell cards for me—that is, except for Lezandro, who has his head bowed down in the crook of his arm.

I gently rub his back and ask, "*Qué pasa?*" but he's inconsolable.

Marina takes him by the hand and walks outside with him. When they return, she pulls the Spanish/English pamphlet from her desk drawer and jots something down on a scrap piece of paper. Lezandro flashes his big toothy smile through his dirt-streaked tears and begins copying her words onto his card.

The room is unusually quiet as everyone, including Marina, prepares to say good-bye. Sitting for the last time in the butt-numbing chairs, I gaze wistfully around the room, drinking in the lives that have blessed me with an enhanced perspective.

Marina decorates a sign with my name sandwiched between two gigantic pink hearts. She places it on the blackboard while the children, one by one, give me their finished cards.

My sweet Enrique leans comfortably into me as I open his. Inside he's drawn a picture of us holding hands—me with yellow hair and him with his heart broken in two.

I give him a gentle squeeze and say softly, "*Gracias, mi pequeño amigo.*"

Mirella, wearing her game face, waves her note in front of the others to gain my attention. I read hers next. Much to my surprise, my impetuous adversary has filled the card with endearing sentiments and plastered it with her prize-winning bingo stickers!

"*Qué lindo!*" I say as I reach for her hand to pull her close. She pretends to be indifferent as I give her a big hug. Then she backs away behind the other children.

Lezandro huddles up close to me, shyly handing me this note. *My heart sad. Love, Lezandro.* Putting my arm around him, I embrace my little buddy and fill myself with this season of my life.

One at a time, the kids grace me with their love. Even Marina artfully decorated a card saying, *Para mi amiga maravillosa con muchos cariños.* And then in English, *heart, friend, affection.*

So this is how the pearl "my cup runneth over" came to be.

My heart sinks as the ball flies over the razor-wired wall—making it clear to me that the kids have never played catch before. Fortunately, I brought another ball along. But first, in anticipation of another aerial disaster, I explain that it's not necessary to use all of their might! They confirm their understanding by eagerly reaching for the new ball. I secure it in Enrique's hand like I'm passing the gold medal–winning baton to Flo-Jo and tell the other boys to back away to catch it.

His inaccurate zeal immediately sends it sailing over the predatory wall. *Crap!* I try not to let the kids see my frustration as I head to my backpack.

Since I don't want the Frisbee to meet a similar fate, I once again demonstrate how to cautiously toss it back and forth. After a few successful flings, Lezandro launches the disc straight toward our towering brick nemesis.

Lost for a moment in my mental cursing, my backpack now empty, it takes me a second to attend to the kids' disappointment. Once I do, I'm forced to consider the possibility of leaving the protected compound. *Should I? We've been repeatedly warned about the dangers of going out alone. Aww, but look at those faces.*

On our way back to the classroom, I wrestle with my dilemma—should I or shouldn't I?—while consoling the kids.

At the doorway, I rally my head and gut to join in with my heart and make the decision to march toward the unknown. I pull back my shoulders and encourage myself as I stride toward the facility's entrance. *You can do this. Don't be a wuss, Alex.*

"*Abierto, por favor,*" I say, smiling at the guard.

The gate closes behind me as I glance up and down the desolate dirt road. *No one around, thank god.*

I steel myself to go where, I presume, no American woman has gone before. I turn to my right, toward the alley, knowing the equipment landed somewhere beyond the back of the two-acre compound.

As the first blind corner draws near, I slow my pace, ready to bolt back to the gate if needed. My body moves in a state of high alert, my senses intensify, and my muscles flexed.

I lean my head forward just enough to see into the alleyway and exhale a sigh of relief.

Safely, I round the corner. A foreboding wooden fence topped with crudely carved spikes and the institute's massive razor-bedazzled wall narrowly flank me. I quicken my step through the claustrophobic passageway. Every few strides, I look back to make sure I'm still alone.

As I approach the next corner, I slow my gait in anticipation of the unknown. *Just one more turn and . . .*

Before I finish my thought, I freeze my footsteps. My ears cock like a Doberman's. My eyes fix to keen my sense of hearing. Fear, persistently looming beneath a flimsy veil of bravery, reveals itself. I listen intently to confirm what I thought I heard, but the sound has been muffled. Still, I know I don't want to be here. My heart begins to race. I slowly peek around the corner to assess the situation, hoping maybe I was wrong about what I'd heard. But once I do, there's no more time to ponder.

I race toward the suspicious man who's dragging a young girl into a beat-up old van. Adrenaline blasts through my body—the sounds of my breathing and beating heart are all I hear as I sprint toward danger. Part of me says, *What in the hell are you doing, Alex?!* but I can't stop myself.

I leap onto the villain's back, blindsiding him. The force of my body knocks the girl free. She runs away down the alley. I squeeze the kidnapper's neck in the bend of my elbow and cover his eyes with my other hand. His attempts to fling me off fail as I lock my lengthy legs around him.

Now what? I don't have an exit strategy! Should I let go and run my ass off, hoping he won't catch me? *Are you crazy?! You know he'll outrun you, you ol' goat!*

But it's too late for me to decide. The goon slams me backward into the wall, cracking my head against it.

# Chapter Twenty-Two
# Lily Speaks

"Henry, I don't know where my mom is," I say, beginning to feel a little panicked. We usually meet inside the gate after the kids eat lunch. "I checked the cafeteria and her classroom, but she's not in either of those places."

Henry ducks his head to step out of the CRP van.

"I'm sure she's around somewhere," he says, unfolding his tall, hunky body while adjusting his glasses.

*Goddamn, he's so gorgeous! Jeez, Lily, this is not the time!*

"Why don't we ask her instructor?"

Henry turns to Mario, our perpetually smiling driver. *"Mario, un momento, por favor."*

*"Sí,"* he replies with his baseball cap pulled down tight around his ears.

"Marina's probably back in her classroom, since lunch is over." I lead Henry under the outdoor overhang that shades us from the intense sun. "Henry, this place isn't that freaking big. I'm starting to get worried."

"I'm sure she's fine, Lily. She was probably helping in the kitchen or one of the other classrooms. Let's wait and see what Marina has to say."

As soon as we enter the room, the kids, run toward us. "Leelee, Leelee!"

"*Buenos días, muchachos.*" I gently shush them and quickly introduce Henry to Marina. We begin questioning her in our recently acquired half-assed Spanish.

"I got some of what she said. How about you?"

"I think she assumed that Alex left early because it was her last day here," he confirms. "They had a farewell party for her, and then she went outside with some of the kids."

Henry and I fumble our way through asking Marina if she has any idea of where Mom could be. Between the two of us, we manage to be the equivalent of one seriously lame Spanish-speaking person, which seems to be enough for the moment.

"*La professora,*" Mirella pipes in, "*nosotros jugábamos.*" Marina explains by dramatically acting out what Mirella is telling her about the balls disappearing over the wall and how "Eye-licks" went toward the entrance when the kids came back to the classroom.

"She wouldn't have gone outside to look for them, would she?" I ask, hoping for a definite no from Henry.

"Mirella, will you show us where the balls went over?" Henry motions a throw toward the wall.

Her eyes widen, and she takes off running. We follow her past the bathroom facility to just beyond the garden where the seniors rake the resistant dirt.

Mirella points to where the stuff disappeared. The seniors come over to see if they can help us.

"What do you want to do, Lily?" Henry says, his deep blue eyes offering both strength and compassion.

"We absolutely need to go and find her!"

With Henry's support, I move into action by asking Marina to search the interior. She organizes the seniors and tells Mirella to go back to the classroom, but the little girl insists on helping.

"Henry, let's check with the security guy to see if he knows anything."

We hurry to the gate, where the laid-back guard verifies that Mom did indeed leave the compound. An uneasy lump I swallowed earlier turns into a humongous rock in the pit of my stomach. *I can't believe she did this. She would have killed me if I'd been the one!*

The gate swings open, and we leave the protection of the institute. Henry leans through the front passenger window of the van, telling Mario to notify Armando of the situation.

The two of us move quickly around the first corner and enter a scary, narrow alley. My fear escalates—not for myself, but for my mom. With each step, I silently plead for a happy ending.

We reach the back of the compound where Mirella said the balls went over. The whole landscape is eerily blanketed by a layer of gritty dirt. Even the barbed-wire fence has a thin dusting on it. Just ahead, however, there is one exception—a dark spot in the road. Henry and I step closer. We cop a squat, hoping not to confirm what we already suspect. Henry touches the puddle of thickened goo with his finger and raises it for inspection. I'm utterly disgusted, but mostly I'm filled with fear. *Chill out. It's not hers. It can't be!*

"Lily, I know this looks bad, but we can't leap to any conclusions." Sadly, his words don't match the look on his face. "We're not positive what this is," he says, regaining his composure, "and even if it is blood, that doesn't mean it belongs to your mum." Henry puts his hands on my shoulders. "We must press on." I look up into his reassuring face. "And besides," he says with an encouraging wink, "our Spanish needs the practice." His eyes smile through the top of his lenses.

We hurry through the maze of creepy alleys in search of anyone who might have information. The few strangers we find don't seem to know anything—or do they? As more time passes, my hope for a happy ending begins to fade.

After another unsuccessful hour and not a single clue as to what happened to Mom, Henry suggests we return to the institute. "Armando should be there straightaway."

"Not yet, Henry—I want to keep looking. Someone has to know something. But if you want to go back, I'll be all right on my own."

"Lily, I'm here for whatever you need."

*He's so amazing. I wonder what it'd be like to be with a guy like him.*

"And you're right about someone knowing something. A tall, blond American woman would, quite rightly, attract attention."

"Thanks for helping. It means a lot to me."

"Whether I was here or not, you'd be doing exactly what you're doing now—only with a lot more hand gestures," he says, coaxing a smile from me.

We begin knocking on doors. With each one that opens, my hopes rise and fall, again and again.

I glance at my watch. Mom's been missing for more than three hours. "Maybe it's time to go back," I say as my mind searches for what else I can do, "but let's take a different route, so we can cover new ground."

Henry and I question every street vendor and local we pass along the way. Some are eager to help; others want nothing to do with us.

I struggle within myself—going back and forth between hope and despair. *Will I find out she's dead? Don't even think it, Lily. But she could be. What will you and Jack do then? Stop it! I'm coming, Mom! Please don't give up, because I won't!*

Henry and I enter a graffiti-clad market. Its bar-covered windows and shady vibe appear threatening, but I let go of my fear. Mom is my only thought.

We scope out the room, its primitive shelves empty except for a small amount of pop, cigarettes, and candy. Two leather-skinned men sit on crates, puffing their unfiltered Oro Negro smokes while the shopkeeper takes a swig of his Inca Kola from behind the counter.

My heart pounds like I've been running for my life. *Could they have harmed her?* The men stare at me—my alabaster presence silencing them. I force a smile, hoping they'll tell us whatever they know.

Henry and I explain the situation as best we can. I think I understand what the man says but don't want to believe it.

I look to Henry. He hesitates and then reaches his hand over to squeeze mine.

"What? Tell me!"

"I think the owner said sometimes there are kidnappings, mostly for human trafficking, but, Lily, I may have misunderstood him. And he hasn't heard anything suggesting that's what happened to your mom."

Inside I'm freaking out. Hideous images of Mom being drugged and sold to the highest bidder play in my head.

"The guy is smug as hell. Are you sure he's telling us the truth?"

"Come on. Let's go. *Muchas gracias,*" Henry says as he leads me by the hand into the street.

I stop, paralyzed in the middle of this wasteland, prepared to kick down every door until I find the woman who has given me everything—the woman who wouldn't give up on me. *What have these people done to her? What will I tell Jack?*

"My mom is our rock, and now I need to be hers," I say out loud. "Henry, what if those men have her? What if they're part of the kidnapping ring? Shouldn't we check them out?"

"Lily, I don't think—"

"I'm going to find out what's going on in there."

"Wait!" Henry says, following me back into the market.

"*El baño, por favor?*" I ask the shopkeeper nicely, but he's quick to tell me that I can't use the bathroom.

I ignore the hardened looks from the other men and, without thinking, try to force an opportunity to search the place by pretending I'm about to puke. "*Enfermo,*" I plead with the owner. He doesn't care that I'm sick—raising my suspicions even more. *What are they hiding?*

I grab the owner's arm and hang on him like he's about to be hurled on. He pushes me away, demanding Henry take me outside.

In that moment, I do the only thing I can think of to save Mom. I rush toward the foreboding back room. The man chases after me, changing his hostile voice to a raised whisper. Henry follows right behind us.

My eyes frantically search the bleak room with its small wooden table, barred window, and scattered empty crates. A black-curtained doorway conceals a darkened room. The store owner pulls at my arm, continuing his emphatic whisper as he tries to prevent me from entering, but I am unstoppable.

"Where is she? I know she's here!" I insist like a nut job. "What have you done with my mom? Mom! Mom!"

And then it happens. In the shadows, with my eyes adjusting to the darkness, I see an infant cradled comfortably in one of the old wooden crates.

"*Bambina, bambina! Mi nieta!*" the man whispers, waving his arms passionately.

*Oh my god, it's a baby. He's babysitting his granddaughter! That's why he didn't want me to come back here!*

My heart sinks because now not only have I not found Mom but I'm mortified for acting bat-shit crazy in front of this sweet old grandpa. "I'm so sorry! *Perdóneme, por favor. Lo siento mucho, señor.* Please forgive me. I had no idea." I grab the shopkeeper's hand, offering him my sincerest apologies. He pushes me away and out of the room.

"Come on, Lily. Let's go," Henry says.

Back outside, in the middle of the road, I gather myself and push away this embarrassing defeat.

"Look, Henry, over there. There's someone we can ask."

I tell my story yet again, and at last, this time, the stranger knows something. The man says that he's just come from the pharmacy, where he overheard a guy asking for bandages. He said he needed them for a foreign woman who was hurt.

My crushed hopes turn to excitement for the woman who is my best friend, my teacher, my everything. *Mom:* one simple word that doesn't begin to describe all that she is to me.

We follow the local through the indistinguishable streets of Villa to the *farmacia*—our urgency leaving a dusty haze behind us.

The pharmacist says he knows the customer who bought the bandages. He steps outside to give us directions to the man's shanty.

All I can think of as Henry and I hurry toward this guy's home is that my nightmare will finally be over. *Please, it's got to be her! Oh, let it be her!*

I knock rapidly on the weathered plywood door and then chew on the inside of my cheek, willing Mom to be inside. Henry puts his arm around me as we stand and wait.

A man wearing a tattered work shirt, crusty jeans, and *ayotas,* sandals made of recycled truck tires, opens the door. I begin to explain the situation, but before I can finish, the man smiles and eagerly invites us in. We duck our heads through the dwarfish entry. Once inside, I lift my eyes. In that moment, the panic and desperation of living my life without my mom vanishes.

Two women and a young girl hover over her as they bandage her head. I run to her.

"Mom, are you all right?" I ask, hugging her tightly while I kneel down beside her.

"I'm okay, honey," she says, gently putting her hand on my head. "These kind people have been taking good care of me."

"What happened to you?" I ask as my eyes fill with happy tears.

"I was unconscious until about ten minutes ago. Hi, Henry," Mom says with a smile. "This young lady is Rosa, and these are her parents, Carmen and Miguel, and her grandmother, Adelina."

Miguel tells us the harrowing story of how Mom saved his daughter from a kidnapper.

"Bloody brilliant, Alex!" Henry says.

Mom smiles and shrugs like it's no big deal.

After Rosa ran home and told her parents what happened, they went back there and found Mom unconscious in the street. They brought her here but didn't know who she was until she came to a little while ago.

"Mom, you have no idea how worried I've been. What were you thinking—leaving the compound? Do you know how lucky you are? You could have been killed! How many times have we been warned? I mean, really. You scared the hell out of me!"

"I'm sorry that I scared you, honey, but I'm not sorry I was able to help Rosa."

"I know, I know," I say. "Just don't ever do something like that again," I scold her. Mom grins. "I'm serious! You have no idea what you put me through!"

"How's your head? We should get you to a doctor."

"I'm fine, honey. I want to go back to the institute and say a proper good-bye to Marina. We can have my head examined later," she says with a smile.

"Really, that's what you're giving me? This isn't funny! I thought I raised you better than this," I tease her back, and then laugh at my insane sense of relief.

# Chapter Twenty-Three

**W**ithout a word or even a glance my direction, Mirella seats herself beside me on the bench near the gate. I look down at her to see a satisfied grin spread across the face of the young girl who helped in the search for me. Marina settles in on the other side while we thoughtfully await the end of our extraordinary time together.

*My dear friend, I wish from the deepest part of my heart that I could bring you with me. You have no idea what you've done for me.* Why can't I find the words to tell her what this journey, and her role in it, has meant to me? But really, we don't need words. Over the past month, we've shown each other how much we care by sharing a knowing look, a mime, a resultant laugh, fumbled words, a hug. No matter what, we've spoken the same language.

"*Amigas de vida, usted y yo.* Friends for life, you and me," I say, pointing back and forth between us. And then, thanking the email gods, I add, "*Gracias por internet. Sí?*"

"*Sí, sí, mi amiga,*" Marina agrees, putting her hands together prayerfully.

After Armando and Lily wrap things up with the police, we rise to say our final good-byes. In the midst of my hug with Mirella, I remember I have a few stickers left in my backpack.

"*Momento, momento!*" I say, unzipping the front pocket and then handing them to her.

Finally, after weeks of unsuccessfully performing my best schtick for her, Mirella reveals her grand, elusive smile. *Aha! Why, you little stinker! You* do *have teeth!*

"*Adios, mi pistola!*" I tease her.

Not knowing what the future holds for Marina and me ever reuniting, we realize the remarkable significance of what we've shared. I bend down to embrace my teacher, my friend. Then, tapping my hand over my heart, I tell her, "*Usted es mi querido amiga para siempre. Gracias por todo.*" Yes, she will remain my dear friend forever, of that I am sure.

On the way back to the CRP house, I bounce up and down in the sweltering van, the heat and dust pouring in through the open windows, and I am awash in spiritual riches.

Before Lily and I head upstairs to pack for our early-morning flight to Cusco, we say our good-byes to Diego and Henry—promising each other that we'll never lose touch.

But I can't just leave without giving my boys something thoughtful to remember me by. After all, I suspect they were the ones who absconded with my mattress a couple of weeks ago simply because I put a Peruvian Baby Ruth in Diego's commode.

So while the guys are downstairs, I invite Lily to help me steal their underwear. Naturally, she's not quite on board at the thought of it, but I play on her sympathies by touching my poor bandaged head. What I won't do for a practical joke.

And this is where the gem "you can't judge a book by its cover" proves to be true. I had absolutely no clue that a proper English gentleman, literary brainiac, musical genius, and grand master of manners would don such loud, colorful undies!

Anyway, again I digress. Back to my thoughtfulness. Taking the contraband to our room, we make quick work of tying them together—one of Henry's, one of Diego's, and then another of Henry's, back and forth.

Lily gets into our deviant mother-daughter experience by throwing her own brand of creativity into the mix. "Let's soak them in water, wring them out, strengthen their knots, and fold them neatly, one on top of the other. Then we can finish by putting them in the freezer."

A big smile takes over my face. "You've learned well, Lily Skywalker."

And so it is with full hearts and Chesire-cat grins that we can honestly say our volunteer work here is done.

# Epilogue

The closer our train rolls toward Aguas Caliente, the more breathtaking the scenery. Small, rustic farms dot the narrow valley landscape as the Andes rise high above them. A solitary plowman works his isolated field in the early-morning light. What rugged lives these people must live, without electricity, plumbing, or modern convenience of any kind. I can only begin to imagine their hardships and solitude—the only sign of outside civilization being the train we're riding on.

Our car is filled with Germans, Brits, Japanese, and two Polish gentlemen, who sit across from Lily and me. We do our best not to knee-kiss them, but it's difficult, given the tight proximity of our seats and the unsettling agitation of the train tracks, perhaps at being laid in such a sacred place.

Soon I will breathe in the reverent air of these mystical mountains—a dream inspired by my youthful imaginings and kindled by readings from more than twenty-five years ago. Machu Picchu is a symbol of the life of adventure and enlightenment I envisioned for myself.

As I gaze out the train window, I notice Lily's reflection. She is smiling and chatting with the Polish men. They are captivated by her friendly exuberance and warmth. Her unassuming beauty is undeniable, but it is her inner beauty that fills me with goodness. What a long, challenging journey we've had, but it has brought us to this wondrous place in our lives. My girl is a confident, self-respecting woman. And so am I—just like my mother was. The three of us may have gotten there in different ways, but we've all had one thing in common—the unconditional love, support, and guidance of our mothers. I have no doubt Lily will pass this legacy along to her children, no matter how hard she may have to fight for it.

The train whistle blows as we arrive at our destination. Lily and I wheel our luggage toward town, along with the other passengers. Most of the tourists veer off toward the center of the village for their hotels and hostels, but Lily and I continue along the turbulent Urubamba River to the Hatucha Towers—a deceiving name at all four stories of it.

The river is frighteningly thunderous as it rages within feet of the walkway. It's so incredibly loud we have to yell to hear one another. "You could power Vegas with this kind of energy!" I exclaim. Yet as fearsome as the Urubamba is this time of year, its chocolaty color and milky consistency make it tempting to reach over the rail to take a sip. It's as if nature's pouring us a giant mug of cocoa!

We reach our hotel with little time to waste. "Meez Feesha," the bellhop says, directing his attention my way. "I take the luggage to your room. You must go quickly and board the bus."

The narrow switchbacks climb steeply up the unguarded road, offering alarming views of the mountain's drop-off outside our window, especially when a returning bus pushes us perilously close to the edge. A heavy mist makes the already mud-slicked road even more treacherous. Keeping my eyes away from the threat of certain death, I focus on the ethereal quality of the lush green peaks and imagine a modern-day Zeus decked out in his rain poncho and explorer hat while perched atop a neighboring summit, defiantly raising his trekking pole.

Once we gather in the parking lot, our guide shepherds the tour group up the ancient stairway to the ruins. Several people move off to the side of the steep granite steps to catch their breath in the thin mountain air.

When Lily and I reach the top, we decide to enjoy a more personal experience and wander away from the flock.

My intuitive daughter is well aware of the importance of this event for me. She knows I need a bit of space to walk with my head in the clouds in order to thoroughly absorb and appreciate the fulfillment of my dream. My life's journey has led me to this place of supreme gratitude for everything that time has brought me. Without all of it, I wouldn't be who I am—a woman blessed with incredible love.

The carefree clouds float to a distant peak as I traverse the mountainside and bask in the warmth of the reachable sun. I stop to breathe in the wonder of a long-gone people. As they once did, I know what it feels like to accomplish something seemingly insurmountable. The ravages of my divorce, a daughter in jeopardy, and the abuse of my spirit have tested me in inconceivable ways. Yet here I stand on this hallowed ground, humbled. In my own way, I have become a trailblazer for my destiny, the entrepreneur of my fate.

There were times when I questioned if I had it in me

to persevere, to learn from my hardships and use them to empower me. These were not easy lessons. If they were, they wouldn't have held such marvelous rewards. The illusive whys of everything don't matter anymore. There is only one answer of importance as to why, and that is . . . to teach . . . Life has taught me some valuable lessons—as it will continue to do. And I wouldn't have it any other way.

I've survived the choices I've made and resolved to thrive from their wisdom. At times it was soulfully painful. Living one moment at a time was all I could manage. And I screwed up plenty along the way. But look at me now! Here I sit on this emerald summit, amid the energy of an iconic people, feeling the essence of my warrior spirit commingling with theirs! I want to beat my chest and shout a war cry! Inside my head I'm doing the running man within the walls of the sacred Temple of the Condor! Go, Alex! Go, Alex!

A radiant grin crosses my face as the harmony of my senses comes to an intoxicating crescendo. I see myself through a panoramic lens, my arms outstretched as I spin on top of the world. Okay, so it all sounds hokey, but really, joy is bursting out of every one of my frickin' pores.

Blinking back tears, I inhale a deep breath of gratitude for the wonderful life I'm blessed to have. I did it! I made it through the bullshit and am so much richer because of it. And still my journey continues. Now, armed with a reawakened, unencumbered awareness of life's infinite possibilities, I am thrilled at the prospect of my eternal education.

Oh, Shirley, if you could see me now!

46545621R00217

Made in the USA
San Bernardino, CA
10 March 2017